A SKINFUL OF SHADOWS

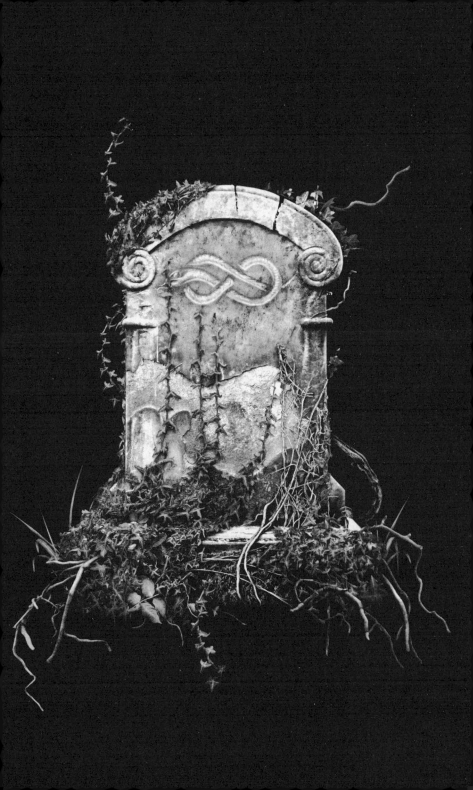

FRANCES HARDINGE

AMULET BOOKS
NEW YORK

A SKINFUL OF SHADOWS

PUBLISHER'S NOTE: This is a work of fiction. Names, characters, places, and incidents are either the product of the author's imagination or used fictitiously, and any resemblance to actual persons, living or dead, business establishments, events, or locales is entirely coincidental.

Cataloging-in-Publication Data has been applied for and may be obtained from the Library of Congress.

ISBN 978-1-4197-2572-2

Originally published in hardcover by Macmillan Publishers Limited, United Kingdom, in 2017.

Text copyright © 2017 Frances Hardinge
Jacket illustrations copyright © 2017 Vincent Chong

Printed and bound in USA
10 9 8 7 6 5 4 3 2 1

Amulet Books are available at special discounts when purchased in quantity for premiums and promotions as well as fundraising or educational use. Special editions can also be created to specification. For details, contact specialsales@abramsbooks.com or the address below.

ABRAMS The Art of Books
195 Broadway, New York, NY 10007
abramsbooks.com

To my goddaughter Harriet,
who shares my hunger for books and
unlikely adventures

PART ONE: LICKING THE CUB

CHAPTER 1

The third time Makepeace woke screaming from the nightmare, her mother was angry.

'I told you not to dream that way again!' she hissed, keeping her voice low to avoid waking the rest of the house. 'Or if you do, you must not cry out!'

'I could not help it!' whispered Makepeace, frightened by her mother's fierce tone.

Mother took Makepeace's hands, her face tense and unsmiling in the early morning light.

'You do not like your home. You do not want to live with your mother.'

'I do! I do!' Makepeace exclaimed, feeling her world lurch under her feet.

'Then you must *learn* to help it. If you scream every night, terrible things will happen. We may be thrown out of this house!'

Behind the wall slept Makepeace's aunt and uncle, who owned the pie shop downstairs. Aunt was loud and honest, whereas Uncle glowered and was impossible to please. Since the age of six, Makepeace had been given the task of looking after her four little cousins, who were always needing to be fed, cleaned, patched up, dressed down or rescued from neighbours' trees. In between times, she ran errands and helped in the kitchen. And yet Mother and Makepeace slept on a bolster in a draughty little room away from the rest of the household. Their place in the family always felt loaned, as if it could be taken away again without warning.

'Worse, someone may call the minister,' continued Mother. 'Or . . . others may hear of it.'

Makepeace did not know who the 'others' might be, but others were always a threat. Ten years of life with Mother had taught her that nobody else could really be trusted.

'I tried!' Night after night, Makepeace had prayed hard, then lain in the blackness willing herself not to dream. But the nightmare had come for her anyway, full of moonlight, whispers and half-formed things. 'What can I do? I *want* to stop!'

Mother was quiet for a long time, then squeezed Makepeace's hand.

'Let me tell you a story,' she began, as she occasionally did when there were serious matters to discuss. 'There was a little girl lost in the woods, who was chased by a wolf. She ran and ran until her feet were torn, but she knew that the wolf had her scent and was still coming after her. In the end she had to make a choice. She could keep on running and hiding and running forever, or she could stop and sharpen a stick to defend herself. What do you think was the right decision, Makepeace?'

Makepeace could tell that this was not just a story, and that the answer mattered a great deal.

'Can you fight a wolf with a stick?' Makepeace asked doubtfully.

'A stick gives you a chance.' Her mother gave a slight, sad smile. 'A small chance. But it is dangerous to stop running.'

Makepeace thought for a long time.

'Wolves are faster than people,' she said at last. 'Even if she ran and ran, it would still catch her and eat her. She needs a sharp stick.'

Mother nodded slowly. She said nothing more, and did not

finish her story. Makepeace's blood ran cold. Mother was like this sometimes. Conversations became riddles with traps in them, and your answers had consequences.

For as long as Makepeace could remember, the two of them had lived in the busy little not-quite-town of Poplar. She could not imagine the world without the stink of coal smoke and pitch that blew in from the great, clattering shipyards, the pattering poplar trees that gave the place its name, and the lush green marshlands where the cattle grazed. London lay a few miles distant, a smoky mass of menace and promise. It was all so familiar to her, as natural as breathing. And yet, Makepeace could not feel that she belonged.

Mother never said, *This is not our home.* But her eyes said it all the time.

When she had first arrived in Poplar, Mother had changed her baby daughter's name to Makepeace so that the pair of them would be accepted more easily. Makepeace didn't know what her original name had been, and the thought of that made her feel a bit unreal. 'Makepeace' did not quite feel like a name at all. It was an offering, a way of 'making peace' with God and the godly folk of Poplar. It was an apology for the hole where Makepeace's father should have been.

Everyone they knew was godly. That was what the community called themselves, not out of pride, but to set themselves apart from all those on a darker road with Hell's mouth at the end. Makepeace was not the only one with a strange, pious-sounding name. There was a smattering of others—Verity, What-God-Will, Forsaken, Deliverance, Kill-Sin and so forth.

Every other evening, Aunt's room was used for prayer meetings and Bible readings, and on Sundays they all walked to the tall, grey, ragstone church.

The minister was kind when you met him in the street, but terrifying in the pulpit. From the rapt faces of the other listeners, Makepeace could tell that there must be great truths shining in him, and love like a cold white comet. He talked of holding strong against the wicked temptations of drink, gambling, dancing, theatres and idle merriment upon the Sabbath, which were all snares laid by the Devil. He told them what was happening in London and the wider world—the latest treachery at court, the plots of foul Catholics. His sermons were frightening, but also thrilling. Sometimes Makepeace walked out of the church tingling with the sense that the whole congregation were shining soldiers leagued against the forces of darkness. For a little while she could believe that Mother and Makepeace were part of something bigger, something wondrous alongside all their neighbours. The feeling never lasted. Soon they were a lonely army of two once again.

Mother never said, *These are not our friends*, but her grip on Makepeace's hand tightened when they entered the church, or walked into the market, or stopped to greet anyone. It was as if there were an invisible fence running around Mother and Makepeace, cutting them off from everything else. And so Makepeace half smiled at the children the way Mother half smiled at the mothers. Those other children, the ones with fathers.

Children are little priests of their parents, watching their every gesture and expression for signs of their divine will. From her earliest days, Makepeace had known that the two of them were never truly safe, and that other people might turn on them.

Instead, Makepeace had learned to find comfort and kinship

in speechless things. She understood the busy malice of horseflies, the frightened anger of dogs, the heavy patience of cows.

It got her into trouble sometimes. Once, her lip had been split and her nose bloodied for screaming at some boys who were throwing stones at a bird's nest. Killing birds for the pot or stealing eggs for breakfast was fair enough, but pointless, stupid cruelty roused an anger in Makepeace that she could never properly explain. The boys had stared at her in bewilderment, then turned their stones on her. Of course they had. Cruelty was normal, as much a part of their lives as the flowers and the rain. They were used to the grammar-school canes, the pig-screams behind the butchers and the blood in the sawdust of the cock-pit. Smashing little feathered lives was as natural and satisfying to them as stamping in a puddle.

If you stuck out, you got your nose bloodied. To survive, Mother and Makepeace needed to blend in. Yet they never quite succeeded.

The night after the wolf-story, without explanation, Mother took Makepeace to the old graveyard.

By night, the church seemed a hundred times larger, its tower an unforgiving rectangle of utter blackness. The grass was tussocky underfoot and greyish in the starlight. In a corner of the cemetery stood a little brick chapel, long unused. Mother led Makepeace inside, and dumped armfuls of blankets in a corner of the dark building.

'Can we go home now?' Makepeace's skin was crawling. Something was close, some *things* were all around her. She felt the queasy tickle of their nearness, like spider-feet against her mind.

'No,' said Mother.

'There are *things* here!' Makepeace fought down her rising panic. 'I can feel them!' With horror, she recognized the sensation. Her nightmares had started with the same prickle of dread, the same sense of encroaching enemies. 'The demons in my dream—'

'I know.'

'What are they?' whispered Makepeace. 'Are they . . . dead?' In her heart, she already knew the answer.

'Yes,' answered Mother, in the same cool, level tone. 'Listen to me. The dead are like drowners. They are flailing in darkness, trying to grab whatever they can. They may not mean to harm you, but they will, if you let them.

'You will be sleeping here tonight. They will try to claw their way into your head. Whatever happens, do not let them in.'

'What?' Makepeace exclaimed, aghast, briefly forgetting the need for stealth. 'No! I can't stay here!'

'You must,' said Mother. Her face was sculpted and silvered by the starlight, and there was no gentleness in it, no compromise. 'You need to stay here and sharpen your stick.'

Mother was always strangest when something was important. It was as though she kept this other self, this wilful, incomprehensible, otherworldly self, in the clothes chest below her Sunday best, for use in emergencies. At these times she was not Mother, she was Margaret. Her eyes seemed deeper, her hair beneath her cap thicker and witchier, her attention on something that Makepeace could not see.

Usually when Mother was like this, Makepeace kept her head down and did not argue. This time, however, terror overwhelmed her. She begged as she had never begged before. She argued, protested, wept and clung to Mother's arm with fierce desperation. Mother couldn't leave her there, she couldn't, she couldn't . . .

Mother pulled her arm free, and gave Makepeace a sharp shove that sent her reeling backwards. Then she stepped back out and slammed the door, plunging the room into pitch blackness. There was a thud of a bar dropping into place

'Mother!' shouted Makepeace, no longer caring whether they were caught. She rattled the door, but it did not budge. 'Ma!'

There was no response, only the rustle of Mother's steps receding. Makepeace was alone with the dead, the dark and the wintry trills of distant owls.

For hours Makepeace huddled awake in her nest of blankets, shivering with cold and hearing the distant vixens scream. She could feel the things haunting the corners of her mind, waiting for their moment, waiting for her to sleep.

'Please,' she begged them, pressing her hands against her ears, and trying not to hear the whispers. 'Please don't. Please . . .'

But eventually her brain fogged with sleep against her will, and the nightmare came for her.

As before, Makepeace dreamed of a dark and narrow room, with an earth floor and walls of singed black stone. She was trying to close the shutters to stop the moonlight leaking through them. She needed to keep it out—it had whispers in it. But the shutters did not meet in the middle, and the latch was broken. Beyond the gap yawned the sickly night, where the stars swayed and glittered like loose buttons.

Makepeace braced herself against the shutters with all her might, but the night breathed the dead things into the room, by the score. They swooped for her, wailing, with their smoky, molten faces. Makepeace covered her ears and closed her eyes and mouth tightly, knowing that they wanted to get in, in, into her head.

They buzzed and whined against her ears, and she tried not to understand them, tried not to let the soft, sick sounds become words. The pale light prised at her eyelids and the whispers seeped and licked at her ears and the air was thick with them when she could not help but breathe . . .

Makepeace woke with a jerk, her heart banging so loudly that it made her feel sick. Reflexively, she reached out for the warmth and reassurance of Mother's sleeping form.

But Mother was not there. Makepeace's spirits plunged as she remembered where she was. She was not safe at home this time. She was trapped, entombed, surrounded by the dead.

A sudden sound made her freeze. A rasping rustle at floor level, startlingly loud in the cold, crisp night.

Without warning, something small and light ran over Makepeace's foot. She screamed reflexively, but the next moment her pulse began to slow. She had felt the brief brush of fur, the tickle of tiny claws.

A mouse. Somewhere in this room a mouse's bright eyes were watching her. She was not alone with the dead after all. The mouse was not a friend, of course. It would not care if the dead things killed her or drove her mad. But it calmed her to think of it, sheltering from the owls and night-prowling beasts. It didn't cry, or beg to be spared. It didn't care if it was unloved. It knew that it could only count on itself. Somewhere, its currant-sized heart was beating with the fierce will to live.

And soon, Makepeace's own heart was doing the same.

She could not see or hear the dead, but she could sense them, pawing at the edges of her mind. They were waiting for her to tire, panic or let her guard down, so that they could strike. But Makepeace had found a little knot of stubbornness.

It was not easy to stay awake, but Makepeace pinched herself and paced through the long, dark hours, and at last saw night yield to the early grey light. She felt shaky and sick, her mind raw and scraped, but at least she had survived.

Mother came to collect her just before dawn. Makepeace followed her home in silence, head bowed. She knew that Mother always had reasons for everything she did. But for the first time, Makepeace found that she could not forgive her, and afterwards nothing was the same.

Every month or so, Mother would take Makepeace back to the graveyard. Sometimes five or six weeks would pass, and Makepeace would start to hope that Mother had given up the project. Then Mother would remark that she thought that 'it would be a warm night', and Makepeace's heart would plummet, for she knew what that meant.

Makepeace could not bring herself to protest. The memory of her desperate grovelling on that first night made her feel sick.

If someone throws aside their pride and begs with all their heart, and if they do so in vain, then they are never quite the same person afterwards. Something in them dies, and something else comes to life. Afterwards, it was as if some understanding of the world had sunk into Makepeace's soul like winter dew. She knew that she would never feel safe or loved as she had before. And she knew that she would never, ever beg that way again.

So she followed her mother to the graveyard each time, stony-faced. She had learned from the little mouse in the chapel. The ghosts were not cruel bullies who could be reasoned with. They were predators and she was prey, and she would need to be stubborn, fierce and alert to survive. Nobody else would save her.

Inch by painful inch, Makepeace started to build her own protections. As the rain thudded and her breath wisped in the cold air, Makepeace recited home-made prayers and invented words of banishment. She learned to brace against the scrabble and buffet of the dead spirits, and to lash out at them, even though the contact sickened her. She imagined herself as Judith from the Bible, standing in an enemy camp with her borrowed sword, a general's blood bright on the blade. *Come near me,* she told the night whisperers, *and I will slice you to pieces.*

And all the while the living things in the graveyard helped keep her calm and sane. Scuttles in the bushes, eerie fluting calls, the flicker of bats—these were now a comfort to her. Even their claws and teeth were honest. Humans living and dead might suddenly turn on you, but wild things just lived on in their brute, wild way, caring nothing for you. When they died, they left no ghosts. When a mouse was killed by a cat, or a chicken's neck was wrung, or a fish was tugged from a river, Makepeace could see their faint wisps of spirit melt away instantly like morning mist.

Makepeace's simmering cauldron of resentment needed an outlet. Instead of complaining about the night trips, Makepeace found herself arguing with Mother about other unrelated things, pushing back and asking forbidden questions in a way she never had before.

In particular, she started to ask about her father. Until now Mother had crushed all such questions with a look, and Makepeace had settled for hoarding the tiny details her mother had let slip. He lived far away in an old house. He did not want Mother or Makepeace with him. Suddenly this was not enough, and she felt angry that she had been too scared to ask for more before.

'Why won't you tell me his name? Where does he live? Does he know where to find us? How do you *know* he doesn't want us with him? Does he even know about me?'

Mother did not answer such questions, but her stormy glances no longer cowed Makepeace. Neither of them knew what to do with each other. Since Makepeace's birth, Mother had decided everything, and Makepeace had gone along with it. Makepeace did not know why she could no longer be docile. Mother had never needed to compromise before and did not know how to start. Surely if she battered Makepeace with the force of her own personality everything would return to normal? No. It would not. Everything had changed.

And then, two years after her first 'stick-sharpening' expedition, Makepeace returned from a particularly bitter, sleepless night in the chapel shivering uncontrollably. A few days later she was burning with fever, and her muscles ached. Within a fortnight her tongue was speckled, and an unmistakable rash of smallpox pimples was spreading across her face.

The world was hot, dark and terrible for a while, and Makepeace drowned in a choking, abysmal terror. She knew she would probably die, and she knew what dead things were. She could not think straight, and sometimes she wondered whether she might already be dead. But the black tide of the disease slowly went out, leaving her still alive, with just a couple of pockmarks on one of her cheeks. Whenever she saw them reflected in her water pail, they gave her a little spasm of fear in the pit of her stomach. She could imagine a skeletal figure of Death reaching out to touch her face with the tips of two bony fingers, then slowly withdrawing his hand.

After her recovery, three months went by without Mother mentioning the graveyard, and Makepeace assumed that the smallpox, at least, had frightened Mother out of her project.

Unfortunately, she was wrong.

CHAPTER 2

On a blandly sunny day in May, Makepeace and Mother ventured into the city itself to sell some of Mother's lace. The spring was mild, but London had been crackling like a storm cloud. Makepeace wished they were not there.

As Makepeace had been changing and becoming angrier, so had Poplar and London. According to the gossip of the teenage apprentices, so had the whole country.

At prayer meetings, red-nosed Nanny Susan had always been full of visions of the end of the world—the sea brimming with blood, and the Woman Clothed with the Sun from the Bible walking down Poplar High Street. But now others were talking in the same way. A couple of summers ago, it was said that during a mighty storm vast clouds had taken the shape of two great armies. Now there was an uneasy feeling that two such armies might really be forming across the land.

The Poplar folk had always prayed hard, but now they prayed like a people besieged. There was a feeling that the whole country was in danger.

Makepeace could not keep track of all the details, but she understood the heart of it. There was a devilish Catholic plot to seduce King Charles, and turn him against his own people. The good men of Parliament were trying to talk sense into him, but he had stopped listening.

Nobody wanted to blame the King directly. That was treason, and might get your ears lopped off, or your face branded with hot irons. No, they agreed that it was all the fault of the King's evil advisers—Archbishop Laud, 'Black Tom Tyrant' (also known as the Earl of Stafford), and of course wicked Queen Mary, poisoning the King's mind with her French wiles.

If they were not stopped, they would persuade the King to become a bloody tyrant. He would turn to false religion, and send out his troops to murder all loyal, God-fearing Protestants in the country. The Devil himself was abroad, whispering in ears, curdling minds, and shaping the deeds of men with sly and subtle hands. You almost expected to see his singed hoof-prints in the roadway.

The fear and outrage in Poplar was very real, but Makepeace sensed an undercurrent of fierce excitement as well. If everything *did* fall apart, if a time of trials *did* come, if the world *did* end, the godly of Poplar would be ready. They were Christian soldiers, ready to withstand, and preach, and march.

And now, walking through the London streets, Makepeace could feel a tingle of that same excitement, that same menace.

'There's a smell here,' she said. Mother was her other self, so it was natural to voice her half-formed thoughts.

'It's the smoke,' said Mother curtly.

'No, it isn't,' said Makepeace. It wasn't a *smell* exactly, and she knew Mother understood. It was a warning tingle of the senses, like that before a storm. 'It smells like metal. Can we go home?'

'Yes,' said Mother drily. 'We can go home and eat stones, since you don't want us earning our bread.' She did not break stride.

Makepeace always found London oppressive. There were too many people, buildings and smells. Today, however, there was a new fizz and fierceness in the air. Why was she even more nervous than usual? What was different? She glanced from side to side, noting the dozens of new placards stuck to doors and posts.

'What are those?' she whispered. It was a pointless question. Mother could not read any more than Makepeace could. The bold black letters looked as though they were shouting.

'Ink-lions roaring,' said Mother. London was awash with raging pamphlets, printed sermons, prophecies and denunciations, some for the King and some for Parliament. Mother always jokingly called them 'ink-lions'. All roar and no claw, she said.

There had been a lot more silent roaring over the last two days. Two weeks before, the King had summoned Parliament for the first time in years, and everyone Makepeace knew had been ecstatic with relief. But two days ago he had dismissed Parliament again in a right royal rage. Now gossip had an ominous rumble, the pale sun seemed to teeter in the sky, and everyone was waiting for something to happen. Whenever there was a sudden bang or shout, people looked up sharply. *Has it started?* their expressions asked. Nobody was sure what *it* was, but *it* was unquestionably coming.

'Ma . . . why are there so many apprentices out on the streets?' Makepeace murmured quietly.

There were dozens of them, she realized, loitering in twos and threes in doorways and alleys, crop-headed, restless, their hands calloused from loom and lathe. The youngest were about fourteen, the oldest in their early twenties. They should all have been labouring away, doing their masters' bidding, but here they were.

The apprentices were weathercocks for the mood of the city. When London was at ease with itself, they were just lads— dawdling, flirting, and jabbing at the world with crude, clever jokes. But when London was stormy, they changed. A dark and angry lightning arced unseen between them, and sometimes they broke out into wild, passionate mobs, breaking doors and skulls with their boots and cudgels.

Mother glanced around at the little loitering groups, and she too began to look worried.

'There are a lot around,' she agreed quietly. 'We will go home. The sun is sinking anyway. And . . . you will need your strength. It will be a warm night tonight.'

For a brief moment Makepeace was relieved, then Mother's last sentence sank in. Makepeace stopped dead, overwhelmed by disbelief and outrage.

'No!' she snapped, surprised by her own firmness. 'I won't go! I am never going back to the graveyard again!'

Mother cast a self-conscious glance around, then gripped Makepeace's arm firmly and dragged her into the mouth of an alley.

'You must!' Mother took Makepeace by the shoulders, staring into her eyes.

'I nearly died last time!' protested Makepeace.

'You caught the smallpox from the Archers' daughter,' retorted Mother without hesitation. 'The graveyard had nothing to do with it. You will thank me for this some day. I told you—I'm helping you sharpen your stick.'

'I know, I know!' Makepeace exclaimed, unable to keep the frustration out of her voice. 'The "wolves" are the ghosts, and you want me to learn to be strong, so I can keep them out. But why can't I just stay away from graveyards? If I keep away from ghosts, I'll be safe! You're throwing me to the wolves, over and over again!'

'You are wrong,' said Mother softly. 'These ghosts are *not* the wolves. These ghosts are mere hungry wisps—nothing in

18

comparison. But the wolves are out there, Makepeace. They are looking for you, and some day they will find you. Pray that you are full-grown and strong by the time they do.'

'You are just trying to frighten me,' said Makepeace. Her voice shook, but with anger this time, not fear.

'Yes, I am! Do you think you are a poor martyr, sitting there at night with those little will-o'-the-wisps licking at your face? This is *nothing*. There is far worse out there. You *should* be frightened.'

'Then why can't we ask my father to protect us?' It was a dangerous angle to take, but Makepeace had come too far to turn back. 'I bet he wouldn't leave me out in graveyards!'

'He is the *last* person we can go to for help,' said Mother, with a bitterness Makepeace had never heard before. 'Forget him.'

'Why?' Suddenly Makepeace could not bear all the silences in her life, all the things that she was not allowed to say or ask. 'Why do you never tell me anything? I don't believe you any more! You just want me to stay with you forever! You want to keep me to yourself! You won't let me meet my father because you know he *would* want me!'

'You have no idea what I saved you from!' exploded Mother. 'If I had stayed in Grizehayes—'

'Grizehayes,' repeated Makepeace, and saw her mother turn pale. 'Is that where he lives? Is that the old house you talked about?' She had a name. At long last she had a name. It meant that she could look for it. Somebody, somewhere, would know where it was.

The name sounded old. She could not quite picture the house it described. It was as if a heavy, silvery mist lay between her and its ancient turrets.

'I won't go back to the graveyard,' said Makepeace. Her

willpower set its pike in the earth, and braced for the onslaught. 'I won't. If you try to make me, I'll run away. I will. I'll find Grizehayes. I'll find my father. And I'll never come back.'

Mother's eyes looked glassy with surprise and anger. She had never learned to deal with Makepeace's new defiance. Then the warmth leaked out of her expression leaving it cold and distant.

'Run, then,' she said icily. 'If that's what you want, good riddance to you. But when you are in the hands of those people, never say that I did not warn you.'

Mother never yielded, never softened. When Makepeace challenged her, Mother always raised the stakes, calling Makepeace's bluff and pushing back harder. And Makepeace *had* been bluffing about running away but, as she stared into Mother's hard eyes, for the first time she thought that she might actually run. The idea made her feel breathless, weightless.

And then Mother glanced at something over Makepeace's shoulder, out on the main street, and stiffened, aghast. She breathed a few words, so faintly that Makepeace only just caught them.

. . . Speak of the Devil . . .

Makepeace looked over her shoulder, just in time to see a tall man in a good coat of dark blue wool stride past. He was only of middling years, but his hair was a flare of white.

She knew the old saying, *Speak of the Devil and he will appear.* Mother had been talking of 'those people'—the Grizehayes people—and then she had caught sight of this man. Was he someone from Grizehayes, then? Perhaps even Makepeace's father?

Makepeace met Mother's gaze, her own eyes now wild with excitement and triumph. Then she turned, and tried to dart for the street.

'No!' Mother hissed, grabbing her arm with both hands. 'Makepeace!'

But Makepeace's own name jarred against her ear. She was tired of 'making peace' with troubles that were never explained. She wriggled free, and sprinted into the main thoroughfare.

'You'll be the death of me!' Mother called after her. 'Makepeace, stop!'

Makepeace did not stop. She could just make out the stranger's blue coat and white hair in the distance, disappearing around a corner. Her past was getting away from her.

She reached the corner just in time to see him disappearing among the crowds, and set off in pursuit. Makepeace was aware of Mother calling her name somewhere behind her, but did not look back. Instead, she pursued the distant figure down one street, then another, then another. Many times she thought she had lost her quarry, only to glimpse a distant shock of white hair.

Makepeace could not give in, even when she found herself hurrying across London's great bridge and into Southwark. The buildings on either side grew dingier and the smells more sour. She could hear laughter drifting from the waterside taverns, and oaths and oar-creaks from the river itself. It was darker now, too. The sun was sinking from view, and the sky had dulled to the colour of stained tin. Despite this, the streets were unusually crowded. People kept getting in her way, and blocking her view of the white-haired man.

It was only when a road spat her out into a large, open space that she halted, suddenly daunted. There was grass under her feet, and she realized that she was on the edge of St George's Fields. All around her seethed a shadowy, restless, raucous crowd, heads silhouetted against the darkening sky. She could not judge how far it stretched, but there seemed to be hundreds of voices, all of them male. There was no sign of the white-haired man.

Makepeace stared around her, panting for breath, aware that she was attracting hard, curious glances. She was dressed in clothes of plain, cheap wool and linen, but her kerchief and cap were clean and respectable, and here that was enough to draw stares. She was also a lone female, and one of less than thirteen years.

'Hello, love!' one of the dark figures called. 'Come to tickle up our courage, have you?'

'Nah,' said another, 'you're here to march with us, aren't you, miss? You can throw stools at those bastards, like the Scottish ladies! Show us your cudgel arm!' Half a dozen men laughed uproariously, and Makepeace could sense menace in the teasing.

'Is that Margaret Lightfoot's girl?' asked a younger voice suddenly. Peering into the darkness, Makepeace could just make out a familiar face, the fourteen-year-old apprentice of the weaver that lived next door. 'What are you doing here?'

'I got lost,' Makepeace said quickly. 'What's happening?'

'We're on a hunt.' There was a fierce, wild light in the apprentice's eyes. 'Hunting old William the Fox—old Archbishop Laud.' Makepeace had heard that name hundreds of times, usually being cursed as one of the King's evil advisers. 'We're just going to go and knock on his door, and say hello. Like good neighbours.' He hefted his cudgel and slapped it hard into his other palm, fizzing and fidgeting with excitement.

Too late, Makepeace guessed at the meaning of all the placards. They had been announcing a great and angry gathering in St George's Fields. The crowd was full of apprentices, Makepeace realized, as her eyes adjusted. All of them were hefting makeshift weapons—hammers, broom-handles, fire-irons and planks—

with a fierce jollity that meant business. They were hell-bent on dragging evil out of its palace and breaking its crown. But in their bright eyes Makepeace could see that it was also a game—a game of blood, like a bear-baiting.

'I need to go home!' Even as Makepeace spoke the words, they had a bitter taste. She had lost her one chance of finding out more about her past, but what if she had lost her home too? Her mother had called her bluff by telling her to run away, and Makepeace had done just that.

The apprentice's brow wrinkled, and he stood on tiptoe, craning to see past the crowds. Makepeace did the same as best she could, and realized that the road she had run down was now clogged with a solid mass of figures, all pouring into St George's Fields.

'You stick with me,' the apprentice said anxiously, as the crowd started to surge forwards, carrying the two of them with it. 'You'll be safe with me.'

It was hard for Makepeace to see past the crush of taller figures, but as she was swept along, she heard more and more voices joining the rallying cries and laughing at the jests. The apprentice army sounded vast now. No wonder they were so confident, so bristling with purpose!

'Makepeace! Where are you?'

The call was almost swallowed by the crescendo of yells and bellows, but Makepeace heard it. It was Mother's voice, she was sure of it. Mother had followed her, and was now caught up in the crowd somewhere behind her.

'Ma!' Makepeace called out as the crowd bore her relentlessly onward.

'There's Lambeth Palace!' came a cry ahead. 'There's lights at the windows!' Makepeace could smell the river again, and could see a great building ahead at the water's edge, with high, square towers, its silhouetted crenellations biting into the evening sky.

From the front of the mob came sounds of furious argument, and the crowd took on a feverish, wavering tension.

'Turn yourselves about!' somebody was bellowing. 'Go home!'

'Who's there ahead?' a dozen voices in the crowd were demanding, and a dozen different answers came back. Some said it was the army, some the King's men, some that it was the archbishop himself.

'Ah, shut your mouth!' one of the apprentices shouted at last. 'Put William the Fox out of doors, or we'll break in and halloo the whole bunch of you!'

The other apprentices responded with a deafening roar, and there was a furious press forward. The patch of sky above Makepeace shrank as she was half crushed by taller figures. There were battle-cries ahead, and the bellow and yell of men fighting.

'Force the door!' somebody was shouting. 'Give 'im the crowbar!'

'Smash their lights!' came another cry.

When the first shot rang out, Makepeace thought somebody had dropped something heavy on the cobbles. Then a second shot rang out and a third. The crowd convulsed, some pulling back, some charging forward. Makepeace took a knee in the gut, and a careless cudgel jab in the eye.

'Makepeace!' It was Mother's voice again, shrill and desperate, and closer than before.

'Ma!' The crowd around Makepeace was thrashing now, but she fought her way through it towards the sound of her mother's voice. 'I'm here!'

Ahead of her, someone screamed.

It was a harsh, brief sound, and at first Makepeace did not know what it was. She had never heard Mother scream before. But as she elbowed her way forward, she saw a woman lying on the ground at the base of a wall, being stepped on by the blind, surging crowd.

'Ma!'

With Makepeace's help, Mother unsteadily rose to her feet. She was ashen pale, and even in the darkness Makepeace could see inky lines of blood pouring down the left side of her face. She was moving wrong as well, one eyelid drooping and her right arm jerking awkwardly.

'I'll get you home,' whispered Makepeace, her mouth dry. 'I'm sorry, Ma. I'm sorry . . .'

Mother stared at Makepeace glassily for a moment, as if she did not know her. Then, her face tensed and contorted.

'No!' she screamed hoarsely, and lashed out, striking Makepeace across the face and then shoving her away. 'Stay away from me! Go away! Go away!'

Caught off balance, Makepeace fell over. She had one last glimpse of Mother's face, still fixed in a fierce and desperate glare, and then took a kick to the face that set her eyes streaming. Somebody else trod on her calf.

'Be ready!' somebody was shouting. 'Here they come!' Gunshots sounded again, as though the stars were exploding.

Then strong hands were hooked under Makepeace's armpits, and she was hauled to her feet. A tall apprentice tucked her over his shoulder without ceremony, and carried her bodily away from the front line, while she struggled and called for Mother. He dumped her in the mouth of an alleyway.

'You run home!' he screamed at Makepeace, red-faced, then plunged back into the fray, hammer raised high.

She never found out who he was, or what happened to him.

Nor did she ever see Mother alive again.

Mother's body was found after the bloodshed and the arrests, after the rioters were thrown into retreat. Nobody was ever quite sure what it was that had struck her in the head, and caused her death. Perhaps a wildly swung poker, perhaps an accidental kick to the head with a hobnailed boot, perhaps a stray bullet that struck her and moved on.

Makepeace did not know, and did not care. The riot had killed Mother, and Makepeace had led her there. It was all Makepeace's fault.

And the people of the parish, who had bought Mother's lace and embroidery when it suited them, decided that their precious churchyard was no place for a woman with a child out of wedlock. The minister, who had always been kind in the street, now stood in the pulpit and said that Margaret Lightfoot had not been one of the Saved.

Mother was buried instead in unconsecrated land on the edge of the Poplar marshes. It was stubbornly brambled, welcoming only the wind and the birds, and as secretive as Margaret Lightfoot herself.

CHAPTER 3

You'll be the death of me.

Makepeace could not forget Mother's words. They were her companion through every daylight moment, every nocturnal hour. She could imagine Mother saying them, but now in a tone steady and cold.

I killed her, Makepeace thought. *I ran away and she followed me into danger. It was my fault, and she hated me for it at the end.*

Makepeace had thought that now she might find herself sleeping in the same bed as her little cousins, but she was still left to sleep alone on the bolster she had shared with Mother. Perhaps everybody sensed that she was a murderess. Or perhaps Aunt and Uncle were no longer sure what to do with her, now that Mother's lace-making was no longer paying for her keep.

She was alone. The little fence that had run around Makepeace and Mother now ran round only Makepeace, cutting her off from the rest of the world.

Everyone else in the house prayed as usual, but with extra prayers for Mother. Makepeace found she could no longer pray the way she had been taught was right, baring her soul before the Lord. She tried, but her insides seemed to be full of a wild, white emptiness like an October sky, nothing she could put into words. She wondered whether her soul was gone completely.

On the second night, alone in her room, Makepeace tried to force the lid off her feelings. She made herself pray for forgiveness, for Mother's soul and her own. The attempt left her shaking, but not from the cold. She was afraid that God was listening with cold, implacable wrath, looking into every rotten crevice of her soul. And at the same time she was afraid that He was not listening at all, had never listened, would never listen.

The effort wore her out, and afterwards she slept.

Tap. Tap, tap.

Makepeace opened her eyes. She was cold and alone in bed, with no curve of Mother's back beside her. The loss was vaster in the pitch blackness.

Tap, tap, tap.

The sound was coming from the direction of the shutters. Perhaps they were loose. If so, they would rattle all night and keep her awake. Reluctantly she rose from the bed and felt her way to the window, knowing the room too well to need a light. She stroked the latch and found it fastened. And then beneath her fingertips she felt a tremor as something tapped the outside of the shutter again.

From behind the wooden slats, she heard another noise. It was so soft and muffled that it was barely more than a tickle in the ear, but it sounded like a human voice. There was something terribly familiar about its tone. Hairs rose on the back of Makepeace's neck.

There it was again, a smothered sob of sound, close against the other side of the shutter. A single word.

Makepeace.

In a hundred nightmares, Makepeace had battled in vain to keep dream-shutters closed and stop maddened ghosts rushing in to attack her. Her hands shook at the memory, but still her fingers rested on the latch.

The dead are like drowners, Mother had said.

Makepeace imagined her mother drowning in the night air, flailing in slow motion with her black hair floating wide. She imagined her helpless, alone, desperate for something to cling to.

'I'm here,' she whispered aloud. 'It's me—Makepeace.' She pressed her ear to the shutter, and this time thought she could just make out the words of the muted response.

Let me in.

Makepeace's blood chilled, but she told herself not to be afraid. Mother would not be like the other dead things. It was different. Whatever was outside, it would still be Mother. Makepeace could not abandon her—not again.

She unlatched the shutter, and opened it.

Outside a few dim stars glimmered in a charcoal sky. A clammy breeze seeped into the room, tickling her with goosebumps. Makepeace's chest tightened with the certainty that something else had entered with the wind. The darkness had a new texture, and she was no longer alone.

Makepeace was filled suddenly with a terrible fear that she had done something irrevocable. Her skin was tingling. Once again she felt it, the tickle of spider-feet across her mind. The reaching, tentative touch of the dead.

She flinched back from the window, and tried to steel her mental defences. But when she thought of Mother, her private incantations became as useless as nursery rhymes. Makepeace closed her eyes tight, but she found herself remembering Mother's face, looking as she had by candlelight on that first night in the chapel. A strange creature, with an unreadable expression, and no softness in her at all.

There was a wintry draught against her neck, the breath of something breathless. A tickle against her face and ear—an escaped strand of her own hair, it had to be. She froze, breathing shallowly.

'Ma?' she asked, in a whisper so faint it barely grazed the air.

A voice answered. An almost-voice. A molten mess of a sound, an idiot slobber, the consonants broken and spilling like egg yolks. It was so close to her ear, it buzzed.

Makepeace's eyes flew open. There—there!—filling her vision was a swirling, moth-grey, distorted face. Its eyes were holes, its mouth a long, wailing droop. She lurched backwards away from it, until her back hit a wall. She stared and stared and wanted to be wrong, even as it lunged hungrily for her eyes with fingers of smoke.

Makepeace closed her eyes only just in time, and felt a cold touch settle on her eyelids. It was the nightmare, it was all her nightmares, but now she had no hope of waking. She covered her ears, but too slowly to stop herself understanding the soft, horrible sounds.

Let me in . . . Let me in . . . Makepeace, let me in . . .

It felt its way across her mind, her defences. It found the cracks made by her grief, love and memories, and tore at them with cruel, eager fingers. It ripped pieces out of her heart and mind, as it dug its way in. It knew the way past her defences, the path to her softest core.

And with the savagery of terror, Makepeace fought back.

She lashed out with her mind at the thing's smoky softness, and felt it scream as she mangled and tore it. The loose pieces of it flailed senselessly like severed worms, and tried to bury their way into her soul. It grappled and clung and raked at her. It could form no words now, only whines and wails.

Makepeace did not mean to open her eyes again. But she did, just for a mere instant, at the very end. To see whether it was gone.

So she saw what the face had become, and what she had done to it. She saw fear and a rictus of something like hatred on its twisted, vanishing features.

It was barely a face at all. But somehow it was still Mother.

Afterwards, Makepeace did not remember screaming and screaming. The next thing she knew, she was sitting on the floor, blinking in the light from her aunt's taper, and trying to answer the family's questions. The shutter was ajar, and banging slightly in the breeze with a *tap-tap-tap* noise.

Aunt told Makepeace that she must have fallen out of bed during a nightmare. Makepeace needed her to be right. It was not completely reassuring, since she knew that ghosts battled in dreams were sometimes real. But, please God, not *this* ghost. This one could not have attacked her, and Makepeace could not have torn it to shreds. The very thought was unbearable.

It had been a dream. Makepeace clung to this idea in desperation.

It was only a week later that rumours spread of a ghost abroad on the marshes. It was said to haunt a particularly lonely stretch, too soggy for the cattle to graze, and striped with stray paths where the footing could be only sometimes trusted.

Some unseen thing startled a wandering pedlar by crashing through the reeds, leaving a mangled path behind it. The local rooks were found to have abandoned their rookery, and the wading birds had fled to other parts of the marshlands. Then the Angel Inn, lurking on the outskirts between town and reedbeds, found itself a haunt of more than just sailors.

'A vengeful spirit,' Aunt called it. 'They say it came at sunset. Whatever it was, it knocked in a door, caused a world of damage and beat some strong men black and blue.'

Makepeace was the only person who heard these rumours with a painful stab of hope as well as fear. Mother's grave was on the edge of the marshlands, not so very far from the Angel. There was a horror in imagining Mother's ghost rampaging maddened, but at least if it was at large, that would mean that Makepeace had not torn it to pieces after all. At least she had not murdered Mother a second time.

I must find her, Makepeace told herself, even as the thought made her sick. *I must talk to her. I must save her.*

Nobody from Makepeace's church frequented the Angel, except Old William during his lapses. Whenever he had reeled home drunk, the minister made an example of him in the sermon, and asked everyone to strengthen him and pray for him. Taking the rutted lane to the inn, Makepeace felt self-conscious, and wondered whether she would be accused of drunkenness the following Sunday.

The Angel's stone buildings were crooked like an arm, cradling its little stable yard. A heavy-jawed woman in a stained cotton cap was sweeping the step, but looked up as Makepeace approached.

'Hello, poppet!' she called. 'Have you come to bring your father home? Which one is he?'

'No, I . . . I want to hear about the ghost.'

The woman did not seem surprised, and gave a curt, business-like nod.

'You'll buy a cup of something if you want a look.'

Makepeace followed her into the darkened inn, and with a pang of guilt spent a coin of Aunt's shopping money on a cup of small beer. Then she was led out through the rear door.

Behind the inn lay a sawdust-covered stretch of bare ground. Makepeace guessed that this was where the inn's entertainments took place when there were enough crowds to merit it—shaven-headed pugilists fighting each other bare-knuckle, cockfights and badger baiting, or less bloody games of quoits, skittles or bowls. Here and there it was blotted dark by old spillages of ale or blood. Beyond this space lay a low wall with a stile in it, and then miles of marshes, the wind-stirred reed-forest shimmering softly in the late afternoon light.

'Come—look at this.' The woman seemed to take a professional pride in showing Makepeace the damage. The back door's bar was shattered, and one of its panels splintered. A window was broken, the leading bent, several of the little panes frost-white with fractures. A cloth sign had been ripped to tatters, only shreds of the image still visible—a pipe, some drums, a dark bestial shape of some sort. A table had capsized, and two chairs had broken backs.

As she listened, Makepeace's heart began to sink. It occurred to her belatedly that none of the ghosts she had ever encountered had left real damage one could see. They had attacked her mind, but never broken so much as a cup.

Perhaps it was just an ordinary brawl, thought Makepeace. She cast a furtive glance at the landlady's worn, canny face. *Perhaps she made the best of the damage, and pretended a ghost caused it, so inquisitive folk would come here and buy drinks.*

The landlady led Makepeace over to two men who were grimly sipping from their tankards in the late afternoon air. Both were lanky and leathery from the sun. They were not locals, and Makepeace guessed from the packs at their feet that they were the travelling sort.

'Come to hear about the ghost,' said the woman, jerking her head towards Makepeace. '*You* can tell her about that, can't you?'

The two men glanced at each other, and scowled. Evidently this was not a story that put them in good humour.

'Is she buying us a drink?' asked the taller of the two.

The landlady looked at Makepeace with her eyebrows raised. Feeling sick, and even more sure that she was being conned, Makepeace parted with another coin, and the landlady hurried off to fetch more ale.

'It came at us out of the dark. You see this?' The taller man held up his hand, around which was tied a grubby handkerchief dark with spots of blood. 'Ripped my friend's coat—nearly knocked my brains out against the wall—smashed our fiddle too!' The fiddle he brandished looked as if someone had stamped on it. 'Mistress Bell calls it a ghost, but I say devil. Invisible devil.'

His anger seemed genuine enough, but Makepeace still did not know whether to believe him. *Everything's invisible if you're blind drunk*, she thought.

'Did it say anything?' Makepeace could not help shivering when she remembered the molten voice from her maybe-dream.

'Not to us,' said the shorter of the two. He held out his tankard as the landlady returned with a jug, and let her top it up. 'After it was done pounding us like a pestle, it left that way.' He pointed out towards the marshes. 'Knocked over a post as it went.'

Makepeace finished her drink, and rallied her courage.

'Watch your step out there, poppet!' shouted the landlady as she saw Makepeace climbing over the stile that led to the marshes. 'Some of those paths look fair enough, but slip under your feet. We don't want your ghost coming back here too!'

The rustle and crunch of Makepeace's steps sounded loud as she set off across the marshes, and she realized that she could hear no birdsong. The only other sounds were the dry music of the reeds rasping stem on stem, and the papery ripple of occasional young poplars whose leaves flickered grey-green and silver in the breeze. The quiet seeped into her bones, and with it the fear that, once again, she was making a terrible mistake.

She glanced back nervously, and was chilled to see that the inn was already a fair distance behind her. It was as if she were a little unanchored boat that had drifted unwittingly from the shore.

And as she stood there, Makepeace was unexpectedly struck and overwhelmed by an invisible wave.

A feeling. No, a smell. A reek like blood, autumn woodlands and old damp wool. It was a hot smell. It itched and rasped against her mind like breath. It filled Makepeace's senses, fogging her vision and making her feel sick.

Ghost, was her one helpless thought. *A ghost.*

But this was nothing like the cold, creeping attacks of the ghosts she remembered. This was not trying to claw its way inside her—it did not know she was there. It blundered against her, hot, terrible and oblivious.

The world swam, and then she barely knew where she was,

who she was. She was swallowed by a memory that was not her own.

The sun stung. The reek of the sawdust choked her. There was a terrible pain in her lip, and she could not shape words. Her ears filled with a buzzing drone and a cruel, rhythmic thud. With each thud, something yanked painfully at her mouth. When she tried to flinch away, a red-hot slice of pain cut across her shoulders. She burned with a rage born of agony.

The wave passed, and Makepeace doubled over. Around her, the world still burned with sunlight, beating drums in her head and making her feel sick. Half blind, she took a clumsy step to steady herself, but instead felt her foot slide from beneath her on the moist, uneven ground. She slithered off the path and landed sprawling among the reeds, hardly feeling them scratch her arms and face. Then she leaned over and threw up, retching over and over.

Her head gradually cleared. The strange agony faded. But she could still smell something, she realized, mixed with a choking smell of rot. And she could still hear buzzing.

It was a different sound now, however. Before, it had been a queasy, heart-grating music. Now it settled into a insectile whirr. The buzz of dozens of tiny wings.

Rising unsteadily to her feet, and pushing the reeds aside, Makepeace advanced further down the slope from the path. With each step the ground grew softer and claggier. She was not the only creature to have come this way, she realized. There were broken stems, gouges in the mud . . .

And beyond them, something sprawled in an overgrown ditch, half hidden by the reeds. Something dark. Something about the size of a man.

Makepeace felt her stomach somersault. She had been wrong about everything. If that was a body, then the ghost was not Mother at all. Perhaps she had just discovered a murder victim. For all she knew, the murderer might be watching her at this very moment.

Or perhaps this was some traveller struck down by the savage ghost, and in need of help. No, she could not run, even though every nerve in her body told her to.

She drew nearer, feeling mud squelch under her shoes with every step. The thing was dark brown, large and mound-like, and jewelled with the quick green-and-black bodies of flies.

A man in a wool coat?

No.

The shape grew clearer. At last Makepeace could see what it was, and what it was not. For a moment she felt relieved.

Then she felt an awful wave of sadness, stronger than her fear or revulsion, stronger even than the smell. She slithered down to crouch beside it, and used her handkerchief to cover her mouth. Then she very gently stroked her hand over the sodden dark shape.

There was no sign of life. In the mud nearby were gouge-marks, from its weak attempts to drag itself out of the ditch. There were bleeding, yellow-edged sores that looked as if they had been left by chains and shackles. She could hardly bear to look at the torn mouth, the seeping gash and trickle of dark blood.

Now she knew that she did still have a soul. And it was on fire.

Makepeace was muddy and briar-torn by the time she reached the backyard of the Angel, but she did not care. A small, wooden stool was the first thing that came to hand. She scooped it up, too angry to feel its weight.

The two travelling entertainers were murmuring fiercely in a corner, and paid Makepeace no mind. Or at least, they paid her no mind until she swung her stool and hit the tallest in the face.

'Gah! You crazy little wretch!' He stared at her in disbelief, clutching his bloody mouth.

Makepeace did not answer, but hit him again, this time in the gut.

'Leave off! Have you gone mad?' The shorter entertainer grabbed at Makepeace's stool. She kicked him hard in the kneecap.

'You left it to die!' she yelled. 'You beat it, and tortured it, and dragged it about by a chain until its mouth tore! And then when it couldn't stand any more, you threw it down in that ditch!'

'What's come over you?' The landlady was beside Makepeace now, a strong arm around her, trying to restrain her. 'What are you talking about?'

'THE BEAR!' bellowed Makepeace.

'A bear?' Mistress Bell looked at the strangers in bafflement. 'Oh! Mercy. Did your dancing bear die, then?'

'Yes, and how we'll make a living now, I don't know!' snapped the shorter man. 'This place is cursed—nothing but bad luck, invisible devils, crazy girls—'

The taller man spat bloodily into his hand. 'That little trull knocked my tooth out!' he exclaimed incredulously, and gave Makepeace a murderous glare.

'You didn't even wait for it to die before you ripped the ring out of its muzzle!' screamed Makepeace. Her head was singing. Any moment now, one of these men would take a swing at her, but she did not care. 'No wonder it came back! No wonder it's raging! I hope you never escape it! I hope it kills you both!'

Both men were shouting, and the landlady was trying to calm everybody down at the top of her voice. But Makepeace could hear nothing over the green-black buzz of anger in her brain.

Makepeace tugged hard at the stool, and the short man yanked back. She yielded to the motion, guiding the stool upwards so that it smacked into his nose. He gave a squawk of pure rage, and let go of the stool, lunging for an oaken walking stick that rested against his pack. The landlady sprinted away, screaming for help, and Makepeace found herself facing two men with bleeding faces and fury in their eyes.

Their wrath was nothing, however, compared to that of the Bear as it charged out of the marshlands.

Makepeace was looking the right way to see it, or almost see it. The Bear was a dark, smoky pucker in the world, four-legged and hump-backed, larger than it had been in life. It galloped towards the trio with frightful speed. Translucent holes marked its eyes and its gaping maw.

The impact knocked Makepeace off her feet. She lay on the ground stunned. The darkness that was the Bear towered over her. It took her a moment to realize that she was staring up at its great, shadowy back. It stood between her and her enemies, as if she were its cub.

Through its murky outline, she could still see her two foes, stepping forward, one raising his stick to strike at her. They could not see the Bear. They could not guess why the downward strike fell awry, batted to one side by the swipe of a great, shadowy paw.

Only Makepeace could see it. Only she could see how the Bear's rage was burning it away, how it spent itself in every motion. It bled wisps as it roared its silent roar. Its flanks seemed to steam.

It was losing itself, and it did not even know it.

Makepeace pulled herself up on to her knees, dizzy with the bear-reek and the song of its rage in her blood. Reflexively she put out both her arms, encircling the raging shadow. All she wanted in that moment was to stop the wisps escaping, to hold the Bear together and stop it melting into nothing.

Her arms closed on darkness, and she fell into it.

CHAPTER 4

'She's been this way for days now,' said Aunt's voice.

Makepeace did not know where she was, or why. Her head throbbed, and was too heavy to lift. Something was trapping her limbs. The world around her was phantom-vague, and voices seemed to float to her from a great distance.

'We cannot go on like this!' said the Uncle-voice. 'Half the time she's lying there like one dead, and the other half of the time . . . Well, you've seen her! Grief's turned her wits. We need to think of our children! They're not safe with her here.'

It was the first time Makepeace had heard him sound frightened.

'What will folk think of us if we cast out our own blood?' asked Aunt. 'She's our cross to bear!'

'We're not her only kin,' said Uncle.

There was a pause, then Aunt gave a great huff of a sigh. Makepeace felt Aunt's warm, worn hands gently grip her face.

'Makepeace, child, are you listening? Your father—what's his name? Margaret never told us, but surely you know, don't you?'

Makepeace shook her head.

'Grizehayes,' she whispered huskily. 'Lives . . . at Grizehayes.'

'I knew it,' whispered the Aunt-voice, sounding awed but triumphant. 'That Sir Peter! I knew it!'

'Will he do anything for her?' asked Uncle.

'He won't, but his family will if they don't want their name dragged through the dirt!' said Aunt firmly. 'It wouldn't look good to have someone with their fancy bloodline put in Bedlam, would it? I'll tell them that's where she's bound if they do nothing.'

But the words were just sounds again, and Makepeace sank into a dark place.

The next few days swam by indistinctly, like pike through murky water. Most of the time the family kept Makepeace bound up in a blanket like a swaddled babe. Whenever she was lucid enough they unwrapped her, but she could not follow what they said, or help with anything. She tottered and stumbled, and dropped everything she tried to pick up.

The smell of cooking pies from the kitchen, usually homely and familiar, now made her feel sick. The scents of the lard, the blood of the meat, the herbs—they were too much, they were blinding. But all the while, it was the smell of the Bear that haunted her. She could not scrub away the dank, warm reek of its mind.

She tried to recall what had happened after she reached for the Bear and the blackness swallowed her, but her memories were a dark swirl. She thought she remembered seeing the two travelling men, though. She had a murky image of them bellowing, their pale faces striped with blood.

Beasts did not have ghosts—at least that is what she had always thought. But evidently they did, now and then. By now it had probably burned itself away into nothingness in its quest for vengeance. She hoped it had been happy with that bargain. Why had it left her so sick? Perhaps, she thought hazily, mad ghost-brutes could infect you with fever.

She thought herself feverish indeed when, one day, she was brought into the main room and found a stranger standing by the hearth. He was tall, and wore a dark blue coat. His beaky face was topped by a shock of white hair. It was the man she had chased like a will-o'-the-wisp on the evening of the riot.

Makepeace stared at him, and felt her eyes fill with tears.

'This is Master Crowe,' Aunt told her slowly and carefully. 'He's come to take you to Grizehayes.'

'My . . .' Makepeace's voice was still rusty. 'My father . . .'

Aunt unexpectedly wrapped her arms around Makepeace, and gave her a brisk, tight squeeze.

'He's dead, child,' she whispered. 'But his family have said they'll take you in, and the Fellmottes will look after you better than I could.' Then she hurried off to gather Makepeace's belongings, teary with tenderness, anxiety and relief.

'We've been keeping her bundled up in the blanket,' Uncle was murmuring to Mr Crowe. 'You'll want to do the same when she's wild. Whatever those rogues at the inn did to her, I think they knocked the wits out of her before someone chased them away.'

Makepeace was going to Grizehayes. That was what she had told Mother she was going to do, on that last fatal day. Perhaps she should feel happy, or at least feel something.

Instead, Makepeace felt broken and empty, like a scooped-out eggshell. The hunt for Mother's ghost had led her to a dead bear. And now, Mr Crowe, who had seemed the key to finding her father, had only led her to another grave.

For years the minister had talked of the end of the world, and now it had come. Makepeace knew it, she felt it. As the carriage bore her out through Poplar, she wondered in her dazzled way why the earth did not quake, nor the stars drop like ripe figs, and why she could not see angels or the shining woman from Nanny Susan's visions. Instead she saw clothes drying, and barrows rattling, and steps being scrubbed as if nothing had happened. Somehow that was worse than anything.

As the carriage lumbered north-west, Makepeace tried to understand what she had been told.

Her father had been Sir Peter Fellmotte, and he was dead. His was an old, old family, and they had agreed to take her in. It sounded like a bittersweet ending from a ballad, but Makepeace felt numb. Why had Mother refused to talk about him?

She remembered Mother's warning. *You have no idea what I saved you from! If I had stayed in Grizehayes . . .*

It was a mistake to think of Mother. Makepeace's head filled with the memory of the nightmare ghost with Mother's features. The malformed voice and the grey face in tatters . . . Makepeace's brain went to the dark place again.

When she came back from it, she felt sick and exhausted once more. She was still sitting in the carriage, but wrapped tightly in a sheepskin blanket so that it pinned her arms. A rope was bound around her, holding it in place.

'Are you calmer now?' Mr Crowe asked her levelly as she blinked in confusion.

Hesitantly Makepeace nodded. Calmer than what? There was a new bruise swelling on her jaw. There was also a bruise in her memory, an indistinct shadowy feeling that she had done something she shouldn't. She was in trouble somehow.

'I cannot have you jumping out of the carriage,' said Mr Crowe.

The sheepskin blanket was thick and warm, but rough with an animal smell. She clung to that smell. It was something she understood. Mr Crowe said nothing more to her, and she was grateful for that.

The landscape slowly changed over the long, damp ride. The first day it made sense to Makepeace, with its misty meadows and thriving, pale green cornfields. During the second day, the low hills raised their hackles. By the third, the fields had yielded to moorland, over which lean, black-faced sheep scrambled.

At last she wakened from a doze to find that the carriage was splashing along a rising road turned to soup by the rain. On either side lay bare fields and pastureland, the horizons guarded by a line of sombre hills. Ahead, behind a small coven of dark, twisting yews, stood a grey-faced house, graceless and vast. Two towers rose above its facade like misshapen horns.

It was Grizehayes. Although Makepeace had never seen it before, she felt an instant recognition, like a great bell tolling deep in her soul.

By the time they arrived, Makepeace was cold, exhausted and hungry. She was unbound and unswaddled, then handed over to a red-haired servant woman with a tired face.

'His lordship will want to see her,' said Crowe, and left Makepeace in her care.

The woman changed her clothes, wiped her face and brushed her hair. She was not unkind, but not kind either. Makepeace knew that she was being tidied for company, not cosseted. The woman tutted over Makepeace's nails, which were ravaged and torn. Makepeace could not remember how or why.

When Makepeace was almost presentable, the woman led her down a dark passageway, silently waved her through an oaken door, then closed it behind her. Makepeace found herself in a great warm chamber with the biggest, fiercest hearth she had ever seen. The walls were covered with hunting tapestries, where stags rolled their eyes as embroidered blood ran from their sides. A very old man was propped up in a four-poster bed.

She stared at him with fear and awe, as her scrambled mind tried to remember what she had been told. This could only be Obadiah Fellmotte, the head of the family—Lord Fellmotte himself.

He was in earnest conversation with white-haired Mr Crowe. Neither seemed to have noticed her entrance. Feeling self-conscious and daunted, Makepeace hung back by the door. Nonetheless their low voices reached her.

'So . . . those that accused us will accuse no more?' Obadiah's voice was a low, rasping creak.

'One killed himself after his ships sank and his fortune was lost,' Mr Crowe said calmly. 'Another was exiled after his letters to the Spanish King were discovered. The third's romances became common gossip, and he was killed in a duel by his mistress's husband.'

'Good,' said Obadiah. 'Very good.' He narrowed his eyes. 'Are there still rumours about us?'

'It is difficult to kill a whisper, my lord,' Crowe said carefully 'Particularly one that involves witchcraft.'

Witchcraft? Makepeace felt a thrill of superstitious terror. Had she really heard that word aright? The minister in Poplar had sometimes spoken of witches—twisted, corrupted men and women who secretly bargained with the Devil for unholy powers. They could put the Evil Eye on you. They could make your hand wither, your crops fail, your baby sicken and die. Causing harm by witchcraft was illegal, of course, and when witches were caught they were arrested and tried, and sometimes even hanged.

'If we cannot stop the King hearing such rumours,' the old aristocrat said slowly, 'then we must stop him acting on them. We must make ourselves useful to him—too useful to lose. And we will need a hold over him, so that he dares not denounce us. He is desperate to borrow money from us, is he not? I am sure we can make some kind of bargain.'

Makepeace continued to stand by the door, tongue-tied, the heat from the hearth tingling over her face. She did not understand everything she had heard, but she was fairly certain that such words and thoughts should never, ever have fallen upon her ears.

Then the old lord looked across and noticed her. He scowled slightly.

'Crowe, what is that child doing in my chamber?'

'Margaret Lightfoot's daughter,' Crowe said quietly.

'Oh, the by-blow.' Obadiah's brow cleared a little. 'Let us see her, then.' He beckoned Makepeace over.

Makepeace's last faint hopes of a warm welcome collapsed. She approached slowly, and halted at his bedside. There was costly lace on Obadiah's nightgown and the cap that drooped over his brow, and Makepeace started helplessly calculating how many weeks it would have taken her mother to make it. But she realized that she was staring, and dropped her gaze quickly. Looking at the rich and powerful was dangerous, like peering into the sun.

Instead, she watched him from under her lashes. She fixed her gaze on his hands, which were loaded with rings. He frightened her. She could see the blue blood in his bunched veins.

'Ah yes, she's one of Peter's,' murmured Obadiah. 'Look at that cleft in her chin! And those pale eyes! But you say she's mad?'

'Meek but slow most of the time, and frantic when the fits take her,' said Crowe. 'The family say it's grief, and a blow to the head.'

'If the senses have been knocked out of her, knock them back in again,' Obadiah snapped. 'No point in sparing the rod with children or lunatics. They're much alike—savages if left unchecked. The only cure is discipline. You! Girl! Can you talk?'

Makepeace gave a start, and nodded.

'We hear you have nightmares, child,' said Obadiah. 'Tell us about them.'

Makepeace had promised Mother never to talk about her dreams. But Mother was not Mother any more, and promises no longer seemed to matter very much. So she stammered a few broken sentences about the black room, the whispers and the swooping faces.

Obadiah gave a small, satisfied noise in his throat.

'The creatures that come in your nightmares, do you know what they are?' he asked.

Makepeace swallowed, and nodded.

'Dead things,' she said.

'Broken dead things,' the old lord said, as if this were an important distinction. 'Weak things—too weak to hold themselves together without a body. They want your body . . . and you know that, do you not? But they will not reach you here. They are vermin, and we destroy them like rats.'

The memory of a molten, vindictive face swooped into Makepeace's mind. *A weak, dead, broken thing. Vermin to be destroyed.* She slammed the door on that thought, but it would not stay shut. Makepeace started to shake. She could not help it.

'Are they damned?' she blurted out. *Is Mother going to Hell? Did I send her to Hell?* 'The minister said—'

'Oh, pox on the minister!' snapped Obadiah. 'You've been raised by a nest of Puritans, you stupid girl. A crop-headed,

48

preachy bunch of ranters and ravers. That minister is going to Hell some day, and dragging his raggle-taggle flock with him. And unless you forget every crazy notion they crammed into your head, you'll go the same way. Did they even christen you?' He gave a little grunt of approval when Makepeace nodded. 'Ah, well, that is one thing at least.

'Those creatures—the ones that want to burrow into your head. Did any of them ever get in?'

'No,' Makepeace said, with an involuntary shudder. 'They tried, but I . . . I fought . . .'

'We must be certain. Come here! Let me look at you.' When Makepeace ventured nervously within reach, the old man reached out and gripped her chin with surprising strength.

Startled, Makepeace met his gaze. At once she smelt wrongness like smoke.

His map-wrinkled face was dull, but his eyes were not. They were cloudy amber and cold. She did not understand what it meant, but she knew that there was something very wrong with Obadiah. She did not want to be near him. She was in danger.

His features crinkled and puckered very slightly, as if his face were holding a conversation with itself. Then he half closed his ancient eyes, and examined Makepeace through the gleaming slivers.

Something was happening. Something was touching the sore places in her soul, exploring, probing. She gave a croak of protest, and tried to squirm out of Obadiah's grip, but his hold was painfully firm. For a moment it was as if she were back in the nightmare, in her own darkened room, with the molten voice in her ear, and the ruthless spirit clawing at her mind . . .

She gave a short, sharp scream, and reached for her soldiers of the mind. As she lashed out in thought, she felt the probing presence flinch back. Obadiah's hand released her chin. Makepeace lurched backwards, falling to the floor. She curled into a ball, eyes clenched shut, fists over her ears.

'Ha!' Obadiah's exhalation sounded like a laugh. 'Maybe you did fight them off, after all. Oh, stop your whimpering, child! I shall believe you for now, but understand this—if one of those dead vermin has made a nest in your brain, you are the one in danger. You cannot scour them out without our help.'

Makepeace's heart was hammering, and she found it hard to breathe. Just for a moment, she had locked gazes with something wrong. She had seen it, and it had seen her. And something had touched her mind the way the dead things did.

But Obadiah was not dead, was he? Makepeace had seen him breathing. She must have been mistaken. Perhaps all aristocrats were just as terrifying.

'Understand this,' he said, without warmth. 'Nobody wants you. Not even your mother's kin. What will happen to you out in the world, I wonder? Will you be thrown into Bedlam? If not, I suppose you will starve, or freeze to death, or be murdered for the few rags you wear . . . if the dead vermin do not find you first.'

There was a pause, and then the old man spoke again, his voice impatient.

'Look at the trembling, damp-eyed thing! Put her somewhere where she cannot break anything. Girl—you must show some gratitude and obedience, and cease these fits, or we will throw you out on the moors. And then nobody will protect you when the vermin come for you. They will eat out your brain like the meat of an egg.'

CHAPTER 5

A lean, young manservant led Makepeace up stairway after stairway, and showed her into a narrow little room with a flock bed in it, and a chamber pot. There were bars on the window, but painted birds on the walls, and Makepeace wondered whether it had once been a nursery. The young servant was barely out of boyhood, and his features were beaky, like the white-haired Mr Crowe. Makepeace wondered blearily whether they were related.

'Count your blessings, and calm your antics,' he said, as he set down a jug of small beer and a bowl of pottage on the floor for her. 'No more shrieking and lunging at folks, do you hear? We've a stick for tricks like that.'

The door closed behind him, and a key turned in the lock. Makepeace was left alone with her bewilderment. *Lunging?* When had she done that? She did not know anything any more.

As she ate the food, Makepeace stared out through the bars at the grey sky, the courtyard, and the fields and moors beyond its surrounding wall. Would this be her home forever, this tower-room prison? Would she grow old here, tucked out of sight and mischief, as the Fellmottes' pet madwoman?

Makepeace could not settle. Her mind was too full. She found herself pacing the little room. Sometimes she realized that she was murmuring to herself, or that the murmur had sunk into her throat and become a guttural noise.

The walls spun as she lurched and turned, their paper peeling like silver birch bark. She was arguing with the heat and noise in her brain. There was somebody else in the room, and they were being unreasonable. But they were never there when she turned.

At last her knees gave, and she tumbled to the floor and lay there. She felt too vast and heavy ever to move again, a thing of mountains and plains. Aches and itches edged across her landscape like travellers. She noted them with disinterest as slumber swallowed her.

And in her dreams she was walking through a forest, but could only take ten steps in any direction before a tree trunk rose up and bruised her. Birds of every sort perched on the boughs, trilling and mocking her. The sky gleamed grey-black like a jackdaw's wing, and her throat was sore from roaring.

Makepeace woke groggily in the early twilight. She stared numbly through the barred window at the violet sky, with its greasy rags of cloud. A bat fleet-fluttered across them for a moment like a dark thought.

She was lying on the floor, not the bed, and she hurt.

Makepeace sat up gingerly, supporting herself on one hand, and winced. She ached all over. Even her hands stung. Peering at them, she noticed dark grazes on the knuckles. Previously some of her nails had been broken, but now several were torn to the quick. There was a tender swelling on her left temple and right cheek, and her exploring fingers found bruises on her arms and hip.

'What happened to me?' she asked herself aloud.

Perhaps she really had fallen into a fit. She could think of no other explanation. The manservant might have threatened her with a stick, but she thought she would have noticed if he had come in and used it.

I must have injured myself. There is nobody here but me.

As if to mock that very thought, she heard a noise behind her.

Makepeace spun round, looking for the source of the sound. Nothing. Only the empty room, and the stretching diamond of light from the window.

Her heart hammered. The noise had been so shockingly clear, like breath against her neck, sending a tingle deep into her inner ear. And yet a moment later she could not have described it.

Gruff. A brute sound. That was all she knew.

And then she smelt something. A reek like hot blood, an autumn woodland, a wet horsey-doggy smell, musky and potent. She recognized it at once.

She was not alone.

That's impossible! It was burning itself out! And we're three days' ride from Poplar! How would it find me? And they destroy ghosts here—how would it get into Grizehayes without anyone noticing it?

But it had. There was no mistaking that reek. Somehow, impossibly, the Bear was in the room with her.

Makepeace backed towards the door, even though she knew it was pointless. Her eyes flicked around the darkening room. There were too many shadows. She could not tell if they were wisping or warping. She could not tell where the translucent eyes were watching her.

Why? Why had it followed *her*? Makepeace felt frightened and betrayed. It had come after its two torturers for revenge, but she had not harmed it at all! In fact . . . back at the Angel, she had even imagined that they had felt a moment of sympathy, of shared pain and rage, and that it had stepped in to rescue her . . .

But it's a ghost. And ghosts only want to claw their way into your head. And it's a beast, and it owes you nothing. Idiot! Did you really think that it was your friend?

And now she was locked in with it. There was no running. No escape.

There was a sudden rough gust of sound at her ear. Red hot. Deafening. Closer than close.

Too close.

Makepeace panicked. She gave a shriek, and fled to the door, hammering it with her fists.

'Let me out!' she yelled. 'You have to let me out! There's something in here! There's a *ghost* in here!'

Oh please, please let the family have left a guard outside my door! Please, please, let someone hear me out in the courtyard!

She ran to the window. She tried to squeeze her face between the bars.

'Help!' she screamed at the top of her lungs. 'Help me!'

The cold of the bars burned against her face. They pressed against her right temple and left cheek, exactly on the bruises. The sensation shocked her into memory. A hazy recollection of a similar moment, forcing her head between the bars. Trying to force her way through, towards freedom and the fair sky.

Makepeace heard her own yell become more guttural, a long, open-throated roar. And now her face was pressing against the bars with bruising force, squirming, trying to force its way through. Her vision was marked by black spots. She could feel her hands scrabbling uselessly against the stonework, the skin scraping painfully from her fingertips . . .

Stop! she told herself. *Stop! What am I doing?*

The truth hit her like a falling star.

54

Oh God. Oh God in Heaven. I am such a fool.

Of course the Bear was able to enter Grizehayes. Of course it's here.

It's inside me.

A blind, angry, desperate ghost was inside her. Her worst fear had happened, after all. And now the Bear would blunder around in her, and smash her mind to pieces. It would bloody and break her body in its frenzy to leave the turret room . . .

Stop!

Terrified, she called up her long-dormant defences again, her angels of the mind. They rallied and raged, and she heard the Bear growl. With a superhuman effort of will she closed her eyes, trapping both herself and the Bear in darkness. It was a night full of silent noise, for her mind was roaring with as much panic as the Bear.

Something happened. A sudden blow shuddered her mind to the core. For a fleeting moment she felt her soul buckle and struggle to right itself. Memories bled, thoughts ripped. The Bear had struck out at her.

And yet it was that blow that shocked Makepeace out of her panic.

Frightened. It's frightened.

She imagined it, a great Bear lost in darkness, friendless and trapped as it had been for so long. It could not understand where it was, or why its body was so strange and weak. All it knew was that it was under attack, just as it had always been under attack . . .

Gently but firmly Makepeace took control over her breathing. She drew in breath after calm breath, trying to slow her heartbeat, trying to banish the fear that the Bear would tear her apart from within.

Hush, she whispered to it with her mind.

She pictured the Bear again, but now imagined herself standing beside it, arms outstretched, as she had stood in that moment when they had tried to protect each other.

Hush. Hush, Bear. It's me.

The silent roaring subsided to an intermittent, silent growl. Perhaps it knew her, just a little. Perhaps it understood that nothing was attacking it now.

I am your friend, she told it. And then, *I am your cave.*

Cave. It did not understand words, but Makepeace felt it gingerly take hold of the idea, like an apple in its jaws. Maybe it had never been wild, but had been reared at a chain's end since it was a cub. But it was still a bear, and deep in its soul it knew what a cave was. Cave was not prison. Cave was home.

As it calmed down, Makepeace wondered how she had failed to notice it in her head. Perhaps her feeling of sickness and strangeness had been the result of contracting her mind to make room for it.

It was *big*, if one could use such a word to describe something spectral. Makepeace could now sense its unthinking power. It could probably crush her mind, as easily as one of its paws might have taken out her throat if they had met in life. But it was calmer now, and she felt its control over her body loosen a little. Now she could at least swallow, relax her shoulders, move her fingers.

Makepeace took a few more moments to muster her courage, then dared to open her eyes. She made sure she was facing away from the window. Bars might mean prison to the Bear, and she did not want to drive it into a frenzy again. Instead, she dropped her gaze to her own hands.

She let the Bear see them, and slowly flexed the fingers so that it knew that these were the only paws it had now. She let it see the ravaged nails, then the bloodied fingertips. *No claws, Bear. Sorry.*

A small, dark ripple of emotion passed through the Bear. Then it lowered Makepeace's head, and licked at the wounded fingers with her tongue.

It was an animal, and owed her nothing. It was a ghost, and could not be depended upon. Perhaps the Bear was simply attending to its own injuries. But the licking was very gentle, as if the wounds belonged to an injured cub.

By the time the young manservant arrived with a switch, to beat Makepeace for 'howling like a heathen and raising Cain', she had made a decision. She would not betray Bear.

Lord Fellmotte had told her that it was dangerous to have a rogue ghost in her head, and perhaps he was telling the truth. But she did not like Obadiah. His gaze made her feel like a mouse in owl country. If she told him about Bear, he would tear Bear out of her somehow and destroy him.

It was risky, keeping secrets from a man like that. If he ever found out that Makepeace was hiding something like this, she suspected that he would be terribly angry. Perhaps he would throw her out on the moors as he threatened, or have her sent to Bedlam to be chained and whipped.

But she was glad that nobody had come running to her rescue when she had screamed. Bear had never been given a fair chance in life. She was all Bear had. And Bear was all *she* had.

So she said nothing as the switch landed a half-dozen solid thwacks across her shoulders and back. They stung, and Makepeace knew they would leave welts. She kept her eyes clenched shut, and did her best to soothe Bear in her mind. If she lost control and lashed out, as she suspected she had before, then sooner or later somebody might suspect that she had a ghostly passenger.

'I don't enjoy this, you know,' said the young man piously, and Makepeace thought that he probably even believed his own words. 'It's for your own good.' She suspected he had never had this much power over someone before.

After he had left, Makepeace's eyes watered, and it felt as if red-hot bars were being pressed against the flesh of her back. The feeling brought back memories, but they were not her own.

The music of guitar and tabor throbbed in her bones, and stirred a recollection of hot coals thrown under her tender, half-grown paws to force her to dance. She tottered, and tried to drop to all fours, only to receive a stinging blow across her soft muzzle.

It was Bear's early memories of being trained as a cub, she realized. She felt a flood of anger on his behalf, and hugged herself because it was the only way to hug him.

They understood something together at that moment, Makepeace and Bear. Sometimes you had to be patient through pain, or people gave you more pain. Sometimes you had to weather everything and take your bruises. If you were lucky, and if everyone thought you were tamed and trained . . . there might come a time when you could strike.

CHAPTER 6

Makepeace was woken by a faint *tink-tink-tink* sound. For a moment she was confused by her surroundings, until the ache of her bruises reminded her where she was. She had not been trusted with a candle or rushlight, so the only light came from the window.

She was startled to realize that there was a head at the window, silhouetted against the deep violet evening sky. As she stared, a hand was raised to tap again at the bars. *Tink, tink, tink.*

'Hey!' came a whisper.

Makepeace stood unsteadily, and limped over to the window. To her surprise, she found that a lanky boy about fourteen years old was clinging to the wall outside. He seemed to be precariously perched on some sort of shallow ledge, one hand gripping the bars to steady himself. He had chestnut hair, and a pleasant, ugly, wilful face, and he seemed unfazed by the four-storey drop beneath him. His clothes were better than hers, almost too good for a servant.

'Who are you?' she demanded.

'James Winnersh,' he answered, as if that explained everything.

'What do you want?' she hissed. She was certain that he was not supposed to be there. She had also heard that folks sometimes visited Bedlam to laugh at the lunatics, and she was in no mood for gawpers or gigglers.

'I came to see you!' he replied, still in a whisper. 'Come over here! I want to talk to you!'

Reluctantly she approached the window. She could tell that

59

Bear did not like being too close to people, and she did not want him to lose control. As the light fell on her face, the boy outside gave a little laugh that sounded half jubilant, half incredulous.

'So it *is* true. You've got the same chin as me.' He touched a cleft in his own chin, just like hers. 'Yes,' he said, in answer to her wide-eyed look. 'It's our little legacy. Sir Peter's signature.'

Blood rushed to Makepeace's face as she realized what he meant. She was not Sir Peter's only child out of wedlock. Deep down, Makepeace had wanted to believe that her parents had been in love, so that her own existence would mean something. But no, Mother must have been a dalliance, nothing more.

'I don't believe you!' Makepeace hissed, even though she did. 'Take it back!' She could not bear it. In the strange, white heat of the moment, she wanted to pull out the bars by their roots and hit him with them.

'You've got a temper,' he said, with a hint of surprise. Makepeace was surprised too—nobody had ever said such a thing of her before, let alone with a hint of approval. 'You *are* like me. Hush—don't go waking the house.'

'What are you doing here?' asked Makepeace, lowering her voice again.

'All the other servants were talking about you,' the boy said promptly. 'Young Crowe said you were mad, but I didn't believe him.' Makepeace guessed that the beaky-faced manservant who had beaten her must have been 'Young Crowe'. 'There's another window on the other side of the tower, so I climbed out of that, then worked my way round, feet on the ledge.' He grinned at his own ingenuity.

'What if you're wrong? What if I'm crazy, and I push you to your death?' Makepeace still felt unreasonably angry and cornered.

Why were there always *people*, living or dead, wanting something from her? Why could she not be left alone with Bear?

'You don't look mad to me,' James said, with annoying confidence, 'and I don't think you've got the strength. What's your name?'

'Makepeace.'

'*Makepeace?* Oh. I forgot you were a Puritan.'

'I'm not!' retorted Makepeace, turning red. The godly in Poplar had never called themselves Puritans, and when Obadiah had described them that way she had sensed that the word was not a compliment.

'Does everyone have a name like that where you come from?' asked James. 'I hear they're all called Fight-the-Good-Fight, Spit-in-the-Eye-of-the-Devil, Sorry-for-Sin, Miserable-Sinners-Are-We-All and things like that.'

Makepeace did not answer. She wasn't sure whether she was being mocked, and the congregation in Poplar *had* included one Sorry-for-Sin, usually shortened to 'Sorry'.

'Go away!' she said instead.

'I'm not surprised they locked you up.' James chuckled. 'They don't like spirit. Listen, I will find a way to get you out of there. Sir Thomas will be back at Grizehayes soon. He's Obadiah's heir—Sir Peter's older brother. He likes me. I'll see if I can put in a word for you.'

'Why?' asked Makepeace, perplexed.

James stared back at her with just as much incomprehension.

'Because you're my little sister,' he said.

Afterwards, Makepeace could not forget those words. She had a brother, it seemed. But what did that really mean? After all, if what James had said was true, then Lord Obadiah was her grandfather, and she had seen no kindness or kinship in the old man's eyes. Just because you shared blood with somebody, that didn't mean that you could share secrets.

And yet James seemed blithely confident that he and Makepeace *were* on the same side.

However, days passed and James did not come back. Makepeace began to fear that she had been too hostile. Soon she would have done anything to see a friendly face.

Young Crowe was not just her warden, he was her judge. If she argued, cried out or was sullenly silent, this was a sign of her melancholy madness. The punishment was a few sharp blows on the shins or arms with his stick.

It was all Makepeace could do to stop Bear striking back, as her vision darkened and his rage threatened to swallow them both. After Young Crowe's visits, Bear would keep her pacing to and fro for hours, sometimes giving a wordless bellow with her voice. There were moments of rapport where he seemed to understand her, and she could soothe him. At other times it was like reasoning with a thundercloud. He did not understand the bars, or Makepeace's limits, or the need to use a chamber pot.

After Bear flung their bowl across the room and broke it, Makepeace's ankles were put in shackles. In the following days, she was held down each morning so that a reddish concoction that smelt of beetroots could be squirted into her nose to cool 'the cauls of her brain'. A little later she was caught weeping and she was given a broth that made her vomit, to rid her of the 'black bile' that caused her 'melancholia'.

Bear was strange and dangerous, and made everything worse. Yet she clung to him. She had a secret friend, and because of this she could hold off despair. She had somebody that she wanted to protect, and who silently raged to protect her. When she slept, it seemed to her that she was curled around something like a small, rounded cub, but also as though something vast and warm had encircled her to shield her from the world.

One day, Young Crowe had her bound to a stretcher, her face covered with a cloth. She was carried, jolted and tilted down stairway after stairway, then into a room that was blisteringly hot and full of the rich, kitchen smells of smoke, meat-blood, spices and onion.

'Sweep out the embers, the bricks are hot enough without them. Help me—we need her head *just* within the oven . . .'

Makepeace struggled, but her bonds held. She felt every jolt as the stretcher was manoeuvred into place, then the searing heat of the oven against her face, even through the cloth. It was hard to breathe, the hot, smoky air burning her lungs. Her skin started to scald and sting, and she cried out in panic, fearing that her eyes would start to fry like eggs . . .

'What are you *doing*, Crowe?' asked an unfamiliar voice.

'Sir Thomas!' Young Crowe sounded rather taken aback. 'We are treating the Lightfoot girl for melancholia. The heat of the oven causes her head to sweat out all the disordered fantasies. It is a tried-and-tested practice—there is a picture in this book—'

'And what were you planning to do after that? Serve her with radishes and a mustard sauce? Take the girl out of the oven, Crowe. I have a mind to speak with her, and I cannot do that while she is being baked.'

A few minutes later, her eyes still blurry with smoke and tears, Makepeace found herself sitting alone in a little room with Sir Thomas Fellmotte, Obadiah's heir.

He had bright, brown eyes, a bluff manner, and a voice that belonged to the outdoors. On second glance she noticed the grey in his long, aristocratically curled hair and the sorrowful-looking lines that scored his cheeks, and guessed that he was not young. His chin had a familiar vertical dent. Belatedly Makepeace remembered that Sir Thomas had been her father's brother.

To her great relief, he did not fill her with same chill dread as Obadiah. As he looked at her, his gaze was warm, human and a little wistful.

'Ah,' he said quietly. 'You *do* have my brother's eyes. But there is a good deal more of Margaret in you, I think.' For a while he stared at her, as if her face were a scrying glass in which he could see the faces of the dead shimmering.

'Makepeace, is it?' he asked, recovering his brisk tone. 'A preachy name, but rather a pretty one. Tell me, Makepeace, are you a good, hard-working girl? James says you're sane as noontide, and not afraid to earn your keep. Is that true?'

Hardly daring to hope, Makepeace nodded vigorously.

'Then I am sure we can find you a place amongst the servants.' He gave her a warm, pensive smile. 'What can you do?'

Anything, Makepeace almost said. *I will do anything if you save me from the Bird Chamber and Young Crowe.* But at the last moment she thought of Obadiah's deathly eyes. *Anything that does not involve waiting on his lordship . . .*

'I can cook!' she said quickly, as inspiration struck. 'I can churn butter, and bake pies, and make bread and soups, and pluck pigeons . . .' Her first encounter with the Grizehayes kitchen had not been a happy one, but if she worked there she could avoid Obadiah.

'Then I shall arrange something,' declared Sir Thomas. He

64

strode to the door, then hesitated. 'I . . . often thought about your mother after she ran away from Grizehayes. She was so young to be alone in the world—barely fifteen, and expecting a child, of course.' He frowned, and twisted one of his buttons. 'Was she . . . happy with the life she found?'

Makepeace did not know how to answer. Right now, her memories of Mother were too painful to handle, like shards of glass.

'Sometimes,' she said at last.

'I suppose,' said Sir Thomas softly, 'that is all that any of us can ask.'

CHAPTER 7

That same afternoon, Makepeace found herself in clean clothes, being introduced to a curious gaggle of other servants. After the darkness and isolation, everything seemed very loud and bright. Everyone was looming and unfamiliar, and Makepeace kept forgetting their names.

The other servant women were wary at first, then beleaguered her with questions, about her name, London and the dangerous world away from Grizehayes. None of them asked about her family, however, and Makepeace guessed that her parentage was already household gossip.

They all seemed sure that Makepeace must be very glad and grateful to have been 'rescued' from her previous home. They also agreed that another hand in the kitchen would be welcome.

'Kitchen's the best place for her, I say,' one woman remarked bluntly. 'She's scarcely handsome enough to wait on the family, is she? Look at her, the little spotted cat!'

'There's a French cook,' another woman told Makepeace, 'but don't you mind him, he's just for show. French cooks come and go like apple blossom. It's Mistress Gotely you'll need to please.'

Makepeace was duly set to work in the kitchen, which seemed vast as a cavern, its ceiling black with generations of smoke. The hearth was so huge that six Makepeaces could have stood in it, side by side. Herbs dangled in bunches from the rafters, and ranks of pewter plates gleamed. Ever since Bear had become her secret passenger, Makepeace's sense of smell had become keener. The kitchen scents hit her with maddening force—heady herbs and spices, charred meat, wine, gravy and smoke. She could feel Bear stirring, confused by the smells and hungry.

Mistress Gotely was in theory just an under-cook, but in practice the queen of the kitchen. She was a tall woman with a strong jaw, a gouty leg, and no patience for fools. And of course Makepeace did seem a fool, clumsy and slow-witted with nerves. She was desperate to prove her worth, so that she wouldn't be sent back to the Bird Chamber. This would have been hard enough without a ghost bear in her head. He did not like the heat, darkness or clatter. The aroma of blood maddened him, and half her mind was busy calming him.

After a baffling, whirlwind introduction to the intricacies of the kitchen, scullery, buttery, ewery and cellar, Mistress Gotely took Makepeace out into the courtyard to see the pump, granary and woodpile.

Grizehayes looked different in sunshine, the grey walls almost golden in places with blots of lichen. Makepeace could see details that made it look more lived in and less like a ghost castle. Rugs dangled from windows to be beaten, smoke trailed from the great, red chimneys. It was a hodgepodge house, old craggy stone alternating with neat grey blocks, slate roofs mingling with turrets and church-like arches.

It's a real house, Makepeace told herself. *People live here. I could live here.*

She blinked up at the sunny walls, then shivered despite herself. It was like watching someone smile with their mouth and not their eyes. Somehow, the house made even the daylight cold.

A seven-foot stone wall surrounded the house, stables and stone-flagged courtyard. Three great mastiffs were chained to the wall. When she drew close they exploded into motion, running to the full extent of their chain, then leaping and snarling at her unfamiliar scent. She jumped back, her heart banging. She could feel Bear's fear as well, like a crimson fog, uncertain whether to lash out or flee the bared teeth.

One grand gate was set in the wall, wide enough for a coach-and-four. Through it she could see only open fields, then drear tufted moorland. She remembered Obadiah threatening to throw her out on to the moors, to freeze or have her brain eaten by wandering ghosts.

Count your blessings, she told herself, repeating Young Crowe's words. *Better to be working in the kitchen here, than chained up in the Bird Chamber. And the Bird Chamber was better than the real Bedlam would have been. And even Bedlam would be better than starving out in the cold, and having my brain eaten by mad ghosts.*

She inhaled a deep breath of the fresh air, and blinked up at the high, heavy sunlit walls. *I am lucky*, she told herself. *Better in here than out there.* Grizehayes was strange and frightening, but it was a fortress. It could keep the darkness out. Even as she tried to convince herself, however, she was wondering why her mother had fled the house, and remembering her words.

You have no idea what I saved you from! If I had stayed in Grizehayes...

Makepeace made heroic efforts to impress Mistress Gotely throughout the day. And then, during the rush to cook dinner, she ruined everything.

Next to the hearth, a little turnspit dog ran in a wooden wheel fixed to the wall, turning it to revolve the great roasting spit over the fire. The ugly little dog's tail was a stump, its muzzle cracked with heat and age, and it wheezed in the smoke. However, it was

Mistress Gotely's habit of tossing embers at its feet to make it run faster that was more than Makepeace could bear.

Vivid in her mind were Bear's memories of his own cubhood, and the coals thrown under his feet to force him to dance. Each time a glowing fragment bounced off the turnspit wheel, showering sparks, she remembered—felt—the searing pain under her paws . . .

'Stop it!' she exploded at last. 'Leave him alone!'

Mistress Gotely stared at her astonished, and Makepeace was taken aback by her own outburst. But she was too full of rage to apologize. She could only stand in front of the wheel, shaking with anger.

'What did you say to me?' The under-cook gave her a meaty cuff about the head, and knocked Makepeace to the ground.

Bear was raging, and Makepeace's cheek stung. It would be so easy to give in and go to the dark place, let Bear take care of the blind rampage . . . She swallowed, and struggled to clear her mind.

'He'll run better,' she said thickly, 'if his paws aren't covered in burns and blisters! Let *me* have charge of him, I'll have him running faster than you ever did.'

Mistress Gotely hauled her to her feet by her collar.

'I don't care how that wilful mother of yours brought you up,' growled the under-cook. 'This is *my* kitchen. *I* do the yelling here, nobody else.' She gave Makepeace a couple of hard, hasty knocks around the head and shoulders, then gave an impatient snort. 'All right, the dog's your problem now. If he's slow, you take his place and turn the spit for him. No whining about the heat!'

To Makepeace's relief and surprise, the old cook seemed in no hurry to report her, or have her chained up again. If anything, afterwards they were a little more at ease with each other, in their own surly, reserved way. They had found the edges of each other's temper, like jagged rocks under a placid skin of water.

When the pair of them finally had their own dinner before the great hearth, the grumpy silence was almost companionable. The cook chewed away at a hunk of the tough, dark bread Makepeace had eaten all her life. To Makepeace's surprise, however, Mistress Gotely handed her a piece of golden-crusted white bread, of the sort the rich ate.

'Don't just stare at it,' the cook told her curtly. 'Eat it. Lord Fellmotte's orders.' Makepeace bit into it gingerly, marvelling at its sweetness, and the way it yielded under her teeth. 'Be grateful, and don't ask questions.'

Makepeace chewed, wondering at this strange show of kindness from the frosty Obadiah. Then she asked questions anyway.

'You said my mother was wilful,' she managed through a mouthful. 'Did you know her?'

'A little,' admitted Mistress Gotely, 'though she mostly worked upstairs.' She said 'upstairs' as if it were as far away as France.

'Is it true she ran away? Or did they throw her out for being with child?' Makepeace knew that such things sometimes happened.

'No,' said Mistress Gotely curtly. 'Oh no, they wouldn't have turned *her* away. She ran off one night of her own free will, without saying a word to anyone.'

'Why?'

'How should I know? She was a secretive creature. Did she never tell you?'

'She never told me *anything*,' Makepeace said flatly. 'I didn't even know who my father was until after she was gone.'

'And . . . you know now?' asked the old cook, giving her a sharp, sideways look.

Makepeace hesitated, then nodded.

'Well, you would have found out sooner or later anyway.' The cook nodded slowly. 'Everybody here knows—it's as plain as the chin on your face. But . . . I wouldn't go talking about it too freely. The family might think you were being impudent and making claims for yourself. Be grateful for what you have, and cause no trouble, and you'll get by.'

'Can *you* tell me what he was like, then?' Makepeace asked.

The old cook sighed, then rubbed her leg, looking affectionate and wistful.

'Ah, poor Sir Peter! Have you met James Winnersh? He was a lot like James. James is a reckless rascal, but he has a good heart. He makes mistakes, but he makes them honestly.'

Makepeace began to understand why Sir Thomas might be fond of James, if he reminded him of his dead brother.

'What happened to Sir Peter?' she asked.

'He tried to leap a hedge too high, on a horse that was worn out,' the cook answered with a sigh. 'The horse went down, and rolled on him. He was so young—barely past his twentieth summer.'

'Why was his horse so tired?' Makepeace could not help asking.

'There's no asking him now, is there?' Mistress Gotely told her sharply. 'But . . . some said that he rode himself ragged looking for your mother. It was two months after she disappeared, you see.' She glanced at Makepeace, and frowned slightly.

'You were a mistake, girl,' she said simply, 'but a mistake honestly meant.'

. . . . .

That evening Makepeace learned that, as the lowliest and youngest person working in the kitchen, she would not be sharing a bed with the other servingwomen. Instead, she would now sleep on a straw pallet under the great kitchen table each night, and make sure the fire did not go out. She was not alone. The turnspit dog and two of the huge mastiffs slept by the fire as well.

Bear was not happy with the nearness of the dogs, but at least he seemed used to the smell. Dogs had loud mouths, cruel mouths, but they were a fact of life. Dog-smell in the markets, dog-smell at night by the campfires.

In the dead of night, Makepeace was jolted awake by a long, rumbling growl, close to her head. One of the great dogs was awake. For a moment she was afraid that it had smelt her and decided that she was a trespasser. Then she heard a faint scuff of footsteps, too light and cautious to be those of the old cook. Someone was coming.

'Come on out!' murmured James's voice. 'Nero won't bite now— unless I tell him to.' He grinned as Makepeace wriggled out. 'I told you I would get you out of there!'

'Thank you,' Makepeace said hesitantly, still maintaining her distance. She was starting to get a sense of how far Bear liked to keep from people when he was not used to them. Even now she could feel his unease, his desire to pull himself up to his full height and snort a threat to scare off the stranger. But she was already standing as tall as she could, and had no more height in reserve.

'You did well getting a job in the kitchen,' said James, settling cross-legged on the great table. 'It's perfect. We can help each other now. I'll keep an eye out for you, and teach you how everything works. And you can tell me anything you overhear. Fetch me things from the kitchen when nobody's looking—'

'You want me to steal for you?' Makepeace glared at him, wondering if this was why he had helped her in the first place. 'If anything goes missing, they'll know it's me! I'll be thrown out of Grizehayes!'

James looked at her for a long moment, then very slowly shook his head.

'No,' he said. 'You won't.'

'But—'

'I mean it. They'd punish you. They'd beat you. Maybe they'd even chain you up in the Bird Chamber again. But they wouldn't throw you out. Not even if you begged them to.'

'What are you talking about?'

'I've been trying to run away for five years,' said James. 'Over and over again. And they chase me down and bring me back here, every time.'

Makepeace stared at him. Was it unusual for rich men to chase down runaway servants? She had heard of rewards put out for runaway apprentices, but she guessed that was different.

'You had nightmares, didn't you?' asked James suddenly, throwing Makepeace off balance. 'Dreams so bad you woke up screaming. Ghosts clawing their way into your head . . .'

Makepeace shuffled away from him a few inches, and watched him with a seethe of distrust and uncertainty.

'I had dreams like that too,' James continued. 'They started five years ago, when I was nine. And not long after that, the Fellmottes sent men to collect me. My mother argued at first. Then they paid her, and she stopped arguing.' He gave a small, bitter smile. 'The Fellmottes don't care about wild oats like us, unless we start having those nightmares. Then they care. Then they harvest us, and bring us here. They heard about *your* dreams, and fetched you here too, didn't they?'

'Why?' asked Makepeace, intrigued. It was true, Obadiah had seemed more interested in her nightmares than anything else about her. 'Why would they care about our dreams?'

'I don't know,' admitted James. 'But we're not the only ones. Lord Fellmotte's cousins visit sometimes, and all of them seem to have a servant or two with that Fellmotte look. I think *all* the Fellmottes collect their by-blows when they turn out to be dreamers.

'They collect us, and they don't let us go again. I found that out when I tried to run off home. I wouldn't try to go back there now—that woman would just sell me to the Fellmottes again.' He scowled, evidently embarrassed.

'By night,' he continued, 'the main doors are made fast with a great bar and chains, and the hall-boy sleeps in front of them. The gate is locked and there are dogs loose in the courtyard. So I slipped out by daylight. But there are bare fields beyond the walls for three miles—I stood out like blood on snow.

'On my second try I got farther—right out on to the moorland. Bitter bleak it was out there, miles of moors and woods. Winds so cold my fingers started to turn black. I stumbled into a village half frozen, and little good it did me. The farmers there took one look at this —' he tapped his chin—'then collared me, and brought me back here. They knew what I was, and who wanted me, and they looked *frightened*.

'Last year, I thought I'd got clean away. Fifty miles, across three rivers, all the way to Braybridge in the next county.' James shook his head again, and grimaced. 'They sent White Crowe after me. You met him, he brought you here. The family use him for important things they need done quietly. He's their shadow hand. And everybody fell over themselves to help him find me—even powerful men. The Fellmottes aren't just a great family. Everybody's afraid of them.'

Makepeace bit her cheek and said nothing. He was probably boasting like the Poplar apprentices did, making much of his adventures, but his words opened up little cracks of unease in her mind.

'But don't you see, now you can help!' James continued. 'They're wise to me, but they won't suspect you. You can act as lookout! Or put aside things that we'll need for our escape—provisions, beer, candles—'

'I can't run away!' exclaimed Makepeace. 'I don't have anywhere else to go! If I lose my place here, I'll be starved or frozen to death before Whit Sunday! Or murdered!'

'I'll protect you!' insisted James.

'How? The country is going all to pieces—everyone says so, and I've seen it! You can't protect me from . . . from mobs gone mad, or bullets! Or ghosts that want to eat my brain! Here I have a bed and food, and that's more than I'll get on the moors! I even ate *white bread* today!'

'Our father's blood buys a few blessings,' James admitted. 'My food's always been a touch better than what the rest of the servants get. I even have lessons sometimes, in between my duties. Reading. Languages. Riding. Maybe you will too. The other servants don't raise an eyebrow. They know whose bastard I am, even if they don't say so.'

'Then why are you trying to run away?'

'Have you seen old Obadiah?' James asked sharply.

'Yes,' said Makepeace slowly, and could not quite keep a wobble out of the word. 'He's . . .'

There was a long pause.

'You can see it too, can't you?' whispered James. He looked stunned but relieved.

Makepeace hesitated, peering into his face. She suddenly wondered whether all of this was a test set up by Obadiah. If she said something disrespectful now, perhaps James would report it, and maybe then she would be turned out of the house or chained up in the Bird Chamber again.

You couldn't trust people. Dogs snarled before they bit you, but people often smiled.

James had a sunburnt face and far-apart eyes. However, it was his scab-knuckled hands that Makepeace noticed most of all. They were the hands of someone reckless, a scuffler and scrapper, but they were also honest hands. The sight of them made a difference somehow. Makepeace allowed herself a grain of trust.

'I don't know what it means!' she whispered. 'But there's something . . .'

'. . . wrong with him,' finished James.

'It feels . . . when I look into his eyes . . . it's like when the dead things in my nightmares . . .'

'I know.'

'But he's alive!'

'Yes! And yet he makes your skin crawl and your thumbs prick? Nobody else sees it but us, or if they do they don't talk about it. And –' James leaned forward to whisper in her ear—'Obadiah's not the only one. The older Fellmottes are *all* like that.'

'Sir Thomas is not!' Makepeace remembered the heir's bright brown eyes.

'No, not yet,' James said earnestly. 'They don't start that way. It's only when they inherit and come into their land and titles that something happens. They change. It's as if their blood turns cold overnight. Even other folks know there's *something* different about them. The servants call them the "Elders and Betters". They're too fast. Too clever. They know too much that they shouldn't. And you can't lie to them. They see right through you.

'That's why we must leave! This house is a . . . roost for devils! We're not servants, we're prisoners! They won't even tell us why!'

Makepeace chewed her lip, tormented by indecision. There *was* something wrong with Obadiah, all her instincts said so. Mother had fled Grizehayes, and taken every pain to make sure that the Fellmottes could not find her. And there was Bear to consider—Bear who might be torn out of her and destroyed if Obadiah worked out that he was there.

But these were all uncertain terrors. The fear of being chained up and beaten again, or cast out to become a starving, ghost-maddened vagrant, was so solid she could touch it. There was also the tormenting thought that perhaps Mother's crazed, tattered ghost was still out there somewhere beyond Grizehayes's protective walls, roaming and looking for Makepeace. The very thought was white-hot with hope and dread, and her mind flinched from it.

'I'm sorry,' Makepeace said quietly. 'I can't run with you. I need a home, even if it's this one.'

'I don't blame you for being frightened,' said James, gently enough. 'But I'll wager my neck we have more to fear here than anywhere else. I hope you change your mind. I hope you change it soon enough to come with me.'

Makepeace was not used to kindness, and it was almost more than she could bear. Since Mother's death, there had been a vast, aching hole in her world, and she was desperate for somebody to fill it. For a moment, Makepeace hovered on the brink of telling James about Bear.

But she bit her tongue and the moment passed. It was too big a secret for somebody she knew so slightly. James might betray her. He might not understand. He might be frightened of her, or decide she was mad after all. Her friendship with him was too new and fragile, and she needed it.

CHAPTER 8

Weeks passed, and Makepeace won the under-cook's grudging approval by being a hard worker and quick learner. She was bottom of the pecking order, so she was always first out of bed, the early morning water-fetcher, ember-carrier, chicken-feeder and kindling-bringer. The work was exhausting, and the heat and smoke still alarmed Bear, but she was starting to learn the tricks of the turnspit wheel, the beehive oven, the dripping pans and the chimney crane for the kettle. She no longer panicked when told to run to the saltbox, the sugar loaf or the meat safe.

Mistress Gotely sometimes saw Makepeace sneaking scraps to the dogs who slept in the kitchen, or letting them lick gravy from her hands.

'Soft-headed little doddypoll,' she muttered, and shook her head. 'They'll eat you bones and all if you let them.' But the gravy had already begun to cast its slow, savoury spell over the dogs' loyalties. None of them growled at her in the night now. In fact, sometimes she slept in a heap with them, their breathing and warmth soothing her dreamless mind, the ugly little turnspit dog nestled in her arms.

As Makepeace hoped, the dogs' friendliness lowered Bear's hackles too. In his head, all beasts, whether human or otherwise, seemed to be divided into 'safe' and 'probably dangerous'. Familiar, safe animals were allowed to get close to him. Unfamiliar, suspicious creatures needed to be scared off with coughs and menaces.

What a frightened cub you are, thought Makepeace.

She had far more trouble with her writing lessons. Once a week, late at night after a long day's work, she was tutored alongside James by Young Crowe, her jailer during her time in the Bird Chamber. To judge by his self-congratulatory smirk, he considered his 'treatments' to have cured her so-called madness.

Makepeace now knew that there was a whole family of Crowes serving the Fellmottes. The other servants, in their blunt, practical way, gave them nicknames to tell them apart. Young Crowe's father, the steward of Grizehayes, was Old Crowe. As James had already told her, the white-haired man who had fetched Makepeace to Grizehayes was White Crowe.

Makepeace had only ever learned to make an 'M' as her 'mark'. She had seen people read, their gaze floating down the lines like a leaf on a stream-current. But when she stared at the letters, they stared back, insect-splats of bulges and splayed legs. Her untrained hand could not shape them. It made her feel stupid. It did not help that she was usually too tired at the end of the day to think straight.

Young Crowe was condescendingly philosophical about Makepeace's lack of learning.

'Do you know what a young bear looks like, when it is fresh out of its mother's womb?' he said. 'Naught but a shapeless mass. She has to lick it for hours until it is cub-shaped, gives it a snout, ears, dainty paws, everything it will need for the rest of its life.

'You are sadly unformed, for one of your years. Like a blob of fat. But we will lick you into shape.'

Makepeace smiled despite herself. She wondered whether Bear had been licked into shape by his mother, in some happy time before all the cruelty. She was charmed by the idea of the little cub gaining its eyes, and blinking up at a big, maternal bear-tongue.

Young Crowe noticed the smile, and dug out bestiaries, so that she could read and copy the words. Makepeace was a lot happier writing about animals.

The Toad and Spider are most poisonous enemies and will fight each other to Destruction, she learned. *The Pelican suckles her Young with her Heart's Blood. The Badger's Legs are longer on one side than the other so that it runs faster on Sloping Ground.*

Makepeace was gradually getting a better sense of Bear's ways. He was not always awake in her mind. A lot of the time he was asleep, and then it was as if he were not there at all. He was more likely to be awake and restless during the grey times of early morning and twilight, but he could not be predicted. Sometimes Bear would surface without warning. His emotions would giddily spill into hers. Her senses would be flooded with his. Bear generally seemed to live in the present, but he carried his memories like forgotten bruises. Now and then he would knock against one of them, and tumble bemused into an abyss of pain.

He was curious and patient, but his fear could whip-crack into rage in an instant. Makepeace lived in fear of that rage. For now the pair of them were safe, but they were one good rampage away from the Fellmottes deciding Makepeace was mad or, worse still, realizing she was haunted.

She was settling in at Grizehayes, and yet she was always unsettled. Even the little signs of preferment—the lessons, the extra spoonful of pottage at lunch—made her uneasy. It reminded her of the geese and swans she was helping to fatten up for the table, and made her wonder whether some hidden knife was waiting for her too.

. . . . .

In the early autumn, the household was thrown into enthusiastic confusion when two long-absent members of the Fellmotte family returned to Grizehayes. One was Sir Marmaduke, a well-connected second cousin of Lord Fellmotte, who had his own grand estate in the Welsh marches. The other was Symond, Sir Thomas's eldest son and heir.

Symond's late mother had done her duty and obligingly turned out eight children before dying of a fever. Four of them were still breathing. The two adult daughters had been advantageously married off. Their nine-year-old sister was in the care of a cousin, and had been quietly promised in marriage to a baronet's son. Symond was the only surviving son.

Symond and Sir Marmaduke had come straight from the court in London, so the whole household was agog to hear the latest news from the capital. In exchange for a few mugs of beer down in the courtyard, the coachman was glad to satisfy his inquisitive audience.

'Earl of Stafford's dead,' he said. 'Parliament arrested 'im for treason. Now 'is 'ead's stuck up on Traitor's Gate.'

There were gasps of dismay.

'The poor Earl!' muttered Mistress Gotely. 'After all he'd done, fighting for the King! What is Parliament playing at?'

'They want more power for themselves, that's all,' said Young Crowe. 'They're robbing the King of his friends and allies, one by one. Not all of Parliament is rotten, but there's a poisonous little hive of Puritans in there, stirring the rest up. Those are the real traitors—and frothing mad, every one.'

'*All* Puritans is mad,' muttered Long Alys, the red-haired laundry maid. 'Oh, I mean no harm by that, Makepeace, but it is true!'

Makepeace had given up trying to tell everyone that she was not a Puritan. Her outlandish, preachy name set her apart. In some respects, she welcomed the distance it put between her and others. It was dangerous to get too close to anyone.

Besides, Makepeace no longer knew who was right, or which way was up. Listening to the Grizehayes folk discuss the news made her feel as though her brain were being turned inside out. Back in Poplar, everyone had known that the King was being led astray by evil advisers and Catholic plots, and that Parliament was full of brave, honest, clear-sighted men who wanted the best for everybody. It had been so obvious! It had been common sense! Right now, the Poplar folk would probably be celebrating the death of the wicked Earl. Praise the Lord, Black Tom Tyrant is dead!

But here in Grizehayes, it was just as obvious to everybody that a power-hungry Parliament driven to frenzy by crazy Puritans was trying to steal power from the rightful King. Neither side seemed to be stupid, and both were equally certain.

Was I raised by Puritans? I believed what they believed back then. Were we all frothing mad? Or was I right then, and am I mad now?

'But this is news the masters could send by a letter!' said Mistress Gotely. 'Why have they come here in person, so sudden?'

'They were bringing something home,' said the coachman, with a mysterious air. 'I had my eye on it for only a second, but it looked to be a parchment, with a wax seal on it the size of your palm.' He dropped his voice to a whisper, despite the dozen listening ears arrayed around him. 'The King's own seal, if I had to guess.'

. . . . .

'It's a royal charter,' James told Makepeace later that day, when they had a chance to talk privately. 'I had the truth of it from Master Symond.'

'Are you and Master Symond friends?' asked Makepeace in surprise.

She had caught a glimpse of Symond, dismounting in the courtyard from a fine grey mare. He was only about nineteen years old, but lavishly dressed in lace and sky-coloured velvets. With his ice-blond hair, and air of courtly elegance, he seemed rare and expensive, like the icing swans Mistress Gotely sometimes made for important guests. He was smooth-featured, and quite unlike Sir Thomas, apart from the little dint in his chin.

To tell the truth, she was rather impressed that James was on close terms with such an exotic creature. She could see James preening himself and wanting to say yes, but his honesty triumphed.

'Sometimes,' he said instead. 'I was his companion when he was growing up here . . . and sometimes we were friends. He gave me these clothes, and these good shoes—they were all his once. He also gave me this.' James pushed up his hair, and Makepeace could see a white scar nicking his hairline over his left temple.

'We were out on a hunt together once, and our horses were a pair of fine-fettled girls. We leaped a hedge, and I took it more cleanly than he did. I knew it, and he knew it. I could see him looking at me like thunder. So just as we were coming to the next hedge, out of the sight of the others, he leaned over and hit me across the face with his whip. I slipped in the saddle, my horse stopped in surprise, and over its head I went, into the hedge!' James laughed, and seemed to find it much funnier than Makepeace did.

'You might have broken your neck!' she exclaimed.

'I'm sturdier than that,' said James calmly. 'But it taught me a lesson. He may look like milk and honey, but there's a lord's pride and temper underneath. He told me afterwards that I'd left him no choice—that he *needed* to be the best. I suppose that's as near as he could get to saying sorry.'

Makepeace thought that this was not near enough, by any means.

'He went away to university at Oxford, and since then Sir Marmaduke has been introducing him at court. Each time he comes back, he's lofty as a cloud at first, and hardly seems to know me. But as soon as we're talking alone, it's like old times . . . for a while.'

Makepeace felt a twinge of jealousy at the thought of James having confidential conversations with somebody else. She had no right to feel that way, and she knew it.

James had become her closest living friend and confidant. She trusted him more than any other human, and yet she had still not told him about Bear. The longer she left it, the harder it was to admit to James that she had hidden something so important from him. After three months, it no longer seemed possible to tell him. She felt guilty about it, and a little sad sometimes, as if she had missed a boat and been stranded forever on a lonely shore.

'So what is this charter?' she asked. 'Did Master Symond say?'

'He hasn't read it,' said James, 'nor does he know what's in it. He says it's deadly secret. He also says the King didn't like it at all, and Sir Marmaduke had great trouble getting him to sign it. His Majesty agreed in the end, but only because the Fellmottes are lending him a fortune, and Sir Marmaduke is helping him sell some of the royal jewels.'

Makepeace frowned. All of this was stirring a murky, ominous memory from her first day at Grizehayes.

'Is the King desperate for money?' She recalled Lord Fellmotte saying those very words.

'I suppose he must be.' James shrugged.

'What do royal charters *do*?' asked Makepeace.

'They're . . . royal declarations.' James sounded a bit uncertain. 'They give you permission to do things. Like . . . building battlements on your house. Or . . . selling pepper. Or attacking foreign ships.'

'So what's the point of a *secret* declaration, then?' demanded Makepeace. 'If the King gave you permission to do something, why wouldn't you want everyone to know?'

'Hmm. That *is* odd.' James frowned thoughtfully. 'But the charter definitely gives the Fellmottes permission for *something*. Master Symond said he overheard Sir Marmaduke saying something about "our ancient customs and practices of inheritance".'

'James,' Makepeace said slowly. 'The evening I first came to this house, I overheard his lordship and White Crowe talking about something. White Crowe was saying that there were people at court accusing the Fellmottes of witchcraft.'

'Witchcraft!' James's eyebrows shot up. 'Why didn't you tell me?'

'I was half mad with fever that day! It's like remembering a nightmare. I've scarce thought about it since.'

'But you're sure they said witchcraft?'

'I think so. Lord Fellmotte said they couldn't stop the King hearing rumours like that, so they needed to stop him acting on them. They needed a hold on him. And then they talked about how the King was desperate for money, and how they might be able to arrange something.'

James scowled at nothing for a while.

'So . . . what if the Fellmottes' "ancient customs" are something evil?' he said slowly. 'Something that might get them accused of being witches? If the King has signed a charter giving permission for something devilish, then he can't ever arrest them as witches, can he? Because if he does, they'll show everyone that charter, and he'll be accused too.'

'If the Fellmottes fall, so does he.' Makepeace completed the thought. 'It's blackmail.'

'I told you there was something wrong with the Fellmottes!' exclaimed James. 'Their "ancient customs" . . . It must be something to do with what happens when they inherit! I told you, they *change*. Maybe they give up their souls to the Devil!'

'We don't know—' began Makepeace.

'We know that they're witches, or close enough!' retorted James. 'Why won't you run away with me? What will it take for you to change your mind?'

This question was answered the very next day.

CHAPTER 9

The next morning dawned sultry but bright, so a handful of servants were sent with pails and ladders to gather the ripe apples from the little walled orchard at Grizehayes. The trees were lush-leaved and bowed over with fruit, and the air sweet with their smell.

Makepeace happened to be there, picking some ripe quinces for Mistress Gotely, when a loud crash sounded from the other side of the orchard. There were a few screams and cries of alarm.

She sprinted towards the sound. One of the stablehands, Jacob, had clearly fallen out of the tallest tree while picking apples. He had always been a joker, Makepeace thought in a daze, as she stared down at his face. It was still creased, as though mid-laugh. His neck, however, was at a new angle, and made her think of the dead chickens on the kitchen table.

Somebody ran to the house to tell Sir Thomas about the accident. He soon appeared, and organized a stretcher. Then everybody was told to leave the orchard.

For a brief moment, Makepeace thought she saw a faint shimmer above Jacob's body. The air briefly creased and whispered. She gave a small, involuntary gasp, and took a step backwards.

Something brushed against her mind, and she was flooded with a scrambled mess of memories that were not her own.

. . . Fear, pain, two children laughing, a grass-stain on a woman's cheek, chilblains and hot cider, dappled apples in the sun, lichen slippery under hands . . .

Makepeace turned and ran from the orchard, heart banging. It was only when she was back in the kitchen, gasping for breath, that she realized that she had forgotten the basket of quinces she needed for the evening meal.

'Well, go back and get it!' shouted Mistress Gotely. 'Quickly!'

Sick with nerves, Makepeace hurried back. At the gate of the orchard, however, she encountered James, who stopped her.

'Don't go in,' he whispered.

'I just need—'

James shook his head urgently. He put a finger to his lips, and pulled her to stand beside him, peering in through the archway. His face was tense, and Makepeace realized that he was more nervous than she had ever seen him.

The orchard was empty of apple-pickers now. One solitary man stalked between the trees. He was unusually tall and strongly built, yet moved with an unnerving, stealthy grace.

'Sir Marmaduke,' whispered James.

Three sharp-eyed greyhounds milled around Sir Marmaduke's feet, quivering with expectancy and excited tension. A bloodhound snuffled the ground.

'What's he doing?' mouthed Makepeace.

James leaned close to her ear. 'Hunting,' he whispered back.

The bloodhound stiffened, and uttered a low, ominous bark. It seemed to be staring intently at an empty patch of grass.

Sir Marmaduke lifted his head. Even from that distance, Makepeace could see that his features were curiously expressionless, but there was something about them that made her innards flinch. It was the same sense of wrongness and horror that had overwhelmed her upon meeting Lord Fellmotte. Sir Marmaduke put his head on one side, as if listening, with a very slight, calm, predatory smile. He remained that way for a time, perfectly and eerily still.

Something moved infinitesimally, shaking a nettle and knocking a drowsy bee into the air. Briefly Makepeace thought she glimpsed a little twist of smoke amid the dancing shadows.

Jacob.

In that moment, Sir Marmaduke leaped into action.

They're too fast, James had said of the Elders. At last Makepeace understood what he meant. One moment Sir Marmaduke was a statue, the next he was sprinting across the grass with incredible speed. People usually tensed for a moment before they ran, Makepeace realized, but Sir Marmaduke had not. The dogs poured after their master, moving like wolves to flank their invisible prey.

The lone ghost fled them, weaving desperately between the trees. As it drew closer to the archway, Makepeace could see it more clearly. It was bleeding shadow in its panic. It was wounded, terrified, uncoordinated. She could just hear its thin, whispery, undulating wail.

It zigzagged, swerving away from the snapping jaws of the dogs, letting itself be hounded this way and that. It could never outpace Sir Marmaduke, and yet the Elder always slowed when he was a step behind it.

He's toying with it, Makepeace realized in horror. *He's hounding it so it burns itself out.*

The ghost was faltering and guttering now, like a grey flame almost spent. It disappeared into the dappled shadow of the nearest tree, and Sir Marmaduke pounced on it at last, his curled fingers closing on something in the grass.

He was turned away from Makepeace, but she saw him bow his head, and raise whatever he clutched close to his face.

There was a thistly, rending sound. Something screamed—a faint, impossible scream that still managed to sound human.

Makepeace gave an involuntary intake of breath, and James clapped a hand over her mouth to stop her crying out.

'There's nothing we can do!' he hissed in her ear.

There were more tearing sounds, and Makepeace could not bear any more. She pulled away from James and ran back to the main house. James caught up with her by the door to the kitchen, and hugged her tightly to stop her shaking.

'That was *Jacob*!' whispered Makepeace. Jacob the jester, always laughing because he was among friends.

'I know,' said James with quiet anger.

'He tore him apart! He . . .' She did not know exactly what Sir Marmaduke had done. She was fairly sure you could not bite a ghost, yet she could not help imagining the Elder rending the helpless ghost with his teeth.

Lord Fellmotte had talked about 'destroying vermin', and Makepeace had never let herself think about that too hard. She had just been glad that no rogue ghosts could attack her in Grizehayes. But now she had seen what 'destroying vermin' meant.

Is that what the Fellmottes would do with Bear's spirit if they found out about him? And what if she or James died at Grizehayes? Would they be hounded to shreds too? She had seen Sir Marmaduke smile, as if he were hunting for sport.

'He enjoyed it!' she whispered bitterly in James's ear. 'You were right about everything! This *is* a roost of devils! Let me come with you!'

. . . . .

The pair of them ran away in the late afternoon. James volunteered to collect kindling. Makepeace arranged to be sent to forage for mushrooms and wild chicory. They met by the old oak, and fled.

As they walked briskly down the lane, trying to look natural, Makepeace thought that her heart would burst from beating too hard. For the first time she wondered if this was why James ran away over and over, so that he could feel this surge of unbearable aliveness. Although James sauntered casually, Makepeace could see his eyes darting from side to side, to see whether they were being observed.

Once the fields yielded to moor, they abandoned the lane and cut across country. Makepeace took out a tiny pinch of pepper she had stolen from Mistress Gotely's treasure chest of spices, and scattered it across the path, to discourage any dog from following their trail.

The undulating moorland path was treacherous. The vivid bracken frequently hid sudden dips, briars, toe-hooking roots and sharp rocks. After they had been slithering and clambering for a few hours, the sun set, and the sky dulled to umber.

'They'll have missed us by now,' said James, 'but I doubt they can track us in the dark.' Makepeace was starting to wonder about the pair's chances of finding their own way once night had fully fallen.

As the light was fading, Makepeace felt Bear wake in her head. He was surprised to find himself free from walls. She felt herself rising on to the balls of her feet and craning her neck upward, as Bear strove to see and smell better.

Her eyes seemed to adjust to the twilight. Not for the first time, Makepeace suspected that Bear's night vision was better than hers. At the same time, she became aware of the scents on the breeze—

gorse pollen, rotting berries, sheep dung and distant woodsmoke.

As the wind changed direction, blowing from Grizehayes, she caught another scent. A familiar animal smell, sharp with eagerness and hunger.

'Dogs!' she whispered aloud, her blood running cold. A moment later she caught the distant sound of tumultuous barking. Peering back the way they had come, she could just make out the tiny, bright pinpricks of lanterns.

'James! They're coming!'

The two siblings picked up their pace, ignoring bruised knuckles and scratches, and keeping to the low paths to avoid silhouetting themselves against the sky. They splashed across a stream to confuse the dogs. But still the company of lanterns gained, and showed no sign of being thrown off the scent.

How do they know where we are?

Distant human voices became audible. One deep, commanding bellow was louder than the rest.

'That's Sir Marmaduke!' James's eyes were bright with alarm.

They scrambled on, flayed by briars and bracken. Makepeace knew she was slowing James down. She was growing tired, and was much less agile than he was. As the sky dimmed, though, he seemed to be having more trouble making out the shadowed dips, rises and snagging roots. Makepeace realized that her brother was struggling in the dark.

The barking abruptly stopped. For a moment Makepeace could not understand why. Then, she imagined great dogs released from their leashes, running silently across the rugged ground . . .

She froze, and stared around at what was now a wasteland of hopelessness. No tree to climb, no building to hide in. Only a steep incline ahead, which perhaps they could slide down to find cover . . .

But before she could voice the thought, a lean, dark, four-legged shape exploded from the undergrowth. It hit James in the chest, knocking him backwards down the slope.

Another dog erupted from the gorse, and Makepeace saw its teeth glisten as it leaped for her face. It was too fast for her, but not for Bear. She watched her arm swing across, clouting the dog away out of the air with a force that shocked her. The dog hit the ground yards away and rolled, then recovered its feet unsteadily.

Beyond it, Makepeace saw two more dogs racing towards her, leaping and zigzagging between the gorse mounds. With a sick sense of unreality, Makepeace saw that they were not alone.

A man was running alongside the dogs, miraculously matching their speed and sure-footedness. A lantern jangled in one of his hands, showing his tall, strongly built figure, plum worsted coat and strangely impassive face.

Makepeace wasted valuable seconds simply staring. Sir Marmaduke's speed was uncanny, impossible. It was like watching rain falling upwards.

She could hear James yelling, amid guttural snarls and rending sounds. She did not know if the dog was tearing his collar or his throat. She had too many enemies, and James . . . James . . .

'Stop it!' Makepeace screamed. 'Please! Call off the dogs!'

Sir Marmaduke gave a curt whistle, and the sounds of struggle ceased. Makepeace stood there panting, ringed about by dogs, willing Bear not to fight or flee. Rustling steps approached, and lanterns bobbed towards her from several directions. James was hauled out of the ditch by Young Crowe, his collar torn to shreds but his skin unbroken.

Apprehending Makepeace was almost an afterthought. In the darkness, she realized, nobody had seen her hurl a large hound away with suspicious strength. Her secret, at least, had survived.

It was a long, cold walk back to Grizehayes. James stared at the ground as he stumbled along, and for a while Makepeace thought that he might be angry with her for slowing him down. But halfway back, he slipped his hand into hers, and they walked the rest of the way hand in defiant hand.

Next morning in the courtyard, Makepeace watched in anguish as James was given a thrashing so harsh he could hardly stand afterwards. Nobody doubted that he had masterminded the escapade and dragged Makepeace along. After all, he was older than her, and a boy.

Makepeace was beaten too, but less severely, and mostly for the theft of the precious pepper. Mistress Gotely was angry and disappointed.

'Some are hanged for less!' she growled. 'I always wondered when the bad blood in you would show. "Cat will after kind," they say.'

Makepeace returned to her work in the kitchen, doing her best to look like a crestfallen penitent. Her thoughts, however, burned with new force and clarity.

Next time we will need a better way to deal with the dogs. I must try to befriend them all, not just the ones that sleep in the kitchen. And our plan must be flawless, or I will not be the one who suffers most. James is brave and clever, but he does not always think things through.

I have drawn the Elders' attention to me. If they watch me, they will see through me. So I must be beneath their notice. I must be unlovely, unremarkable, boring. I must be careful and patient.

I will find a way to escape from here, even if it takes me years.

As a matter of fact, it did.

PART TWO: GOTELY'S CAT

CHAPTER 10

A lot can change in two years and a season.

Twenty-seven months is long enough for a place to seep into your bones. Its colours become the palette of your mind, its sounds your private music. Its cliffs or spires overshadow your dreams, its walls funnel your thoughts.

Humans are strange, adaptable animals, and eventually get used to anything, even the impossible or unbearable. Beauty living in the Beast's castle doubtless had her routines, her little irritations and a great deal of boredom. Terror is tiring, and difficult to keep up indefinitely, so sooner or later it must be replaced by something more practical.

One day you wake up in your prison, and realize that it is the only real place. Escape is a dream, a lip-service prayer that you no longer believe in.

But Makepeace was used to fighting against the slow poison of habit. Her life with Mother had taught her how to keep herself unrooted. *This is not your home*, she reminded herself, again and again and again.

Fortunately, Makepeace had Bear, whose hot and turbulent instincts told her, over and over, that she was in a prison, loaded with chains she could neither feel nor see. Then there was James. It was harder for the siblings to meet now, since James had been given new duties that gave him less time with the other servants. He was now the personal servant of Symond, Sir Thomas's blond-white heir, and had become his errand boy, companion, sparring partner and personal footman.

In spite of the household's efforts to keep the siblings apart, however, the two snatched opportunities to meet in secret and hatch plans.

In two years and a season, you can learn a lot about escape planning. Makepeace discovered a flair for it.

James came up with bold, cunning schemes, but never noticed their flaws. He was confident, she was doubtful and distrustful. But doubt and distrust had their uses. Makepeace had an eye for problems, and a quiet cunning when it came to solutions.

She hoarded every chance penny she was given, and secretly spent them on a threadbare change of clothes, in case disguises were needed in a hurry. She learned the rituals and habits of all Grizehayes's inhabitants, and discovered the old house's myriad hiding places. She stubbornly worked on her penmanship, so that she could try her hand at forgery if required.

Two years and a season taught her to be a cautious, patient thief, squirrelling away oddments that might be useful on the run—a small knife, a tinderbox, some paper, candle stubs. She had powder to lighten her face and hide her pockmarks, and charcoal to darken her brows. Makepeace collected unwanted or ill-guarded rags, and in the quiet times before sleeping had gradually stitched them together to create a makeshift rope, just in case one was ever needed.

She had even secretly drawn her own map of the local area on the back of an old playbill, adding to it gradually whenever she learned of another landmark.

And from time to time, to everyone's disgust, James and Makepeace tried to escape from Grizehayes, and were dragged back in disgrace.

In two years and a season, you can learn from your failures. You can discover patience and cunning. You can teach everybody to overlook you.

Makepeace learned to hide in plain sight. Eventually she was treated as part of the kitchen, like the ladles and tongs. By the time she turned fifteen, she had become accepted. Trusted. Taken for granted. The other servants now saw her as a surly extension of the grumpy old cook, rather than a real person with secret thoughts. 'Gotely's Shadow', they sometimes nicknamed her. 'Gotely's Echo'. 'Gotely's Cat'.

Makepeace was as unlovely as she could make herself. Her clothes were always baggy and ill-fitting, and often streaked with dripping or flour. Her hair had started to learn the same defiant witchiness as her mother's, but like the other servant women she kept it carefully wrapped up in a turban-like linen cap. Her expressions changed slowly, and she let people think that her thoughts were similarly slow. They were not. They were as quick as her fingers, the deft, calloused hands that nobody gave a second glance.

She kept most people at arm's length. Over the years, some Bear-ness had bled into her behaviour. Because Bear did not like people approaching too quickly or coming too close, neither did she. When strangers wandered within five feet of her, it made her feel angry and frightened, as if they were charging at her screaming. She could feel Bear wanting to draw himself up and menace them, to make them back away. He tried to snort low, guttural threats, and these escaped her throat as angry-sounding coughs. Makepeace had earned a reputation for fits of sour temper, and territorial defence of the kitchen.

'Don't go running into there without warning,' the errand boys were cautioned, 'or Gotely's Cat will swipe you with her ladle.' But the household made a joke of it. Nobody guessed at the Bear-temper Makepeace had learned to keep in check.

Over time Bear had learned to accept the kitchen, in spite of the heat and noise. He knew all its smells now. He had rubbed himself against the door jambs to make them his, so the kitchen felt safer. Just as slowly, Makepeace had introduced him to the idea of promises and bargains. *Hush now, Bear, and later I will let us run in the orchard. Don't lash out, and later I shall steal us a fistful of the scraps meant for the poultry. Hold back your rage now, and some day, some day, we shall escape to a world without walls.*

The two tiny smallpox marks on Makepeace's cheek had never faded. The other serving women sometimes nagged her to do something about them, cover them with powder or fill the pits with fat. She never did. The last thing she wanted was for anyone's gaze to linger on her.

I am not worth your attention. Forget about me.

James, on the other hand, was attracting notice. Whenever Symond went away to attend court or visit relations, James would be left behind, and would become just another servant. But whenever Symond returned to Grizehayes, James's star would rise again, and his spirits with it. The two were thick as thieves, and suddenly James knew all the doings of the family, the court and the nation.

The servant women still teased him, but their tone was different now. He was now a seventeen-year-old man, not a boy, and it was whispered that he had prospects.

. . . . .

In two years and a season, a country can fall apart. Cracks prove deeper than anybody expected. They can become crevasses, and then chasms.

News came piecemeal to Grizehayes. Sometimes it arrived in sealed letters that went straight to Lord Fellmotte's room, but then trickled down through the household in overheard fragments. Sometimes pedlars and tinkers brought word-of-mouth news, seasoned with rumour and gore.

These scraps could be patchworked into a picture.

As the Year of Our Lord 1641 wore itself out and yielded to 1642, the tension between the King and Parliament became ever more dangerous.

London was simmering and divided. Mobs clashed, rumours spread like wildfire, and the King's party and Parliament's supporters were convinced that the others were plotting against them.

For a while it seemed that Parliament was winning the battle of wills.

'I don't understand the whole of it,' said Mistress Gotely, 'but they say Parliament wants to do more and more without the King's say-so. By the time they've finished, the King won't be a king at all—just a poppet with a crown. He should show them a bit of right royal wrath.'

Apparently the King thought so too.

On the fourth day of January 1642, King Charles marched to the House of Commons with hundreds of armed troops, to seize the five men he thought were Parliament's ringleaders.

'But when he got there,' said Long Alys, who had heard the news from Young Crowe, 'those men had escaped! They must have had spies to tip 'em off. And the rest of Parliament would not tell the King where they were gone, and faced him down! And now the trained bands of London are told to protect Parliament, against their own King! Oh, they're all showing their traitors' colours now.'

A line had been crossed, and everyone could feel it. Until now, both sides had been raising the stakes, sure that sooner or later the other's nerve would break. But now weapons had been brandished. There were rumours that Parliament was raising an army against the King, and pretending it was for a war in Ireland.

'Of course, the King's gathering his own troops as well!' Old Crowe was overheard saying to his son. 'How else can he protect his crown and his people against Parliament?'

'They're both strutting like cocks and showing their spurs, and hoping it won't come to blood,' was the less charitable view of one of the stablehands.

This cannot be happening, was the feeling everywhere. *Surely there is a way to prevent this! Surely nobody wishes for war!*

But in August of 1642, in a field at Nottingham, the King had his royal standard raised and fixed in the ground. Its silk rippled as he read a declaration of war.

That same night the King's standard blew down in a storm, and was found in the mud.

'It is an ill omen,' muttered Mistress Gotely, rubbing at her gouty leg. She always claimed that she could feel coming storms as pains in her leg, and sometimes said that she could sense bad luck too. 'I wish it had not fallen.'

When a country is torn in two, it splits in surprising zigzags, and it is hard to guess who will find themselves on one side and who on the other. There were stories of families divided, friends taking up arms against each other, towns where neighbour warred against neighbour.

Parliament held London. The King had made his base in Oxford. There was some talk of peace negotiations, but many more accounts of battles.

At Grizehayes, however, the war always felt distant. There were preparations, of course. The men in the villages drilled on the commons, and green uniforms were made up for a local regiment. The Fellmottes ordered weapons and ammunition as well, and had the defensive walls of the great house repaired. Yet the idea that war could reach the Fellmotte stronghold seemed absurd.

We will never change, said its grim, grey walls, *and so nothing will really change, for we are all that matters. We are the great rock amid the world's sea. The doings of other men may wash and crash around us, but we are eternal.*

CHAPTER 11

In the season of bitter winds and long nights, Christmastide finally arrived. With its feasting and merry-making, it mocked the grey skies and defied the barren fields. It was a bright arrow through winter's dark heart.

For most people, the twelve days of Christmas were a very welcome break from work. However, there was no rest for the feast-makers. Makepeace was run off her feet preparing tarts, pies, soups, collops, roast fowl of every size, cold meats and iced extravagances. She was even put in charge of roasting the vast boar's head, a patched and monstrous thing whose cooked snout still had an honest piggishness. Makepeace did not feel bad about cooking dead beasts and birds. They would have understood the belly's need to be full, the hungry taking of life to stretch out one's own life.

To see Makepeace doggedly working, you would not have guessed at the secret plan burning in her heart like a cool and quiet fire.

As usual, James had struck the first spark.

'Twelfth Night!' he had whispered to her one evening. 'Think of it! The house will be full to the rafters! It's the one night of the year when everybody from the farms and villages is allowed to feast in the hall at Grizehayes. The courtyard gates will be open, and the guard dogs muzzled. So . . . when the crowds start to leave, we slip out too. They won't miss us for hours.'

As Makepeace ran breathlessly from task to task, her mind was picking away at the scheme, It was a good plan, and *could* work, with enough cunning. But there were risks. Even if they got away, the siblings would be left homeless and friendless in the depths of winter, amid bare, hungry fields. She was not even sure she could count on Bear's night vision, since he was 'awake' much less in colder months.

Worse, many of the other Elders would be visiting Grizehayes for the feast.

We'll have to stay out of their way, James had said. *Or they'll know what we're planning. They'll see through us, right to the bone.*

By the time Twelfth Night finally arrived, Makepeace was exhausted, and had several new burns on her hands and arms from spitting fat, hastily handled skewers and jostled kettles.

The great hall was trimmed with sprigs of holly, ivy, rosemary and bay, and in the huge, blazing fireplace could be seen the charred and glowing remnants of the Yule log, its ribbons long since burnt to shrivelled rags.

Trappings of heathenry! the Poplar minister would have exclaimed. *They might as well be sacrificing a bull on an altar to Baal! Christmas is a Devil's snare, baited with ale, idleness and plum duff!*

Nobody else seemed alarmed by it, though. The villagers started to arrive in the afternoon, in nervous, jocose groups, marvelling at the carvings and clustering around the warmth of the hearth. A little cider lent them some confidence, and the time-blackened beams of the hall echoed with their raised voices and laughter. By the time the sun was setting, the hall was packed.

The servingmen were run off their feet ferrying plates of food to the hall, and carrying ale and cider from the cellar, along with the few barrels of drinkable wine left over from the newly deceased year. There were always too few hands at the ready, so Makepeace found herself scampering between kitchen and hall, bearing plates of tongue, bowls of pale and lumpy brawn, and platters of cheese and apples.

Over by the hearth she could see James filling the cups of the 'better kind' of visitor. Unlike Makepeace, he was considered handsome enough to wait upon the family and honoured guests. He was quick of wit, well-proportioned and athletic, with a pleasant-ugly face and an easy charm. Nobody seeing his good-humoured smile would guess that he was planning his escape that very night.

Wait for me at midnight in the chapel, he had told her. *Nobody will be there tonight.*

A great oaken throne placed near the hearth was clearly intended for the lord of the manor, but neither Lord Fellmotte nor Sir Thomas was in evidence. Instead it was occupied by Symond, who seemed to be revelling in his lordly role. He was surrounded by other courtly young bloods, also in their early twenties. If gossip spoke truly, they could all boast of eminent families or powerful patrons.

The whole festival bore the marks of Symond's interference. He had come back from court a self-appointed expert on elegant dishes, extravagant masques and the scandalous dresses that the ladies of fashion were almost wearing this year. On his insistence, Mistress Gotely and Makepeace had been struggling to stuff birds with other birds, and make marchpanes in the shapes of sailing boats.

According to James, Symond had said he *needed* to be the best at everything. Perhaps it was just lordly vanity and a wish to be admired, but for a moment she wondered if the family's golden boy was trying a little too hard. Why did he have so much to prove, and who was he trying to prove it to?

Wassailers arrived at the door with a fiddler, declaring in song that if they were not given drink and meat they would set upon the company with clubs. Everybody cheered uproariously and stamped their feet, and the singers were welcomed in. A great wassail bowl of hot, spiced lamb's-wool ale was brought in, golden apple pulp floating in its depths. A single piece of bread was pulled out of the bowl and ceremoniously presented to Symond, who accepted the toast with a gracious dip of the head.

Amid the laughter and uproar, Makepeace saw one of Symond's friends slap his lace handkerchief into his cup of ale, and crumple it into a sodden ball to throw at his friend's face. She felt an unexpected sting of anger.

Stop being a Puritan, she told herself. *It is his handkerchief and his ale—he can spoil them if he wants.*

And yet the waste enraged her. Somebody had worked for weeks to make that lace, stitch by careful stitch. Unknown sailors had braved terrible dangers to carry the soup's spices from other lands. She herself had spent some time preparing the lamb's-wool ale. The young blade's little show of 'lordly high spirits' had wasted more than money or fine goods; it had wasted other people's time, sweat and effort without a thought.

Makepeace was still gnawing on this thought when she noticed that the joyous crowd near Symond's throne was hushing and respectfully parting to let a single figure pass.

Lady April was one of the Elders. She was not tall, and yet the sight of her seemed to chill the merriment and wildness out of everyone. The lace trim of the old woman's black cap threw a perforated shadow over her puckered brow, bony nose and wrinkled eyelids. Her face was covered in the paint known as tin glass, leaving her skin eerily white with a metallic gloss. Her mouth was a vermilion sliver. She looked like a portrait come to life.

Makepeace felt her own skin crawl and her blood chill. Was James right about the Elders seeing what you were thinking at a glance? She pulled back into the crowd, afraid that Lady April might turn an icy gaze upon her, and immediately know about all her schemes and the runaway pack of provisions and supplies Makepeace had hidden in the chapel.

The handkerchief-thrower, however, failed to notice Lady April's approach. He scooped up his handful of sodden lace and hurled it again, only to gawp aghast as it flopped against the hem of Lady April's cloak. All colour instantly drained from his face, and his grin was replaced by a look of pitiable terror.

Lady April said nothing, but she turned her head very slowly to gaze down at the tiny patch of dampness marring the tassels of her cloak. She straightened and stared directly at the culprit, the muscles of her face motionless.

The young courtier's face crumpled in panic. As she turned and moved out of the great hall into the corridor, he followed her, imploring, apologizing and twisting his cuffs. His friends watched the old woman go, all wearing the same frozen look, and nobody made mouths behind her back. Even on this night of misrule, Lady April was not funny.

Caught up in the scene despite herself, Makepeace edged over to the corridor so that she could watch the old woman and her accidental assailant. Lady April glided on implacably until she came to a place where a wine hogshead had been tipped over and its dregs spilt. She looked down at the pool of deep purplish-red, and waited. After a few moments' blankness, the young man hesitantly took off his expensive-looking cape, and laid it down over the spillage. Still she waited, only advancing one toe to prod at the cape, where dark stains were soaking up through the bright cloth.

Slowly the young culprit got down on his knees, and Makepeace saw him lay his hands flat on the cloth, palms down. Only then did Lady April deign to advance, hem raised just shy of the ground, slowly and deliberately using his hands as stepping stones.

Normal people could not see the strangeness of the Fellmottes in the same way Makepeace and James did, but apparently even powerful men saw plenty to fear in Lady April.

By the time the lantern clock showed eleven o'clock, Makepeace's heart was pounding. She needed to sneak off to the chapel soon, or there was a risk that she would find herself dragged away for another chore, and miss her midnight appointment.

The huge Twelfth Night cake was carried in, to a storm of applause. It was duly carved up, its pieces pounced upon with glee. Whoever found a bean in their piece would be the Lord of Misrule for the night. The world would be turned upside down, and the lowest vagrant might find himself as master of the feast, everybody else duty-bound to obey his whims . . .

A space was cleared for a group of newly arrived mummers. Two of them, dressed as St George and a Saracen knight, set upon each other with wooden swords. Everybody gathered around, roaring with enthusiasm.

Nobody was paying any attention to Makepeace, and this was as good a time as any to slip away. She turned and elbowed her way through the crush, then out of the great doors into the icy cold of the courtyard beyond. She took in a deep lungful of biting winter air, then turned and blundered straight into a man who had been standing nearby.

By the light from the doorway, she could just make out the lace of his cuffs and cravat, the velvet of his long coat, his brown eyes and the tired lines of his face.

'Sir Thomas! I am sorry, I—'

'My fault, child. I was looking at the upper realms, not this one.' Sir Thomas gestured upward. 'I love nights with this watery haze. It looks as though the stars are dancing.'

A little startled, Makepeace looked up. There was a slight clamminess to the cold night air, and the stars did indeed seem to waver and twinkle.

'You should be inside, claiming your piece of the cake,' said Sir Thomas with a smile. 'Don't you want your chance at the bean? Wouldn't you like to be queen for a night?'

The idea of forcing Young Crowe to grovel and serve her had a wicked appeal. But the last thing she wanted right now was to be the centre of attention.

'I wouldn't be a real queen, sir,' she said hesitantly. 'Tomorrow I would be low enough to be kicked again. If I had played "Queen" high and mighty, I would pay for it later. Everything has its price.'

'Not at Christmas,' said Sir Thomas cheerfully.

'Tell that to the geese,' muttered Makepeace, then flushed, realizing that this had not been a very polite response. 'I . . . I am sorry.' Why was Sir Thomas so determined to talk to her, tonight of all nights?

'The . . . geese?' Sir Thomas still seemed unruffled, his smile patient. Not for the first time, Makepeace thought it strange that a man like this should be Obadiah's son and Symond's father.

'For weeks I've been fattening them,' Makepeace explained gingerly, 'for tonight's feast. The geese, the capons, the turkey. They gobbled up all the food I laid down for them, and never knew there would be a price to pay in the end. Maybe they just thought they were lucky. Or perhaps they thought I was being kind.

'All the folks in there, eating capon pie and roast goose . . . they're making a bargain too, aren't they? Tonight they get to sit by a great fire, and eat themselves sick, and sing up a storm. But in exchange, they're supposed to show they're grateful by working hard and being obedient the rest of the year, aren't they?

'At least they know what bargain they're making. Nobody warned the geese.'

She was speaking a lot more forcefully than she had intended. The dread that she herself was a 'fattened goose' had never stopped haunting her.

'Would it have made anything better for the geese if they had known what might happen?' asked Sir Thomas. His tone had changed, and now he sounded very serious. 'What if knowledge only brought them fear and misery?'

Makepeace felt the hairs rise on the back of her neck, and was suddenly fairly sure that neither of them was talking about geese any more.

'If I were them,' she said, 'I would want to know.'

Sir Thomas sighed, his breath misting about his face.

'I had a conversation very like this,' he said, 'with another young woman, sixteen years ago. She was of your years, and . . . I see her in you. Not in any feature I can name, but some gleam of her is there.'

Makepeace swallowed. Not long before, she had been desperate to leave the conversation. Now answers seemed to be tantalizingly within reach.

'She was with child,' Sir Thomas continued. 'She wanted to know why my family were so keen for her child to be raised on the Grizehayes estates. She suspected something ill in the whole affair, but did not know what.

'"Tell me," she said. "Nobody else will." And even though it meant breaking promises, I did. And then she asked me to help her run away.'

'You helped her?' exclaimed Makepeace in surprise.

'Sometimes folly strikes us like lightning. She was my brother's lover. I was married, and too dull a fellow to take a mistress. Yet it came to me suddenly that this was the one woman to whom I could refuse nothing. Even though it meant that I would never see her again.

'Yes, I helped your mother. I have spent the last sixteen years wondering whether I made the right decision.'

Makepeace slowly raised her face, and met his eye directly.

'Please,' she said. 'Tell me why I was brought here. Tell me why I should be frightened. Nobody else will.'

For several breaths, Sir Thomas stared out in silence at the faint and restless stars.

'We are a strange family, Makepeace,' he said at last. 'We have a secret—one that could harm us greatly if it was known. There is a talent that runs in the family, a gift of sorts. Not everybody in our family has it, but there are always a few in each generation. I have it, and so does Symond. So does James. And so do you.'

'We have nightmares,' whispered Makepeace. 'We see ghosts.'

'And they are drawn to us. They know that there is a . . . space inside us. We can host more than ourselves.'

Makepeace thought of the swarms of clawing ghosts, and then of Bear, her own greatest secret.

'We're hollow,' she said flatly. 'And dead things can get in.'

'Ghosts without a body fray and perish,' said Sir Thomas, 'so they try to claw their way into us to take sanctuary. By then, most of them have become tattered and crazed. But not all ghosts are mad.'

They were near the heart of the matter now, Makepeace could feel it. Her skin was crawling.

'Imagine,' said Sir Thomas, 'how great a family would be, if no experience, no skills, no memories were ever lost. Suppose every important *person* could be preserved. The blessing of centuries of accumulated wisdom—'

It was at precisely this moment that a polite cough sounded from the doorway. Young Crowe was standing there, silhouetted against the light from the hall.

'Sir Thomas,' he said. 'Forgive me, but Lord Fellmotte is asking for you.'

'I shall be with him soon,' said Sir Thomas, and seemed surprised when Young Crowe did not immediately withdraw.

'Forgive me,' Young Crowe said again. 'I was asked to tell you . . . that you are to be most fortunate tonight.'

The colour drained from Sir Thomas's face, making him look older and more tired.

'Tonight?' he exclaimed, aghast. 'So soon? It seemed that there would be years . . .' He recovered command of himself, and slowly nodded. 'Of course. Of course.' He took two deep breaths, and stared at his own hands as if wanting to make sure they were still there. When he looked at the watery stars again, his expression was stricken and wistful.

He turned to Makepeace and managed a smile.

'You should go in and ask for some cake,' he said. 'Be queen for a while if you can.'

With that, he followed Young Crowe back through the door.

CHAPTER 12

Makepeace was haunted by Sir Thomas's forlorn expression, but she could not stop to wonder at it. Too much time had been lost already. She hurried to the chapel.

The door swung open quietly, and she was surprised to find that a couple of candles were lit. Perhaps somebody had been praying there, after all. There was no sign of James. She settled down to wait, hoping that she had not missed him.

Even after two and a half years, the glittering chapel still made Makepeace uneasy. In Poplar it had been drilled into her that God wanted churches to be plain. So she had been scared and shocked by the Grizehayes chapel's statues, paintings and dangerous smell of incense. She had sat through that first service terrified that she had fallen into a nest of Catholics, and was probably going to Hell.

'I don't think the Fellmottes *are* Catholics,' James had once tried to reassure her. 'At least, I don't think *they* think they're Catholics. They just like . . . old ways of doing things.'

Nowadays, she was no longer sure who was going to Hell. The Fellmotte chapel was so sure of itself, so *old*. It was hard to argue with anyone who had centuries on their side.

On Sundays, the Fellmottes sat in their own raised gallery at the back of the church, reached by a private corridor from their chambers. *Already closer to Heaven than the rest of us*, thought Makepeace. Perhaps they had an arrangement with God, the way they did with the King. Perhaps when the Day of Judgement came, and the seven seals were opened, God would slap the Fellmottes on the back and let them through into Heaven with a wink.

Makepeace could hope for no such special treatment. Instead, Makepeace had been secretly offering up her own rebel prayer.

Almighty Father, when my ashes return to the earth, take me not to Your palace of gold and pearl. Let me go where the beasts go. If there is a forest in Your forever where the beasts and birds run and howl and sing, let me run and howl and sing with them. And if they drift away to nothingness, let me join them like chaff on the wind.

The door creaked open. Makepeace's spirits soared, and then sank. It was not James.

Instead Young Crowe and Old Crowe could be seen, assisting Lord Fellmotte into the room. Lady April and Sir Marmaduke followed after, with Sir Thomas a few steps behind. Makepeace ducked down again, and huddled behind a sarcophagus, her mind racing. Why were they all here? Did they suspect something?

'I thought we had agreed that nothing was to be done until it could not be helped,' Sir Thomas was saying. 'I was not prepared—'

'Your affairs should always be in order,' his father interrupted. 'You know that. It is true, we intended to live out our span in the usual fashion, but events are moving too fast. The King missed his chance to seize London, which means that this ridiculous war will continue longer than expected. If the family is to prosper in these times, we must be able to act freely and quickly. Lord Fellmotte cannot be bedridden.'

'Must it be tonight?' asked Sir Thomas. 'Can we not let my son enjoy this evening, and talk of this again in the morning?'

'The family are gathered, and there is no good reason to delay.'

Makepeace heard the door open and close again. The next voice that spoke was Symond's.

'Father—is it true?' He sounded calm. Too calm, in the way that flames sometimes look blue.

'Come, Symond, step aside with me a moment,' said his father. To Makepeace's dismay she could hear the pair's soft steps approaching. They came to a halt not far from her hiding place.

'Will they spare you?' Symond's voice was tight, precise and level. 'Have they decided?'

'You know that they cannot make promises.' For once, the bluff Sir Thomas sounded a bit evasive. 'There are always risks, and only so much room.'

'You have skills and knowledge useful to the family! Do they know about your studies into navigation and the stars? The devices in your room—the astrolabes and pocket dials!'

'Ah, my poor toys.' Sir Thomas gave a sad little laugh. 'I do not think the family are very impressed by those, alas. Symond—what will be, will be as God wills it. I was born to this destiny. I have prepared for it my whole life. Whatever happens, this Inheritance is my duty and my privilege.'

'We are ready for you, Thomas,' said Lady April, in a glassy, precise voice.

The five Fellmottes could be heard retreating to other end of the chapel, near the altar. Chairs scraped against stone, and then Lady April began intoning something in a low, steely voice. It had the solemnity of a psalm or incantation.

Makepeace sat hugging her knees. Cold seeped from the stone flags, and the marble against her back. Her bones ached with it. It seemed to her that every carving, every memorial slab, every heraldic device on the stained-glass windows was breathing cold into the air.

Something was happening, something deathly secret. What

would happen if she was discovered, or if James blundered in and was caught?

Lady April's voice was no longer the only sound. There were whispers now, as faint as the rending of cobwebs. They rustled and undulated, and then Makepeace heard a very human gasp, followed by a long, choking gurgle.

She could not resist raising her head just enough to steal a look.

Sir Thomas and Lord Obadiah were seated side by side, on throne-like wooden chairs. Obadiah was slumped, his jaw hanging loosely. Sir Thomas had his back arched as if convulsing, his mouth and eyes wide open.

As Makepeace watched, she thought she saw a shadowy something slowly ooze from Obadiah's ear. It seemed to pulse and quiver for a moment, then darted towards Sir Thomas's face and vanished into his gaping mouth. He gave a stifled croak and his expression spasmed, like a rippled puddle reflection. Two more tendrils of shadow started to seep out of Obadiah's eyes.

Makepeace ducked back into her hiding place, trying to breathe quietly. After a while, the ominous noises ebbed, and there was a long silence.

'Donald Fellmotte of Wellsbank, are you there?' asked Lady April.

'Yes,' came the rasped response.

'Baldwin Fellmotte of the Knights Hospitaller, are you there?' Lady April called on name after name, and received a husky 'yes' each time.

'Thomas Fellmotte,' she asked at last, after seven other names, 'are you there?'

There was silence.

'He was a loyal servant of the family,' said Sir Marmaduke,

'but it seems his mind was not strong enough to endure his Inheritance. Obadiah was the same.'

'What happened to him?' asked Symond, still eerily self-contained. 'Where did he go?'

'You must understand that there is only so much space inside a single person, even one with your gift,' said Lady April. 'Sometimes there are casualties, and a mind is crushed and extinguished.

'Right now, however, you have another duty. Your grandfather's body is untenanted, but still breathing. He should not be left in this state of indignity. You should be the one to release him from it, Symond.'

Makepeace pressed firmly against her ears and clenched her eyes shut. She did not move a muscle until she was quite sure that all the Fellmottes had left the chapel.

When Makepeace staggered back into the festivities, the jubilant, human noise shocked her like a blow. There was so much sound in the air that it hardly seemed breathable.

In the main hall, she found James. He was seated in the lordly chair by the fire, a crowd around him laughing at his jokes, and a large tankard of ale in one hand. A great plate of sweetmeats and Shropshire cakes were placed to one side of him, and one brawny fellow was capering and pretending to be his jester.

Makepeace understood at last why James had failed to keep their appointment. He had taken his slice of the Twelfth Night cake. He had found the bean. He was Lord of Misrule. When he saw her, his face fell, and he quickly rose and led her by the arm to a quieter corner.

'It cannot be midnight already,' he began, but then seemed to notice her ashen look. 'Little sister—what has happened?'

In hushed tones, she told him everything.

'The Elders are full of ghosts, James! That is why we cannot bear to look at them! That is why they change when they Inherit! Ghosts of their ancestors pour into them and take them over!'

'But why did they collect *us*?' James stared at her. 'They cannot want us to inherit anything!'

'Can you not see? We are *spares*, James! Sometimes heirs die, or go away for a while. If an Elder drops dead, they need somewhere to put the ghosts in an emergency! We're vessels—that's all we are to them!

'James, we need to leave! Please! How quickly can you get away?'

James had listened to her with horror, but now she saw a glimmer of conflict in his honest face. He glanced over his shoulder at his new-found throne. She should have guessed how much it meant to him, to be lord for a day. When would he get another chance like this?

'It's too late tonight,' he said uncomfortably. 'You're in no state to run for miles, anyway. Let us talk about it again in the morning.'

With a feeling of deep hopelessness, Makepeace watched her half-brother walk back to his waiting throne, and his little throng of courtiers.

Thomas, the new Lord Fellmotte, returned to the hall some time later, with Symond at his side. If Symond had been discomposed for a time, he now seemed to have recovered from it completely. He sat beside his father, surveying the scene with a feline serenity.

Thomas no longer strode or laughed. He moved differently from before, with an eerie stiffness. There was no longer any warmth in his face, and his eyes had the basilisk gaze of Obadiah.

CHAPTER 13

Grizehayes in winter appeared its true self—colourless, eternal, untouchable, unchangeable. It numbed the mind and froze the soul, and made all dreams of escape seem childish.

There was a 'new' Lord Fellmotte in residence, but Makepeace knew that he was no newer than the grey towers. These days Thomas Fellmotte sat bent over, as though used to an aged spine. Suddenly he had an appetite for rich foods and the best brandy. Watching him savage a roast chicken leg, his teeth scraping the meat from the bone, Makepeace could imagine the eager ghosts inside him. Too long had they been trapped in an ailing, crippled frame filled with agues and aches. Now they had teeth again, and a stomach strong enough to bear a little luxury.

'Thomas should have taken better care of this body!' Makepeace overheard him mutter one day. 'We are racked with backaches from all his riding, and our eyes are dim from his reading! We might have taken his body sooner if we had known how he would wear it out. His memories are a jumble, as well, like an unsorted library . . .'

The 'Lord Fellmotte' ghosts did not speak like guests. They seemed to feel that Thomas's body was a property that had always belonged to them, and that they had reclaimed it from a negligent tenant.

Everything had changed. Nothing had changed.

And yet as days grew lighter, rumour whispered of change nonetheless. Spring was coming to Grizehayes, and so was the war.

. . . . .

One May morning before dawn, as Makepeace collected snails in the kitchen garden, she overheard low voices speaking behind the wall.

She often gathered snails and earthworms to make snail water, Mistress Gotely's favourite gout medicine. However, Makepeace had her own reasons for always doing so at such an early hour, while the household were still abed. It meant that nobody else would see her dropping to all fours in the kitchen garden, and letting Bear contentedly amble her body through the cold, dew-laden grass. As long as she stayed in the right part of the garden, the enclosing wall concealed her from Grizehayes's windows.

It was such a simple thing, but it made Bear feel less trapped. This was his cool, green territory, a domain of damp scents and mysteries. Every time, Makepeace felt her eyes sharpen, until she could see in the dim light as clearly as full day. Today she dug at the turf with her fingers, rubbed against a tree and snuffed at the dandelion clocks, breaking them with her nose. She was a little too slow to stop Bear licking a fat beetle off her wrist and eating it.

Then she froze, with the beetle-taste still in her mouth, as she heard quiet, urgent voices and the crunch of footsteps . . .

'Well?' There was no mistaking Lord Fellmotte's rasping creak of a voice.

A second male voice answered. It sounded like Sir Anthony, an Elder who had arrived late the night before. He was second cousin to the new Lord Fellmotte, and Makepeace suspected that his ghosts were a fierce gaggle of soldiers, with a couple of cooler heads thrown into the mix.

'It is as we thought. The rebel troops are moving in on the garrison at Geltford.'

Startled, Makepeace pricked up her ears. Geltford was only forty miles from Grizehayes.

'Hmm,' said Lord Fellmotte. 'If the rebels take Geltford, they will turn their attention to us straight afterwards.'

'Let them,' Sir Anthony said bluntly. 'I pity them if they try to besiege Grizehayes.'

'If the King loses Geltford, it will weaken his hold on the county,' Lord Fellmotte said thoughtfully.

'Do we care?' asked Sir Anthony. 'We have declared for the King, but if we keep our troops at home we can claim we are guarding our lands for his sake. We can hold back, and let this silly little war burn itself out.'

'Ah, but we need the King to win this idiotic war!' retorted Lord Fellmotte. 'If Parliament wins, then King Charles will be weakened, and too poor to pay us back all the money we have loaned him! Besides, we have a hold over this king! He can never prosecute us for witchcraft! If those ranting Puritans sniffed out the truth of our traditions, they would be howling about necromancy in a second. We cannot let them get too powerful.

'The King must win this tussle, and if we do not help him he will make a sow's ear of it. We have *seen* war, and most of this soft, milk-sucking generation have not! No, the King will need us.'

'Could we broker a peace?' suggested Sir Anthony. 'What does Parliament *want?*'

'They say that all they want is for the King to stop claiming new powers for himself.'

'Is he?'

'Of course he is!' exclaimed Lord Fellmotte. 'So are they! Both sides are right. Both sides are wrong. But the King is too stubborn to make terms. He believes he is God's own chosen, so anyone who disagrees with him is a traitor.

'Have you ever met him? King Charles is a *little* man, and he knows it. His legs never grew out properly. His father would have had them put in iron bands to stretch them when he was a child, and perhaps that would have done him some good, but no, the good lady taking care of him would not hear of it. So he has grown up with the cold stubbornness of a *short* man. He does not know how to back down, for he cannot bear to feel *little*.'

'Then what shall we do?' asked Sir Anthony.

'Send messengers,' Lord Fellmotte replied. 'Call in favours. Use threats. Find the great names who are wavering, and harry them to the King's cause. And in the meanwhile . . . ready the regiment. We shall not let the rebels have Geltford. They cannot cross the river if we hold Hangerdon Bridge.'

On the other side of the wall, a young under-cook crouched on all fours, fingers numb from the cold of the dew, her mind whirring as she forged plans.

'The regiment is marching, James,' said Makepeace that evening. 'This is our chance.'

Ever since Twelfth Night, James had looked a little distracted and shamefaced whenever he bumped into Makepeace. It had become difficult to collar him for private conversations. Today, however, Makepeace had successfully dragged him to the passage that led to the old sally gate. She had once wondered whether the gate could be used as a means to sneak out of Grizehayes, but the way was blocked by a locked door and a heavy portcullis. Nonetheless, the passage was an excellent place for secret conversations.

Her cherished, home-made map was spread on her lap. There

were several pieces to it now, drawn on to the faded pages of old ballad-sheets, crudely charting routes to London and other big towns.

'I know,' whispered James, nibbling at his thumbnail. 'The regiment leaves tomorrow. Sir Anthony is leading it, and taking along his son, Master Robert. Master Symond is going, too—he told me himself.'

Makepeace had never been able to think of Symond the same way since Twelfth Night. He had been made to watch his own father becoming possessed. And what about Lady April's order that he should 'relieve' his grandfather's empty shell of life? Had the family forced him to smother the old man with a pillow? And yet he had seemed so calm straight afterwards. She did not know whether to pity him or recoil from him.

James never seemed willing to talk about it, and Makepeace was haunted by suspicions that Symond had taken him into his confidence. The thought stung her to the quick, but she tried to smother her own jealousy.

'Then it's the perfect time to run!' she whispered back. 'The Elders are getting involved in the war at last, so they'll be busy and distracted—the Crowes too, I fancy.

'All the local villages are full of soldiers' wives packing bags to follow the regiment. Think of it! Upheaval, confusion, big crowds on the march that we can hide in if we please!'

Makepeace looked at her brother, and saw what she should have noticed straight away. There was something that he was afraid to admit, yet itching to tell her. He was bristling with suppressed excitement.

'What is it?' she asked, gripped by foreboding. 'What have you done?'

'I asked to go with the regiment—attending upon Master Symond. I was turned down . . . but I have joined the militia that will be guarding Grizehayes and the villages. Don't look at me like that! This is good news—a chance! For both of us!'

'A chance for *you* perhaps. A chance for you to have your head blown off by a cannonball!'

'I will probably never even see fighting! And I will be Prudence on two legs.'

'You will be full of swagger and hellfire, and green as a willow! The other soldiers will give you all the dangerous tasks, and cheat you at dice.'

'Yes, Mother,' said James with mock-solemnity, his ugly, charming smile double-creasing both cheeks. Usually the old nickname warmed her, but today it stuck in her craw. She was being humoured. 'Listen, Makepeace! If there *is* fighting, I can prove myself, and then the Fellmottes will have to acknowledge me. Once I have power in the family, I will be better able to protect you!'

Makepeace stared at him.

'Power in the family?' she repeated. 'We agreed to *leave* the family! We agreed that we wanted nothing from them, and would run as soon as we could! Or has the plan changed?'

James's gaze dropped, and she knew the plan *had* changed. It came to her that it had been changing for some time, even before Twelfth Night.

She had felt him slipping away from her and the promises they had made. His talents were being recognized at Grizehayes. Should he not learn as much as he could before they ran away? Before they committed their final act of defiance and ingratitude, should they not get as much out of the family as they could? And ever so gradually, these ideas had yielded to another thought: *If I can become powerful at Grizehayes, do we really need to leave at all?*

'We're not children any more,' James said, a little defensively. 'I'm a man now. I have duties . . . to the family, to the King.'

'Leaving this place is not a children's game!' retorted Makepeace, her face hot.

'Is it not?' James snapped. 'Do you really think we could ever escape the Fellmottes with . . . these?' He nodded towards the map pieces. 'It has always been a game, and one we can never win. The Fellmottes will always find us, Makepeace! I need to face the world as it is. I need to play by their rules, and play well.'

'It's the bean in the cake,' muttered Makepeace, with quiet fury.

'What?'

'The bean in the Twelfth Night cake! Chance made you Lord of Misrule for the night, and you could not resist it! You threw aside all our plans, just so that you could have everyone bowing and obeying and calling you "my lord". Even though it was all a sham and make-believe.

'You promised we'd escape together, James. You *promised.*'

And this was the crux. Amid Makepeace's worry about James, there was a miserable, childish feeling that he was betraying her.

'You've never been happy with my escape plans!' hissed James. 'If you had been less timid . . .' He trailed off, then began again, in a quiet, sharp tone. 'So let's escape then, shall we? Tonight? What shall we do, then? Steal a horse?'

His gaze was too level, too defiant. He did not mean it.

'We'd have to change horses quickly.' Makepeace could not help spotting the flaws. 'You remember how quickly the horse tired last time, with two riders? Last time they caught up with us before we reached the river.'

'Then we head towards Wincaster—'

'Wincaster? The town where the other regiment is garrisoned? They'd take our horse for their cavalry!'

'See?' snapped James, frustrated and triumphant. 'You're *never* happy!'

Makepeace took a moment to steady her temper, and met his eye.

'There's a market fair in Palewich the day after tomorrow,' she said evenly. 'I can persuade Mistress Gotely to send me there to buy piglets and spices. That puts money in my pocket, and they will not expect me back for hours.

'I have kept a wax Fellmotte seal—we can heat it and put it on a fake letter. You can slip away, and if anyone challenges you, you can show the letter and pretend you're taking it to the regiment.

'We meet, and buy a horse that the family will not recognize. We change clothes, and take the old lane past Wellman gibbet. I have enough provisions to last us three days without needing to beg or buy food—we can sleep in the Wether caves the first night, and then in any barn we can find after that.'

It was not a perfect plan, but it was better than his, and suited to the chaos of the moment. James's gaze faltered, as she knew it would.

'Let's talk about it again another time,' he said, then put an arm around Makepeace's shoulders and gave her a little squeeze. 'You need to trust me!'

He was the only creature on two legs that Makepeace did trust. But as she stood there, she could feel that trust bleeding out of her. She wriggled out from under his arm, and sprinted away down the tunnel, the damp walls hurling broken echoes of her steps.

CHAPTER 14

The day of farewells was moodily sunny, and smelt of sun-simmered heather and the rosemary in the kitchen garden. In the bustling stables and courtyard, the dogs picked up on the mood, barking, whining and trotting nervously behind one person, then another.

Makepeace was kept busy preparing provisions in the kitchen, groggy from a poor night's sleep. She had never had a serious argument with James before, and it had left her feeling sick and unmoored. The memory of her last quarrel with Mother gnawed at her mind, and she was haunted by a superstitious dread that if she did not make peace with James, something terrible would happen.

Even when she came up to the courtyard, there was no chance to speak with her brother, for he was busy helping Symond Fellmotte prepare for his departure.

Symond was muffled in a good coat of oiled elk-hide, his boots and ruff gleaming, his gold-white ringlets aflutter on the breeze. The restlessness of his gloved hands and slush-coloured eyes were the only signs that he was not perfectly at ease. Not for the first time, Makepeace was struck by the contrast between Symond's ice-blond self-control and James's easy vagabond grin. And yet, as Makepeace watched them murmur earnestly together, she sensed their closeness. This was a part of James's life in which she had no share, a world of male daring and camaraderie.

The broad-shouldered Sir Anthony was first to mount up. His horse did not like him, for they seldom liked the Elders and

Betters. But like every animal on the estate, it was cowed into quivering, absolute obedience. The next horse was taken by his son Robert, a tall, dark-browed young man who seemed to spend his life glancing at his father for approval.

Before Symond could saddle up, Lord Fellmotte came out into the courtyard and ceremonially embraced his son. It was a clasp without warmth, like that between buckle and strap. Makepeace wondered what it could possibly be like, to be hugged by your father's ghost-infested shell.

Symond did not even flinch. If he was upset or nervous, none of it showed in his face.

That night, Makepeace slumbered uneasily in her little bed under the kitchen table, lulled by the breathing and dream-growls of the dogs who lay by the hearth.

A little before dawn, a clatter from the corridor outside jolted her fully awake, and she scrambled out of bed. Within a minute she was edging towards the doorway, a carving knife held defensively in one hand and a lighted taper in the other.

A dark figure appeared in the doorway, one hand raised reassuringly.

'Makepeace, it's me!' it whispered.

'James!' she hissed. 'You scared me out of my wits! What are you doing here?'

'I needed to talk to you.' James's eyes were wide and intent. 'I'm sorry about what I said before. I'm sorry I didn't listen to your escape plan . . .'

'I'm sorry too,' Makepeace whispered quickly, wanting to cut off any excuses. 'I know you can't run from the militia. I shouldn't have asked. You'd be a deserter—'

'Never mind that!' James glanced over his shoulder briefly. 'Do you still have that wax seal? The Fellmotte seal, the one you were talking about?'

Makepeace nodded, shaken by this change of direction.

'Here!' He hurried forward and thrust a bundle of folded paper into her hands. 'Can you put the seal on the outside of this?'

'What is it?' Makepeace asked, surprised. It crackled drily in her grip.

'It doesn't matter—once it's sealed, it'll look like a dispatch. I can pretend to be a messenger—just the way you said.'

'Do you mean . . . we're going ahead with the plan?' Makepeace could not quite believe it.

'Are you still willing? Can you get to Palewich fair this afternoon?' James's face was alive with something; possibly anger.

'Yes.'

'Then be at the old stocks at two o'clock. There's . . . a lot happening. But if I can get away—'

'I'll be there,' she said quickly. Something had happened, she realized, something that had turned James's volatile temperament about-face. If she could up sails swiftly enough, perhaps she could catch this sudden gust.

James reached out quickly and squeezed her hands.

'Put the seal on the papers and hide them somewhere. Don't let anybody else see them!'

'I'll give them to you tomorrow,' Makepeace whispered.

'I need to go—the others will be waking soon.' James gave Makepeace a brief hug, and then hesitated for a moment, staring into her eyes. 'Makepeace . . . whatever happens, I *will* come for you. I *promise*.' He squeezed her shoulders, then hastened away into the darkness.

There was no time to lose. Dawn was coming, and Makepeace would not have the kitchen to herself for long. She slipped to the buttery, removed a loose brick and retrieved the wax seal. It was intact, just slightly bleached and crumbly at the edges.

Makepeace would have liked to glance through the papers, to find out which documents James had snatched up in his haste, but it was nearly dawn. Every time she heard the floorboards creak, she imagined that it was Mistress Gotely hobbling her way to the kitchen.

She heated a knife against the embers, then used the blade to melt the flat base of the seal. Very carefully, she pressed the seal into place, so that it held the little bundle closed.

Then, hearing the distant *tap, tap, tap* of Mistress Gotely's walking stick, Makepeace hurried to one of the great salting troughs, in which meat was left to dry. Wrapping the bundle in a cloth, Makepeace buried it in the brownish grains of salt, flush with the stone edge of the trough.

Makepeace's heart was kicking against her ribs in an agony of hope.

The next day, the house felt bereft, uncertain.

As the other servants gossiped, wondered and worried, Makepeace kept herself busy and her face placid. All the while she was thinking to herself: *This may be the last time I clean this tankard. Perhaps this is the last time I bring Mistress Gotely her tea.* She had not expected these thoughts to give her such a pang. Habits, places and faces grew into you over time, like tree roots burrowing into stonework.

Makepeace hoped to talk to James again, but fate was against her. Old Crowe the steward had been taken ill overnight, so

James had to run extra errands. At last, she managed to intercept him in the courtyard, and thrust a cloth-covered package into his hands. It contained bread, cheese, a thin sliver of rye cake and the concealed papers. James took the package from her, with a look full of meaning.

As Makepeace had predicted, it was not hard to persuade Mistress Gotely to send her to the fair with money to buy pigs, spices and other household wares.

Trust was like mould. It accumulated over time in unattended places. Trusting her was convenient; distrusting her would have been inconvenient and tiresome. Over the years, Makepeace had become encrusted with other people's inattentive trust.

Nobody seemed to pay attention to Makepeace as she walked across the courtyard, carrying two large, well-padded baskets. And then, as she strolled out through the gate, Young Crowe fell into step with her.

'I hear you're heading to the fair?' His manner was deliberately offhand. 'Always best to have a companion on these country lanes.'

Makepeace's blood chilled.

It was not the first time Young Crowe had shown a protective streak. Ever since she was thirteen, and thus old enough for a certain kind of man to consider her fair game, she had been aware that he was acting as an unlikely guardian. To her shame and discomfort, Makepeace has been glad of the interventions. She knew, however, that this was not due to chivalry or fondness. He was just protecting valuable Fellmotte property. Apparently this was more important than looking after his sick father.

'Thank you,' she said, and managed to sound shy rather than dismayed.

They walked to Palewich fair. With Young Crowe dogging her steps, Makepeace had no choice but to wander the stalls, buying the goods on the old cook's list. All the while she watched the sundial on the church clock tower.

Bear never liked throngs, or market noises and smells. Makepeace could feel his unhappiness as pains in her own body and hot, muddled flashes of memory. She recalled being ringed around by mocking, furless, shouting faces, and feeling the sting of maliciously flung stones.

Nobody will do that to you any more, she told Bear, her own anger rising protectively. *Never, never again. I promise.*

As it neared two o'clock, she took a chance, and lost Young Crowe in the crowds. She made her way to the old stocks, and waited, hiding behind an old yew tree.

Two o'clock became quarter past, became half past two.

James did not come.

Perhaps some accident had angered him, and made him ready to run, and now some other incident had put him back in good temper again. He had done well at something, or been praised by one of the militia officers. He had found himself with comrades he liked.

He was not coming. Makepeace felt something in her chest wrench, and wondered if it was her heart breaking. She waited to see how that would feel. Perhaps hearts broke like eggs, and spilt, and stopped working. But all she felt was numb. *Perhaps my heart already broke and never grew back.*

At a quarter to three, Young Crowe found her again. She made excuses, and ate humble pie until the taste of it made her feel sick. He walked her home, rather sullenly.

Her heart sank as Grizehayes came into view. *Here you are*

again after all, the grey walls seemed to say. *Here you are, forever.*

She re-entered the kitchen to find Long Alys eagerly spilling the latest gossip to Mistress Gotely.

'Have you heard? James Winnersh has run away! He left a note, found this morning! He's run off to join the regiment! Well, we should not be surprised. Everyone knows how disappointed he was when they wouldn't let him go!'

Makepeace fought to keep her face mask-like. James had run away after all, but not with her.

'Did he tell you what he was planning?' Alys asked her, keen-eyed and ruthless. 'You were always his little friend, weren't you? I thought he told you everything.'

'No,' said Makepeace, swallowing down her hurt. 'He didn't.'

He had taken her plan, her wax seal and her help, and then he had ridden out into a new, wide world, leaving her behind.

CHAPTER 15

James was at the heart of all the gossip for the next few days. White Crowe was sent after him, and most of the household fancied that he would be brought back soon enough.

On the fourth day, however, it became clear that something was badly amiss. Young Crowe and other servants could be seen running this way and that, searching the house and carrying letters. Then, while Makepeace and Mistress Gotely were preparing dinner, the kitchen door was flung open.

Makepeace looked up in time to see Young Crowe march into the kitchen, with none of his usual smug nonchalance. To her bewilderment he strode straight up to her and grabbed hold of her arm with startling force.

'What in the world—' began Mistress Gotely.

'Lord Fellmotte wants to see her,' he snapped, 'right now.'

As she was dragged out of the kitchen, Makepeace tried to gather her ragged thoughts and keep her balance. Somehow she had been caught out. Lord Fellmotte suspected something, and she did not even know what.

Young Crowe would explain nothing as he dragged Makepeace up the main stairs and into the study that was used by Lord Fellmotte.

Lord Fellmotte sat waiting for her, and never had his stillness looked less serene. As she walked in, he turned his head to watch her approach. Not for the first time, Makepeace wondered which of the ghosts within him had moved his head, and how they decided such things. Did they vote? Had they all taken on different tasks? Or had they worked together for so many lifetimes that they were used to acting as one?

Lord Fellmotte was not a man. He was an ancient committee. A parliament of deathly rooks in a dying tree.

'I found her,' declared Young Crowe, for all the world as if Makepeace had been hiding.

'You ungrateful little wretch,' said Lord Fellmotte in a voice as slow and cold as frost. 'Where is it?'

Where was what? Surely he could not mean the wax seal? She had stolen it months before.

'I'm sorry, my lord.' She kept her eyes lowered. 'I don't know what . . .' From under her lashes she saw him stand up and draw closer. Her skin crawled at the proximity.

'No lies!' rapped Lord Fellmotte, so loudly and suddenly that Makepeace jumped. 'James Winnersh recruited your help. You will tell us all about it. Now.'

'James?'

'You have always been his favourite accomplice, his obedient dog. Who else would he turn to if he was planning something desperate?'

'I didn't know he was planning to run away!' Makepeace said quickly, and then remembered too late that Elders knew when you were lying. She *had* known that he was planning to run, just not the way he would do so.

'We have been kind to you here, girl,' snapped Lord Fellmotte. 'We do not need to remain so. Tell us the truth. Tell us about the sleeping draught you made at his request.'

'What?' The unexpected question took the wind out of Makepeace's sails. 'No! I made no such thing!'

'Of course you did,' Lord Fellmotte said coldly. 'Nobody else in the house apart from Mistress Gotely could have done so. In fact, you are lucky that this was not a matter of murder. The steward is an old man, and that draught laid him perilously low. It might easily have stopped his heart!'

'The *steward?* Old Master Crowe?' Makepeace was now completely bewildered.

'James brought my father a cup of ale the night before the regiment left,' said Young Crowe coolly. 'He was insensible within an hour. He could still barely stand next morning, and is weak even now—'

'We know why he was drugged,' Lord Fellmotte continued relentlessly. 'We know that James stole his keys, so that he could raid the muniments room, then put the keys back afterwards. Where is it, girl! Did James take it with him? *Where is our charter?*'

Makepeace stared at them open-mouthed. She only knew of one charter, the mysterious document from King Charles himself, giving permission for the Fellmotte family traditions.

'I know nothing of this!' she exclaimed. 'Why would James steal a charter? I never made him a sleeping draught—and if I had, I would make it well enough not to risk drugging some poor soul into the hereafter!'

There was a long silence, and Makepeace was aware that Lord Fellmotte was walking around her, studying her closely.

'You may be telling the truth about the sleeping draught,' he said very softly, 'but you are hiding *something.*'

Makepeace swallowed. The bundle of papers James had asked her to disguise and hide had been large—possibly large enough to hide a charter inside. Makepeace tugged at her memory of their last conversation as if it were a piece of knitting, finding the loose places, the dropped loops of not-quite-rightness. At the time she had thought that James seemed angry and indecisive. Now she could see that his manner had been odd and evasive.

Why, James? And why did you leave me here to take the blame?

'Well?' asked Lord Fellmotte.

If Makepeace wanted to buy some mercy from the Fellmottes, now was the time to tell them everything she knew. She took a deep breath.

'I am sorry, my lord—I know nothing,' she said.

Lord Fellmotte drew himself up angrily, but Makepeace never found out what her sentence would have been. At that exact moment, there came a respectful but rapid tap at the door.

His lordship's expressions were as ever hard to read, but Makepeace thought she saw a flicker of annoyance.

'Enter!'

Old Crowe came in, stooped lower than usual, evidently aware that he was intruding.

'Forgive me, my lord—you said that if my brother returned you were to be notified immediately . . .'

Lord Fellmotte frowned, and was silent for a few seconds. Makepeace imagined the ghosts hissing and conferring within the shadows of his skull.

'Send him in,' he said curtly.

There was a pause, and White Crowe entered, still wearing his riding boots, his white hair starred with rain. His hat was in his hand, but he looked as though he wished he had more hats to take off. His face was sweaty and haggard, as if he had travelled far and slept little, and his eyes were very, very frightened.

'My lord . . .' he said, and then trailed off, his head bowed.

'Have you found the Winnersh boy?'

'I traced him, my lord. He really had caught up with our regiment and joined it.'

'Then I assume you bring a message from Sir Anthony?' Lord Fellmotte asked briskly. 'Does he send word of the regiment?'

'My lord . . . I . . . I do bring news of the regiment.' White Crowe swallowed. 'Our men joined with the other troops and headed for Hangerdon Bridge, as planned . . . but we encountered the enemy before we could take it, my lord. There was a battle.'

Makepeace's heart dropped away. She thought of proud, reckless James charging towards bristling lines of pikes, or dodging musketfire.

'Go on.' Lord Fellmotte stared at White Crowe stonily.

'It was . . . a terrible battle, my lord, full of confusion and carnage. The fields were still piled high with . . .' He trailed off again. 'I am sorry, my lord. Your noble cousin Sir Anthony . . . is now with God's mercy.'

'Dead?' The muscles tightened in Lord Fellmotte's jaw. 'How did he die? Were things done *properly*, Crowe? Was Sir Robert on hand and ready?'

White Crowe was shaking his head. 'Sir Robert was lost as well. Besides, there was no chance, no time for anything to be done. There was an unexpected . . . reversal.'

For a moment, emotions flickered across Lord Fellmotte's features, like firelight across an old, stone wall. There was shock, anger and indignation. There was also something like grief, but it was not the sorrow of a living man. It was the grief of the cliff that remains after a landslide.

'And my son?'

White Crowe opened his mouth, and his voice caught

in his throat. He darted a nervous glance at Makepeace, evidently reluctant to speak before her.

'Out with it!' shouted Lord Fellmotte. 'Does Symond live?'

'We have every reason to believe so, my lord.' White Crowe closed his eyes and exhaled for a brief moment, as if steadying himself. 'My lord . . . nobody knows where he is. This letter was found bearing his seal. It is addressed to you.'

Makepeace dug her fingernails into her hands. *What about James?* she wanted to scream. *Is* he *alive?*

Lord Fellmotte took the letter, broke the seal, and read. Little convulsions trembled through his features. His hand began to shake.

'Tell me,' he said, his voice low, 'of the battle. What did my son do? Tell me the truth!'

'Forgive me!' White Crowe stared at his feet for a few seconds, then raised his gaze. 'Our regiment started with the rest of the foot, in a line of companies along the ridge of Hangerdon Hill, each with its own commander. And after the first charge our men were placed a good way forward—too far for shouting—so all eyes were on Sir Anthony. He would point his horse in the direction they were to advance.

'But while they were still waiting for orders, Sir Anthony was seen slumping, and sliding off his horse. Master Symond, who was right next to him and supporting him, called out that a musketball had taken Sir Anthony under the ribs. But as he took your cousin's weight, the horses seemed to jostle each other, and Sir Anthony's horse came forward a little on to high ground. And our men, who were already a good distance forward, took it for a signal. They charged—not with the rest of the army, but away at an angle—towards a heavy mass of the enemy.

'Master Symond handed Sir Anthony down to his followers, and shouted that he was taking control of the regiment. He said that he would ride down and get the men to pull back—and ordered Sir Robert to come with him . . .' White Crowe hesitated again. 'But he did not pull them back, my lord. When he reached the front, he led them right into the teeth of the enemy.'

What happened to James?

'Go on.' Lord Fellmotte's teeth were clenched now, his face blotched, one hand gripping the other.

'It was only common soldiers that said so,' White Crowe continued unwillingly, 'but they claimed that Master Symond was last seen pulling his colours from his hat, and riding away cross country.'

'Was Sir Anthony truly struck by a musketball?' asked Lord Fellmotte, his voice husky and unrecognizable.

'No, my lord,' said White Crowe very quietly. 'He was run through with a long blade.'

Makepeace's jaw dropped as she understood. She had been so busy worrying about James, she had failed to see where the explanation was heading. *But . . . that's impossible! Symond has always worked so hard to be the golden boy, the family's darling! Why would he throw it all away now?*

'My son . . .' Lord Fellmotte swallowed with difficulty. 'My son has betrayed us—betrayed *everything*. He has the charter! He dares to threaten us with . . .' He stopped, and gave a slow, shuddering sigh. One corner of his mouth was drooping, and his eyes were glassy.

'His lordship is taken ill!' Makepeace could no longer hold her silence. 'Call the physician!' Next moment she remembered that his physician and the local barber-surgeon had left with the regiment. 'Call *somebody*! Fetch a cup of good brandy!'

As White Crowe ran to sound the alarm, Makepeace hurried to the side of Lord Fellmotte, to stop him falling from his chair.

'My son,' said Lord Fellmotte, very softly. Just for a moment, the expression of his eyes reminded Makepeace of Sir Thomas before his Inheritance. His tone was one of numb surprise and deep sadness, as if Symond had just run him through.

PART THREE: MAUD

CHAPTER 16

Ten minutes later, a small murder of Crowes were gathered around Lord Fellmotte. White Crowe, Young Crowe and Old Crowe the steward all stared at the lolling form of their master, as if the moon had fallen and broken at their feet. A goblet of brandy had been brought from the kitchen, and Makepeace held it to the invalid's lips.

'My lord—my lord, can you hear me?' Old Crowe peered into his master's face. 'Oh, this is bad. This is most perilous bad.'

Lord Fellmotte's face was the colour of old china. His eyes were still alive, and through them Makepeace could see the ghosts glittering and seething with black fury, like beetles scrambling about on a burning log. However, somewhere within the complicated machinery of his body, some cog had moved awry, and now he could scarcely move.

Makepeace wondered if there was anything left of the original Sir Thomas within his mortal shell. Perhaps, perhaps not. But the heart that beat was his, and perhaps hearing of his son's betrayal had broken it. Maybe there had been just enough of him left to destroy the whole machine.

'We must move his lordship to his bedroom,' declared Old Crowe. 'Discreetly—the other servants must not know that he is laid this low. The family would not want to show such weakness at this time.'

Makepeace helped, and nobody stopped her. Once his lordship was safely installed in his chamber, the Crowes held a quick, whispered conference, their beaky noses almost touching.

'We need a physician,' Old Crowe muttered. His little black eyes moved to and fro, as if he were telling abacus beads with his mind. 'We should send a man to ride round Palewich, Carnstable, Treadstick and Gratford, and find out whether there is any doctor that did not leave with the regiment.' He turned to White Crowe, and asked the question that had been burning in Makepeace's head. 'What happened to James?'

'James?' White Crowe looked slightly taken aback.

'Yes, James! Did James survive?'

'I did not see him myself . . . but yes, I hear he was seen alive after the battle.'

James was alive. Relief sent warm prickles over the skin of Makepeace's face and neck.

'Then where is he?' asked the old man. 'Did he flee with Symond?'

'No.' White Crowe shook his head. 'As I hear it, he stayed with the men and fought bravely, even when they were hardest pressed. I assume that he is still with the army, but I did not tarry making a list of the survivors. There was a great deal of confusion after the battle, and I thought that I should bring the news as soon as possible.'

'You made no effort to trace him?' Old Crowe's face turned a dusky plum colour. 'You of all people should know better! If his lordship does *not* mend, then the masters will soon need a new vessel! Symond is fled, Robert is lost, and the rest are scattered across the country. We need James!'

Makepeace held her breath. Her mind had been focused upon her half-brother's fate and her uncle's collapse. Suddenly she was presented starkly with her own danger. Very soon the Crowes would remember that they did *not* need James.

'We will find him if he can be found,' said Old Crowe. 'And we must contact the rest of the family, or as many as we can reach. This is a matter for them to decide.'

He gave Makepeace a glance of suspicion and hostility.

'As for that girl . . . she may be a part of this nest of vipers. In any case, we cannot have her running loose, talking to the other servants or trying to send word to James. Lock her up.'

Thus it was that Makepeace found herself locked in the Bird Chamber once again. Only when she heard the key turn after her, and knew herself alone, did Makepeace let herself slump against the wall.

The smell of the room woke Bear. He recognized the barred window, the cold and the peeling walls. His memories were foggy, but he knew it was a place of pain.

Oh, Bear, Bear . . . Makepeace had no comfort to give him.

What did Symond tell you, James? How did he persuade you to help him steal that charter? What did he say he would do once he had it? Did he promise you power, or fame, or freedom?

Did you know that he was planning to kill Sir Anthony, and betray the whole regiment? No. Of course not. You wanted to be a hero. You wanted to serve the King. You wanted to be part of a brotherhood of arms. You only knew half the plan, didn't you?

'Oh James, you *mooncalf!*' she muttered aloud. 'Why did you make a plan with him instead of me? You trusted the wrong kin!'

After four days of gruel and solitude, Young Crowe came to summon Makepeace from the Bird Chamber.

'Make yourself presentable,' he said sullenly. 'The Elders wish to speak with you—in the Map Room.'

Heart pounding, she followed him down the stairs.

Hush, Bear, she thought, wishing that she could hush her own mind. Bear could not understand what was happening, but she suspected that he could sense her own subdued panic. She could feel him shifting uncertainly. *Hush, Bear.*

Buried in the heart of Grizehayes, the Map Room was windowless. Its light flickered from candles in little alcoves, their plasterwork louring with soot. The walls were divided into panels, on each of which was painted a different battle map. Most were great Christian triumphs—the Siege of Malta, the Siege of Vienna, and battles against the Saracens during the Crusades. Blue seas writhed around tiny identical ships. Generals loomed giant-like next to the minute ranked tents of their troops.

Seeing the shadowy outlines of three Elders waiting there silently, Makepeace wondered whether any of the ghosts within them had been at those battles. Perhaps they remembered seeing those painted sails billow, and those stitched cannons belch smoke.

As she entered with Young Crowe, two of the three seated figures looked up at her.

The first was Sir Marmaduke. Again Makepeace was daunted by his sheer size, and shivered as she remembered fleeing from him across the dark moors. The sight of him gave her a twinge of physical panic, like a mouse freezing at the sound of an owl's call.

The second was Lady April, with her tin-white, knife-edge cheekbones and small, claw-like hands. She sat at the edge of her chair, watching Makepeace with unnerving, unblinking attention.

Makepeace's gaze moved to the third figure, and the world seemed to twist out of shape. It was far younger than its companions, and yet there it was, in a green velvet coat and embroidered shoes. Every inch of that figure was as familiar to her as the lines of her own hands, but transformed by unutterable strangeness, like a thing from a nightmare.

He raised his head at last to look at her, and his mouth moved in a smile. She knew every detail of him so well—the double creases in his cheeks, the tiny nicks and scars from tumbles and fights, and his honest, scrapper's hands.

'James,' she whispered, feeling her mind darken with despair.

The smile was not his, and behind his eyes dead things looked back.

CHAPTER 17

'No,' said Makepeace, very quietly. Her voice came out so faint and flat that she could hardly hear it. *No, not James. I can bear anything but this.* She was aware of the Elders talking nearby, but their words fell around her like so much hail. 'James,' she said again. Her mind seemed to have broken its axle.

'God's feathers, is she an actual imbecile?' snapped Sir Marmaduke.

'No, but she doted on her half-brother.' Elder James gave Makepeace a wraith-eyed smile that was almost tender. 'She was his faithful tool. They have been playing a game of sorts, imagining themselves captives like the princes in the Tower, and hatching little escape plans together. The spark and genius of the plans was always his. She was devoted, but too timid really for such a conspiracy.'

Makepeace clenched her teeth, and fought for self-control. If she lost her rein on her emotions now, all hell and Bear might break loose.

'And you are sure she knew nothing about the theft of the charter?' asked Lady April, in her glassy, chiselled voice.

'Oh, she hid it for James overnight, but she had no idea what it was.' Elder James's mouth puckered briefly with sour amusement. 'She was James's cat's paw, just as James was Symond's instrument. Neither of them know where Symond has gone. Neither knew that he planned to flee.'

Even as she reeled with shock and anguish, Makepeace's

mind was struggling to take the truth on board. James was possessed. Her brother was now an enemy.

With a chill, she remembered Lord Fellmotte speaking of Sir Thomas's memories as 'a jumble, like an ill-sorted library'. The ghosts in James would have access to his memories. Everything James had known was now known to the Elders. Every secret conversation, every plan, every shared secret . . . the very thought made Makepeace feel sick and cold.

James must have been captured and dragged back to Grizehayes, so that Lord Fellmotte's ghosts could be poured into him. And yet, even as this occurred to Makepeace, she felt a pang of doubt. The voice with which the new Elder spoke did not belong to James, but it did not sound much like Lord Fellmotte either.

'Has it really come to this?' Sir Marmaduke demanded, looking Makepeace over with undisguised disdain. 'Look at her! How can we think of using this pockmarked little slattern?'

'We do not have the luxury of time!' retorted the James-Elder. 'Lord Fellmotte is sinking fast.'

'Well, perhaps we must use her as a temporary bolthole, until we have something better?' suggested Sir Marmaduke.

Lady April gave a startling hiss of disapproval.

'No! You know the risks we take every time we move abode! If we keep pouring ourselves from vessel to vessel like so much wine, some of us will be spilt. Have we not lost enough kin of late?'

'Indeed!' snapped the James-Elder. 'Remember, during *our* last Inheritance, we lost two members of our coterie! After Symond ran us through, we lay bleeding for five minutes before that boy ran back to aid us. We were lucky that all seven of us were not lost.'

So that was it. The ghosts within James had not come from Thomas Fellmotte after all. They came from Sir Anthony, whom Symond had murdered on the battlefield. James must have run back from the fracas to help his dying relative, just in time to be possessed by Sir Anthony's ghosts.

Numbly Makepeace realized that this had left her in terrible danger. James now had no room for the ghosts inside Sir Thomas. There were no other gifted within reach. At long last, the Fellmottes' gaze had fallen upon Makepeace.

James and his stupid heroism . . . Makepeace closed her eyes, and tried to breathe. She could feel a heat building in her, a wordless, helpless rage and grief. *Hush Bear, hush.*

'Is this girl even schooled?' Sir Marmaduke was asking.

'She can read and write,' Young Crowe answered quickly, 'and has a good seat in a saddle, but little more than that. She is hard-working, but not a creature of parts . . . It seemed so unlikely that your worships would ever consider her a suitable home.'

'Worse and worse,' growled Sir Marmaduke. 'You know how much easier things are when they are suitably trained! Wearing some unschooled clod, you might as well be trying to dance a gavotte in riding boots. Vessels like that can take *months* to break in, and we do not have months! There is a war on, and we need Lord Fellmotte's coterie at full strength!'

'We have debated this to death!' snapped Lady April. 'There *are* other spares, but they are needed—tailored—reared for specific destinies. More to the point, they are all elsewhere, most of them fighting in the King's name! Lord Fellmotte is fading. We need to act *now*.'

'A woman cannot inherit Lord Fellmotte's title or estate,' pointed out Sir Marmaduke, but he was starting to sound pensive rather than argumentative. 'At the moment Symond is the heir in the eyes of the law.'

'Leave that to us,' said Lady April. 'We shall be sending dispatches to Oxford very soon. We shall have the King declare Symond a traitor.'

The casual tone took Makepeace's breath away, and she could not help being a little impressed. *We shall have the gardener cut back that hedge. We shall have my tailor take in the sleeves. We shall have the King declare Symond a traitor.*

'As for the other difficulties,' continued Lady April, 'the Crowes have them in hand. When Symond is disinherited, the next in line is yourself, Sir Marmaduke. If you were to let the title pass to your second son, Mark, who does not stand to inherit your own estates, then we might marry him to this girl once he returns from Scotland. Officially, your son would take the title of Lord Fellmotte and control of the estates . . . and unofficially he would accept the guidance of his wife.'

The Elders settled into silence, their features flexing and rippling. Three different conferences were taking place. Three ancient, deathly committees trying to reach a decision.

'A cook is hardly a suitable match for our son,' demurred Sir Marmaduke.

'She can be *made* suitable,' said Lady April. 'Crowe—what do you have for us?'

Young Crowe cleared his throat, and opened a large, leather-bound book.

'My father has found records of one Maud Fellmotte, daughter of Sir Godfrey Fellmotte and Elizabeth Vancy. They were from a minor branch of the family, all now dead, may God reward them. Little Maud lived just long enough to be baptized, then went to her eternal reward. If she had lived, she would be fifteen years old . . . the same age as Makepeace.

'Let us suppose that Maud never died. She lived on, and became a ward of the family in one of their Shropshire properties. And now she is brought back to Grizehayes, so that she can become engaged.'

So this was the way Makepeace would be transformed into a 'suitable match'. She would be given a new name, a new history, new parentage and a new future. Makepeace the under-cook would not just die, she would vanish like a soap bubble and leave no trace.

'But . . . people must remember the real Maud!' Makepeace blurted out, amid rising panic. 'There must be a slab with her name in the family crypt!'

'Her close kin are all dead and the household scattered,' Young Crowe rejoined reassuringly, directing his words to the Elders, not Makepeace. 'And names can be chipped away.'

Makepeace imagined the Crowes taking a chisel to a little memorial slab. Then she imagined them chipping away her own name, her face, her very self.

'Maud is a little dead girl in the ground.' Makepeace knew she had to hide her feelings, but this was a step too far. 'I cannot steal her name.'

'It is not stolen, but given!' Young Crowe gave her a rictus smile of annoyance. 'Think of it as a hand-me-down.'

'But if I take on a new name, everyone will wonder at it!' exclaimed Makepeace in desperation. 'I am known here! In the house, on the estate, in the villages. If you dress me as a lady and call me Maud, nobody will be fooled! They all know who I am!'

'*Nobody cares*,' Elder James interrupted coldly. 'You are of no consequence. You have nothing that we have not given you. And nobody in this whole county will raise their voice against us. If our dogs chased you across the moors until you dropped, nobody would help you. And nobody would breathe a word about it afterwards.

'You are who we say you are. And if we say you are heir to a destiny greater than you ever deserved, and wealth beyond your merits, then that is what you will be.'

Hush, Bear. Hush, Bear.

Makepeace's new prison was more luxurious than the last. It was a green silk chamber with lacquered furniture and a bed with embroidered hangings. It had been redecorated when it was thought that Symond might marry an heiress. In the clothes chest was fine, clean linen, a skirt of silvery silk, a summer blue velvet bodice with pearls along the neckline, and a white cap trimmed with lace so fine a spider might have spun it.

There was even a bowl with two hard, yellow oranges in it. Makepeace had occasionally cooked with oranges, and marvelled at the exotic, stinging smell of the peel when it was cut, but she had never eaten such rare fruit. Now the sight of them made her feel sick.

For a while, all she could think about was James. Brave, foolhardy James, always so in love with his own plans, and unable to see the flaws in them. Why hadn't he told her about his scheme with Symond? Perhaps he had been proud to have outgrown her, and to be hatching schemes with a fellow man instead of his younger sister. And now there was no more James, only a shell of ghosts like their uncle.

Or was he quite gone? Makepeace found herself desperately

scrabbling for hope. Two ghosts from Sir Anthony's coterie had been lost during the Inheritance, so that must mean that James had five spectral intruders instead of seven. If that created a little more room, perhaps his personality had not been crushed to nothing just yet. He was young, angry and stubborn. Perhaps he was still fighting. Perhaps he could be saved, somehow.

However, right now she also needed to think about saving herself. Symond had fled. Sir Robert was dead. The war had scattered all the other spares and heirs. Lord Fellmotte was sinking fast.

When he died, the Fellmottes would tear her open, and rip out Bear when they discovered him. Then seven ancient, arrogant ghosts would crowd into her, and she would feel her own mind stifle and die.

Perhaps Sir Marmaduke's son would refuse to inherit the estates and marry her. Surely it was possible? How could he want such a fate? Who would want to marry a rough-handed girl brimming with the ghosts of his grandfathers? How could he walk down the chapel aisle with her, and slide a ring on to her finger, under her watchful, dead gaze? How could he bear to take a monster like that to his chamber and father heirs on her?

But it would do no good, she realized. By the time Sir Marmaduke's son was told of the arrangement, she would long since have been taken over by the Fellmotte ghosts. Even if he protested it would be too late to save her.

Makepeace made a quick search of the room. As she expected, the windows of her chamber were too small for her to squeeze through. She might have been able to signal through them, but there was no friendly eye outside to see. Her door was bolted from the outside. The embroidered sewing box contained no scissors or even pins, nothing she could use as a weapon.

Makepeace pressed her fingertips hard against her skull and tried to think. The Elders knew everything James knew. But James had not known everything.

There were hiding places she had never told him about, discoveries she had never mentioned. He did not know about the ivory device she had stolen from Sir Thomas's precious collection of navigational paraphernalia, or the rag-rope she had quietly lengthened whenever an unwanted scrap fell into her hands. Most important of all, she had never told him about Bear.

I trust you, she had often told him. But was that true?

No, she realized, with a feeling like grief. All these years, even while she plotted with James, in her heart of hearts she had been waiting for him to betray her. When at last she had looked into his eyes and seen a host of dead enemies staring back, her mind had filled with a storm. But there had been an eye to that storm, a quiet core where a calm, relieved voice was saying: *Ah, there it is at last. No more waiting for the sword to fall.*

She had always loved James. But she had never truly trusted him. Somehow, this was the saddest realization of all.

A news-sheet on the dressing table caught her attention. As usual, reading it was a slow and painful process, but she was keen to see whether there was any news of Symond, and to learn the progress of the war.

The sheet had clearly been printed by someone staunchly loyal to the royal cause. Half the stories depicted the King's troops surviving through courage and divine intervention. The other half ranted about rebel troops committing terrible crimes, cutting down women and children, hacking off the heads of stone saints, and burning hayricks. There were plenty of tales of miracles. He described the bitterly cold night after the Battle of Edgehill, and the way that wounded men had seen their injuries glowing with a soft uncanny light, only to find them partially healed when morning came.

One story caught her attention.

There was a soldier coming out of Derbyshire who barely survived a battle where many were lost and was after sadly transformed in manner and countenance. He said that he was afflicted with a ghost of one of his dead comrades who let him neither sleep or rest but whispered in his head and caused him to move and speak strangely. In Oxford one chirurgeon called Benjamin Quick operated on the soldier by boring a small hole into his skull with a device of his own invention, and afterwards the patient was quite returned to himself and never more complained of ghosts.

Makepeace read the story and reread it. Once again, a tiny candle of hope was flickering into life. It was possible that the doctor had simply cured a man of fever or delusion, but what if the soldier really had been haunted? Could you drive out a ghost using some new trick of science and medicine? That possibility had never crossed her mind before.

If there was still some trace of James inside his body . . . perhaps this doctor could save him.

CHAPTER 18

On Sunday, when the time came for the service, Makepeace took her new place in the raised gallery with the family.

After the Amens, the servants were allowed to trail out of the chapel, but the Elders remained seated. Makepeace had no choice but to stay with them. At last the living footfalls faded, and a crypt-like silence settled.

The priest spoke again.

'In the late Battle at Hangerdon Hill, Almighty God in His infinite mercy took many of His servants from this world, and gathered them at His side where they shall stand in glory forever.'

And he spoke of the two long-dead Fellmottes that had been lost to the world when Symond's knife ended his uncle's life. Robyn Brookesmere Fellmotte, Knight Commander under Henry III, and victor at the battles of Crake and Barnsover. Jeremiah Fellmotte of Tithesbury, Privy Council member under four kings.

Now and then Makepeace thought she heard a faint, reptilian exhalation from the Elders behind her. Perhaps that dry hiss was all they had to offer instead of tears. They had lost comrades and relatives that they had known and counted upon for centuries.

Perhaps, also, this loss had cruelly reminded them of their own fragility. One quick stab and some mischance could rob them of eternity. They might find themselves smokily screaming like the commoner ghosts they despised, and melting into air.

The names of Sir Robert and Sir Anthony were only mentioned briefly. Their tragedy was secondary. They were bottles that had broken, spilling a vintage of great worth.

Makepeace knew that the Elders saw her the same way. She herself was meaningless. She was only a fleshly container, waiting to be given meaning.

After chapel, a dressmaker measured Makepeace, and a cobbler examined her feet. More new clothes would be needed for her, now that she was 'Maud'. She was not consulted on the colour or style, of course.

And then, in the early afternoon, Lady April came to inspect her.

'Open your mouth,' she said, and when Makepeace did so unwillingly, she peered closely at Makepeace's teeth. She insisted that Makepeace take down her hair, and then raked a fine-toothed comb through it, and stared at the slender prongs for signs of lice.

Then there were questions, all asked in the same cold dispassionate tone. Did Makepeace have fleas? Any itches or pains? Did she still have her maidenhead? Did she get any headaches? Backaches? Moments of dizziness? Did she ever drink strong spirits? Were there any types of food that made her sick?

After this, Makepeace was told that she was to have a bath.

Makepeace received the news with trepidation. She had never had a real bath before, and she had heard people say that they were dangerous. The water could seep in through the holes in your skin, bringing all manner of sickness with it. Like most people, she usually just rubbed herself clean with a rag, and even then didn't strip herself bare, but took off a few garments at a time so that she would not get cold. Nakedness would be a fine way to catch a chill.

In spite of her protests, the family's big wooden bath was

hauled out and placed in her new chamber in front of a blazing fire. Feet thundered on the steps as Makepeace's fellow servants carried buckets of hot water up from the kitchen.

'Can I have a screen around the bath, to keep away the draughts?' Makepeace felt her face redden. She was in no hurry to remove her clothes in front of Lady April. Lady April had a woman's body, but Makepeace knew that the hidden gallery of ghosts inside her would probably be male. If the Fellmottes preserved the ghosts of those they considered 'important', this was unlikely to include many women.

'How quickly you learn to be delicate!' It was hard to tell whether Lady April's tone was contemptuous or approving. Her smile was too thin to read.

But a sheet was duly hung up around the bath to make a little tent, holding in the steam and keeping out prying eyes. Once it was in place, Lady April left the room.

We are about to wade into a warm river, Bear. Do not be frightened.

Keeping her shift on, Makepeace carefully stepped into the water, which was already starting to cool, and sat on the edge of the bath. Bear was nervous, but calmed when the water did not bite. Makepeace tried not to think of her pores opening, to create thousands of tiny holes in her defences. However, there was something luxurious and groggily soothing about the warmth and steam. She gingerly splashed water on to herself, and watched her blisters pale and soften.

A faint rattle at the far side of the room told her that the door had opened again, and then the sheet-screen parted to show Beth-around-the-house, one of the maids. She was holding a brush and a washball of grated white soap mixed with dried petals. Bear caught its scents of ash, oil and lavender, and was confused by them. He was uncertain whether soap was dangerous or food.

'Beth!' It was Makepeace's first chance to talk to one of the other servant women unobserved since her 'promotion'. She lowered her voice to a whisper. 'Beth . . . I need your help!'

Beth flushed, but did not raise her gaze. She knelt by the side of the bath as if she had heard nothing, and she began dutifully making a lather.

'I'm a prisoner, Beth! It's a pretty cage, but it has a lock on the door, and someone guarding it day and night. I am in danger here, and I do not have much time. I need to get away from Grizehayes!'

But Beth would not look at her. It was too late to claim a friendship. Makepeace had always been careful not to care too much about the other servants, sensing the invisible divide waiting to gape between them. Now she could see that Beth must have regarded her the same way. Who could blame her? Why grow too fond of a piglet being fattened for the feast table?

Then, just for a moment, Beth did meet her eye. *Please*, said her frightened gaze. *Please don't.*

'They ordered you not to talk to me, didn't they?' whispered Makepeace. 'But they can't hear us now. And I won't tell them.'

Beth gave her another quick glance, and this time Makepeace could not mistake the look of fear and distrust. *Yes, you will*, said the look.

And Makepeace understood. Makepeace herself would not report Beth to the Fellmottes, but soon Makepeace would not be Makepeace. She would be a vessel, and her new occupants would rifle through her memories at their leisure and discover Beth's little disobedience.

'Give me the brush,' said Makepeace, her spirits sinking. 'I can scrub my own back.'

Beth's lip trembled, and she cast a desperate glance over her shoulder.

'No!' she whispered, face twisted with panic. 'Please don't send me away! I . . . They told me to wash you . . . to look for pimples or sores or scars . . . signs of sickness . . .'

So that was why the bath had been ordered. She was still being assessed for her desirability as a residence. Nonetheless, she could not fight the suspicion that she was also being laundered like linen, so that she was ready to be worn.

'Then tell them about every wart!' snapped Makepeace. 'Every scar, and corn, and blister. Why stop there? Tell them I'm still mad, and I fall down in fits. Tell them I'm pox-ridden and pregnant.'

They'll take me anyway, but I want them to feel sick when they do. If I can make them feel one grain as sick as I do, that is a victory.

Bear, Bear, forgive me, Bear. I promised you we would be free some day, but now we never will.

I wanted to protect you. That's why I kept telling you to hush and hold back, so nobody would know about you. I kept you quiet. I made you meek. I never meant to tame you, Bear, but I did.

Sorry, Bear.

As night fell, she saw a carriage pull into the courtyard, and halt. There was to-ing and fro-ing around it, and for a while she dared to hope that one of the other heirs or spares had returned, or that Symond had been found. But nobody got in, and nobody got out, and the carriage just waited there, the twilight plating its wood in dull silver.

Not an hour later, they came for her.

The little table was heavy enough to use as a weapon, but light enough for her to lift. When the door opened she was standing behind it, and swung her table at the first person to enter with all her might. She had hoped that it would be one of the Crowes, who were at least ordinary mortals.

But it was not. It was Sir Marmaduke, with many lifetimes' memories of feints and deflected blows. He reached out and tweaked the table from her grasp, fast as an adder's strike. She barely saw his motion as the wooden weight was ripped from her hands.

She fought them as they tied her wrists and ankles. She tried to kick out at them, and thump them with her head, even as they carried her downstairs. She fought them all the way to the chapel.

CHAPTER 19

The chapel had become a haunted place. Only half a dozen candles burned, lonely lights amid the darkness. They illuminated marble plaques, an alabaster knight, a wooden effigy of a noble at rest, flanked by stumpy wooden mourners. Makepeace could guess whose memorials they were. It seemed that the eternal dead were the only bright things, the only real things, glowing in the well of darkness.

But Makepeace was real. The bite of rope into her wrists was real. The bruising grip from Sir Marmaduke and Young Crowe was real.

'Mistress Gotely!' she shouted, her voice echoing blasphemously throughout the chapel. 'Beth! Alys! Help me!' They would not come to her aid, she knew that. She was alone. But the other servants might hear her, and it would mean something to be remembered. She wanted them to know that she had not gone willingly or quietly. If they remembered that, she would still be *something*, if only a scar on their memories, a pang of guilt they tried to ignore.

One candle stood on the altar, which was spread with a crimson cloth. Deep red, mourning red. The embroidered silver cross spilt over the edge of the altar like the cleft in a tongue.

Before the altar stood two chairs, just as they had on Twelfth Night. One was an invalid chair, in which reclined Lord Fellmotte. His head lolled to one side, and his eyes glistened in the candlelight, moving, moving, like insects trapped under glass.

The second was the throne-like chair in which she had seen

Sir Thomas convulse on the night of his Inheritance. Makepeace was forced into it, her bound wrists digging into her back. Young Crowe wound a rope around her middle and tied her to the chairback.

'Stop making an exhibition of yourself!' hissed Lady April, emerging from the shadows. 'You are in a house of God—show some respect!'

'Then let God hear me!' It was the only threat Makepeace could think of, the only power she could call on more dreadful than the Fellmottes. 'God is watching—He sees what you are doing! He will see you killing me! He will see your devilry—'

'How dare you!' retorted Lady April. For a moment it seemed that she would strike Makepeace, but then her raised hand lowered again. Of course she would not bruise a cheek that very soon would belong to Lord Fellmotte.

'Our traditions have the blessing of both Churches,' the old woman hissed, 'and six different popes. It is God that has blessed us with the ability to live on, gathering wisdom over centuries. And in our turn we have served Him well—many Fellmottes have joined the Church, and risen to become bishops, even archbishops! God is *on our side*. How dare you preach to us?'

'Then tell everyone!' snapped Makepeace. 'Tell the world how your ghosts steal the bodies of the living! Tell them you have God's permission, and see what they say!'

Lady April drew closer. She pushed stray strands of Makepeace's hair out of her face, and slipped a band of cloth around Makepeace's neck, just under the chin. Makepeace could feel it being tied to the chair behind her.

'I will tell you,' Lady April said icily, 'what is ungodly and unnatural. Disobedience. Ingratitude. Impudence.'

Makepeace knew that the old woman meant it. Lady April's ghosts believed there was a natural order to the world, bright and shining. Just as flames rose and water ran downhill, so everything found its ordained level. It was a great pyramid, with the lowly multitudes at the bottom, then the middling sort, then the nobility, and finally Almighty God as the shining pinnacle—each rank gazing at the levels above with submission and gratitude.

For Lady April, disobedience was more than rudeness, more than a crime. It defied God's natural order. It was water flowing uphill, mice eating cats, the moon weeping blood.

'You're the Devil's own pups,' snapped Makepeace. 'There's no goodness in obeying *you*!'

'Crowe,' Lady April said coldly, 'hold her head.'

Young Crowe grabbed Makepeace's head, and held it still while she tried to jerk free. Lady April seized her jaw and forced it wide open.

'Help!' was the last thing Makepeace was able to shout, before a broad wooden tube was forced into her mouth, holding it so far open that her jaw ached. It was a stupid thing to shout, a waste of her last word. No friends would rush to her aid.

A nervous voice creaked from the entrance to the chapel.

'My lord, my lady . . .' Old Crowe was standing in the doorway.

'Does this look like a good time?' snapped Lady April, still gripping the tube wedged in Makepeace's mouth.

'Forgive me—a campfire has been sighted, out on the moors. You gave orders that if there were any sightings . . .'

'We will look into it,' Sir Marmaduke murmured quickly to Lady April. He started towards the door, then hesitated, his face performing the shifting Elder frown. 'Do you still mean to travel tonight?' he continued under his breath. 'If enemy troops are close, the roads will be dangerous.'

'We are quite aware of that,' Lady April told him curtly, 'which is why *this* must be done quickly so that we can leave. We have urgent dispatches and money for the King—we must travel tonight if we are to meet with our messenger. We cannot afford to find ourselves trapped here.'

'Then give your signet ring to somebody you trust, and send them instead!' insisted Sir Marmaduke.

'If we trusted anybody, we might.' Lady April's lean mouth thinned and puckered for a moment. It seemed that her face muscles had long since forgotten how to smile. 'Go! We will handle this. Tell Cattmore to have the carriage ready—we will be down shortly.'

Sir Marmaduke strode from the chapel, followed by Old Crowe, and the door closed behind them.

'We need her mouth and eyes open,' said Lady April.

Young Crowe, still gripping either side of Makepeace's head, moved his thumbs to peel up her eyelids and force her eyes open. Her eyes watered, and the world became blurry.

She was being opened up, so that it was easier for the ghosts to get in. Makepeace writhed and screamed wordlessly, and tried to twist her hands free.

'It is far too late to complain now, Maud,' Lady April went on. 'You agreed to this. You agreed with every night that you slept under our roof, and with every meal at our expense. Your flesh and bone is made from our meat and drink—it is *ours*. It is too late to cry over the reckoning. This is your chance to show your gratitude.'

Makepeace could feel dampness flowing down her cheeks. Her

eyes were watering with the pain of being held open, and she felt stupidly angry that Lady April would think she was crying. The others' faces were smudges now, peach-tinted with the candlelight.

'My lords,' said Lady April, in a far more deferential tone, 'the path is made ready.' And Makepeace knew that she must be addressing the ghosts waiting inside Lord Fellmotte. 'The girl is troublesome—it might be best for your Infiltrator to come first, to subdue her, and make all ready for your coterie.'

Infiltrator? Makepeace had never heard the term before, but it sent a chill down her back.

There was a long pause. But the silence had a texture, a prickliness, like the air just before rain. There was a sibilance tickling at Makepeace's ears. Whispers—a faint, papery, scrabble of sound.

Then Makepeace saw a wisp of something flicker between Thomas Fellmotte's lips, like a serpent-tongue of smoke. His jaw fell open, and it crept out a little further, coiling hazily, then swelling, a soft, snaking plume of shadow. It did not thrash or flail or melt away. It began advancing with sinuous purpose, seething towards her.

Makepeace screamed, and twisted, and tried to push out the tube with her tongue, but in vain. The whisper was louder now. A single voice, but the words indistinguishable, only dusty splinters of sound. She could see it nosing this way and that like a blind thing, edging ever closer to her face. It was smoke, and not smoke. It strangled light.

And then, with one fluid motion, it seethed up over her face and poured into her mouth. Her vision darkened and twisted as it slid into her eyes.

The Infiltrator was inside her mind, and she screamed, and

screamed, and could not have stopped screaming even if she had wanted to. She could feel it, sliding around in her thoughts, moth-soft, probing, insistent. It forced its way into the secret recesses of herself, and it was wrong, wrong to feel it there, like a great worm twisting inside her head. She struck out at it with her mind, but it flexed against her, forcing her back, crushing her against the walls of her own skull to make room for itself.

But Makepeace's scream was not just one of terror. There was rage in it too. It became a roar, and she was not the only one roaring.

Suddenly she could smell Bear and taste Bear. Her blood was like hot metal. Her mind was on fire. Somewhere in her skull, she felt Bear strike out, a clumsy swipe with a terrible shadowy strength. The impact juddered her to the bone and sickened her, but she felt it tear into the Infiltrator, which jerked and flailed like a scalded snake.

There was a terrible creaking crack, and Makepeace realized that she was biting down through the wooden tube. Splinters pushed their way into her gums as the wood gave way. She strained at the bonds holding her wrists, and they broke. She grabbed at the straps around her chest and neck, and yanked at them until they gave.

Lady April jumped backwards with a speed that belied her age. Young Crowe did not, nor did he dodge Makepeace's great, swinging blow, which struck him in the temple and hurled him across the room. He hit the pew so hard that its oaken mass tipped backwards, knocking over the next like a domino.

Makepeace stood, spitting out broken wood and plumes of ripped ghost. Her surroundings came to her in pulses. Thought was a lost gull in a storm. She was Bear, and Bear was she.

A pulse of awareness. Lady April plucking a bodkin from her sleeve, with the swiftness born of centuries of practice, and holding it in front of her. She was shouting something at the top of her voice. Calling for help? Help from the living? Help from the dead?

Another pulse. A red stripe of pain across her chest. Lady April was dragonfly-fast. Lady April's bodkin was red. But pain and sickness were just notes in the storm-music that filled her head.

Young Crowe at her feet, winded and stunned, one arm twisted badly. He looked up at her, and she saw a madwoman reflected in his dull eyes. And then his gaze flicked to something behind Makepeace. Lady April picking up his sword. Lady April ready to lunge.

Then Lady April's cold, cold eyes looked deep into Makepeace's own, and saw Bear.

Makepeace saw the shock in those ancient eyes, saw the question. *Girl, what have you done?*

And in that moment Makepeace's hand-paw struck out with skull-denting force. The shock of the blow jolted every joint in her arm. A pulse of dark. A pulse of light. Lady April crumpled on the floor. Smaller now. An old woman sleeping.

Bleeding.

Makepeace stood and gasped for air, as her thoughts and vision throbbed in and out of clarity. Where was she? The chapel. Pools of light. Broken wood. Two bodies on the floor. Pain spilling over everything, or maybe coloured light from the window.

Think. Think!

She stooped, unwillingly, to touch Lady April's wrist. Every moment she feared that ghost-snakes would writhe from the old Elder and leap for her own mouth. But she had to know.

There was a pulse, a sullen, relentless tremor of life. Nearby, she could see that Young Crowe was also breathing.

Makepeace thought of the smoke-snake forcing its way into her mind, and for a moment felt a terrible temptation to stamp on Lady April's skull and crush it like an egg. But she did not. *They deserve to die*, she thought, groggily, *but I do not deserve to be a murderer.*

'Think!' she whispered to herself. 'Think!'

Her gaze fell upon Lady April's silver signet ring. She stared at it, her thoughts shifting to form a plan. No, something too foolhardy to be called a plan. It was a desperate, ridiculous gamble, but it was all she had.

Makepeace dropped to her knees, and unfastened Lady April's hooded cape. Her paws hurt as she fumbled with the clasp. No— her hands. Her hands hurt.

She removed the signet ring and gloves from the wizened hands. She snatched the old woman's purse and a bag that hung at her belt. Then she quickly put on the cloak, gloves and the ring, and pushed her other thefts into her pockets. As an afterthought, she picked up the bodkin as well.

Makepeace paused just once, to glance across at the other throne where Lord Fellmotte lay slumped, his eyes following her. He still looked like Sir Thomas, and it felt cruel to leave him there, but she had no choice.

'Sorry,' she whispered.

It was ten o'clock, and even in her Bear-drunk state, Makepeace knew the best route to avoid attention. Over the years, she had memorized the different passages, knew where one could hide, which routes muffled your steps and which echoed them.

All of this was second nature to her, which was just as well, since today her first nature was no longer behaving naturally.

Makepeace only just managed to duck into the shadows of a windowseat when Sir Marmaduke came striding past. She held her breath until he had gone. He was not running, so presumably he had not heard Lady April's cries. As soon as he reached the chapel, however, he would see the devastation. In mere minutes the alarm would be sounded.

She scampered to the Long Gallery, removed the helm from a suit of armour, and retrieved one of her runaway packs and her carefully stitched rag-rope from inside.

There was no time to sneak out through the kitchens. She could not risk leaving by the main entrance either. At a distance or in the dark she might pass for Lady April in her stolen clothes, but there would be too many people and candles in the Great Hall for her to go unrecognized.

She had to stake all or lose all.

Hastily she tethered one end of her rag-rope to an old torch bracket on the wall, then eased the nearest casement open. It was a first-floor window set in the side-wall of the house, looking down on a shadowy expanse of flags around the corner from the main courtyard.

Heart in mouth, she tossed the loose end of the rag-rope out of the window, and clambered out on to the sill. Wrapping the rough cloth of the rope around each hand, she began to climb down the wall, scrabbling in the dark for toe-holds in the mortar-cracks between the stones. She could hear the raking sound of her own breath, and the *snap-snap-snap* of her careful stitches tearing, one at a time.

The rope gave when she was still four feet from the ground, but she managed to land with no more than a bruising jolt. Pulling her hood down over her face, she stalked around the corner of the house with as much confidence as she could muster.

Through the fabric of the hood, she could just make out the outline of the waiting carriage, and the silhouette of the driver seated on its roof. She hoped that he saw only Lady April's cloak, and would not wonder why his mistress had unexpectedly emerged from around the side of the house.

She held up her gloved hand so that the ring glistened in the faint moonlight. The driver's silhouette nodded deferentially and touched his forehead.

The carriage door was open. She moved to enter, daring to raise her head as she did so . . . and came face to face with Mistress Gotely.

The old cook was stooped inside the carriage. A basket of muslin-wrapped shapes sat on the seat inside. Provisions for Lady April's journey, no doubt.

Mistress Gotely stared at Makepeace in shock, one hand to her own chest, breathing heavily. Makepeace knew that she had been recognized, and could only guess how guilty and dishevelled she must look. She could only stare back at the broad, sullen face of her mentor, tormentor and companion—the woman she had liked, but never trusted with anything important.

Makepeace felt her mouth move to shape the word that Beth had whispered to her.

Please.

After a long moment, Mistress Gotely lowered her eyes.

'Apologies, my lady,' she said, clearly enough for the driver to hear. 'God speed you on your journey.'

And she stepped out past Makepeace, dropped an awkward, gout-skewed curtsy, and hobbled back towards the house.

Hardly daring to believe in the chance she had been given, Makepeace climbed quickly into the carriage. She banged twice against the roof, and the driver whistled up the horses. The carriage lurched into motion.

Thank you, Mistress Gotely, she thought silently. *Thank you.*

There was distant shouting somewhere in the house. Makepeace thought she could hear Sir Marmaduke's voice.

'Close the gates!' came the faint words. 'Close the gates!'

But she heard it only because she was listening for it, and the driver did not seem to hear it at all. For the clipper-clop became a trot, and now they were out of the courtyard and through the gate. The trot became a canter, the limes that flanked the road raced past, and then they were on the main road and away, the moorland's rugged, indifferent face silver-stubbled in the moonlight.

PART FOUR: JUDITH

CHAPTER 20

The carriage windows were curtained. Overhead, a shuttered lantern rocked on a ring set in the ceiling, narrow beams of candlelight dancing on the walls.

Makepeace felt cold and sick, and could not stop shaking. Everything hurt. Bear had saved her by striking out at her captors, but he had done so with her body. Now she started to feel the bruises and strains. She could only hope that she had not broken bones or lost teeth.

There was blood in her mouth, but also the moth-dust taste of the Infiltrator that Bear's swipes had torn so easily. Who had that spirit been? Perhaps some veteran of a dozen lives? Had they tried to scream in their last moment of existence? She could not feel sadness for them, only a hollow horror when she remembered coughing up plumes of torn ghost.

Makepeace's thoughts would not run straight. She could feel Bear's exhaustion, but he also seemed restless and confused.

Bear? Bear—what's wrong?

For the first time ever he did not seem to hear her. He seemed bee-stung, too blind with some discomfort to notice her. She breathed deeply, trying to calm him.

What was Sir Marmaduke doing now? She imagined him charging into the courtyard, and finding her gone. He would give orders, have horses saddled, set off in pursuit . . .

The carriage was travelling fast, but not as fast as riders at full gallop. The broad road towards London cut a bold stripe across the moor, with open land on either side. The carriage would be visible a mile away. If it stayed on the main road, it would be overtaken in no time.

Where was she? She tweaked aside the curtain, and peered out. Trees slid by, black embroidery against the dark silver sky. A milestone marker passed, then a great crag shaped like a man's fist, its pale stone livid against the dark heather.

Makepeace had spent years weighing up escape routes, and noting which tracks were sheltered from view. If she was where she thought she was, then up ahead there should be . . . Yes! There! The spiked silhouette of a lightning-shattered oak. She took a deep breath.

'Driver!' she called, over the echo of hoofs and rattle of harness. 'Turn left!' Her voice was hoarse from roaring, but she tried to imitate Lady April's rasping, imperious tones. 'After the broken tree!'

The driver gave a nod and reined in the horses. If he noticed anything odd about her voice he gave no sign of it. Perhaps one yelling voice sounded a lot like another over the rattle of wheels.

He turned the carriage carefully just after the tree, and eased it on to a rugged old drover's lane, flanked by high, quivering mounds of gorse. The carriage jolted, jerked and tilted, until Makepeace feared that they might throw a wheel.

And then, just as Makepeace was feeling a little safer, the carriage slowed and halted, the driver calming the horses with low whistles. Makepeace opened her mouth to call up a question, then caught the sound that her driver had already heard.

Somewhere behind them, probably on the broad, straight road to London, galloping hoofs were echoing into the night. One horse, maybe two.

Makepeace closed her eyes and prayed that the carriage was hidden by the high gorse, and that its broad roof was not gleaming in the moonlight like the back of a great beetle. Bear's rampage had left her too drained and battered to leap out and run.

The galloping hoofs grew louder. Louder, until it seemed they must be a stone's throw away. But they did not break rhythm. They passed, and faded.

The riders had not spotted the carriage. And the driver had not recognized them as men from Grizehayes. The carriage eased into motion once more, and Makepeace's heart slowed to a less painful rhythm.

Devil take you, Sir Marmaduke. I hope you're halfway to Belton Pike before you realize you've overshot us.

Evidently Lady April's driver was used to travelling stealthily. For now, this was proving unexpectedly useful. When the path forked, she bade him take a rough hunting trail into the woods. The black trees closed in protectively. Bracken and dead sticks crackled between the spokes.

By lantern-light, she checked her injuries. Her teeth were intact, though she had to pick a few splinters out of her gums. Lady April's bodkin had punctured the skin of her shoulder, but not deeply. There were a lot of bruises, however, and a sharp pain in her left elbow. Looking back, she thought she remembered a soundless, velvety, tearing sensation in the joint when she hurled Young Crowe across the room.

Her body wanted to sleep, so that it could start fixing itself, and her head grew treacherously heavy. She jerked herself awake, over and over, but at last exhaustion closed itself around her mind like the fingers of a soft, dark hand.

'Hey!'

Makepeace lurched into wakefulness, the shock of it making

her stomach swim. She blinked painfully into the light of a lantern. Beyond it she could just make out the pale, jowly face of a man, creased with confusion and suspicion. He was standing at the door of the carriage, staring in at her.

Then Makepeace remembered where she was, and why. The staring man must be the driver. What had Lady April called him? Cattmore?

'Who the devil are you?' he demanded.

He must have been expecting Lady April, Makepeace realized. The cloak, the ring, the gloves. And now he had found a battered-looking girl of fifteen in his carriage.

What could she do? Make a break for it? Beg him not to betray her?

No.

'Take that light out of our eyes, Cattmore,' Makepeace said, with all the steely authority she could muster. Remembering Lady April's rigid posture and thin, red lips, she straightened her back and narrowed her mouth to a line. 'Our sleep must not be interrupted. We shall need to be well rested when we reach our destination.'

It was a gamble, a desperate and dangerous gamble. She was staking everything on the driver knowing enough about the Fellmotte Elders to know that they did not always *look* like Fellmotte Elders.

The lantern wobbled. Makepeace could sense Cattmore's indecision and dismay.

'My . . . lady? Is that you?'

'Of course,' Makepeace rapped sharply, her heartbeat thundering in her head. 'Do you think we would trust anyone else with this?' She held up one hand, letting the signet ring catch the light.

'No, my lady—forgive me, my lady.' He sounded cowed and remorse-filled, and Makepeace had to suppress a sigh of relief. 'I . . . I was not aware that you had . . . moved residence. May I ask—'

'You may not,' Makepeace snapped quickly. 'Suffice to say, we have had a very trying day.' Thankfully her borrowed nobility allowed her to be rude and dodge questions. 'Why have you stopped? Are we at our destination?'

'No, my lady—I . . . I thought I heard you rap on the roof.'

'You were mistaken,' Makepeace said quickly. And yet her bruised right hand did feel newly sore, as if it had struck against something. 'How long before we arrive?'

'We will be at the safe house in another hour, I think. Er . . . when we arrive, how would you like to be introduced to the others, your ladyship?'

Others? Makepeace's thoughts scattered in panic, and it took all her willpower to herd them together again. Did she dare impersonate Lady April in a meeting with these 'others'? If they knew the lady well, they would soon see through her.

For a moment she considered asking the coachman to drive her somewhere else instead, but that would certainly revive his suspicions. Makepeace's pretence was fragile as an eggshell. One good prod would crush it entirely.

'Tell them that we are an agent of Lady April,' she said. That seemed the safest option.

'Yes, my lady. What name should I use?'

A picture from an old book of pious tales sprang to Makepeace's mind. An angry woman with a sword in one hand and a severed head in the other.

'Judith,' she said on impulse. 'Judith Grey.'

The coachman touched his forehead and withdrew.

Makepeace slowly let out a breath, then frowned at her stinging knuckles. Had her hand really knocked against something loudly enough for the driver to hear?

Could Bear have taken control of her body again while she slept? His unfamiliar restlessness unsettled her. For three years he had been her soulmate and second self, but now she did not know what was wrong with him, and could not ask.

He is still confused and frightened after the fight, she told herself. *That is all.*

In an hour, she would have to bluff her way through an encounter with the 'others'. She did not have long to prepare. If she was to pass herself off as an agent on Lady April's business, she needed to know what Lady April's business was.

There was a chest on the floor of the carriage. It was locked, but she found the key for it in Lady April's purse. It held so many coins that it made Makepeace feel a little dizzy. This could only be the money for the King.

Lady April's bag contained a slim package of papers and a tiny bottle. Makepeace uncorked the bottle and sniffed cautiously, fearful of poison, but the contents smelt of garden artichokes.

Makepeace examined the papers by the light of the candle. Reading had always been a struggle but, curiously enough, this night of all nights it did not seem so hard. Whatever the reason, she was glad of it. Some of the papers seemed to be battle reports. Some tiny slips of paper bore only a strange cipher, in characters that Makepeace did not recognize.

Makepeace no longer had any doubt. Lady April was a spy.

One letter, written in a bold and elegant hand, caught her attention:

Salutations to my Friends and Kinsmen,

If this Missive is in your Hands, then by now I have either relieved myself of my Command or Perish'd in the Attempt. If the Latter, then no doubt you will hide my Actions for the Sake of your beloved Family Name. If the Former, then by now I have traded my Colours for Better Ones.

You will call me a Turncoat of course, but of late I have found my Sense of Duty Leaning towards Parliament. I would rather be a Traitor to the King than to my Conscience. I must admit however that my Conscience might have proven less Tender had I known for certain that I was properly valued by my Kin. Alas I was left to Wait upon your Mercies and Pray that you might find me Worthy to join your Ranks. I no longer choose to Gamble my Life and Soul on your Good Graces.

I Pity the Regiment but my new Friends could not be expected to Take my Conversion on Trust without some Evidence of my Good Faith.

I have taken a Trifle from the Muniments Room to ensure my Safety. If you should move against me, or if I should Espy a Murder of Crowes from my Chamber Window, then Parliament shall have the Charter and Copies will be Sent to every Gutter Printer from Penzance to Edinburgh. The World will know you as Monsters, and the King as a Friend to Monsters, and then we shall see how the Wind blows.

Be sure that no Gratitude will stay my Hand if I

think myself in Danger. Blood is Blood, but a Man has a Duty to Save the Neck God gave him.

Your most affectionate Kinsman,
Symond Fellmotte

It was all Makepeace could do to resist crumpling the letter into a ball. So this was the jaunty message that had caused Lord Fellmotte's heart to break, and shattered his health in a single blow! Symond had not simply deserted; he had defected to Parliament's forces. He had planned his betrayal in advance and in cold blood.

I Pity the Regiment but my new Friends could not be expected to Take my Conversion on Trust without some Evidence of my Good Faith . . .

Makepeace read that line over and over. He had deliberately drawn James and the regiment into mortal peril, and left them there. He had been willing to sacrifice them all to win the approval of his new allies.

She did not blame him for wanting to escape his Inheritance. After all, she had been trying to run away for years. She could not even blame him for backstabbing the Elders. But she could blame him for betraying James and a whole regiment of his tenants and servants, men who had followed and trusted him.

So the golden boy Symond had not been happy after all, or at least not happy enough. He would have accepted the rich burdens of lordship, even played host to immortal spirits, had he been certain that in time his ghost would have been preserved like theirs. But he had not been certain. And apparently he had been laying plans and awaiting his moment, just like Makepeace.

No, not like me. He's no better than the other Fellmottes. Another

rich man bent on what he thinks the world owes him, and willing to
pay any price, as long as it's in the blood of others.

Makepeace let out a long breath, and tried to calm herself. At least now she knew that Lady April had planned to pass on letters, military information and evidence of Symond's treachery to a messenger destined for Oxford. Makepeace was not much the wiser, but perhaps wise enough now to play a game of hints.

She had another pressing problem, though. Lady April knew where the carriage had been heading. Once the old woman had recovered enough to speak, the Fellmottes would be hot on Makepeace's heels again. Furthermore, after the meeting the driver might expect to take 'Lady April' back to Grizehayes or her own estates.

As Makepeace wiped her face and tucked her braided hair back under her cap, she tried to form a plan.

The carriage arrived at the safe house during the early hours. It was strange to have the door held open for her, and a hand offered to help her alight. Bear's keen sight pierced the darkness, and let Makepeace see a little of their surroundings. They were out of the woods, albeit just in a literal sense, and only a few straggling trees marred the dull, misty horizons.

The carriage was parked beside a lonely house backed up against a hillock, next to a greenish, dripping waterwheel. The millpond was heavily choked with weed, but here and there water gave a brief sabre-flash of reflected moonlight.

An elderly couple opened the door quickly to her driver's knock, and quietly bowed her in. They showed every sign of expecting Makepeace, or somebody at least.

'Is all well?' asked the coachman as the couple led them through dark, cold passageways that smelt of mice and last year's hay.

'Quiet enough these last few months,' answered their hostess. 'But we have had our share of billets. Parliament's troops settled on us like a plague of locusts and ate our pantry bare.' Her eye fled quickly and fearfully to Makepeace, as if dreading her disapproval. 'There was nothing we could do about it, I swear!'

Makepeace was shown into a narrow little parlour, with a fierce fire of spitting, wet logs. There she found the 'others' waiting for her. Both were women and, to judge by the hum of conversation as the door opened, women that knew each other. They hushed as Makepeace entered.

One was tall, and the hair that peeped out from under her high-crowned hat was an unabashed red. There were half a dozen tiny circles of black taffeta glued to her face. Makepeace knew that such patches were fashionable, but six was too many even for fashion. These probably hid pockmarks, and Makepeace guessed that this woman must have had an even worse brush with smallpox than her own.

The other woman was old and broad-faced, with tired, tightly braided hair the colour of weathered rope under her coif. Her eyes were blue, like little scraps of sky. Common as washday, Makepeace thought, and very far from stupid.

They gave Makepeace a dip of the head as she entered, but did not start talking again until their hostess had left the room. The red-haired woman took a careful look at Lady April's ring and seemed satisfied. There were quick, oddly informal introductions. The redhead was 'Helen Favender' and the old woman was 'Peg Corble'. Makepeace had the feeling that these names were about as real as 'Judith Grey'.

'We were expecting somebody else,' said Helen. Her voice had a touch of a Scottish accent, and Makepeace wondered if hers was one of the families that had travelled from Scotland to England with the previous King. There was a silver ring on her finger, and Makepeace guessed that even her bluntness came from the confidence of gentry. She was a horse with a bit of wildness, but one that had been well-fed and allowed space to kick up its heels.

'My mistress intended to come herself,' Makepeace said quickly, and not entirely untruthfully. 'Another emergency arose—she had to change her plans quickly.'

'Nothing too grievous, I hope?' asked Peg, her gaze sharp with concern and curiosity.

'She would not tell me,' Makepeace said quickly.

'Did you bring the money for His Majesty?' asked Helen, and seemed reassured when Makepeace passed across the chest and key.

'Yes . . . but there has been a change of plan.' This was the leap. 'My mistress has ordered me to travel with you to Oxford.'

The two women exchanged a sharp look.

'Travel with us?' said Helen. 'Why?'

'There is a message for one there that she would have me pass on in person—it was not to be entrusted to paper.' Makepeace hoped that this story was plausible and vague enough.

'And yet she entrusted it to you,' remarked Helen wryly. 'Has she used you for this kind of business before?'

'Some private matters for my ladyship—'

'What sort of matters?' interrupted Helen.

'Ah, do not pluck the poor little hen!' said Peg reprovingly. 'She cannot reveal her lady's private doings!' But above her kindly smile her eyes were questioning.

'This is a twist in the road, and I wish to know the reason for it!' Helen retorted. 'And . . . child, you are younger than I like for this business. We shall be bluffing our way past enemy troops! It is no game—if we are caught, then we shall have a holiday in the Tower if we are lucky—'

'*You* might, perhaps,' Peg remarked drily. 'I'm more likely to have my neck stretched till it's lovely and swan-like.'

'And if one of us is unweaned to shadow-work, it is more likely that we *will* be caught!' Helen continued.

'I am not untried!' Makepeace protested. 'I will not let you down—I promise!'

'Lady April always plays her own game,' said Helen, and raised her hands in a gesture of exasperation. 'So does everybody! If all who love the King could keep in tune with each other, we would have the rebels routed by now. But we are all fiddlers in the dark, sawing away at the same strings and poking each other in the eye.'

'Please do not send me back!' said Makepeace, changing tack. 'My lady would never forgive me.'

'This message you must pass on—it is really so important?' asked Peg.

'Important enough that I was followed on the road,' declared Makepeace, in a moment of inspiration. 'There were riders on the moors, chasing the coach.'

'Are you sure you lost them?' Peg asked sharply, immediately seeming less maternal.

Makepeace nodded. 'Yes—but I did not like it. It was as if they knew I would be passing. Is this place safe? How many people know of it?' Every moment she spent in this so-called safe house, she knew that she was at risk.

194

'A good question.' Peg met Helen's eye, and raised one eyebrow. 'We had planned to stay here a day . . .'

'. . . but perhaps we should not wait that long,' finished Helen. 'The horses will need a few hours to rest, and so will we, but let us be gone tomorrow morning.'

Makepeace noticed that, however grudgingly, she had been included in the 'we'. Helen was not happy to find an unknown girl accompanying her, but she had not yet refused to take her.

She knew that Helen was right. The mission to reach Oxford *would* be difficult and dangerous. But she could not forget the story about the doctor Benjamin Quick, who had rid a patient of his 'haunting'. According to the news-sheet, he had done so in Oxford.

If she could find this mysterious ghost-defeating doctor, maybe he could show her some way of fighting the Fellmottes. She could not give up on James, or the hope that his true self still existed. With the help of the doctor, perhaps she could save him, before it was too late.

CHAPTER 21

Makepeace woke with a start, with the bleary impression that something had just nipped sharply at her forearm. She was very cold, the world was very dark, and there were cobbles under her bare feet.

Where am I? How did I get here?

Her fuzzy thoughts rallied. She had gone to bed in the little garret room put aside for her, with the flock bed and the extra blankets.

She was holding a large, metal ring. Before her the darkness yielded to deeper darkness, from which came soft snorts, and the sound of hoofs shifting on straw. She was standing in front of the stables, holding the door open. Above her the stars glittered.

What was I doing?

Surely Bear had not crept down to eat the horses! He had hungrily considered it during Makepeace's first ever riding lesson, and it had been hard to persuade him otherwise. But that had been a long time ago.

Bear—why did you bring me out here?

There was a silence, then Makepeace seemed to hear a low rumble of a growl inside her head, so cold and deep that it might have been the coal-hearted earth answering her. It was not a friendly noise. She felt it as a warning, a noise of utter enmity.

'Bear,' she whispered, aghast, but there was no reply. Something about Bear had changed, and she did not know what. She was reminded of dogs raising their hackles when they caught the smell of a stranger. Or dogs snarling at a friend after going mad in the sun. Her blood ran cold.

Just then, she heard a faint murmur. It was not Bear, nor did it come from inside her head.

Makepeace edged towards the sound, and found herself peering around the side of the stables, towards the front of the house. The shutters at one of the windows were slightly open, the slit bright with candlelight. A male silhouette was leaning close to the window, whispering to someone within.

For a moment Makepeace felt utter, panicked certainty that the man must have been sent by the Fellmottes. They had found her, they had come for her. Then she recognized the voice of her hostess from inside the window.

'Go quick!' she whispered. 'Head to Aldperry, and ask for Captain Maltsey. Tell him that the Royalist she-intelligencers are back—and that I kept my word.'

As the man obediently scurried away, lantern in hand, Makepeace understood. This was nothing to do with the Fellmottes. Her hosts were working for somebody else entirely.

Shivering with the cold, she felt her way along the front of the house until she found the door, then slipped inside as quickly as possible. She climbed the inky, narrow stairs, then rapped furtively on the door opposite her own, praying that she had picked the right room. She was relieved when Helen appeared at the door, hair wild, taper in hand. Makepeace stepped in through the door, and closed it before speaking.

'We need to leave.' Quickly she described what she had heard. 'They've betrayed us. They've sent a man to tell Parliament's troops that we're here.'

'I should have guessed!' Helen exhaled through her teeth. 'They've been so cowed this time, and they never were before.' She glanced at Makepeace, and frowned. 'So why were you down by the stables, anyway?'

'I walk in my sleep sometimes,' Makepeace said quickly, and received a sceptical look from Helen.

'Hfft, maybe she does,' said Peg, who was awake now, and gathering her possessions with calm practicality. 'It's hardly likely she was running away like *that*.'

Makepeace realized, to her great embarrassment, that she was only wearing her long-sleeved shift, which doubled as her undergarment and nightdress. She hugged her arms around herself defensively.

Helen frowned, brought the taper closer, and pulled one of Makepeace's sleeves back. By the light of the flame, the yellowish-brown bruises on Makepeace's arm were clearly visible.

'You've been ill-used,' said Helen quietly. 'Hmm. I start to see why you do not want to face Lady April without having carried out her orders.' She gave Makepeace an odd, cool glance with a hint of sympathy. 'Come—get dressed before the night air makes you ill.'

As Makepeace pulled down her sleeve again, she noticed something else. Besides the bruises, a little patch of her forearm was pinkish, as though fingers had recently pinched the flesh hard.

The coachman was woken quietly, and told to prepare the carriage and the two horses belonging to Peg and Helen. Back in her room, Makepeace dug out her runaway pack, and retrieved her change of clothes. The old russet jacket she had secretly bought from the market. The faded, smoke-grey skirt was one she had put aside some six months before, and showed more

198

petticoat than it once had, but there was nothing to be done about it. She tucked all her hair under a dingy linen cap.

When she returned, Helen and Peg gave her brief glances of approval, and did not seem surprised to see her transformed from lady to ill-dressed servant. They were spies, and perhaps used to such metamorphoses.

The coachman, however, looked at her aghast. He seemed even more concerned and surprised when he learned that Makepeace would not be returning with him.

'Take a long route back,' she told him, in her best imitation of Lady April's manner. 'And tell nobody where I have gone—not even members of my family.' He would almost certainly crack under Fellmotte questioning, but this might buy her some time.

By the time Makepeace mounted up behind Peg, there were streaks of light in the sky. Their hostess appeared in the door as they were departing, confused and protesting. Makepeace felt a little pity for her, even as the mill house receded behind them and vanished among the trees.

The Fellmottes had taught Makepeace to ride, but this had not prepared her for many hours on horseback. Bear never made such things easier. He could smell horse, and was always confused at finding himself straddling another animal. Her horse was skittish, and she wondered whether it could smell Bear.

Bear was still restless, feverish and strange. He had always been a wild thing, of course, but Makepeace had grown used to his brute warmth and unruly, changeable moods. She had spent three years bargaining wordlessly with him—sharing his pain, soothing his fears, reining in his urge to lash out. But this was different. For the first time in years she was afraid of him.

Sometimes his mind would nestle against hers as normal, but then he would draw back and utter a long, low growl that chilled her. What if he had been injured in his battle with the Infiltrator, and it had changed him somehow? Was he starting to forget who she was? What could she possibly do if he turned on her? He was inside all her defences.

Over and over, she tried to make sense of the way she had woken at the stable door. It had felt exactly as though somebody had pinched her arm. Bear might bite, but he did not pinch. So who or what had woken her? Makepeace did not know what would have happened if she had not been nipped awake. She tried not to think of Bear going on a rampage. She hoped she would not have woken up covered in blood, among dead and screaming horses.

Groggy with her injuries and lack of sleep, Makepeace felt like one in a dream. She was not used to seeing green hills that sloped gently, without erupting in crags or stretching in stark, barren wilds. She was outside the Fellmottes' sprawling estates at long last, and she could not believe it. It did not seem real.

For the last three years, Makepeace had lived in fear, trapped under the chilling gaze of the Elders. Now she was terrified of being caught again, but at least she felt alive. The Fellmottes might catch up with her at any moment, but for this breath, and this, and this, she was free.

Both Makepeace's companions seemed comfortable in the saddle, and even chatted as they rode. The trio had decided upon their roles now. Helen was, of course, a gentlewoman travelling with her two servingwomen. Whenever they passed some travelling newsmonger, loaded down with printed sheets, Helen would slow her horse.

'What news? What do you have for sale?'

She bought corantos, piping-hot tales of the latest happenings filled with hearsay and gore, and separates, reports of Parliament's latest doings.

''Tis all rebel rot,' Peg said a little reprovingly as Helen pored over her latest news-sheet. 'We are in Parliament-held land now.'

'Indeed,' answered Helen. 'But we must know the enemy's tunes if we wish to sing along. And I believe our friend here will wish to read this.' She leaned across to pass the paper to Makepeace.

Most of the pamphlet was sizzling with righteous fury. The King's men were burning down churches with women and children inside! The wicked French Queen wanted poor, noble England under the evil sway of the Pope! Prince Rupert was in league with the Devil! His dog 'Boy' had survived every battle, and therefore was clearly a familiar bringing orders from his Infernal Master!

It was strange to bump into such beliefs again after so long. Catholic spies, the wicked Queen—it was like being back in Poplar! But since arriving in Grizehayes, Makepeace had grown used to hearing everything from the Royalist side, and now the news-sheet gave her a frightened, unsteady feeling in her stomach. For three years she had been breathing in other people's certainties, and she now realized that her opinions had quietly shifted towards everyone else's without her noticing.

'Look at the bottom of the page,' said Helen.

Scanning downwards, Makepeace spotted the name 'Fellmotte'. It was a list of those who 'have sided with the King and Papists against Parliament and our most ancient rights' and whose estates were to be 'sequestered'. All of the most eminent Fellmottes were on the list.

'*Sequestered*—what does that mean?' asked Makepeace.

'It means forfeit,' answered Helen. 'It means that if Parliament has its will, they will seize the Fellmotte lands, plunder them of all they can, then hand them over to someone of their liking.'

'Somebody like Master Symond,' murmured Makepeace under her breath. She had imagined that he was only making a break for freedom. But perhaps his ambitions stretched further. Perhaps he was making a bid for the whole of the Fellmotte lands.

'Your kinsmen will fight against it, I am sure,' Helen said crisply. 'They have friends in London, and money enough to buy a host of lawyers.'

Occasionally the trio passed bands of soldiers. Most did not wear uniforms, just sashes or pieces of paper in their hats to show their allegiance. They often made a show of stopping the three travellers, and sometimes asked for a 'toll', which Helen paid each time without a murmur.

Sometimes there were murmurs about confiscating the horses for the troops, but such suggestions wilted before Helen's confident, genteel outrage. Class was her armour and weapon, and for now it was still serving her well. Makepeace wondered if it would work so well against a Parliamentarian officer or gentleman.

Helen had lent Makepeace a sun-mask, of the sort ladies wore to keep their complexions fair. She was glad of its concealment now, and glad of Helen's confidence and willingness to handle conversations.

When they stopped for the night at an inn, she collapsed exhausted into bed, but her sleep was broken. Over and over she jerked awake, her nose filled with the smell of Bear.

Even when she slept, her anxieties did not.

Makepeace dreamed that she was back in the little upstairs

bedroom at her old home in Poplar. She was very young, and sitting on a woman's lap, trying to read a coranto with news of the war. It was very important that she understand it, but the letters kept moving and telling different stories.

The woman said nothing. Makepeace felt that she should know who the woman was, but something stopped her from turning to look at her face. Instead, she watched the woman's hand reach out and slowly scratch an 'M' into the grime on the wood of the door jamb.

It was the key to everything, Makepeace was sure, but she could not make sense of it. All she could do was stare and stare at the letter, until her mind darkened into a deeper sleep.

On the afternoon of the second day, the trio left the main road and took a winding lane to an isolated house where a solitary man was waiting with a wagon full of barrels. He levered up the lid of one so that Helen could inspect the contents.

'And the gold is inside?' she asked.

'Every penny we could gather,' he answered. 'The personal fortunes of three great men, who would languish in the Tower if it was ever known that they had done this. All our hopes rest with you—tell His Majesty that we have answered his call in his time of need! God bless you, and see you safely to the King!'

Makepeace's mouth turned dry. She had thought that Helen and Peg were simply trying to slip into Oxford with messages for the King and Lady April's gold. But no, apparently they were about to smuggle a king's ransom past an entire Parliamentarian army. The barrels looked very obvious. Makepeace wanted to ask what else was in them, but was afraid to reveal how little she knew of the plan.

'Will they not be searched?' she whispered to Peg instead.

'No, child,' Peg answered. 'God willing,' she added in an undertone, and Makepeace felt less than reassured. 'Anyway, necessity is our master. The King's cause is desperate—if he cannot pay his troops, he has no army. He must have this gold . . . and we cannot carry all of it on our persons, not this time. You'll see, there is only so much you can hide on yourself before your knees start to give. Last time I nearly swooned right into a sentry's arms.'

Sure enough, Makepeace was soon being shown how to conceal some of Lady April's coins inside the lining of her stays, in her shoes, in the rolled braid of her hair and in dropped pockets under her skirt.

Riding in the wagon with her two companions, Makepeace felt an odd excitement building inside her. She was in a fellowship of sorts, even though she was there under false pretences.

'We are most likely to be searched when we are ten miles from Oxford,' Helen told her. 'For two months the rebels have been sending men to talk to the King, to see if there is a chance of peace. While they talk, they have agreed that for now the rebel troops will stay ten miles clear of the city, and the King's troops will not venture outside that circle. Neither side measures it too carefully, though, so there are raids and clashes aplenty, but they make a show of honouring it.

'But it means that just outside that ring, Parliament has camps and garrisons set, champing at the bit and keeping watch, to make sure no help comes to the King.'

As they drew closer to Oxford, Makepeace noted, to her surprise, that there seemed to be a lot of people on the road, and not all of them soldiers. Some were clearly carrying baskets of wares for sale—pans, flour, capons, herbs.

'Market day,' murmured Peg over her shoulder. 'All the better for us if we are not the only ones travelling to the city.'

'Are all these people going there?' Makepeace asked. 'What about the Parliament troops ahead? Won't they all be stopped?'

'Oh no, the army won't stop people going to market!' Peg winked. 'How else would they find out what's happening in Oxford? That's how they get their spies in—a goodly number of them, anyway. And it puts the locals out of humour if they cannot do their business or find ways to fill up their pantries.'

'Hush now, chickens,' said Helen. 'I see soldiers ahead.'

The village they were entering showed the marks of war. The fields were trampled, and the narrow road gouged to mud by more traffic than it had been designed to take. There were soldiers everywhere, standing in doorways, dragging unwilling horses, or leaning out of windows to smoke clay pipes. To Makepeace's country eyes, they looked like a full army. Then she glanced past the drifting smoke from the smithies, and saw the *real* army.

In a field beyond was a forest of weather-stained tents. To her startled gaze it seemed to her that there must be thousands of men and horses—too many to take in.

'You can stare,' said Peg drily, who had noticed Makepeace watching the troops sideways. 'It would look strange if you did not.'

Makepeace remembered the murals in the Map Room, with their vivid blues and reds, and the miniature army tents neatly arranged in rows, as if seen from a great height. This encampment of dull canvas, with its dusty horses and rutted ground, was shockingly real in comparison. It had a chorus of smells—damp wood ash, gunpowder, oil and horse dung. There were surprising numbers of women as well, scouring out cooking pots, carrying firewood, and in some cases suckling tiny infants. The whole scene was chaotic and brutally practical.

Those sentries standing to lacklustre attention in the middle of the road, with the dusty restlessness of stray dogs in the summer heat, had real blood that might be spilt. They had real shot in their muskets that might be fired. It might be fired at her. After all, what was she now? An adventuress. A she-intelligencer. A spy.

'Have your papers ready,' said Helen, 'and take off your sun-mask. Courtesans wear masks too, remember—we will never get past the camp if they take us for *those*.'

Makepeace felt her stomach turn to acid as they rode slowly up to the waiting men, who were shielding their eyes from the sun and squinting at their approach. Two carried muskets, and the sun gleamed off the metal with lazy menace.

'Where are you heading?' called one of the sentries.

'Oxford,' said Helen, with startling confidence.

The sentries looked askance at the wagon, then back at Helen and her 'servants'. They were unlikely to be mistaken for farmers taking goods to market.

'Sorry, mistress, but we cannot allow anyone to provision the enemy army.'

'Read this.' Helen produced her paperwork. 'I have permission from Parliament. See—the barrels are mentioned in this letter.'

The first sentry blinked at the papers, and Makepeace felt a sting of sympathy as he passed it to the next in line. The paper was promptly handed on again to the tallest sentry, apparently the only member of the group who could read.

'So . . . you're a washerwoman?'

'A laundress,' Helen corrected him with quiet gravitas. 'One that has attended upon royalty and ladies of court.'

'And those barrels are full of soap?' The sentries gazed at her with a strange mixture of hostility, doubt and deference. Helen had all but declared herself a Royalist. And yet she was a lady of quality, and a lady bearing a letter from Parliament.

'The finest Castille soap, made with the purest thistle ash,' declared Helen. 'You can see the assay-marks on the barrels.'

'Spanish muck,' muttered the sentry. 'Has Oxford no soap or washerwomen?'

'Of course,' answered Helen promptly. 'But none suitable for His Majesty's clothes and person. Do you think he can get any old crone to scrub his silks with mutton fat and lye?'

We are going to die, thought Makepeace with a strange calm. *Our cover story is completely mad.* The letter from Parliament could only be a forgery. The sentries were bound to realize this, and call their superior officer, and everyone on the wagon would be arrested. She was very aware of the sun's heat on her face, the weight of the gold hidden in her clothes, the scent of dry mud baking, a lone buzzard circling above in the summer blue. She wondered whether spies were shot or hanged.

The sentries were conferring under their breath, casting occasional glances at the women on the wagon. The word 'search' reached her ears.

'Me? No!' she heard one mutter in response. 'I'm not groping a royal laundress!'

One of them cleared his throat.

'We will need to look in the barrels, mistress,' he said.

'Of course,' said Helen.

The youngest sentry came over and rolled down one of the barrels from the wagon, then carefully prised it open. Makepeace was sitting closer than the others, and caught the distinctive reek of smoke and olive oil. Sure enough, the barrel was filled with misshapen, greasy white oblongs of soap, glossy and slippery from the heat. The young sentry unwillingly leaned down and stirred them around with his hands, grimacing.

'Well—get on with it!' called one of his friends.

'It looks like soap.' He wrinkled his nose. 'It stinks like soap.'

'I don't think it will help your enemies much,' suggested Peg. 'Or do they fight better when they're clean?'

The sentries glanced at the queue of people forming behind the wagon, then back at the large number of barrels.

'All right, all right,' muttered the taller sentry, the reader. 'Let them through.'

Peg clicked and gave a flick of the reins, and the good-natured horses trundled into motion again.

Makepeace realized that her heart had been cantering, and took a deep breath. The sky was a burning blue, and there were fingernail crescents dug into her palms. She felt oddly exhilarated.

'Where did you get the letter?' she whispered once they were far out of earshot of the sentries.

'Parliament,' answered Helen. 'Oh, it is quite real.'

'They gave you special pass as a laundress?'

'Of course. He is the King.' Helen gave a lopsided smile. 'God's appointed. They cannot help but revere him, even as they fight him. Rebelling against him is only treason. Leaving him to wallow in common filth would be sacrilege.'

'They want His Majesty defeated and brought to heel,' Peg explained. 'But they do not want him smelly.'

So this was the world in all its tomfoolery. Armies might clash, multitudes might die, but both sides agreed that the King must be able to wash his socks.

The world was turning cartwheels, Makepeace realized, and nobody was sure which way was up any more. Rules were breaking, but nobody was certain which ones. If you had enough confidence, you could walk in and act as if you knew what the new rules were, and other people would believe you.

CHAPTER 22

After passing the Parliamentarian soldiers, they followed the road down into a low broad valley with the village of Wheatley strung along it. Its ancient stone bridge had once spanned the gleaming curve of the river Thame, but now part of its length had been knocked down, and there was a makeshift drawbridge mounted at the far side of the gap.

The soldiers who held it were Royalist troops from Oxford, though, so they were easily persuaded to lower the drawbridge, and the wagon rolled on. The horses struggled up a steep hill. Then, as the road descended, Makepeace caught a few glimpses of the city in the valley below through gaps in the trees—hints of church towers and spires, toast-coloured stone and frayed blue strands of chimney smoke.

'This was a fair-looking county not long ago,' murmured Peg.

The countryside closer to Oxford looked as though the end of days had come upon it. The meadows and farmland were rutted and ravaged, hoof-marks gouging the earth as though the Four Horsemen had ridden by. Copses were clumps of newly shorn tree stumps. Most of it seemed to be flooded too, puddles gleaming amid the clods like crescents of sky.

Ahead, two freshly dug earth mounds flanked the road, offering crude protection to the bridge beyond. Far off to her right, Makepeace could just make out more new earthworks, a brown, slope-sided ridge hugging the city's northern side. She supposed it was a protective wall, but it looked as though the wounded landscape had reared up like a great beast to defend itself. On the earthy slopes she could see figures toiling with spades and barrows.

'They don't look like soldiers,' she murmured. There were men and women of all ages, and even a few children.

'They're Oxford civilians, doing their part to protect the city,' said Helen.

'Well, it's that or pay a fine,' muttered Peg. 'If I was faced with the same choice, I'd probably be up there with a spade.'

Beyond the bridgehead earthworks, the road crossed a grand, many-arched stone bridge that spanned a tangle of river tributaries. They rode past a beautiful, sandy-gold building that Peg told her was Magdalen College, and approached the aged grey walls.

At the gates, a sentry glanced at Helen's papers upside down, then waved their group on. They rolled carefully in through the gate . . . and into Oxford.

It was Makepeace's first city since London. It was beautiful and horrible, and she knew straight away, without being told, that there was something wrong with it.

The street was fair and broad, the houses high and grand. But it was the stink that struck her first and hardest, turning over her stomach. Every lane she passed seemed to have its own reeking ditch, lumpy with rot and waste. In one alleyway she saw the remains of a dead horse, its eyes white and its hide jewelled with flies. Not far away, children were gathering puddle water in ewers.

Too many faces in the crowded streets were taut, gaunt and scabbed. There was a hungry edge in the air, a taste of desperation drawn out for too long. Everything felt flayed and skinless, like the land outside.

It was the beauty that made everything worse. Makepeace boggled at the great buildings, with their fair columns, stone flourishes as fine as lace, and towers that would grace a cathedral. They lifted their heads high, but their hems were drenched deep in stench and filth. It was like seeing a fading court beauty, still in her finery, but mad with age or the pox.

Helen stopped the wagon outside Merton College, and gave orders. As the barrels were unloaded, Makepeace stared up at the college's golden stone and grand chimneys.

'We have been assigned lodgings,' declared Helen. The trio followed a young man who led them through a couple of streets and pushed open the shop door of a whitebaker, a man who made fine, white bread for the better class of person. The baker himself, a skinny but well-mannered man of forty, looked resigned when told that he had received more guests.

He even managed a hollow rictus of a smile when Helen handed him several pieces of paper.

'What are those?' Makepeace whispered to Peg.

'Payment—or they will be once the war is won,' Peg said stoutly. 'Then all loyal servants of the King will be able to present those tickets and be paid what they are owed.'

Makepeace started to understand why the baker looked unhappy, and why the shelves of his shop were so bare. The paper tickets were nothing but promises from the King, and probably not much use for keeping the wolf from the door.

The three new arrivals were shown to a single tiny room with a poor flock bed and the smallest of windows.

'I am sorry we have no better,' said the baker wearily, 'but we are jammed to the gills. We already have an officer, a candlemaker, a goldsmith's wife and a playwright staying with us. So many flee to Oxford for safety—you know how it is.'

'Did you ever hear of a doctor called Benjamin Quick?' Makepeace asked.

'No, I do not recall the name.' The baker's brow furrowed. 'But if he knows his physick, he will be busy and much in demand. Did you know that we have the camp fever here now?'

'Camp fever?' Makepeace's companions exchanged glances, looking surprised and alarmed.

'The soldiers brought it back with them from the camps outside Reading,' explained the baker, failing to keep the bitterness from his voice. 'My wife has been brewing cures—but I fear that making it costs us dear because of the nutmeg, so we must ask coin for it.' Nutmeg was a rare spice known for its healing virtues, and its nigh-magical ability to protect against plagues and other ills.

'We'll only stay until our business is done,' said Helen briskly, 'and we'll gladly pay for some of your wife's cure while we're here. Judith—come with me when I go to the King's court. If your doctor is of good standing, somebody will know of him.'

Makepeace had no choice but to agree. What excuse could she give for shunning the King's court-in-exile? The idea made her nervous, however. She had no idea how to be courtly, and there was an outside chance that one of the Fellmottes might be there, or a friend of theirs who had visited Grizehayes. She would just have to hope that nobody would be expecting to see an erstwhile kitchen servant at court in silks and velvets.

Left alone in their room, Makepeace and Helen tried to make themselves passably ready for 'court'. Makepeace changed back into her rich clothes, and hid her calloused hands under gloves. Peg borrowed curling tongs from their hostess, and spent an hour laboriously curling the hair of her companions. She then carefully powdered their faces because they both looked grey as death with tiredness.

Two nights of broken sleep had left Makepeace with a sickly, floating sensation. She was exhausted, but glaringly awake, and wondered whether she would ever sleep again. Bear, on the other hand, seemed to have worn himself out, and was slumbering.

Makepeace *liked* Helen and Peg, she realized with a little pang. If they ever found out that she had been lying to them, they would probably hand her over to be tried as an enemy spy, but she did not hold that against them. She liked the way they planned for danger with humour and good sense, and without boasting, toasting or waving rapiers at the rafters.

Peg declared that she herself would stay behind to keep an eye on the group's possessions.

'This is a hungry city,' she said. 'Even honest folk forget themselves sometimes. The Devil has no better friend than an empty belly.'

'But we brought money for the King!' said Makepeace, thinking of the fortune in gold. 'Can he not pay people with coin now, instead of those paper tickets?'

Peg gave a small, sad laugh. 'Oh no—that will all be spent straight away on the army's overdue wages! If he had not found the gold . . . well, the whole garrison would have rioted and torn the city apart. Trust me, that would have been far worse for the townsfolk.'

'Give a man a sword and pistol,' said Helen, 'and leave him

hungry for a few weeks, and everybody will start to look like the enemy.'

'Do not look so sad!' Peg said phlegmatically. 'Thanks to us, His Majesty's forces will not crumble or go rogue just yet. For all we know, perhaps we have just turned the tide of the war!'

Makepeace felt her stomach lurch. For somebody who felt no great loyalty to either side, she seemed to have become surprisingly involved in the war. She had wondered about fleeing to Parliament to seek sanctuary from the Fellmottes, but perhaps she had burned that bridge now. If Parliament ever found out that she had smuggled bullion in His Majesty's service, they might not be understanding.

'Christ Church is where the King holds court now,' said Helen, leading Makepeace through the streets. 'If he is not out hunting he will be there at this time, I think.'

If he is not out hunting. Oxford sat in a ravaged wasteland, ringed about with Parliament's troops. But of course the King left the city to go hunting. Of course he did.

Christ Church took Makepeace's breath away. To her eyes, the college looked like a great palace, its carved stone golden-brown like the best pastry.

At the gatehouse, Helen's papers were examined again, and the pair of them were allowed to enter. Stepping through that entrance was a moment of enchantment.

The smoke, stink and crowds were left behind in an instant. Beyond the dark covered entrance lay a wide, grassy courtyard where well-dressed gentlefolk walked, sat and played instruments. Glossy, well-fed dogs loped and lolled on the grass. A couple of the gentlemen seemed to be playing tennis. Over to one side, a few animals grazed. High, softly golden walls watched on every side, shielding the little paradise.

There was something uncanny about it, as though King Charles were a fairy king who had somehow magically transported his entire palace into the heart of the desperate city.

Helen greeted friends, exchanged pleasantries and archly turned compliments away with a flick of her fan. Then an earnest-looking bearded man drew her aside for a conversation, leaving Makepeace standing alone and acutely self-conscious. To make matters worse, she was almost certain that two men at the far side of the garden were watching her.

One of them looked slightly familiar, but it was only when she noticed his lavish lace cuffs that she recognized him. It was the handkerchief-thrower who had made such an abject apology to Lady April at Twelfth Night.

Perhaps he had recognized her too, in spite of her new clothes. Perhaps everybody had noticed the clumsiness of her gait, and could smell three years of mutton grease and hearth-ash marinated into her skin.

Then she saw him mutter something to his companion, and stroke his fingertip down the middle of his chin. Makepeace felt the sunlight grow cold. It was the cleft in her chin that had caught his eye, then. It was still possible that he had not recognized her, but he might well have guessed at her Fellmotte blood.

Her first instinct was to hide behind one of the laughing groups, and look for a way to sneak out of the college. But what good would hiding do now? She had been noticed. Even if she fled now, those young men would probably gossip about seeing a young girl with a Fellmotte chin.

Instead of hiding, she raised her head at a moment where the young men were looking at her. She met their eye and stiffened slightly, as if startled by their brazen staring. They both gave extravagant, apologetic bows, and Makepeace smiled at them in what she hoped was a charming and courtly way. Evidently her smile was welcoming enough for the pair to feel able to approach.

From a distance they had seemed like the same perfectly groomed peacocks as before. When they were closer she could see that war had scuffed them. Both looked tired under the powder. Their fine coats were less well-brushed, and their boots had seen more action than polish.

How strange, thought Makepeace, looking at their faces. *Four months ago they looked so much older than me, but now they seem like boys. They look too young for a war.*

'We frightened you,' said the handkerchief-thrower. 'We are ogres, and should be punished by your cruellest rebuke. Forgive my rudeness, but I thought that we might have met.'

'I am not sure,' said Makepeace, trying to soften her accent a little. 'I think I may have seen you with one of my cousins . . .' They had not recognized her as a Grizehayes servant, she was almost certain of that now. She was at court, and must be someone of decent birth.

The handkerchief-thrower exchanged a knowing glance with his friend. 'I fancy I know the cousin you mean. A close friend of ours. Is he well?'

'I . . . have not seen him of late,' Makepeace said cautiously. She was a little taken aback by their cheerful tone. Could they really be talking of Symond as a 'close friend'? Maybe they had not heard about his defection.

'Oh, no, of course not,' he said affably. 'Now I remember,

Symond has turned into a double-dyed traitor, and is forsworn by his family for ever more, eh? No fatted calf for our boy.' He winked at Makepeace as she stared at him surprise. 'Do not worry. We are party to the joke, you see?'

'Oh.' Makepeace managed to smile, despite her bewilderment. 'That is . . . good. How . . . did you find out?'

'Symond told us by letter.' The handkerchief-thrower leaned forward confidingly. 'Yours is not the only family betting on both dogs in the fight. I know of a few younger sons who have "turned to Parliament" with their kin's secret blessing. If the rebels win, and the Fellmotte estates are confiscated, Parliament will gratefully give them to Symond, so at least the lands stay in the family. That's the Fellmotte plan, eh?'

It took Makepeace a second or two to understand what he meant. So some noble families were playing a dangerous game, to make sure that their ancestral lands were not lost to their bloodline even if the 'wrong' side won. It made sense for some noble families to take such drastic measures, but she was quite certain that Symond's defection was real. The Fellmottes' rage and shock had seemed perfectly genuine.

'He has written to you?' This was intriguing. 'Have you written back to him?'

'We let him know the gossip, to stop him perishing from boredom,' said the handkerchief-thrower. 'He says he is surrounded by wild-eyed Puritans—a grim-jawed pack who pray at him day and night, and won't let him have any fun.'

Idiots, thought Makepeace. *Sending the 'gossip' of court to an enemy officer. No wonder he wanted to stay in contact with these geese!*

For a moment she considered shattering Symond's lie and telling his friend the truth. But if she did, a chance might be lost.

'Then you can help me!' she said instead. 'I need to contact my cousin urgently. Can you tell me where a letter will find him?'

'Do your family not have your own ways of reaching him?' He looked surprised.

'We did, but that is all undone . . . The messenger he chose is dead –' Makepeace thought that she had better leave the lie vague—'and now we must contact him urgently. There are many matters he was handling for the family and he is the only one that knows the details.'

'If you give me a message, I can add a few lines to my next letter,' he suggested, a slight frown of suspicion creasing his brow.

'Forgive me—I cannot! They are delicate family matters . . .' Makepeace hesitated, then decided to risk her trump card. Discreetly she pulled Lady April's signet ring out of her pocket, and showed it so that only her two companions could see it. 'I am here on behalf of my betters.'

The handkerchief-thrower instantly went grey with fear. Clearly he had lost none of his terror of Lady April. If she was the spymistress for the Fellmotte clan, this was hardly surprising. Makepeace felt an unexpected thrill at the reaction. It was a strange and heady thing, this borrowed power. It was giddying to cause fear instead of feeling it.

'I do not know where he can be found,' he said hastily, 'but he has told me where to send letters. I address them to "Mistress Hannah Wise" and send them to a farm just north of Brill, belonging to a family called Axeworth. I think somebody else collects them from there.'

'You are very kind,' said Makepeace primly. 'I know I can trust you to tell nobody.' She was putting away the ring when she felt a tug at her sleeve. Helen had reappeared at her side.

'Judith—His Majesty is ready for us.'

Makepeace jumped, and it took a moment for her to understand what Helen had just said. *His Majesty is ready for us.* Not 'me', but 'us'. She had an audience with the King of England.

Panic overwhelmed her as Helen gripped her gloved hand and pulled her across the quad to an open door. They stepped into a cool darkness, scented with rose-water, past walls painted white, and wood panels the colour of dark honey. Courtiers stepped aside to let them through. As Makepeace passed them she could smell their perfumes, rich with cinnamon and musk.

The room beyond was richly appointed, with a high ceiling, tall windows, silk hangings and some crests mounted high on the walls. Several people stood around the room, but in the centre sat a man in a high-backed chair. King Charles I of England, Scotland and Ireland. Makepeace dropped her gaze quickly, too used to finding herself before the Fellmottes. If he looked into her eyes, would he not see right through all her lies? If the Fellmottes could do so, then surely God's appointed could do the same?

'Kneel,' murmured Helen quietly. Makepeace followed her lead, and dropped to her knees.

It was only as Helen began to give an account of their journey, and pass over documents and reports to the royal attendants, that Makepeace dared to glance furtively at the King from under her lashes.

He was a little man, as Lord Fellmotte had told Sir Anthony. There was something stiff and careful about the way he moved. In fact, he was stiff altogether, as if ready to bristle at the world for noticing his littleness. His beard was elegant and pointed. There were bows on his shoes. His face was mournful, lined, and marked by a rigid uncertainty. There was something tense and waiting to happen in his manner—perhaps outrage, the baby sibling of dignity.

The King listened to Helen's report, and nodded.

'Inform our friends that all will be repaid once the rebellion is crushed. In striking at me, the rebels strike at God Himself—they cannot prosper. Their defeat is certain. And rest assured we shall remember who our friends have been, and who have proven treacherous or backward in offering help.' Then, to Makepeace's dismay, he turned to face her. 'Mistress Grey, I believe you too carry reports for me?'

For a moment Makepeace's mind went utterly blank. The King's habit of describing himself as 'we' was all too like the Fellmottes. But her skin did not crawl as he looked at her, nor did she feel as if she were being peeled like a fruit. The King could not see into her soul.

She stumbled through an account of Symond's defection, and produced his letter. The King read it, and the jaw behind his narrow beard tightened.

'Please carry my respects back to Lord Fellmotte,' he declared coolly, 'but impress upon him that this charter *must* be recovered. Our good name is at stake, as well as that of the Fellmotte family. Is it known where the traitor Symond Fellmotte has gone?'

'Not yet,' answered Helen, 'but we shall find out who his friends were at court. Then we may discover who is harbouring him.'

'Go with my blessing, and bid others offer you what help they can,' answered the King. 'In the meanwhile, we are not insensible of the service you have both done our nation this day.'

He slightly extended a hand, allowing each of them in turn to move forward and touch his fingertips briefly. It was said the touch of a king's hand could cure scrofula, but his fingers felt human, and slightly moist with the heat.

Makepeace felt a little dizzy, but not with awe at the man before her. It was as if History were walking at his heels like a vast, invisible hound. It followed him, but he did not command it. Perhaps he would tame it. Or perhaps it would eat him.

Helen wanted to stay at the college, to learn all the latest news from those recently arrived from other parts of the country. Apparently she was also keen to visit an astrologer she knew.

'They say that a few months ago Prince Rupert saw fire fall from the sky near here,' she explained, 'and break apart with a great crack into balls of flame. Everyone agrees that is an omen of *something*, but nobody can decide what it means. I would like to have a learned man unravel it, in case it will affect the war.' She gave a wry but rather forced smile. 'What a time we live in—even the stars are falling.'

Helen had, however, found somebody who knew of Benjamin Quick.

'They have not seen him lately,' she said, 'but they knew where he was staying a few weeks ago. If you are lucky you may find him there still. He is living with a chandler near Quater Voys, just opposite the penniless bench.' Helen fumbled in her pockets, and pulled out a small, corked bottle. 'Before you go, take a spoonful of our hostess's cure! There is disease abroad, remember?'

Surprised, Makepeace obeyed. The 'cure' tasted of sweet, strong wine, nutmeg and other spices. The moment was bittersweet too. Helen had doubted Makepeace's intentions and abilities at first, but now that they were safely arrived she seemed determined to mother her.

'Carry this.' A small muslin bag was placed in Makepeace's hand. 'Keep it close to your face, to purify the air you breathe and keep yourself safe.' The bag rustled when Makepeace pinched it, and when she held it up to her nose, she could smell dried flowers. 'This city is full of foul airs—no wonder everyone is falling sick!'

Quater Voys turned out to be a great, crowded crossroads, thronged with a lot of the market-day visitors. Makepeace found the chandler's shop, with its hanging yellow-white candles, and entered. A little old woman with a bitter mouth was sweeping the floor.

'I'm looking for Master Benjamin Quick, the doctor,' Makepeace said quickly. 'Is he still living here?'

'Just about,' said the old woman with a sour little grimace. 'But not for long, I fancy. If you hurry, you might just catch him. Up in the attic room.'

Makepeace hurried up a creaking flight of stairs, and then scaled a ladder to the attic. Wide-eyed children watched her silently as she climbed.

The attic was dusty and dark, with a low, slanting roof, and one tiny window to let in the light. For a moment she thought it was unoccupied. She saw a travelling chest and a few books tied into a bundle with cord, next to a grimy, unkempt flock bed. Her first feeling was relief. The doctor could not have left yet. He would hardly depart without his belongings.

Then she realized that some of the rucks and rumples in the bed linen were not cloth. One beaky fold was actually a pale face, so bloodless that it was almost greyish. Long hands were just visible, gripping the blanket. There were faint, purplish blotches on his cheeks and hands.

At the same time the smell hit her. It was a stink of disease and fouled clothing. Was he dead? No, there was a slight tremor in his hands, an awkward bob of his Adam's apple.

'Master Benjamin Quick?' whispered Makepeace.

'Who is there?' His voice was very faint, but slightly irritable. 'Is my soup . . . ready yet? Will it reach me before I meet the Author of my Being?'

'I am sorry,' said Makepeace.

'Sorry' was a weak word for her emotions. It was all she could do to swallow down her pity and disappointment. Everything Makepeace had braved to reach Oxford had been in vain. The man before her was dying. His fingernails were blue as a drowned man's, and the sockets around his eyes were hollowed and dark. She was sorry for him, sorry for herself, sorry for James.

'You're not the chandler's girl,' said Quick, frowning and turning his dim eyes to peer in her direction.

'No,' said Makepeace sadly. 'My name is Makepeace Lightfoot.'

'You have my sympathy,' said the doctor faintly. He squinted. 'Are you some sort of Puritan? What do you want with me?'

'I came to ask you to help a patient.'

'Patients . . . have proven bad for my health.'

The doctor coughed again.

'Is there nothing that can be done for you?' asked Makepeace, still scavenging for scraps of hope.

'We should . . . call a doctor,' mumbled Quick, deadpan, then gave a faint, breathless chuckle. 'Ah, no, we have one. It is . . .

camp fever. I have seen enough cases . . . I know . . . nothing to be done.' His gaze slid off her blearily, and then he looked confused and frightened. 'Where are you? Are you gone?'

Makepeace was still lurking near the hatchway. Her little bag of dried flowers suddenly seemed a pitiful defence against the foul airs of the attic. She did not know how easily the fever might jump from one person to another. Furthermore, she had been given a bath barely two nights before, so her pores might still be open to every disease.

Yet she could not bear to leave the doctor to die alone. She drew closer, until the doctor's wandering gaze fixed upon her, and she saw a hint of relief in his hollowed face.

'I am still here.' Makepeace stooped to pick up a wooden box by the side of his bed. 'Is this your medical box? Is there nothing I can give you?'

'Tried . . . everything to stop the epidemic.' It was not clear whether the doctor had even heard her. 'Killed the cats and dogs, ordered the beer boiled longer, visited the sick . . .' His eyes came to rest on a pile of pieces of paper, and he gave a small cough of a laugh. Even from a distance Makepeace could see that they were like the tickets given to the whitebaker: promissory notes from the King. 'I was . . . paid well for it all. I die a rich man. Rich in promises, anyway.'

This long speech seemed to have unravelled him, and he coughed for a while, his entire frame shaking. His gaze settled on Makepeace again, and he blinked, as if he were having trouble seeing her.

'Who are you?' he asked dustily. 'Why are you here?'

Makepeace swallowed. She did not want to torment a dying man with questions, but there were other lives in the balance.

'You saved a man who said he was haunted. You took the ghost out of him. How did you do it?'

'What? I . . .' The doctor made slight gestures with his hands, as if turning a screw on something invisible. 'A device . . . hard to explain.'

'Doctor.' Makepeace leaned forward, and willed her voice to pierce the fog of his fever. 'I am trying to save my brother. He has five ghosts in his head, and if they are not taken out he will lose his mind. Please—where is the device? Is it here? Could someone else use it?'

'No . . . it needs a skilled hand . . .' Quick stretched out a hand towards a pile of his belongings near his bed. For a moment she thought he was pointing out the device, but then she realized that he was vainly reaching for a small, battered bible. She picked it up and placed it on his chest so that he could curl his hands around it. 'Why do you ask me this now? I shall soon be . . . a ghost . . . myself.' Every word clearly cost him effort. 'My research . . . so many hopes and plans.' He looked at the pile of tickets again. 'At the end . . . nothing but empty promises.' The hands gripping the bible shook, and she realized that he was terrified.

A ghost. An idea struck Makepeace, and it chilled her as if the sun had gone in.

'Could you have saved my brother?' she blurted out. 'If you were well, could you have done it?'

'What?' Quick's gaze fogged with confusion.

Makepeace swallowed, mustering her courage, and staring into the snake eyes of her own plan. The very idea of it made her feel sick, but James's life was at stake, possibly even his soul.

'I can save you if you promise to save him,' she said.

Quick stared at her, and made a faint, wispy sound in his throat.

'When you die, I can catch your spirit before it floats away,' said Makepeace, her heart beating faster. 'I can keep you in this world. You would haunt me. You would go where I go, and be my passenger, but you would still see and feel and think, through me. I could even let you use your skills through me sometimes.'

'Monstrous . . . impossible . . .' Quick looked alarmed by her now, but there was also a tiny, agonized gleam of hope.

'It *is* possible!' insisted Makepeace. 'I have done it before!'

'You are . . . already haunted?' The doctor's brow creased with suspicion, doubt and superstitious fear.

'The other ghost is a brute, but an honest one,' Makepeace explained hastily, wishing she had not mentioned her other lodger. 'He is my friend.' She felt miserable and cruel, but she persisted. 'Could you save my brother? Will you save him?' She was not even sure whether she wanted to hear a 'yes' or a 'no'.

'Are you devil-sent?' Quick's voice was almost inaudible.

'I am sent by desperation!' Makepeace's nerves were fraying at last, worn thin by fear and lost sleep. 'Do you think I *want* you in my head for the rest of my life? Do you think I offer this lightly?'

There was a long pause. Now the doctor's breathing and eyelid flickers were so slight that several times Makepeace thought that they had stopped altogether.

'God help me,' whispered the dying man. For a moment Makepeace thought this was a 'no', but then she met his eye and she realized that it was a 'yes'. 'God forgive me for this! Save me . . . and I will save your brother.'

And God help me too, thought Makepeace, as she took his hand. His breathing was growing fainter, and his eyes seemed to look through her.

'When the time comes, do not be frightened,' she said very

softly. 'Find me, move towards my face. I will let you in . . . but you must approach gently, like a guest. If you rage and rend, Bear will tear you to pieces.'

There was a long silence, during which second after second fell away into the unforgiving past. The moment where life became death was so quiet, so still, that most people would have missed it. Makepeace did not, though, because she was a Fellmotte. She saw the tiny, shadowy wisp of vapour seep from the doctor's mouth into the air, and begin twitching in smoky distress.

It looked very much like the Infiltrator spirit that had crept out of Lord Fellmotte. Perhaps all souls looked the same when they were naked, stripped of flesh and blood, finery or buckskin.

Makepeace was suddenly terribly afraid. But she had come so far, so very far, and already dared so much. She leaned forward, fighting her urge to recoil from the foul airs of the sickbed, and brought her face close to the thrashing ghost.

She drew in a deep, shivering breath, and felt the doctor's spirit slide coldly in through her nose and mouth, and into her throat.

CHAPTER 23

There was a terrible rushing cacophony inside Makepeace's head, like clouds at war.

Something banged sharply against the back of her head. Makepeace was staring up at the rafters, where spider-webs hung thick with dust. She had fallen backwards, she realized. There was a tightness across her chest that left her gasping for air.

She could hear the doctor yelling, his voice impossibly distant and yet tingling with closeness. God in Heaven! What Hell is this?

At the same time there came the bass rumble of Bear's growl, confused and menacing.

'Both of you!' Makepeace whispered, struggling for breath. 'Calm down! There is room for everyone!' She sincerely hoped that this was true.

There is a Thing in here! screamed the doctor. It is not even human! A wild animal!

'I told you as much!'

When you said 'brute', I thought you meant a brutish man! declared Quick. An uncouth oaf!

'No—an animal! A bear!'

I can see that now!

Makepeace struggled to sit up. She did not look towards the doctor's corpse. Things were quite confusing enough already with his thin voice echoing in her head. Her head reeled, and it was all she could do not to throw up.

She clutched at her head. At the same time she reached for

Bear in her mind, and imagined running her fingers through thick, dark fur. He quietened a bit, but there was still a lurching, dangerous storminess to him. Bear did not trust the doctor, she could tell. Bear did not like his soul's smell.

Makepeace was startled back into her senses by creaking footsteps down below.

'Young woman, what are you yelling about?' It was the old woman down in the chandler's shop. 'What is happening up there?'

Not a word about my death! hissed the doctor urgently. Or that old cat will kick you out and steal everything down to my shirt. She'd have done so already if she wasn't afraid I'd cough on her. The doctor sounded a lot more coherent, now that he was free of his fever-ridden body.

'Sorry!' Makepeace called down. 'I was upset . . . the doctor was talking about hellfire . . .'

Oh, thank you so much. That will do wonders for my enduring reputation. You could not come up with another story?

Well, never mind. You must go through my pockets, and take everything you find. My books too—and my tools and purse are hidden under the mattress.

'If I walk out with my arms full, I'll be hanged for theft!' hissed Makepeace. 'I'll carry as much as I can hide beneath my cloak. Where's your device for pulling out ghosts?'

Ah, the cranial elevator. It is in a thin black pouch inside my box of surgical tools. I shall need my books, too, if I am to be of use to your brother. And there are some things that I would not wish to leave behind—my good gloves, my boots, my pipe . . .

'I'll take the tools, your purse and a few of the books,'

Makepeace said quickly, 'but none of your clothes. If I die of your sickness, then both our ghosts will be left without a house. And forgive me, but I don't smoke a pipe.'

Nauseous, she slid a hand under the mattress, trying not to notice the way the doctor's arm lolled as she did so. Her fingers found hard corners, and she pulled out a slender wooden box and a leather-bound notebook, and hid them in her skirt pocket. His purse had only a few scant coins, but she took it anyway. The books she tucked under one arm, so that they were concealed by her cloak. As an afterthought she took the paper tickets as well. They might prove to be empty promises, but paper itself was valuable.

As Makepeace descended again, past the silent children and the chandler's wife, she was sure she must look guilty. The sour-faced woman gave her a searching look.

'Still alive, is he?' she asked with slight disdain.

'Sinking, I think,' said Makepeace.

'You don't look too good yourself.' The woman narrowed her eyes, suspicious, and withdrew a step. 'Sodden with sweat, you are, and a feverish look too. You can keep your distance, and get yourself out of my house!'

Grateful for the chance, Makepeace obeyed and hurried out into the daylight.

I suppose there is no chance of hearty tot of rum? suggested the doctor as Makepeace hurried along through the streets. I think I could make use of one.

'An innocent young maid like me?' Makepeace whispered sarcastically.

I can recommend its fortifying virtues on medical grounds. O Almighty have mercy, this is intolerable! You walk without symmetry—this jolting—do you need to *lollop* so? I am seasick! And your posture is dreadful, I can feel every kink in your spine . . .

'If you talk too much,' Makepeace murmured, 'you will wear yourself out.' Bear certainly seemed to tire after too much exertion, and she found herself hoping that the doctor was the same.

She reached her lodgings, where Peg was happy to leave 'Judith' in charge of the belongings for a while. Makepeace was relieved to find herself alone, or as alone as she could be. She sank down on to the bed, her head full of clamour.

The doctor was shouting again, with a mixture of panic and imperiousness in his tone.

You there! What are you doing! Come back here—I'm talking to you!

'There is no point shouting at him!' Makepeace muttered through gritted teeth. 'You'll just anger and confuse him more! He cannot understand you. He's a bear!'

I'm not a perfect simpleton! retorted the doctor. Of course I am not wasting words on the bear! I am talking to the other!

Makepeace wobbled, and put out a hand to support herself as the doctor's words sank in.

'What?' she whispered. 'What other?'

There is another spirit in here. A third human spirit, as well as you and I. Are you saying that you did not know?

'Are you certain?' hissed Makepeace.

As sure as I can be of anything in this maelstrom!

Someone was there just now—fled from me—slithered away and hid—would not answer me. But she is still there somewhere.'

'*She?*' croaked Makepeace.

Yes. It was a woman, I am sure of it. A smoky, maimed thing. Savage, frightened.

Makepeace covered her mouth with both her hands and heard herself make a small, lost noise. Her mind filled with a nightmare image that she had tried so hard to forget. A savage, swooping thing with an all too familiar face, that had clawed and clawed to get into her mind, even as she tore it apart . . .

Mother.

Makepeace had tried not to think about her for years. Now memory came for her, dragging a smoky train of shadow, sorrow, guilt and bewilderment.

Makepeace had hoped against hope that the whole episode had just been a nightmare. Deep down she had always feared that she really had shredded Mother's ghost. But it had never occurred to her that the spirit might have succeeded in invading her mind.

Perhaps it had. Perhaps all this while Mother's mauled spirit had been lurking in the dark corners of Makepeace's head, and . . . doing what? Gnawing away at the soft parts of her mind like a worm in the wood? Hating her, and waiting for a chance for vengeance?

'Where is she?' asked Makepeace in panic. 'What is she doing? What does she look like?'

I do not know! exclaimed the doctor. It was but a glimpse, and I saw her with my mind, not my eyes. She is gone now, I do not know where.

· · · · ·

Makepeace was finding it hard to breathe. She pressed her hands against the side of her head and tried to concentrate. Her chest had tightened with fear, but also an agonizing yearning. A foolish, desolate part of her felt that a crazed and vengeful Mother was better than no Mother at all.

Perhaps Makepeace had been given a second chance to make her peace with Mother. Even if Mother was a thing of terror now, perhaps Makepeace could soothe and calm her, the way she had soothed and calmed Bear.

What is wrong with you? demanded the doctor.

'I may know who she is,' Makepeace admitted.

Who, then? he asked. A friend? An enemy?

'I do not know which she is now.' Makepeace's words tumbled out. 'She was my . . . my mother, but we parted badly and . . . death sometimes changes people.'

If the she-ghost really was Mother, however, she had lain quiet for three years. She did not seem to have set about eating Makepeace's brain 'like the meat of an egg'. Was it possible— just possible—that Mother's ghost did not mean her harm, after all?

Makepeace recalled the sudden, well-timed pinch to her arm, which had woken her in the stable. It had allowed her to overhear her host's treachery, and possibly stop Bear eating the horses. She remembered her most recent dream—sitting on the unseen woman's lap, and watching her scratch out an 'M'. It was the only letter Mother had ever learned to write. 'M' for 'Margaret'.

Perhaps Mother was still on her side. Makepeace's surge of hope was more painful than her fear.

What if she is an enemy? The doctor's sharp tones cut through her reflections. *What can you do about it?*

The question shocked Makepeace back into her senses. She needed to plan for the worst, however sick the thought made her. What could be done about a foe already inside someone's head? It crossed her mind that she had recruited the doctor to deal with just that kind of problem. If he could banish ghosts from James, then perhaps *in extremis* he could do the same for her.

Makepeace laid out the late doctor's belongings on the bed, and examined them. With some trepidation, she opened the pouch containing the 'cranial elevator'. It was an alarming-looking metal device, its long, thin drill attached to a metal crossbar with jointed extensions.

Be careful with that, said the doctor.

'How does it work?' she asked.

Do you really have the stomach for such matters? Well, it is rather ingenious. The drill is used to bore into the patient's skull, and then the bridge section is braced against his head, so that when the screw is turned, the drill-part is slowly withdrawn, raising the dented part of the skull—

'You need to make a hole in the patient's head?' exclaimed Makepeace. She was thinking of James again now, and was not sure what horrified her more: the thought of drilling holes in him, or the prospect of trying to do so while he was strengthened by angry, powerful ghosts.

Of course. How else would you relieve the pressure on the brain?

'What if the patient does not . . . like the idea?'

Well, of course you would have a couple of stout fellows

hold him down. You might want to put some lint in his ears as well. Some patients dislike the sound of drill grinding bone.

'Is that the only way?' Makepeace felt misgivings tingling in the pit of her stomach. She had no 'stout fellows' to back her up. 'Can you not use the device . . . from a distance, somehow?'

From a distance? Of course not! This is a surgical device, not a wand!

'What did you mean when you said the drill raised the dented part of the skull?' Makepeace asked slowly. There was a pause, and when the doctor continued, Makepeace thought she detected a slight defensiveness.

I understood that you were acquainted with the details of my earlier case. A soldier was struck a glancing blow to the head by a bullet, at such a distance that it only dented his skull. The pressure on his brain, and build-up of blood inside the skull, caused him to become wild and fanciful, so that he was convinced that he was haunted. Once I raised the dent and dealt with the haemorrhage inside, he returned to his senses . . .

'You lied to me!' gasped Makepeace. 'You promised to save my brother! He has five ghosts inside him! Real ghosts, not blood on the brain! How will your drill help with that?'

Well, how was I to know that you were being so literal?

'I was offering to house your soul after your death!' retorted Makepeace. 'It might have crossed your mind!'

I was hardly at my best! The fever was heavy on me, and I was in the throes of mortal terror!

Remembering the hazy, unfocused face of the doctor before his demise, Makepeace could not deny that he had a point. It might have been a misunderstanding, and even if he had deliberately misled her, could she blame a desperate, dying man for clutching at a chance straw?

She still felt sickened and furious, but mostly with herself. She had fought so hard to avoid having more ghosts poured into her head. In a moment of folly she had taken one on willingly, and all for nothing.

I shall do everything I can, of course, the doctor continued, still sounding a little nervous. If there is a way to help your brother, you have a better chance of finding it with me than without me. I doubt any chirurgeon will ever have a better chance to study this spiritual phenomenon.

'This changes everything,' Makepeace said. 'I need to think.' Whatever happened, she needed to leave Oxford. If the Fellmottes sent agents to the King's court, they would hear about the young girl with the cleft in her chin. So where should she go?

She could head west, deeper into Royalist territory and away from the front line, perhaps into the heart of Wales itself. She might escape notice there in some small village, but that would mean abandoning James. The longer he was left full of ghosts, the less likely it was that his own personality would survive. Even though the doctor was unable to banish spirits, she could not give up on saving James.

She could try to cross the lines and flee deep into Parliamentarian territory. The Fellmottes might be less willing to send agents after her there, but it would look bad for her if the rebels ever found out about her short career as a bullion-smuggler.

What kin did she have to call on? Her aunt and uncle

presumably still lived in Poplar. But her aunt and uncle had given her away and, besides, London and Oxford were glaring at each other across the map, each one bristling in readiness for the other's attack. The roads in between would be thick with armies, road-blocks, earthworks and spy-hunters.

Reluctantly Makepeace allowed herself to consider the option she had been trying to avoid. She had one kinsman who belonged to neither the Poplar parish nor the powerful Fellmotte cadre.

Symond.

He had murdered Sir Anthony, but then again Sir Anthony had been a shell full of ghosts. Makepeace despised Symond for abandoning his friends and his regiment, but the two of them had the same secrets and foes. The enemy of her enemy was not her friend, but he might prove a useful ally of convenience.

Most important of all, he had been brought up as a Fellmotte heir. He might well know more about the Fellmotte ghosts than she did. He might even have some idea whether it was possible to flush the ghosts out of James.

It would be a risk. The last Fellmottes to trust Symond had ended up dead or haunted. But not so long ago, Symond and James had been close as twins, and Makepeace could only hope that not all of that affection had been feigned. She would also need to give him some good, solid reasons not to betray her.

'Doctor,' she said at last. 'Do you know a good way of leaving Oxford? I need to travel to Brill, and then onwards into land held by Parliament.'

Why in the world would you want to do that? That whole area is ragged from raids by both sides. And crossing the lines to enter land held by the enemy is an absurd idea! I died recently, and I am in no hurry to enjoy the experience again just yet.

'There is a man I must find, Dr Quick.' Makepeace took a deep breath. 'And it is not safe for us in Oxford. Have you ever heard of the Fellmottes?'

The noble house, with fingers in every pie and gallants in every knightly order? Of course I have!

'They are more than that! They are hollow, Doctor. They can hold ghosts inside them, just as I am housing you. I am of their blood—I have their gift—and the Fellmottes have plans for me, wicked plans. I have run from them, but they will come after me.'

You juggling little Jezebel! You never told me that! When you came to tempt my soul, you might have mentioned that I would be trapped inside a renegade and runaway, pursued by one of the most powerful families in England!

'There was scarcely time!'

Well, I am sorry to have been precipitate in my demise! How thoughtless of me to have died so quickly! Why did you run from the Fellmottes, anyway? Did you steal from them? Tell me that you—we—are not with child and fleeing from disgrace?

'No!' hissed Makepeace. 'I was running for my life! They would have filled me full of ghosts—Fellmotte ghosts—until there was no room for *my* soul. And that would have been the end of me.'

There was a pause.

I cannot tell whether you are telling the truth, **the doctor said, sounding intrigued rather than offended.** How interesting. I am inside your mind, but not quite inside your thoughts. Nor are you inside mine, I must suppose. We are still somewhat mysterious to each other.

It was true, Makepeace realized. Bear's mind had no words, but she felt his emotions like vast wind-buffets. She could hear the doctor like a voice in her head, but his thoughts and feelings were fleet and difficult to read, like a glancing moth-flutter against her skin.

Maybe souls learned to read each other over time. The Fellmotte ghosts had had lifetimes to hone their cooperation, so that they could work together fluidly and rapidly. Perhaps they eventually saw each other's thoughts daylight-plain. Or perhaps they each still had a nugget of secret self that they hid from each other.

The Fellmotte ghosts also seemed to be able to raid and rifle the memories of their living host. Clearly the doctor could not read Makepeace's memories yet. Perhaps he would, though, in time.

We must forget this plan of travelling to Brill, **the doctor muttered.** Heading into enemy territory is out of the question. We must find a way to make terms with the Fellmottes. We cannot afford to have enemies that powerful.

'No!' hissed Makepeace. 'There is no talking to them! And that is not your decision to make!'

This is ridiculous, **murmured the doctor, and for a moment Makepeace was not sure whether he was addressing her or talking to himself.** Listen, young woman. I cannot possibly leave all decisions to you. Like it or not, there are now four souls aboard this fleshly ship, and we are in sore need of a captain. As far as I can see . . . I am the only possible candidate.

'What?' exclaimed Makepeace. 'No! This is my body!'

We are all its denizens now, **persisted the doctor.** Your age and sex make you unsuited to command, not to mention that you have made fugitives of us all! And our other travelling companions are a half-mad banshee of an intruder, and a bear! I am the only person fit to lead this circus!

'How dare you!' Anger rose in Makepeace like a storm. This time it was not Bear's wrath but her own, and it frightened her. She could feel no limit to it.

That is scarcely a reasoned response—and we must settle this rationally! The doctor also seemed to be losing his temper. You have obviously been blundering at every turn! You did not even know how many ghosts you were hosting! You should be grateful that I am willing to step in!

'One more word,' breathed Makepeace, 'and I will drive you out! I can! I will!' She did not know for certain that she could, but the words felt true as she said them, with Bear's growl throbbing in her blood. 'I ran from the all-powerful Fellmottes—from hearth and home, from *everything*—because I would not be their puppet. And I have nothing, but I have my own self. And that is *mine*, Doctor. I shall not be the Fellmottes' toy, and I will not be yours. Play tyrant with me, and I shall hurl you out of doors, and watch you melt away like smoke in the wind.'

There was another long pause. She could feel the doctor's emotions shift, but she could not tell what they were, or what the movements meant.

You are very tired, **he said slowly.** You are worn to a rag, and I had not noticed. We . . . have both had a trying day, and I have chosen a bad time for this conversation.

You are right, I am lost without you. But if you take a moment to think calmly, you will realize that you need me, too. Your mother's ghost is possibly dangerous, and certainly mad, and roaming around inside your walls. You cannot see her. So you need an ally, one who can do more than growl. An ally who can watch out for her, and tell you what she is doing.

Makepeace bit her lip. Little as she liked to admit it, the doctor had a point.

If you have your heart set upon this plan of yours, he went on, then let us see if we can find a way to survive it. Brill is north-east of here, and only ten miles away as the crow flies, but that distance matters.

Our troops hold a goodly number of garrisoned towns and fortified houses nearby, to guard the roads and bridges around Oxford—Islip, Woodstock, Godstowe, Abingdon and so forth—but if you head east as far as Brill, you are wandering outside the protective circle. There is a great house at Brill that is still in the hands of the King's men, thank God, but a good deal of the countryside around them is pocked with Parliamentarians.

If you plan to walk there, you will not need to cross any bridges, so we may avoid being stopped and questioned. But it will be perilous travelling cross-country. It seems this is a war fought in paddocks and roadsides. Ambush may be crouched behind any hedgerow or cattle trough.

Makepeace had to concede that all of this was useful information. The doctor was arrogant, but very far from stupid.

'I will need to plan,' Makepeace agreed. 'I will need directions before I leave . . .' She was starting to realize just how much fatigue was wearing on her nerves.

What a leaden thing you are! murmured the doctor. I

believe you are quite sick from weariness. When did you last sleep properly? He sounded rather medical and disapproving.

'We have been dodging Parliament's boys across several counties,' Makepeace retorted. 'I stole a wink or two when I could.'

Then for God's sake sleep now, woman! the doctor rapped out, not unkindly. If you do not sleep, then you will sicken, whether you catch the camp fever or not! And then where will we all be? If you are determined to captain this vessel, don't you at least have a duty to your passengers?

'I . . .' Makepeace hesitated.

She barely knew the doctor, and was halfway to deciding that she did not like him, but she could not go without sleep forever. Like it or not, Quick was right. She did need an ally. And she could not recruit his help without admitting her predicament.

'I . . . have caught myself sleepwalking recently,' she confessed. 'I have been . . . afraid to sleep.'

Indeed? Quick seemed to digest the news. Another hand pulling your strings, perhaps? Or maybe a paw?

Makepeace did not answer. He did not press her, but after a few moments she thought she heard a sigh.

I shall stand sentry while you sleep, and wake you if you start to wander, or if either of the others try anything. Whatever I may think of your decision-making, you seem the lesser of three evils.

The thought of deep, uninterrupted sleep was so heady that Makepeace felt sick. As she lowered her heavy head on to the bed and closed her eyes, the darkness was almost unbearably sweet.

'Do be careful, Doctor,' she murmured, as she let herself relax. 'Bear does not like you. If he thought you were trying to hurt me . . . I'm afraid he might tear you to shreds.'

CHAPTER 24

'Judith?'

Makepeace opened her eyes with difficulty. They felt sticky. There was a sour taste in her mouth, and her throat was swollen. She wanted to close her eyes again.

A woman's face hovered over hers, indistinct in the dim room. Was it evening or dawn? For a moment Makepeace could not remember where she was, or what time of day it was likely to be.

'Judith, what ails you? You're grey as clay!'

Helen put out a hand towards Makepeace's forehead, but then pulled it back without touching her. She looked frightened and conflicted.

'Your brow is slick,' she murmured. 'I told you to keep that posy close to your face!'

'I am not ill!' Makepeace insisted, and tried to sit up. Her stomach convulsed, and she fell back again. 'I am just . . . tired.' She could not have fallen ill so fast, could she? It had been but a few hours since she had sat by Quick's deathbed.

Helen said nothing, but backed away and dropped into a chair, one hand over her mouth. Her eyes moved to and fro as she made calculations.

'I am leaving Oxford tonight,' she said at last. 'Peg has already left. I must head north towards Banbury—Symond Fellmotte's favourite tutor lives there, and might have news of him. Besides, there is talk of Parliament's forces moving against the city. If they start firing their mortars at the walls, I will be trapped here. I had thought to take you with me.'

'I need to leave as well!' said Makepeace quickly.

Helen was shaking her head.

'I cannot take you like this,' she said. 'It would be dangerous enough if we were both well. I cannot *carry* you, Judith. And it would be perilous to your health.'

Listen to me, said the doctor. She is right. You cannot move now.

You have the camp fever.

'No!' hissed Makepeace. 'I cannot be ill now! I *will* not be ill!'

You have no choice.

Makepeace was gripped by a terrible fear. Her mind had been under assault before, but now it was her body being attacked from within. She remembered Benjamin Quick's sickbed, and his soul steaming out of his husk.

'I am sorry,' said Helen, apparently with real regret. 'I will leave you the rest of the medicine, and half my purse—but I cannot stay for you. His Majesty's orders must come first.'

Do not panic, said the doctor. I am here, and I know the disease. You are younger and stronger than I was. We shall see you through this.

'Nobody must know that you are ill,' said Helen, as much to herself as to Makepeace. 'They are setting up quarantine cabins outside the city in Port Meadow. If your fever is reported, you will be dragged out there, and then I would not give three pips for your chances. I will pay the landlord to hold his tongue and keep you fed. I bet he'd do more than that for a fistful of actual coins.'

She scooped up her belongings, and raised her hood over her head.

'God protect you,' she said.

For a moment Makepeace could only think of bitter things

to say. But Helen was giving what she could, and owed 'Judith' nothing. Makepeace's gaze fell on the little patches that hid Helen's pockmarks. She had suffered a hearty tussle with the smallpox, then—a duel with Death. She could not blame Helen for fleeing from a sickroom and a sick city.

'You too,' she said.

Makepeace's eyelids drooped again for what seemed only a moment, but when she raised them again, Helen was gone.

I will not die. It was all Makepeace could think, and she thought it over and over. *I will not die. Not yet. I have not had my chance. I have not been all that I can be, or done all that I can do. Not yet. Not yet.*

At one point she became aware of the doctor's voice in her head, quietly and calmly insistent, as if talking to a small child.

That was a knock at the door, child. They have probably left food outside. You must get up now and go to the door. We need food, do we not?

And she rose, oh so groggily, and staggered to the door, her head pounding. There was a bowl of soup outside. Makepeace tried to stoop for it, but her knees gave way, and she sat down awkwardly. With great effort she dragged it into the room along the floor, then closed the door.

Eating was a marathon task. Her head was so heavy that she had to rest it against the wall, and kept nearly falling asleep.

Another spoonful, the doctor urged. Another. Come on, now. Here . . . let me use your hand. So Makepeace let him take control of her right hand, and guide a spoonful of soup to her mouth, then another, then another. She felt like a very young child, and for some reason this made her want to cry.

That is better, the doctor said. Now you need to take your

medicine. Under his guidance, Makepeace crawled to his medical bag, and pulled out a little green glass bottle. Just a little sip for now. More later.

The medicine made her mouth stickier, and the reeling of the room grew worse. Bear didn't like the smell.

'I can't stay here,' Makepeace whispered, as her blood galloped in her ears and temples.

You have no choice, said the doctor. Rest is your only possible cure. You must sleep or you will die.

Makepeace was not willing to die.

Her sense of time melted. There was another knock on the door, and she did not know why, because she had already eaten the soup. But this was new soup, the doctor told her. She had to open the door and eat the new soup. Why had they come with more? The doctor told her it was suppertime. Hours had passed. She ate the new soup. A little later, she had to move again to use the chamber pot. Shifting herself around the room was like dragging a hill.

The grooves of the floor pressed against her face. Why had she chosen to sleep like that? *Knock, knock.* New soup. The doctor was getting better at manoeuvring her hand and the soup spoon now. Even though she knew who was moving it and why, it was uncanny to watch her own limb moving like that.

'Why are you not dizzy too, Doctor?' she croaked.

I am, a little, he answered, but you are tied to the body more strongly than I am. Its ills affect you more powerfully. Your strength is your weakness. My weakness is my strength.

The doctor was talking about medicine again. Yes, it was medicine time. Drag, drag, dragging herself to his bag, sipping from the bottle.

She had fever-dreams. She could swear that there were others in the room, talking in hushed voices. But when she blinked her tired eyes and peered around her, she was alone.

Seconds stretched out like sleeping lions. Hours passed in a blink. The sky beyond the window was grey. Then it ached with sun. Then it was bruise-coloured and the light was fading. Then it was a pit of deep and blessed darkness. Then the whole cycle began again.

This made Makepeace anxious, but she could not remember why. There was something she needed to remember, and somewhere she needed to be, but they were lost in the fever fog of her brain.

Murmur, murmur, murmur. It was happening again. Imaginary voices holding a conversation above Makepeace's head. But this time they were *not* imaginary. Makepeace opened her eyes a little. The door was slightly ajar, and through the aperture she could see the face of her host and that of a thin woman, who Makepeace assumed was his wife.

'We can't keep hiding her and feeding her forever!' whispered the woman, glancing at Makepeace with a mixture of pity and exasperation.

'That red-haired lady paid us the first good coin we've seen in a month, and she asked us to tell *nobody* about the young lady until she is well again.' The landlord's words were staunch enough, but he wore a small, uncertain frown.

'But what if this fellow asking after her really *is* her friend, as he says he is? Let him take her! If anyone finds out we haven't reported a case of camp fever—'

'I tell you, it's no such thing! Look at her—no chills or rash.'

'The rash comes later, and you know it!' exclaimed his wife. 'She's barely been abed three days!'

'And she's been in town only four,' her husband answered sharply. 'Did you ever see camp fever take hold that fast?'

'Perhaps she brought it with her!' The wife sighed. 'You should not have turned the gentleman away. We must send someone after him, and tell him the truth.' The older woman stared down at Makepeace for a moment, her face tired, troubled and not unkind.

The door closed.

With a titanic effort, Makepeace managed to pull herself up to a sitting position, her back against the wall. Desperately she scrabbled for her slippery thoughts.

Three days. She had been sick for three days. That . . . was bad; she remembered that now. She was not supposed to be here still. There was danger. She had been noticed at court. If the Fellmottes came asking after her, somebody would remember seeing her with Helen. Somebody would remember where Helen had lodged.

A man had been asking after her. Perhaps the Fellmottes had already found her.

Steady, murmured the doctor.

'I . . .' She swallowed. 'We . . . We need to go. Now.'

You know you cannot. You have no strength.

'I must!' Makepeace's voice sounded croaky and husky, but talking made her feel more solid, more alive. 'I need to go before that man comes back . . . the Fellmottes . . .'

Calm yourself, said the doctor, and think. Our hosts will not send for him now. It is getting dark. If you sleep now, the fever may break, and then we can . . .

Makepeace tried to stand, and fell to her knees again.

Listen to me! Listen! The doctor sounded frustrated and regretful. *I understand your panic, but I am telling you as a doctor that you cannot—must not—exert yourself in your current state! You need to respect your limits. You do not know what is happening to your body right now, but I do.*

'Sorry, Dr Quick,' whispered Makepeace. She crawled on hands and knees over to her cloak, and dragged it awkwardly around her shoulders.

Well . . . at least take some of the medicine first, to defend yourself from the night humours.

'No. I . . . I always sleep after the medicine.' Her feet were like lumps of lead, but she pulled her shoes on to them anyway.

For God's sake, you can't even stand!

Makepeace took deep breaths, grabbing hold of the bed's footboard to steady herself, then hauled herself up . . .

. . . and stood.

Unsteadily she scooped up her bundle of belongings and the doctor's bag, and took step after wobbly step towards the door. She had to concentrate on placing each foot, but she reached the door, opened it, and stepped out on to the darkened landing.

Stop this madness! hissed the doctor. *Stop it!* He abruptly took control of her hand and tightened it around the door jamb to stop her continuing.

Angrily she wrested control back again. But now she was aware of a dangerous rustle of whispers at the back of her head. This time she was sure she was not imagining it.

Do whatever you must, the doctor said, and this time Makepeace knew he was not talking to her.

As Makepeace started to descend the stairs, she suddenly felt her left foot rebel against her. It twisted under her, obeying a will that was not her own, and she fell. The edges of the steps bit into her legs and side as she bumped and slid down the full length of the stairs, with a deafening rumble.

There were confused voices from the floors above and below. Bare footsteps approached. Figures appeared in nightclothes, tapers in hand.

She struggled to her feet, assisted by a couple of helping hands.

'Thank you . . . I . . . I need to leave . . .' Makepeace's voice sounded husky and thick.

'At this time of night?'

Makepeace could make out hints of suspicion in the blurry faces around her.

'Miss, are you well?'

She blundered past the hovering figures, and opened the front door. The cold of the night air made her gasp.

'Why, there she is!' came a call from the street. Too late, Makepeace noticed the whitebaker's wife, hurrying back towards the house. There was another figure at her side, a male figure.

A great wave of panic rose up inside Makepeace. She knew that silhouette. She knew it as well as her own name, and her childhood nursery rhymes. He stepped forward into the light, smiling up at her with his arctic eyes.

It was James.

CHAPTER 25

For a moment Makepeace stared in horror, then her survival instincts took over. She threw herself sideways, hoping to dodge past James, but he moved with lightning speed to seize her shoulders and pull her back.

Uncanny speed. Elder speed.

'There, now, Maud—what's wrong?' He was smiling again, with a smile that looked terribly wrong on his ugly-handsome face. 'Don't you recognize me?'

'Let me go!' In desperation she turned to the whitebaker's wife. 'He's not my friend!'

'You seemed to know him for a moment.' The other woman frowned in confusion.

'She did.' James forcibly wound one of Makepeace's arms through his, pinning it against his ribs. 'Maud, it's me—James! Your own brother!'

'Oh . . . now I think I can see the likeness.' The baker's brow cleared, and Makepeace could see the other faces showing signs of comprehension and relief.

'He's not my brother!' Makepeace tried to pull her arm free, then struck out at James's face with her free hand. 'For God's sake, listen!'

Voices were raised in concern. Restraining hands settled on Makepeace's arms and shoulders. Calming things were murmured to her. She was dragged into the parlour, and pushed down into a chair.

'There, now, flower.' The baker's wife still looked a little uneasy. 'Your brother has ordered a chair to carry you to his lodgings—you can stay here in the warm until it gets here.' She glanced at James. 'Do not take her words in ill part, sir,' she added in a whisper. 'It is just the fever talking. She will know you very well soon enough, I am sure.'

'Oh, she will,' said James. There was only one candle in the room, flickering on a little table by Makepeace's chair, and by its light his features seemed to quiver and dance.

'Listen! Listen to me!' Makepeace was still groggy, but she managed to pull herself up to a sitting position in her chair. '*He is not my brother.* Look into his eyes. Look at him! He's a devil. Don't leave me alone with him!'

The baker's wife's eyes flitted to James's face and rested there for a moment. Then her gaze dropped again, and she hurried from the room. Makepeace suddenly realized that even if she succeeded in convincing her landlady, it would achieve nothing. The strange man might be a devil, but he was taking a troublesome invalid out of the house.

The door clicked shut behind her. Brother and sister stared at one another.

'James,' said Makepeace, as quietly and steadily as she could. 'We promised we would never abandon each other, do you remember?'

'He did not abandon you,' said the Elder. 'He simply remembered his duty to the family at the last.'

'Did he? How many of you had to hold him down to help him "remember his duty"?'

'Is *that* what you imagined?' Again, a small rictus tremor

of amusement. 'You thought that the boy tried to fight us? No. He submitted himself willingly. Despite all his flaws and follies, he redeemed himself at the end.'

'I don't believe you,' whispered Makepeace.

'You should,' said the Elder. 'I know him better than you do now.'

Makepeace remembered the bean in the Twelfth Night cake, and the way James had thrown aside their plans to become Lord of Misrule. The allure of lordship, power and a title had called to James in a way that it never had to her. She could even imagine him convincing himself that he was strong enough to hold his own against a gaggle of ghostly guests.

'James, you idiot,' she whispered.

'You, on the other hand, abandoned your duty,' continued the Elder. 'Never mind your brother—what about *us*? What about your duty to *us*? And who helped you escape? Who placed that beast in you? *Who gave you that rope?*'

That was what was bothering the Elder most, Makepeace realized. Even now, the ghosts could still not believe that she might have managed her escape alone. She might have found it funny, if she had not been so angry.

'Oh, to Hell with all of you!' shouted Makepeace, reckless with rage. 'Are you still planning to take me back and fill me with Lord Fellmotte's ghosts? Are you all blind or stupid? *I'm rotting with the camp fever.* So go ahead, pour them in! We can all watch our skin blister and our brain melt together, till we're ready for a winding sheet!'

A moment later, Makepeace's throat contracted and trembled as another mind took control of it. With a horrible queasiness, she felt her own tongue squirm in her mouth without her permission.

'The girl is mistaken.' The voice came from her own throat, but it was not her own, and it rasped against her throat. 'She is not infected.'

'Ah,' said James, with every sign of satisfaction. '*There* you are, my lady.'

Makepeace gagged, trying to regain control of her throat, and feeling panicky and breathless. Who was talking through her? Its voice was cold and controlled. It did not sound like Mother. Nor did it slur or rave, like the attacking Mother-ghost of Makepeace's nightmare.

'She is only drugged with opiates,' continued the voice. 'The beast is weakened by the drug as well—its spirit is so tangled with that of the girl. There is another spirit too, a doctor of middling merit whose drugs we have used.'

Traitor! thought Makepeace as she understood at last. She had never been ill. She had been tricked into drugging herself into semi-consciousness. *Dr Quick, you liar! I should have let your sick old spirit soak into your deathbed like spittle.* She could feel his sallow ghost weighing down her arms, ready to stop her if she tried to struggle or run. *You snake*, she thought. *You idiot!*

'Hold her still, then,' said the Elder. He opened Dr Quick's bag, and drew out the little bottle of 'medicine'. He pulled its cork and sniffed at it carefully. 'This time we will take no chances.'

Bear! Makepeace called in her own head. *Bear!* But Bear was cloudy and confused. He was angry and could hear her, but he did not know where to swing his paws.

She tried to struggle as James came over and took hold of her chin, but the drugs and ghosts in her system weighed her down to the chair. She could feel the subtle malice of the doctor and the unknown other as they exerted all their willpower to stop her moving. The bottle was held to her lips, and a large dose poured into her mouth. She tried to spit it out, but she could feel her mouth and throat convulsing against her will, in an attempt to make her swallow.

'Good,' said James, his voice cold and distant. 'Once she is unconscious, my lady, begin scouring her out. We will need those other spirits removed if there is to be room for Lord Fellmotte's coterie.'

What? Dr Quick was shouting inside Makepeace's head. *That is not what we agreed, my lady! You promised that the Fellmottes would give me a place among them! Tell him! Tell him!* Makepeace's limbs suddenly felt slightly less leaden. The flustered doctor was no longer helping to pin her down.

With all the force she could muster, she kicked away the little table, toppling the candlestick.

She only meant to plunge the room into darkness, but the candle tipped back and fell against James's cloak. The flame caught a tasselled fringe, and hungry tongues of gold licked up the cloth. James yelled a curse from another century, and tried to tug loose the cloak's fastening at his throat. At the same time, Makepeace hurled herself out of the chair, and scrambled towards the door on hands and knees, spitting out the drug as she went.

The unknown Other was trying to claw at her mind, commandeer her limbs and sabotage her motions. However, now it had to contend with the doctor. Makepeace could sense the two of them wrestling with silent fury, as she grabbed her possessions and scrambled into the hall.

She dragged back the bolts of the front door, opened it and flung herself out on to the street. Behind her in the house she heard a cry of pain, and more swearing. Elders were ancient and terrible, but apparently still flammable.

Makepeace ran. The cold air stung some clarity into her groggy brain. Bear was with her now, staggering, grumbling but aware that she needed his strength. Her steps rang out on the cobbles, and soon another set of steps were echoing behind her, faster than hers and more deft.

She turned a corner, and found herself in an unexpected pool of light.

'Stop!' Half a dozen armed, scruffily dressed men stood in her way, each wearing a dingy sash, their leader holding a lantern aloft. It was a patrol of some sort. She made to duck round them, but one of them grabbed her by the arm. 'What's the hurry, mistress?'

Makepeace looked back, and saw James sprint forward into the candlelight, eyes alight with rage. He would sell them a story and talk them round in moments. Or he would if she gave him the chance.

'You said you would hide me!' she screamed at James, to his obvious astonishment. 'You said it was safe to go out on the streets! But now they've caught us! I don't want to go to the quarantine cabins!'

During the shocked silence that followed, Makepeace could see the patrol guards noticing her greasy pallor and shivers for the first time. The man who had grabbed her arm hastily released it, and the group moved to surround her, maintaining a slight distance.

'You have the fever?' the lantern-holder demanded.

'It's not my fault!' wailed Makepeace, and had no difficulty in letting tears come to her eyes. 'I don't want to die!'

James's face contorted with frustration. Within him, the ghosts were doubtless raging. Somehow the situation was slipping through their fingers.

'She is not ill,' he said quickly. 'My sister imagines things sometimes—'

'The girl's as grey as ash!' exclaimed the leader. 'She can barely stand! Sorry, friend—I don't blame you for trying to protect your sister, but we must follow orders.' He hesitated, then frowned a little. 'And you've been tending her, have you? Perhaps you'd better come with us as well.'

'Do you have any idea who I am?' snapped James. 'I have powerful friends that you would not wish to cross—'

'And we have orders,' retorted the guard.

James's ice-cold eyes flitted over the six guards with a calculating look. Perhaps the Elders inside him were weighing up whether to kill the whole patrol. They could do it, no doubt, but there would be consequences.

He turned, and fled into the darkness. One guard started to give chase, but soon gave up and returned.

'Sorry, mistress,' said the patrol leader, 'but we must take you to the huts outside the city. They will look after you there.' He sounded less certain than he wanted to be.

I really hope, murmured the doctor, that there is a second half to your plan.

Led through the darkened streets of Oxford, Makepeace felt as if she were walking through some cold underworld. At long last, Quick's drug was loosening its hold on her, but the scenes around her were dreamlike in themselves.

Makepeace had grown so used to Grizehayes. She had silently seethed against the house, but its long pauses, the contemplative chill of its high walls, and the wind's uninterrupted conversations with itself had become part of her bones. Even its sounds were familiar to her—she could identify every creak, clink or distant voice. Here, every distant laugh, bark, smash or hoof-clatter was unknown to her, and it made her feel unmoored.

The streets were darkening, but not yet dark enough for the link-boys to be out. Now and then a great college building loomed against the violet sky. A few candles flickered in windows.

Once, her escort led her to the side of the street, so that a strange procession could waltz past. There were gentlemen in fine clothes, with cobweb-fine lace at their collars, bows on their shoes, ostrich plumes on their hats and lustrous, curled hair down past their waists. They were making a show of dancing down the murky, slippery street. A gaggle of musicians swayed beside them, playing flutes and guitars, while behind them giggled a small horde of ladies, masked and hooded like courtesans.

Makepeace knew that these were living men and women, but there was something phantasmal about the parade, like the carvings of dancing skeletons she had sometimes seen in graveyards. Even knee-deep in disease and disaster, the court was determined to be the court. Silly, decadent, gorgeous and bold.

At the gates, the patrol exchanged muttered words with the sentries. The gates swung open, and the group emerged into a cold wind, the sky wide and unforgiving above them. The earthworks were even more vast in the fading light.

In spite of the sharp night air, and the sense of being exposed to the wide gaze of the sky, Makepeace felt slightly relieved. Oxford had made her feel trapped, she realized. She had already spent too much of her life imprisoned by ancient walls.

Ahead, the broad road continued towards the river, and Makepeace could see the soft glow of lanterns from guard posts on the bridge. She turned her head away from it, staring out across the lightless fields to her right. She blinked hard, welcoming her night sight.

Bear, I need your eyes. I need your nose. I need your night-wits and forest-wisdom.

'I'll walk you to the quarantine camp,' the patrol leader was saying. 'You'll need a lantern to light your steps.'

'Thank you,' Makepeace said quietly. 'But I will need no such thing.'

Before her escort could react, she sprinted from their little pool of lantern-light into the darkness, her feet pounding the soft, treacherous clods of the field. The guards called after her for a while, but did not pursue. In a lost city, how could they chase down every lost soul who became a little more lost?

PART FIVE: NO MAN'S LAND

CHAPTER 26

After the lantern-light, the darkness was shocking. Makepeace could hear nothing but her own panting. One of her feet twisted on a tussock and she nearly fell, biting her tongue as the shock jolted her spine. The next false step might turn her ankle, but if she hesitated she would be caught. She raced onward, deafened by her own panting, and put her trust in Bear.

And Bear, who had been confused by the crowds, the streets, the medicine and the human stinks, realized that now they were running. This was something that he understood. He wanted to drop to all fours, but sensed that Makepeace could not run that way.

Seen through Bear's eyes, the darkness was not complete. There were details just visible, storm-cloud grey against the black. Ruts and furrows. Hummocks of half-built earthworks. The outlines of trees far ahead flanking a path.

Makepeace zigzagged between the mounds, until she was running along the tree-lined path. Only when she was out of breath did she pause for a moment.

I think we have lost our pursuers, murmured the doctor.

Shut up, Dr Quick, Makepeace retorted in her head. Stealth was vital, so she did not dare answer out loud. Fortunately, the doctor seemed to hear her.

You have some right to be angry, he said. I acknowledge that I made an error of judgement.

I said, shut up. I need to concentrate. Makepeace swallowed her annoyance, and tried to focus on Bear's sense of smell. *Trust me, we're not alone out here.*

The guards would make no serious attempt to follow her, she suspected. A contagious girl was not their concern outside the city, and they had little chance of finding her in the dark. But James would not be deterred so easily. She was sure that he must have followed her and her escorts through the streets. Bribery, bullying or connections would see him through the gates. He would soon be hunting her.

If you want to make yourself useful, Doctor, Makepeace whispered grimly, *keep an eye out for 'my lady'.* That was what both the doctor and James had called the unknown spirit who had briefly taken control of Makepeace's powers of speech. Whoever she was, she was an enemy, and could strike at any time.

Tenderly Makepeace drew out of her pocket a little ivory object.

That is a diptych dial! The doctor sounded both scandalized and fascinated. How did you come by such a thing?

Makepeace did not bother to answer. The Fellmottes had been dismissive of Sir Thomas's precious collection of navigational devices. Taking it had barely felt like theft.

She had long since worked out the meaning of its etched lines and numbers. It was a miniature sundial, designed to be carried around in the pocket, and the inside of the lid was a moondial. Right now, however, she was more interested in its tiny compass.

'North-east to Brill,' she mouthed to herself, then turned the little box around until the arrow pointed to the 'N' and set off in the 'NE' direction.

The wind changed direction, blowing from behind her, and Bear uttered a deep growl. There was a smell on the wind. It was almost human. It was almost James.

Ahead, across the charcoal-grey field, Makepeace glimpsed the jet-black seam of a narrow, twisting river, almost hidden by trees. She headed for its concealing shadow, and followed it until she came to a place where the bank was rutted. It was a ford, but even with Bear's night sight she could not tell how deep the water was.

A solitary moorhen made her jump by bursting from cover and sputtering a line of white foam across the surface of the river. Somewhere far behind her, Makepeace heard a brisk snap of a twig, as if somebody had given a start.

There was no time for caution. Makepeace hitched her skirts to the knee, took off her shoes and stockings, and clambered down the bank, the cold mud giving perilously under her feet. Her first step into the icy river brought it up to her knees. As she waded across, the current threatened to knock her off balance, but she managed to scramble up the soft slippery bank on the other side.

She donned her shoes and socks again, then carefully she slipped through the undergrowth and carried on walking. She had doubtless left barefoot tracks in the mud. If her pursuer was James, he would have centuries' experience of second-guessing enemies, and hunting all kinds of prey. However, unlike Makepeace, he probably could not see in the dark.

The hours of darkness were Makepeace's friend, so she carried on walking. She stayed alert, trying to sense 'my lady', but the mysterious ghost seemed to have gone to ground again. However, she could feel the doctor hovering insistently inside her mind.

Mistress Lightfoot, he began at last, we must talk.

Must we? Makepeace was brimming with bile. *What can you say that I will believe?* She had trusted that calm, doctor's voice.

She had obediently sipped his medicine as he tricked her into the Fellmottes' hands.

I was deceived—I was betrayed.

You *were betrayed?* exclaimed Makepeace. *I took you in! I scavenged you from death!*

You did so for your own reasons, not for pity! snapped the doctor, and then were was a long silence as if he regretted his outburst. We have both acted in haste. Have we not?

His words had some truth in them, but Makepeace was still wary. Like medicine, truth could be used as a poison by someone cunning enough.

You despise me, she snarled quietly, *just as you despise Bear. I am a kitchen girl. He was a dancing brute on the end of a chain. Why would you care what we think? We are* nothing. *When would our wrongs ever bother you?*

Well, now you must *care. We are your judges, Bear and I, lowly as we are. Make us trust you, Doctor. Give an account of yourself.*

The Bear is hardly— began the doctor.

Do not say a word against him, warned Makepeace, with a growl in her thoughts. *I can trust him as I can no other.*

The beast is loyal, conceded the doctor quietly. That is certainly true. I think it would fight for you against the world.

I do not have its passionate devotion to you—I will not pretend that I do. I made an alliance against you, thinking that it was my best chance of self-preservation. I was mistaken. You only trusted me because you needed another ally. You still do. I no longer have a reason to betray you. We do not need to like one another to be useful to each other.

The choice is yours. You can have your Bear tear me apart, or we can talk, and try to form a useful alliance.

Everything the doctor said in his clear, precise voice frayed at Makepeace's temper. Humans always betrayed you sooner or later. For a brief moment she wondered what it would be like if the great armies on the march destroyed each other and every human in the country, leaving only empty fields and forests where she might wander with Bear.

The idea made her feel serene for a moment, but next instant the cold sadness of it sank in like dew.

Talk, she told the doctor grudgingly.

You have an enemy in your skull, said Quick, *as you know. A subtle foe, mistress of a thousand tricks. I thought her mad when I first glimpsed her, but she is not. She is merely mangled—wounded. And she is very dangerous.*

Somewhere in Makepeace's head, something gave a hiss of anger and warning. *Silence, Doctor, not another word . . .*

The doctor hesitated, but continued, his voice now a trifle fearful.

Her name is Morgan, he said. *Lady Morgan Fellmotte.*

The Other was not Mother. For a few seconds that was the only thought in Makepeace's head. She had known it already, but the doctor's words killed her last doubts. Makepeace was overwhelmed with relief, but at the same time a terrible feeling of emptiness and loss.

In her lifetime she was a spymistress and intelligencer, the doctor went on. *For the last thirty years she has been part of the coterie of ghosts that inhabit each Lord Fellmotte. About a week ago, when the coterie was hoping to move into your body, she was sent ahead to—*

'Infiltrate,' whispered Makepeace aloud.

The Other was the Infiltrator. At last Makepeace understood. The ghost that had slithered into Makepeace's brain in the chapel had been wounded by Bear, but had not been destroyed after all. Of course it was so. Of course. She had been so obsessed by the idea of a vengeful Mother-ghost she had been unable to see past it.

It is one of her appointed tasks, said the doctor. Taking over a new mind is a dangerous business, so an Infiltrator is often sent first to scout out the domicile, subdue threats and make room for the coterie. However, the lady was not expecting your brain to be guarded by a large, angry ghost-bear. She was badly wounded, and so she hid in the corners of your mind.

Oh, Bear, thought Makepeace, struck by realization and remorse. *You knew. You kept growling and I didn't know why. You could smell her.* In her mind she put out a hand to stroke Bear's muzzle. He had not been snarling at Makepeace at all, but at an intruder she could not see.

Ever since, Quick explained, Lady Morgan has been trying to sabotage your escape and get word to the Fellmottes, but without you noticing her presence. She only dared act when your guard was fully down—when you were asleep.

My sleepwalking! Makepeace's mouth was dry. It had been caused by Morgan all along, not Bear. *I nodded off in the carriage escaping Grizehayes. She must have rapped on the roof so that the driver would stop and discover me.*

No doubt, said Quick. She has also been leaving secret marks and messages at every stop to make it easier for the Fellmottes to track you. She even left a letter in a Fellmotte carriage telling them that you were heading to Oxford.

So that was why Makepeace had found herself standing outside the stables of the safe house in the dead of night. It took her a moment to work out why Morgan had pinched her arm to wake her. Morgan must have overheard their hosts sending word to the Parliamentarian soldiers, and woken Makepeace so that she would realize her danger. After all, the Fellmottes would hardly want Makepeace falling into the hands of the enemy.

It also made sense of the dream in which the mysterious lady had scratched an 'M' into the door jamb. Perhaps some part of Makepeace's sleeping brain had realized that her body was getting up, sleepwalking to the door and leaving a mark for others to find. 'M' for Morgan, not Margaret.

The night after my death, Dr Quick went on, when I promised to guard your sleeping, I did so in good faith. Once you were asleep, however, Lady Morgan approached me with a proposition. She told me that you were a virtual lunatic who would almost certainly destroy me in a fit of temper, and . . . at that time I was in a mood to listen to her. She promised that if I helped the Fellmottes capture you, the family would allow my spirit to dwell alongside theirs as a reward.

We needed to prevent you leaving until the Fellmottes arrived, so we dosed you with an opiate. When you woke, I persuaded you that your torpor was a sign of illness, and that you needed to keep drinking your 'medicine' at regular intervals.

I take no pride in this. It was a low scheme, beneath me. All I can say is that I believed that I was fighting for my survival.

How had Makepeace missed all the clues? Even her new-found ease with reading should have told her that she was using someone else's skill.

Instead, she had suspected Bear. Poor loyal, bewildered, angry Bear.

Everybody betrayed her, so why expect otherwise? But it turned out that distrust could fool you and endanger you, just as trust could.

Have you made a decision? asked the doctor quietly.

Makepeace trudged on for a little while without answering. Overhead a scattering of stars trembled in the hazy night, each of them pure, cruel and lonely.

You've been a total fool, Doctor, she answered silently. *A dupe and a gull. So have I. We need to be cleverer from now on, or we're both lost.*

She heard him give an almost inaudible sigh of relief.

Do you still mean to push on to Brill, and then into enemy territory? asked the doctor after a while.

Yes, she replied. *James is at our heels. I must do something he does not expect from me. We must go somewhere he cannot easily follow. We must find friends he cannot win round.*

Gracious God—are you thinking of joining the enemy?

Makepeace hesitated. She was reluctant to discuss her plans with the doctor after his treachery, let alone within hearing of the elusive, ever-listening Morgan. However, there was no hope of a true alliance if she kept Quick completely in the dark.

My cousin Symond has turned to Parliament's side, she explained. *He is a treacherous, murderous snake, so the Fellmottes will probably expect us to stay away from him. But Symond might be our best chance of survival if we can make an ally of him.*

Makepeace did not mention the rest of her plan.

The royal charter that Symond had stolen from the Fellmottes was his master card. If it really did reveal the terrible truth about the Elders, then it would be devastating if it was made public. The Fellmottes would probably be accused of witchcraft, and the King too for protecting them. It might even turn the tide of the war.

Symond had it. The Fellmottes wanted it back. The King had sent Helen to recover it. Parliament would probably give anything to acquire it if they found out it existed. Whoever had the charter in their possession had power in their grasp.

Makepeace felt that it would be no bad thing if she had it instead.

CHAPTER 27

The damp ground made for slithery walking. Makepeace kept her eye on the diptych dial's compass, and tried to hold to her bearing, even when this meant scrambling through thickets, streams and hedges.

There was a cream-coloured moon aloft now, and the fuzzy shadow on her moondial told her that it was about two or three of the clock. A few birds were already scraping the night air with questioning notes. Night was her friend, but dawn was only a few hours away.

Most of the drug was out of her system now, she fancied, but she was finding herself groggy from fatigue. She realized that she had not enjoyed unbroken or undrugged sleep since leaving Grizehayes. At one point she entered an almost trance-like state, the rhythm of her feet heavy and automatic, and was only woken by an urgent whisper from the doctor.

Mistress Lightfoot! Your left hand!

Makepeace jerked awake, and became aware that the fingers of her left hand were just releasing something soft. She halted, and immediately spotted her crumpled handkerchief on the ground, its whiteness vivid against the dark earth. She stopped and picked it up.

Lady Morgan is still trying to leave our friends a trail, Makepeace remarked. *Has she dropped anything else?*

I believe not, said the doctor. I have been watching out for such things.

You must realize that this is hopeless, said another voice,

274

as hard and level as a blade. It was the same voice Makepeace had heard forced out of her own throat back in Oxford, and she knew it must be Morgan. *You cannot fight me forever.*

Yes, I can, answered Makepeace fiercely. *I was fighting you even before I knew you were there. Now I do know, and now I have allies.*

You must sleep sometimes. Your attention will drift now and then. Even your accomplices cannot always watch for me. An absent-minded moment is all I need to seize mastery of your hands, or harm you, or make you whisper words you instantly forget.

I could even trip you and dash your brains out if I wanted.

Maybe, said Makepeace, *but I do not think you will. Lord Fellmotte would not like it if you chipped his vessel, would he? And if I die, so do you.*

If it were not for me, you would be in the hands of the rebels already, said Morgan. Her voice was cold but not old, and Makepeace wondered whether she had died before her time. *You have no idea how much I have helped you already. What do you think would become of you if I stopped helping?*

Who knows? Makepeace shrugged defiantly. *Perhaps Parliament's men will capture me, and torture the Fellmotte secrets out of me. How would you like that, my lady?*

I could start pruning your mind like a tree, suggested Morgan. *How would you like that?*

Bear would never let you. Makepeace fought down her fear.

That disgusting animal is an infestation, not a friend.

He is worth a hundred of you! snapped Makepeace. *When did you people decide that you were the only ones allowed second chances? You already had lives full of power, and riches! You had chances most people could only dream of!*

275

You have no idea how hard I worked to earn my immortality! Morgan sounded genuinely angry, her voice razor-sharp. I spent every second of my life slaving for the family, to make myself too valuable to lose. I *had* no life of my own. I earned my after-life. That was the bargain I made.

Well, you never made a bargain with me, so it counts for nothing, said Makepeace curtly. *I choose who lives in my head. And if you're my enemy you have no place in it!*

Makepeace closed her eyes, trying to sense Morgan in the dark space of her own mind. Where was she? There! For a second there was a flicker in her mind's eye—a foggy image of a sharp-faced woman, eyes gleaming amid pits of shadow.

She tried to snatch at the ghost with her mind. Something slithered away into hiding, like a rat's tail against her skin. Makepeace reached for the elusive tickle of otherness . . .

. . . and then felt a shock of the mind, as if something had slammed in her face.

There was a sudden feeling of anguished terror, and a searing, muddled blare of memories. She remembered darkness, screams, cobbles under her feet and blood like ink running down either side of an open eye.

The spasm ended, and Makepeace found that she was on her knees, gasping.

What happened? asked the doctor.

I tried to catch Morgan. Makepeace picked herself up, still reeling from the mental blow, and put away her handkerchief. *How does she hide from me? Where does she go?*

I am not completely sure, confessed Dr Quick, but there appears to be a part of your mind that is closed off from the rest. I think she is using it as her lair.

. . . . .

After a couple of hours, Makepeace realized that the ground was steadily ascending, the little thickets and copses becoming less frequent.

I think I know where we are, remarked the doctor. Unless I am mistaken, the town of Brill is at the very top of this hill.

Then we need to be careful, said Makepeace. *We must skirt round the town, and find out a farmhouse to the north.*

Take a new bearing, suggested the doctor, a touch more northerly, and I think we shall pass to the north of the town.

The sky was just beginning to pale in the east when Makepeace caught the smell of woodsmoke, courtesy of Bear's sharp senses. She adjusted her course accordingly, and after a while glimpsed the farmhouse. There were a couple of low buildings, dank-thatched and grey-walled, backing on to a little paddock where a few skinny, threadbare chickens pecked at the dark rotting leaves in search of food. A rooster perched proudly at the summit of a large, overturned wheelbarrow.

It was early for callers, but Makepeace could not wait for dawn. She rapped at the door, and was surprised when it was quickly yanked open. An old man peered out, holding the door open only a few inches. Makepeace could just make out his foot braced against the door, as though he thought she might shove her way in.

'What do you want?' His eyes were bright and antagonistic, his hands and arms still strong from years of work.

'I'm looking for the Axeworth farm—'

'You won't find them here,' the old man snapped. 'This was their place, but they left a few days ago. Too much trouble here.'

'Do you know where I can find them?' asked Makepeace.

'Try Banbury.' The door slammed in her face. She knocked, then knocked again, but there was no reply.

Hmm. The doctor's voice was hesitant and wary. Lady Morgan . . . says that he is lying.

Makepeace remembered all too well the Elders' eerie ability to tell when somebody was lying. Morgan was not, of course, a very trustworthy source. She might be laying a trap of some sort. Then again, it was also possible that Morgan had her own reasons for wanting Makepeace to track down Symond. The canny Elder might still be hoping to reveal his location to the other Fellmottes.

Makepeace took a few steps back, studying the house and garden.

I think she's right, Makepeace admitted after a few moments. *If the Axeworths ran off, they left their chickens, their tools and two bundles of firewood. There's a barrow over there they could have used to carry their heavy goods. Why would they leave it behind?*

The wind freshened for a moment, and it seemed to Makepeace that the grey sky became greyer, the damp of the air more insidious. There was a note in the wind. It was a little like the sound made by blowing across the neck of a glass bottle, except that Makepeace had the unpleasant feeling that she was the bottleneck. She flinched involuntarily, and put her hands over her ears.

What is it? asked the doctor.

There's something . . . Makepeace was conflicted, trying to listen and trying not to listen. The faint, fluting note had a shape to it. As she listened, it wavered, wailed and became a repeated word.

Hell . . . Hell . . . Hell . . .

There's a ghost here! said Makepeace urgently. *We need to leave!*

But as she turned away from the house and took a step back

towards the path, an invisible something threw itself against her. She could feel it beating against her mind like damp, mad wings. In shock, she threw up her arms in a useless attempt to defend herself, and recoiled a few steps into the garden.

Chickens scattered. As she felt her heel thud against the wheelbarrow, Makepeace looked down, and froze.

Whoever had tried to hide the body had not done a particularly good job. They had curled it up like an unborn babe, covered the bulk of it with the overturned wheelbarrow, and tried to hide those parts that stuck out with leaf mulch and moss. Through the twigs and dank leaves, Makepeace could clearly see a hand, mushroom-pale. It was an adult hand, but not a particularly old one, though calloused with use.

The voice of the ghost was louder here, and Makepeace could hear the repeated word properly.

Help . . . Help . . . Help . . .

'Oh, you poor, sorry wretch,' she muttered, sadly. 'Nobody can help you now.'

'Hey!' The old man was advancing, a gardening fork brandished in a threatening fashion. 'What are you doing there? If you're looking for something to steal you're too late—we're pared to the bone!'

'No!' Makepeace stared at the points of the fork, wondering if the corpse at her feet had holes in its chest to match those spikes. 'I was just leaving!'

The old man glanced at the barrow at her feet, then back at Makepeace's face, and his expression crumpled.

'You're going nowhere,' he shouted. 'Ann! Come out here!'

A woman in her thirties ran out into the yard, took in the situation at a glance, and snatched a hand-scythe from a hook on the wall. Like the old man, she wore a tragic expression, made up of desperation, fear, anger and despair.

There were vivid red smears on the woman's left sleeve and across the front of her dress.

That is fresh blood, the doctor said suddenly.

I guessed, replied Makepeace, as she backed a few steps.

She was cornered. If she turned tail and fled through the garden, she would have to tear her way through the hedge at the back. If she darted for the path, she would have to dodge the weapons of the old man and the woman. Either way, she knew she was too exhausted to outrun them.

Listen to me, said the doctor. The corpse under the barrow is nearly blue. That blood is fresh. It did not come from our dead man.

Makepeace's brow cleared, and she looked at the woman anew.

'You're injured,' she said. 'Or somebody in that house is, anyway.' The old man and the woman exchanged glances.

Help . . . Help . . . Help . . .

'Let me see them,' Makepeace said impulsively. 'I can help them. My last master was a chirurgeon, and he taught me a few things. I have tools! I can show you!'

There was a long pause, then the woman called Ann beckoned with her scythe.

'Come on, then.'

Dr Quick, thought Makepeace, *I really hope you're as good as they say.*

So . . . we are proposing to help these murderers? asked the doctor as they neared the door. We are not intending to run, then, once we are in front of the house?

No, answered Makepeace.

She knew that she was too tired to run, and she strongly suspected that Bear and the doctor were also drained by the efforts of the night. Besides, she had a presentiment that if she tried to flee, she would find herself with a faceful of ghost again. She had a new suspicion about its wishes.

The little cottage was sparse and dark inside. The smell of blood hit Makepeace immediately, and for a moment reminded her of cutting up fresh hares and partridges in the Grizehayes kitchen. Underlying it, though, was another aroma, a sickly smell of rot.

The source of the smell was obvious. A man the same age as Ann was huddled next to the embers of a fire, wrapped in blankets. He was pale and greasy-looking, and his left shoulder had been roughly bandaged with torn linen, which showed stains ranging from crimson to black.

Well, that bandage will need to be changed for a start, said the doctor. There is all manner of nastiness there, I can smell it. Send somebody to boil some fresh linen. God's own truth, I would boil the whole house if I could.

'When did you take this hurt?' asked Makepeace.

'Two days ago.' The patient's eyes were watchful and a little feverish.

Two days, and I'll warrant the wound has not been properly cleaned, muttered the doctor. No wonder he has taken an infection. We'll need to take a look at it.

Makepeace reached towards the bandage, but the patient pulled back, eyeing her with fierce suspicion.

'I think I see how it was,' Makepeace said, slowly and deliberately. 'Royalist soldiers and Parliament men found each other out and started killing each other, using your cottage for cover. They left a corpse behind, and one of them hurt you by mistake in the dark. That's what happened, isn't it?'

Her three hosts glanced at each other.

'That's how it was,' agreed the patient firmly, and some of the tension went out of the room. Makepeace peeled back the bandage, and struggled not to gag as a smell of rot filled the room. The wound was a long slit, the edges swollen and reddened.

'His flesh is rotting,' said Ann, who was hovering nearby.

Ah, said the doctor, that is a sword cut. That young fellow under the barrow must have been a soldier, and he gave some account of himself before he met his end. No maggots yet, but a touch of gangrene. We'll have to cut that out, and scour out the wound . . .

Makepeace listened to his instructions, then turned to the patient's family.

'Boil some strips of fresh linen if you have them,' she said, 'and bring me some salt and vinegar.'

Of course, the doctor remarked thoughtfully, if we could taste the patient's urine, I could learn a lot from that.

Not with my tongue, you don't! Makepeace thought firmly. She had limits.

Carefully she took Dr Quick's box of tools out of her bag, trying not to let her hands shake. Biting her lip, she attempted to let the doctor take control of her hands.

He had mastered her hands before, when he had spoonfed her during her stupor, but this time she was fully awake, and somehow that made things harder. Watching her own hands fumbling with the catch of the box without her controlling them sent a tingle of panic through her. The doctor seemed just as jittery.

Your hands are too small, he was muttering, *and too clumsy. How can I make precise cuts with these . . . blundering meat gloves?*

Makepeace's hands took hold of a small bladed tool, dropped it, then picked it up again. Her fingers were shaking more than ever. The metal felt strange and cold in her grip.

She watched her own hand carefully extend the tool towards the wound, the very tip of the blade used to gently ease back the edge of the cut. It made her feel sick to watch it, and to be so close to the wound. The tool was too sharp, the angle wrong, the flesh too vulnerable. Despite herself she flinched, and snatched back control of her hand. The tool twitched and nicked the edge of the wound, and the patient gave a hiss of pain.

For God's sake, do you want me to do this or not? If you fight me for control of your hands, we may kill this man! You need to trust me!

'Sorry,' Makepeace whispered aloud. Despite the cool room, she could feel the tickle of sweat running down her back.

She released three long, slow breaths, and then let the doctor take control of her hands.

As she watched, Makepeace tried to pretend that the hands belonged to somebody else. That helped a little. Somebody was demonstrating surgery to her, and she needed to watch every moment, even when her stomach curdled. Nonetheless, she had to grit her teeth as the discoloured flesh was carefully cut away, and tweezers used to remove tiny clotted rags from the wound, presumably fragments of the patient's sleeve.

'He's bleeding again,' Ann said nervously.

'That is as it should be.' Makepeace parroted the voice in her mind. 'The blood will help wash out the wound.' She braced herself as she prepared the swab of salt and vinegar. 'I am very sorry . . . but this will probably hurt a good deal.'

The next two minutes involved a lot of screaming, and by the end of it Makepeace was wondering whether chirurgeons ever threw up. By the time the wound was bandaged again in fresh linen, Makepeace was feeling drained and shaky. The old man brought her a bowl of gruel, but a few minutes passed before her stomach was steady enough for her to eat it.

Afterwards, Ann offered her a bed, and Makepeace accepted it. She guessed that she would not be allowed to leave until it became clear whether her ministrations had done the patient any good. If she was going to be a prisoner, she decided she might as well get some sleep at the same time.

He may well die despite our efforts, the doctor said quietly. I think I should warn you of this now. I am very good at what I do, but my job is hard and a sword's task is easy. Humans are fragile things, and breaking us is far easier than fixing us. Since the start of this war, most of my patients have died.

The army knows that often there is nothing to be done. I do not think these people will be so understanding. Mistress Lightfoot, you will need a plan for our escape should that man be carried off to the arms of the Almighty.

But Bear had other ideas. He was tired, and now was the time to sleep. There was a beautiful, brute simplicity to it. When sleep came for Makepeace, it felt a little like sinking into warm folds of dark fur.

Makepeace woke hours later, feeling more clear-headed than she had in a long while. A thin, milky sunlight filtered through the open door.

Ann brought her more gruel, a little bread and some good news. The patient was still weak, but his pulse less 'wild', and his fever fading.

'Those tools,' said Ann. 'I suppose the chirurgeon died and left them to you.' Her tone was cloudy with deliberately unasked questions.

'Yes,' said Makepeace, meeting her eye. 'That's exactly how it was.'

When she joined the rest of the family in the main room, the mood was less antagonistic. As she suspected, they were the Axeworth family, the very people she had been seeking.

'I need your help,' she explained. 'I know messages are dropped here—letters for a Mistress Hannah Wise. Do you know where they're taken, after they leave here?'

Again there was an indecisive exchange of looks, and this time it was the old man who answered.

'We'll tell you. After all, we won't be handling those messages any more. We'll be leaving here as soon as my son is well enough to travel. We're not supposed to know where the letters go, but the messenger who picks them up is fond of a drop or two.' He mimed downing a drink. 'There's a house by the name of Whitehollow. That's where he drops them off.'

'Do you know where it is?' asked Makepeace eagerly.

The old man shook his head.

'Never mind,' Makepeace said quickly. 'Thank you for the name. I'll find it.'

'I wish we could spare you provisions for your journey,' said

Ann, 'but we have little enough for ourselves. The soldiers have stripped our cupboards bare.'

'Soldiers from which side?' asked Makepeace.

'Who knows? Both, I warrant. There's not much to tell them apart.' Ann retrieved a cloth bundle from under a floorboard, and unwrapped it on the table. 'You can take your pick of these, though, if there is anything you fancy.'

Makepeace could see at a glance that the huddle of items in the bundle must have belonged to the dead soldier. There was a much thumbed devotional book with a few letters between the leaves, a sturdy pair of boots and a recently cleaned sword.

'We have a use for the boots,' admitted the old man. 'The rest we will probably bury. We dare not sell them in case questions are asked. Take whatever you please.'

Makepeace thumbed through the devotional book, which was apparently called *The Practice of Piety*. Parts had been underlined, and there was a fanciful little doodle of an angel in one margin. A flower had been pressed in the front cover, and Makepeace imagined the young soldier, out of his home county for the first time, plucking and preserving a bloom he had never seen before. Opposite the flower was written the name 'Livewell Tyler'.

What sort of nonsense name is 'Livewell'? demanded the doctor. It is every bit as bad as yours! And look at these prating prayers! I think our dead man is a Puritan.

For some reason, Makepeace could not bear the thought of the well-loved book rotting in the earth. She was about put it in her pocket when some of the letters fell out.

They were all scrawled in the same youthful, uncertain hand, and signed '*Your loving sister, Charity*'. To judge by the brief addresses at the top, young Livewell Tyler had been posted in a number of different places. The address on the last letter caught Makepeace's eye: '*Whyte Holow, Buckinghamshire.*'

Back outside the house, Makepeace took a moment to pause on the path. She could still hear the faint voice in the wind.

'The farmer will live,' she whispered. 'You can stop now.'

What are you doing? asked the doctor. If that is the soldier's ghost, we have just saved his murderer!

If he wanted help for himself, he would have been trying to claw his way into my head, like most ghosts, Makepeace told the doctor silently. *But he didn't. He just flapped at me like a wounded bird. He was trying to stop me leaving the cottage. He wanted me to help them.*

The wind settled, but the wispy, fluting note continued, tickling at Makepeace's brain.

Will . . . live? I am not . . . a murderer?

'No, you're not,' said Makepeace gently. 'You were afraid you were going to Hell, weren't you?' She was surprised by how well the ghost had held its mind together, given its unhoused state.

The wind rose again, and subsided in ragged gusts.

I am . . . going to Hell. The fluting voice was filled with a grim certainty. *Not one of the Saved . . . but the farmer will live . . . will live . . . that is . . . that is good . . .*

'What makes you think you're going to Hell?' demanded Makepeace.

. . . Deserted my post . . .

Makepeace could almost taste the bitterness of his shame on the wind.

. . . So hungry . . . tried to steal a chicken . . . farmer warned me off with a rake . . . drew my sword and struck him. Struck

*him with my sword. Mad . . . hated him . . . mad with hunger. I
am a . . . coward. Thief. Sin of wrath . . .*

I told you he was a Puritan, said Dr Quick.

Makepeace thought the doctor was probably right. There was
something about the ghost's way of talking that reminded her of
the apprentices in Poplar. She wondered how many of those boys
had signed up to fight, with their hearts full of fire, and worn-out
bibles in their top pockets. This Livewell Tyler sounded young
and fierce like them, but for now all his fierceness was turned on
himself. She remembered his calloused hands, and wondered what
hammer or scythe he had thrown aside for a sword.

He was a deserter, and apparently stupid enough to have died
over a chicken, but somehow he had held together his hazy spirit
for two days through his sheer determination to save the man who
had killed him. He had done this even though he thought his own
soul was irrevocably lost.

. . . A thief and a coward . . .

The voice was becoming more broken, blurred and anguished.
Despite the wan daylight, Makepeace could just about see its
smoky shape as it started to twist and writhe. It was turning upon
itself, tearing shreds from its own spirit.

Fascinating, remarked the doctor, who was apparently
observing the same phenomenon.

'Stop it,' she whispered. 'Livewell Tyler . . . please, stop it!'
Left to itself, the ghost would drive itself mad, and torture itself
to pieces.

Oh please, no, said the doctor, as if detecting the drift of her
thoughts.

'Listen, Livewell!' Makepeace hissed, willing the tortured spirit to notice her. 'How do you feel about second chances?'

I . . . have earned none . . .

'But I have!' Makepeace changed tack. 'I am fleeing from wicked men who would endanger my very soul. I need to find a place called Whitehollow. Will you help me?'

CHAPTER 28

Makepeace trudged mile after mile after mile, trying to ignore the incandescent rantings of Dr Quick.

What were you thinking? he demanded. *Why would you recruit a member of the enemy? Is our little cadre not divided enough?*

Master Tyler knows the way to Whitehollow, Makepeace pointed out defensively. *Besides, we might need somebody who understands soldiering.*

For all we know, he may decide to cut our throat, muttered the doctor. *Will he ever give up that infernal noise?*

Back at the farm, Makepeace had explained her 'gift' to Livewell, and it had seemed that he understood what she was suggesting. His spirit had calmed, and stopped tearing itself apart. After she breathed in his ghost, however, he had fallen silent for an hour. Then he had started praying, fervently and relentlessly. He had been doing so ever since, despite all Makepeace's attempts to talk to him.

Makepeace would not admit it, but she was starting to wonder if the doctor was right. Perhaps taking on Livewell's spirit *had* been a stupid, rash thing to do. But watching his ghost unravel had been unbearable.

He probably needs some time to adjust, she told the doctor.

Well, he cannot have it! snapped Quick. *Soon we will cross the border into Buckinghamshire, and then we will need some actual directions from him!*

While walking, Makepeace had seen the sun reach its wan

summit, then start to descend again as the afternoon wore on. Ever since leaving the Axeworth farm, she had been trudging non-stop, never daring to pause. Somewhere James would be hunting for her.

Makepeace knew that she was passing through no man's land, and that there would probably be troops from either side roaming around. She hugged the hedgerows in the hope that she would not be seen from a distance. Soldiers meeting a lone traveller in such a place might be suspicious or arrest her. Worse, they might even be dangerous.

Soon she would be in lands held by Parliament. If she *was* caught and searched, Lady April's ring or the King's paper tickets would mark her as a Royalist. A little reluctantly, she halted in a little thicket, and buried them at the foot of an alder.

As she prepared to step out of the thicket into a meadow, she was brought up short by a sharp whisper in her head.

Get back!

She reflexively stepped backward into the shadow of the trees, and ducked down behind a high troop of nettles. Only then did she realize that the praying had stopped. The whisperer had been Livewell. Looking out across the meadow, she saw a tiny brilliant glint wink from behind a hedge.

Spyglass, whispered Livewell.

Makepeace held still. After what felt like a little age, two men with muskets slung over their shoulders climbed through the gap in the hedge, and walked away. She stayed where she was until she was sure they were gone.

Thank you, Master Tyler, she said as she carefully set out again.

'Twas a matter of habit. It was a rather surly response, but at least he had not resumed his prayers.

Master Tyler, Makepeace tried again gently.

What is it, witch? snapped the dead soldier. He sounded harrowed but defiant.

Makepeace flinched, startled. All the reassuring words she had prepared abandoned her.

I am not a witch! she protested. *I told you what I am! I told you about the Fellmottes!*

I know what you said, answered Livewell, his voice quivering but determined. You were very clever, and I was weak. You told me that the King is friendly with witches, and that I could help you against them. I told myself that this would be doing God's work! But you use the Fellmotte witchcraft. You bind spirits to yourself. You are served by a great beast. *I* am the one making deals with a witch . . . and I have let you claim my soul!

If I was a witch, she answered, *why would I bother claiming your soul? You're so sure it's hell-bound already. Why wouldn't I just leave it where it was and pick it up on Judgement Day?*

You want me to lead you to Whitehollow, Livewell answered promptly. Maybe you mean harm to our men there. For all I know, you plan to poison them or curse them. I betrayed my brothers-in-arms once, by abandoning them. I won't betray them again.

He sounded frightened, but resolute. Perhaps he was braced and ready for Makepeace to hurl devilish curses on him and then swallow his soul with a gulp. She closed her eyes and sighed angrily.

If I'm a witch, she asked, *why don't I fly across the miles instead of walking my feet bloody? Why didn't I turn into a hare to hide from those soldiers, instead of squatting in a nettle patch? Why don't I send my imps to fetch a partridge pie and a big mug of ale right now? I wish I was a witch!*

But I'm not. I don't have magic, just a hand-me-down curse I never asked for. I'm flesh and bone—bruised flesh and weary bones right now. The only dark masters I ever had were the Fellmottes, and I've run myself sleepless fleeing from them.

I do want to believe you, the young soldier said, rather less fiercely. If the Fellmottes truly are witches, and if you really are their enemy . . . then let us warn everyone about them!

I have no proof! exclaimed Makepeace. *They would call me madwoman—or witch, just as you did!*

But if we could open everyone's eyes, he exclaimed, it might change the course of the war!

Makepeace hesitated, knowing that she was about to make everything worse. However, dishonesty would be a poor beginning to their relationship.

I am sorry, Master Tyler, she told him, *but I do not give two crushed peas who wins this war.*

Instantly chaos broke out in her head.

That is too bold! declared the doctor. To weigh His Majesty as lightly as those rebels in the Parliament—

How can you say that? Livewell sounded equally incensed. How can you not care whether our people are safe and free?

Oh, stop your howling, Puritan! snapped Dr Quick. You and your kind would bring us to a joyless world with no merriment, no beauty, nothing high and mysterious to lift our souls!

And you would rather see the King rise up as a bloody tyrant, cutting the heads off anyone who argued with him! answered the soldier. Where's the 'joy' and 'beauty' in that?

How dare you, you lousy, beggarly—

You're very lucky we're both dead, sir! Or I would—

'Stop shouting in my head!' erupted Makepeace aloud. Several nearby birds took off in fright. 'No, I do not care. Why should I? Nobody has shown me why I must die for the King, or why I should love Parliament better than my own hide! I wish to live! And I have more than a dram of sympathy for everybody else who just wants to live!'

There was a long pause.

I cannot blame you for that, I suppose, Livewell said at last. I tried to save my own skin too. He gave a small, uncomfortable little laugh. Forgive me. I have no right to ask you to risk your life, just because I failed to live mine well. You're a young maid. I should be trying to keep you from harm.

Remorseful Livewell was somehow harder to deal with than angry, suspicious Livewell. Makepeace had offered him a second chance. Maybe he had seen it as an opportunity to redeem himself. What redemption could she possibly offer him?

So what is your plan? he asked quietly. Why do you want to go to Whitehollow?

There is a man I need to find there, she explained. *A treacherous man, but he might know a way to fight against the Fellmottes.*

And then? he asked. What do you want to do after that? If the war doesn't matter to you, what does?

The blunt, simple question knocked Makepeace back on her heels. What did she want? She realized that she scarcely knew. For so long, her mind had been filled with thoughts of what she did *not* want. She did not want to be chained up, or imprisoned, or filled with ancient ghosts. She did not want to live in fear of the Elders. But what did she actually want?

I want to save my brother, she said slowly. *He's full of Fellmotte ghosts. I want to chase them out and free him, so I can cuff him and tell him he's an idiot. And . . .*

Her mind crowded with memories. Jacob's ghost screaming. Sir Thomas's frightened face. James with dead things behind his eyes. And the icy, snake-eyed Elders, so sure of their rights to others' lives . . .

There was a mountain of a wish in her heart. It was dark and looming, daunting and unscalable, but she looked directly at it at last.

'And,' she said aloud, 'I want to be the Fellmottes' undoing.'

Now that sounds like a cause worth the whistle. For the first time, Livewell sounded like he might be smiling.

The walk was easier with Livewell's directions, and more pleasant without the incessant praying. Makepeace explained a little of her history, and Livewell gradually opened up about his own. He had been a cooper's son in Norwich, brought up in his father's trade. He had learned his letters in the local grammar school, and started teaching them to his younger sister.

Then the war had broken out, and he had enlisted at the first chance.

I had no doubts, he said. How could I stay at home, hammering barrels into shape, when this war was beating the world into a new shape? This is a fight for the country's soul! I wanted to do my part! It was like a hunger and thirst in me . . .

He trailed off. Even his zeal had a touch of sadness.

By the time the shadows started to stretch, Makepeace had walked over fifteen miles, and Livewell was certain that they had crossed into Buckinghamshire. She was exhausted, her feet were blistered, and her legs and injuries ached. She was also very hungry. She had used up the provisions from Mistress Gotely over the last few days, and the gruel the Axeworths had given her had been thin and meagre.

Bear felt the hunger too, and that was something he understood very well. Makepeace could sense his rumbling unrest, and his sudden curiosity about every rustle in the hedges.

Makepeace found that she had had unexpectedly halted, and that she was looking up into a nearby tree. There was a dark spiky blot that looked a little like a bird's nest. Makepeace could sense Bear thinking of the oozing innards of eggs, the crunch of fledglings. But peering up at a different angle she could see it was not a nest after all, just a tangle of twigs. Instead, she found her mouth opening, and her teeth fastening on the tender, spring leaves of the tree.

Bear! Makepeace told him, spitting out the mouthful of leaves. *I can't eat those!*

But Bear was indomitable now. With Makepeace's hands he reached down to grab an old piece of rotting log, and ripped it open to show its flaky inside. Makepeace found herself licking off the scurrying ants, their taste a peppery tingle against her tongue.

Livewell gave a squawk of alarm and shock. Going feral was probably not the best way to convince him that she was not secretly a demon in female form.

Makepeace sighed, and dropped herself down on the bank of a nearby stream, then pulled off her shoes and stockings.

No cloven hoofs, she pointed out drily, then lowered her feet into the water, and felt the cold water pleasantly numbing her blisters. *And I don't vanish at the touch of running water, either.*

A thin, dark shape in the water caught Makepeace's eye. The little fish was gone almost as soon as she noticed it, but it had clearly captured Bear's attention too. Makepeace's mouth was watering, and she did not know whether it was from her hunger or his.

She found herself lurching to her feet again, and had placed one foot in the water, damping her hem, before she was able to take back control again.

Stop! And yet, did she really want to stop Bear catching a fish if he could manage it? *Wait just a little.* She could not afford to get her clothes wet, for she would have no means to dry them if she was sleeping in barns, and they would chill her to death. She carefully hitched up her skirts and shift, tucking and tying them just below hip height.

Then she let Bear stride her into the stream, feeling the cold, rushing pressure of the water, and the slither of wet, weed-covered stones under her feet. At first the cold was pleasant, but after a while it started to bite. Her mind fidgeted as well, thinking of time lost and pursuers behind them. Bear, on the other hand, was patient as a mountain. After a while Makepeace was infected with his alert calm. The pain of the cold water became simply something that was, like the blue of the sky. Her mind-fidgets eased.

There! With reflexes not her own, Makepeace raked at the water with the spread fingers of one hand, and a fat, brown perch was scooped out of the stream. It flew through the air and landed on the bank, where it flapped and flexed, trying to flick itself back into the water.

Makepeace found herself lurching out of the water to land on all fours, slapping one palm down on the fish's head, and sinking her teeth into the middle of the still-living fish.

'Stay where you are!' came a sudden shout. Looking up, Makepeace saw a man in worn clothes pointing a drawn sword at her. He had just stepped through a gap in the high hedgerow, and seemed as shocked to see her as she was to see him. There was a dingy sash over his coat, so she guessed that he must be a soldier, but it was too muddy for her to guess which side he belonged to.

Makepeace was aware of the picture she presented. The live fish between her teeth spasmed, its tail nearly hitting her in the eye. She took it carefully out of her mouth, even as its juices made her want to swallow it whole, and pulled her skirts down over her bare legs.

'What have you found?' An older soldier stepped through the hedge, a broad-nosed man with a healing cut above his right eyebrow.

'There's something amiss with her,' the younger man said, never taking his frightened gaze off Makepeace. 'She was half stripped, and leaping about like a wild thing! She had her teeth in a raw fish, champing it like an animal—'

'And so would you if you were hungry enough!' Makepeace retorted quickly.

The older man frowned slightly.

'Where are you from?' he asked. Both soldiers had the same accent, and Makepeace guessed that her own had given her away as a stranger.

'Staffordshire,' said Makepeace promptly. She hoped that the county was far away enough to explain her accent, but close enough that she might have walked the distance.

'You're a long way from that county,' said the older soldier, his face darkening with suspicion. 'What brings you from home?'

Makepeace had hoped that the conversation would not reach this point. She stared at the two men, trying to guess which army they served. A cover story that would please one side would enrage the other.

I know that man! Livewell said quietly. The younger one — that's William Horne. He was in my regiment.

They were Parliament men. Makepeace chose her story accordingly.

'My stepfather threw me out,' she said. She rolled up her sleeve, and showed the fading bruises on her arm. 'He is fierce for the King's cause. I am not, so he beat me and told me that if I came back he would kill me.'

Sympathy briefly glimmered in the man's eye, but then cooled again into distrust.

'You must be very frightened of him to flee across three counties,' he said.

'I did not think to come so far!' Makepeace let a little of her real weariness and desperation creep into her voice. 'I was looking for work, and chasing rumours of it across the land—'

'Work?' The older soldier's eyes were now steely and hostile. 'Do you think we're stupid? This valley's seething with raiding parties! Who would come *here* to look for work?'

Tell them God sent a vision, telling you to come to Whitehollow! Livewell said urgently.

What? asked Makepeace silently, bewildered.

One of the generals collects prophets and astrologers! he told her hastily. He keeps them safe at Whitehollow — like prize hens.

'I *had* been seeking work . . . but then the Almighty sent me a vision of a place that I must go,' said Makepeace, trying not to flush bright red. 'A house by the name of Whitehollow.'

Both men stiffened, and exchanged glances.

'What did it look like in your vision?' demanded the older man.

'A great house of red brick,' Makepeace said, repeating Livewell's murmured words. 'High on a hill, ringed about by woods.'

'A spy could have that description,' said the younger man in an undertone. As the two soldiers whispered, however, Makepeace was listening to Livewell's urgent voice in her head.

'I have seen *you* in a vision, William Horne,' she said.

The young man nearly jumped out of his boots.

'It was two months ago,' she said. 'You were in a village church with two other soldiers. It was a wicked church, full of gaudy, devilish ornaments . . . so you'd come there by night to smash everything you could. You splintered the altar rail, and broke the stained-glass windows. You hacked the carvings on the pews.

'Then one of your friends took down the crucifix with its man-figure, and smashed it against the slabs.'

William Horne visibly flinched. The older soldier seemed untroubled, though, or if anything rather approving.

'You all stopped to stare at the smashed pieces of the Christ face,' Makepeace went on. 'A terror came on you all . . . but none of you admitted it. You all grew fiercer, more eager to smash and tear. You tried to outdo each other, so you wouldn't have to look at those broken eyes on the floor.'

William was staring at her now, with a hypnotized look of superstitious fear.

'You were the one who brought in your horse to drink from the font—to show you weren't frightened. You all watched its big, white mouth lapping at the water, and you laughed. But the echoes of the church made it sound like a host of devils were laughing along with you . . . and you all ran.'

The old man gave his companion a questioning glance. William Horne swallowed and nodded.

'It was in Crandon,' he said faintly. 'It shook us all up. And one of the others—the fellow who smashed the cross—he was never the same after. It broke him inside. He . . . went missing a week later.' He looked at Makepeace again, eyes wide with fear and doubt. 'How did you know how the laughter sounded?'

'Enough,' said the older man firmly. 'You were doing the Lord's work. Put it out of your mind.' With the back of his hand, he pushed aside his comrade's sword hilt, so that the trembling blade was no longer pointing at Makepeace. 'Put it away, William.'

He turned to Makepeace again.

'Make yourself decent, mistress, and come with us.'

Makepeace rose and adjusted her skirt, then put on her stockings and shoes, her teeth belatedly chattering.

Thank you, she said in her head.

I hope I have not made all worse. Livewell sounded almost as shaky as William. It was the only plan I had.

Some of the dangerous tension seemed to have left the air, but Makepeace knew that she had just raised the stakes. She had intended to approach Whitehollow stealthily and perhaps observe it for a while, to see whether she could spot Symond. She had not planned to march straight in through the front door, and risk coming face to face with him.

On the one hand, it looked like she would be escorted to Whitehollow. On the other hand, her hopes of arriving discreetly had just died a painful death.

PART SIX: WHITEHOLLOW

CHAPTER 29

The older soldier turned out to be one Sergeant Coulter, and six more men were waiting in the lane. The troops kept up a brisk pace, making few allowances for Makepeace's weak and weary legs, but they did not surround her like a prisoner.

They paid her little attention. This allowed her to finish eating the raw fish, and continue talking to their dead comrade in her head.

Why did *you desert?* she asked abruptly. The story of the church had intrigued her. She was fairly sure she knew the identity of the man who had gone 'missing'.

I was a coward, Livewell answered automatically, then fell silent for a while. I do not know, he confessed at last, and sighed. After I broke that image of Christ in the church, I could not forget the way its broken face looked back at me. Those eyes, so bright and empty and sad . . . I had a notion that they were sad for me. A week later, I killed my first man, and when I was standing over him his dead eyes had just the same look.

And after that I had a fancy in my head, that when I met the enemy they would all have cracked faces, and eyes that were sad for me. I don't know why, but the fear of it stopped my sleep and made my hands shake. One day I slipped away and started walking . . .

There was little Makepeace could say. She started to wonder whether it was such a good idea to bring Livewell back to a camp full of his erstwhile comrades.

After several miles' walk, they took a lane that wound through up a wooded slope and past a stately gatehouse, until it reached the great house at the top of the hill. Whitehollow was a square, red-brick manor about half the size of Grizehayes. The lawn before it might once have been a well-groomed ground for promenades, but now it was untrimmed, cropped only by half a dozen soldiers' horses. A few marble ancestral busts lay on the grass with their heads splintered. It looked as though they had been shot apart.

Whatever the house might once have been, it was now a military stronghold. Nearly everyone seemed to be a soldier rather than a servant. Having served in Grizehayes, it was jarring for Makepeace to walk into a great house and notice all the little tasks left undone, and the defiant acts of vandalism.

On the inside of the main door, papers had been nailed to the carved oak panels, some of them news-sheets trumpeting military victories, some religious tracts sizzling with zeal. The fireplaces had not been raked out properly for a while, and there was thick mud trodden up the stairs by many feet. A fine, carved chair had been broken apart for firewood, and several old chests lay open, their locks hacked out. Apparently righteousness didn't rule out looting.

For now, however, Makepeace could see no sign of Symond. What would she do if she came face to face with him? Could she signal to him somehow, and beg him not to reveal her identity? Why would he heed her if she did?

The sergeant stepped aside for some quiet, animated conversations with a small group of other people, nodding occasionally in Makepeace's direction. She was attracting a lot of fearful, inquisitive, appraising stares, and felt herself turning beetroot red.

One woman in fine but faded clothes seemed to be fixing Makepeace with a particularly intense gaze. Her face was lined in a way that made Makepeace think of a rain-streaked window pane. She seemed much the same age as Mistress Gotely.

That is Lady Eleanor, muttered Livewell, sounding as if he would have liked to swear.

Who is she? asked Makepeace.

The general's favourite prophetess, he answered. She made a lot of enemies here, so I hoped she had gone by now. Unpaid debts. Quarrels. And sometimes she tells people that they are doomed to die—that never goes down well.

Is she ever right? Makepeace tried not to stare back. *Do people die when she says?*

Yes, Livewell admitted reluctantly. They usually do.

Makepeace's pulse raced. It was bad enough that she had to bluff her way as a visionary, without doing so in front of a real prophetess. And what would this lady think of some young, ragged upstart rival?

Is she a proud woman? she asked suddenly.

Proud? Livewell sounded perplexed. Yes, she—

Makepeace did not wait for him to finish. Instead, she approached the little group boldly, and then dropped a low, long curtsy in front of Lady Eleanor.

'My lady!' she said, with as much awe as she could manage. 'I have seen you in my visions, raised above the world, with a great shaft of sunlight falling upon you and blessing you! There was a book in your hands, filled with light!'

Coulter looked startled, but Lady Eleanor's expression brightened into an exultant and magnanimous smile. Makepeace suspected that there was now much less chance of being denounced by her fellow prophet. If Lady Eleanor had made many enemies, she would probably not kick away somebody who treated her like a queen.

When Makepeace was brought in to talk to some of the higher-ranked officers, Lady Eleanor's arm was firmly looped through hers.

Makepeace was glad of an ally over the next two hours, which she spent being interrogated to within an inch of her life.

The three officers were not rude. They regarded her with the wary respect and suspicion you might show towards an unexpected lion. But they were relentless and steely, and pounced on every inconsistency.

Who was she? Where was she from? Who were her family? She explained that she was Patience Lott, daughter of a cabinet-maker called Jonas. She invented a sickly mother, a younger sister and a small and nameless hamlet on the edge of the moors. All of this could be checked and disproved, but not quickly, and she doubted they would send anybody to Staffordshire to do so just yet.

Another officer asked her lots of knotty religious questions. Had she lived a good life? How well did she know her Bible and her prayer book? Groggy and exhausted, Makepeace stumbled a few times, giving answers that would have been right in Grizehayes but wrong in Poplar, but managed to bluff her way through, with the help of Livewell's whispers.

Then, heart hammering, Makepeace began to describe her 'visions'. The room was deadly hushed, apart from the scratch of pens noting down her every word.

'I saw the King sitting in a great throne, but he was too small for it,' she said, hoping she sounded portentous enough. 'There was a huge dog behind him that he did not see. Over his head flew six owls with wings as black as death. He threw down food for them, but they caught up his shadow instead and carried it away in a scroll-case.'

She did not dare look at Lady Eleanor, in case the prophetess's expression was hardening into suspicion and contempt. But nobody interrupted her.

'Go on,' said one of the officers. 'What else have you seen?'

With growing confidence, Makepeace invented more wild dreams. Her tiredness made it easier. Everything was dreamlike already.

'I saw fire falling from the sky, and where it fell it set people's hearts aflame. They ran through the world, and the flame jumped to the heart of everyone they met, until everybody was burning . . .'

Makepeace could not have said later when she started to enjoy it. She could feel herself transforming before the soldiers' eyes. She was no longer just a muddy, battered vagabond. Being a prophet changed everything. Your bruises showed you were a martyr. Your rags proved how long you had wandered in the wilderness.

She had walked into the room wearing God like a robe.

'Now tell us what the visions mean,' said the most senior officer at last.

Makepeace blanched, suddenly realizing the enormity of what she was doing. She was claiming that God was speaking through her. If these men realized she was lying, then what would they do to someone who committed such blasphemy? But if they did believe her, perhaps her 'visions' would affect their battle plans. A careless, ignorant word of hers might cause men to march, or even die.

An army of Livewells or Jameses, dying on her word. It was power, raw power, but she did not want it.

'I do not know,' she said abruptly. 'I . . . came here because I know Lady Eleanor is the only person who can understand them.'

To Makepeace's relief, Lady Eleanor was delighted to translate them. Makepeace sat there, shaky and dry-mouthed, while the older prophetess went into scriptural raptures.

At last the officers seemed satisfied, and let Makepeace go. She left the room with Lady Eleanor, wondering how much mischief she had done, but was stopped just outside by Sergeant Coulter.

'When you saw a vision of Whitehollow, did you see any of the people living there?' he asked quietly. 'Perhaps a young lord with white hair?'

Makepeace shook her head, her curiosity piqued. His description sounded a lot like Symond.

'If your visions show you someone of that sort, and he looks to be doing something ill, let me know.' The sergeant exchanged a look of understanding with Lady Eleanor, who nodded.

'Who did he mean, my lady?' Makepeace asked, after the sergeant had moved away.

'Young Lord Fellmotte,' answered Lady Eleanor, not quite quietly enough to be discreet.

Lord Fellmotte indeed! Even though Makepeace was no longer a member of the Fellmotte household, she found herself secretly bristling at Symond's cheek in claiming the title. But then again, as far as Parliament's side were concerned, perhaps he was the rightful lord. After all, they had denounced the rest of his family, and were trying to seize their lands.

'Is his lordship at Whitehollow at the moment?' asked Makepeace, trying to sound casual.

'No—he is on some business for the general, and will not be back until tomorrow evening. And if my advice were followed, he would not be permitted to return at all!'

'You do not trust him?' asked Makepeace.

'No, I do not!' exclaimed the prophetess. 'Neither does Sergeant Coulter. Lord Fellmotte claims to have joined our side in the war, but we think that he is still one of the King's malignants. The sergeant has his bags and pockets searched now and then, looking for signs of treachery.

'You must understand, I have fathomed the mysteries of names. The letters of "Symonde Fellmotte" can be rearranged to "sly demon meltt foe"! Of course such a man is not to be trusted!'

Makepeace managed to keep a respectful straight face until Lady Eleanor had departed.

That woman, said Dr Quick, is entirely insane.

I hope so, said Livewell grimly.

Why? asked Makepeace, surprised.

She says the world will be ending soon, he replied.

At the end of that day, Makepeace decided that there was no greater luxury than a glowing fire, a hot bowl of soup and the chance to sleep on a dry mattress, even if it was just a straw one at the foot of Lady Eleanor's bed. It was all she could do to stop Bear licking the soup bowl clean.

What do you intend to do when this Symond returns here tomorrow? asked the doctor, after the lights were out, and Makepeace was trying to sleep. How do you propose to stop him denouncing you as soon as he sees you?

It was a good question. Makepeace knew she would need to speak with Symond alone, but on her own terms. He would need a very strong reason to listen to her, and she did not think that appealing to his conscience or sense of kinship would do her much good. She would need some power over him.

She needed to find the charter. Could he be carrying it around on his person? She did not think so. According to Lady Eleanor, Sergeant Coulter was having Symond's pockets and belongings searched regularly. Symond would be a fool to risk someone finding a paper with the King's seal on it on his person.

Where had he hidden it, then? He would want it to be somewhere close to hand, so that he could check on it and grab it in a hurry. With luck, it was somewhere at Whitehollow. If only she could find it before he returned, she would have all the power she needed.

CHAPTER 30

The next day, Makepeace began discreetly searching for the charter.

She woke early to find that some plain, clean and respectable clothes had been left out for her. Since everybody now seemed to assume that she was Lady Eleanor's pet and hanger-on, she decided to play the part by running down to the kitchen to make her new 'mistress' breakfast. There she talked to the cooks, and befriended a skinny, honey-coloured cat who apparently went by the name of 'Wilterkin'.

The kitchen was smaller than the one at Grizehayes, and fiercely hot. She soon decided that, in Symond's shoes, she would never have hidden the charter there for fear of the precious wax seal melting.

Nobody stopped a young prophet wandering around the house. She supposed the soldiers were a little afraid of her, but they would be curious too, and would remember if she did anything odd. If she looked like she was searching, they might yet suspect her of being a spy.

On the second floor, she found Symond's room. There was no mistaking his blue coat, and the crest on his travel case. He had been given one of the better beds, and a little privacy. Nobody was nearby, so she took a risk and hastily searched the room. She found no sign of the stolen charter, which did not surprise her at all. Symond was too clever to leave it somewhere so obvious, and she was probably not the first person to search the room.

In fact, she was quickly starting to realize that most of the house had been searched, torn up, ravaged and looted. In some places wooden panels had been splintered to see whether there were cavities behind, and some of the mattresses slit open. Nearly every floor was littered with debris.

'Did this house insult your mothers or something?' Makepeace asked a young private who was polishing boots, and bored enough to make conversation.

'Well, it made fools of us,' he admitted. He glanced over his shoulder to make sure nobody saw him gossiping with a seer, then beckoned her over and pushed open the nearest door. Beyond it lay a grand four-poster bed that had been stripped of nearly all its fine, embroidered hangings. 'Do you see the hidden door over there?' Opposite, Makepeace could indeed make out a door-shape, covered in the same brown fabric as the surrounding wall. Some of the fabric had now been peeled away at the right-hand edge, to show the pale wood underneath, but it had clearly once covered the whole door, camouflaging it against the wall.

The young soldier crossed the room and tugged at a little metal ring to pull the door open. 'There's a secret room, do you see?' Behind it a tiny room held only a simple mattress, a jug and a chair.

'When the war broke out, the de Velnesse family who lived here chose the King's side,' he explained. 'All the rest of us hereabouts—and the trained bands, the local soldiery—chose Parliament. So a great mass of us turned up at Whitehollow to arrest the knight who lived here. His wife surrendered the house, swore he had left already, and welcomed our troops in to be her guests.

'It turns out her husband was hidden away in the secret room. The dinner she served us was drugged, and that night her husband tiptoed out—right past all the men sleeping in this room—and the two of them ran off with all the jewels and plate they could carry.

'So I suppose we thought, if the house has one surprise like that, why not more? Maybe there's treasure they couldn't carry hidden away here somewhere. We can't count on getting paid, so why not find our wages where we can? And if it means ripping up the house of traitors, so much the better.'

The conversation was interrupted by the arrival of a senior soldier, who gave his private a disapproving look. Makepeace walked away looking as imperious and all-knowing as she could manage.

Elsewhere she found a few loose floorboards, but there was nothing beneath them. To judge by the fresh sawdust, optimistic soldiers had levered them up in the hopes of discovering some secret cache.

They're stealing everything but the walls, Livewell said quietly, sounding a little taken aback.

Righteous armies are just made of folks, Makepeace said as kindly as she could.

Livewell did not answer. Perhaps he was seeing his fellow crusaders in a new light. Or perhaps he was feeling slightly better about the Axeworths' chicken.

By the end of the morning, Makepeace was desperately racking her brains. Back in Grizehayes she had become very good at finding hiding places for things. Where would *she* have concealed the charter?

It had to be somewhere indoors. Even if the charter was carefully wrapped, there was too much danger of damp in an outdoor hiding place. Inside the chimney pieces? No, like the kitchen they would be too hot. The wash-house and the icehouse would be too damp. Besides, Symond was a lord—he would probably avoid the places where the servants were always busy, because he knew them less well, and could not be sure how often everything was checked, used or cleaned.

Most important of all, it had to be somewhere that would be overlooked by a whole garrison of soldiers bent on searching and dismembering the house in search of loot. It couldn't be tucked inside anything that was likely to be examined, hacked open or stolen.

It is now past noon, murmured the doctor. Symond Fellmotte might return at any moment.

I know. The soldiers were trooping off to eat, and for a little while most rooms would be empty. Makepeace knew that this might be her last chance to find the charter.

Could he have hidden it in plain sight among other papers? No, the expensive parchment would be obvious, and it was all too likely that it would be picked up and glanced at. Unless . . .

Makepeace slipped down to the main hall again. The papers nailed to the inside of the great main door flickered and fluttered in the breeze. A cunning man might slip a parchment under these posters for a time. But when she tugged corners aside, there was no sign of a hidden charter. Her pride and excitement turned to disappointment. For a moment she felt personally aggrieved with Symond for failing to use such an inspired hiding place.

He had not hidden his tree in a forest of other papers. Where, then?

It must be somewhere nobody would think to look. What if they thought they *had* looked there already? What if they thought it had already yielded all its secrets?

A hasty check—no the broken chests seemed to have no false bottoms. But what about the secret room? She hastened back to the master room, and pulled open the once-secret door using the metal ring. No, the hidden room behind had been pretty thoroughly searched. Even the mattress was slit, its stuffing pulled out.

Then inspiration crept quietly into Makepeace's mind, like a cat on to her lap. She turned her head to look at the door she was holding open. The once-camouflaged door, with its brown cloth covering now partly peeled back.

When everybody else looked at it, they saw a door that had hidden a secret room. It would never cross their minds that it had secrets of its own.

Very carefully, Makepeace slipped her hand between the wood and the brown covering, and slid it downwards, questing. Her fingertips touched parchment.

Not half an hour later, she looked down into the courtyard from a high window, and saw a man dismounting. Even at a distance, she knew him at a glance. Symond Fellmotte had returned to Whitehollow.

Heart banging, she hurried to his room, taking pains to avoid being seen. There was just enough time for her to hide behind the door before it opened.

A man entered the room, and stooped to loosen one of his riding boots. There was no mistaking him, even though the poor light dulled his hair to a greyish, tired colour, like weather-worn wheat. When Makepeace closed the door behind him, Symond swung around, one hand reaching reflexively for his sword hilt.

'I'm here to speak with you!' Makepeace hissed, holding up two empty hands.

Symond froze, staring at Makepeace, his sword halfway out of his scabbard.

'Makepeace from the kitchen.' His tone was flat with utter disbelief.

'If you kill me, you'll never see your precious charter again!' blurted Makepeace hastily.

'What?' The colour drained from Symond's face.

'I found it in the secret door and took it out. I'm the only one who knows where it is now, Master Symond.'

He scowled, and the sword slowly scraped its way out, until he was levelling it at her.

'Who are you?' he asked slowly. 'You cannot be Makepeace.'

'Yes, I can,' Makepeace told him firmly. 'The Fellmottes have not infested me, if that is your fear. They have tried more than once, though. I have you to thank for that.' It was not completely true that she was Fellmotte-free, but it didn't seem like a good idea to mention Morgan straight away. 'I ran away from Grizehayes. It was the only way to stop them pouring their ghosts into me.'

'What about James?' Symond cast a careful glance around the room. 'Is he here too? Let me talk to him.'

'No. I came alone. I have you to thank for that too.'

'Alone?' Symond seemed to be recovering from his shock. 'You stupid little baggage! You've just wandered into an enemy garrison, full of my well-armed friends, and told me that you've stolen from me. Tell me where my charter is, or I'll let some air into your veins, then hand you over as a spy.'

'Will you?' said Makepeace, her heart thudding. 'What would

your new friends say if I told them about the charter? You can't have shown it to them, or stories of Fellmotte witchcraft would be screaming from every news-sheet. And they're not *really* your friends anyway, are they? Lots of them think you're a Royalist spy. Imagine what they'd say if they found out you were hiding a decree with the King's seal on it.'

For a moment Symond's expression dulled, and she realized that he was really, truly angry. She thought he might run her through, in spite of the loss of the charter. Then the corners of his mouth gave a little shrug, and he slowly slid his sword back into its scabbard again.

Makepeace realized that her blood was surging with excitement, as it had while she was gold-smuggling.

'Why are you here?' Symond narrowed his eyes and studied her. 'Why run to me?'

'Who else has the same enemies, and knows them for what they are? Who else would believe me?' Makepeace gave a sour laugh under her breath. 'I don't even have James any more.'

'What happened?' Symond asked sharply. 'Is he dead?'

'He lives, after a fashion.' Makepeace bit her tongue, trying not to sound too angry or bitter. 'Your knifework on Sir Anthony left some ghosts without a home . . . and James was to hand.'

Symond's brows rose at the news, but Makepeace could not tell whether he was shocked, remorseful or just processing the information.

'He should have run,' he said quietly.

'Not everybody finds it easy to abandon their comrades,' said Makepeace darkly, then reminded herself that she was trying to set up an alliance. 'Do not worry, I am not here for revenge.

Perhaps I should be, but I would rather survive. We do not need to like one another to be useful to each other.' Makepeace realized that she had echoed Dr Quick's words.

'So what do you want?' Symond's tone was now almost conversational, but Makepeace sensed that the anger had not gone. 'Is this blackmail?'

'No. I would rather be your friend, Master Symond. But you are not always kind or honest with your friends. I took the charter to stop *you* betraying *me*.

'I need an ally, and a place to hide. But most of all, I need to know more about the Fellmottes and their ghosts. You were the heir. You were being prepared—you must know more than I do. There must be ways to protect ourselves against them. To fight them.'

'I *am* fighting them,' Symond remarked drily, 'but I am getting Parliament's army to do it for me.'

'That is not enough!' Makepeace said fervently. 'I need to know how to battle ghosts that are already in a body. I need to save James.'

'To save *James*?' The young Fellmotte shook his head. 'It is too late. If he has Inherited, he is lost.'

'He Inherited five spirits, not seven,' Makepeace parried. 'Sir Anthony lost two ghosts after you left him for dead. James might not be crushed to nothingness yet.'

'His chances are small,' Symond replied, but he looked a little thoughtful.

'But is it not worth the gamble?' Makepeace could only hope that Symond had some grains of real affection for James. 'He was your childhood playmate—you grew up together. He trusted you. He was so loyal to you that he helped you steal from the Fellmottes!'

'I always liked his company,' Symond said, in a carefully level tone. It reminded her of the flat, precise way he had talked on the night of his father's Inheritance. 'When I talked to him, I could pretend that the world was simple. It was like taking off armour.' He sighed, and shook his head again. 'He should have deserted when I did. I am not his keeper.'

Makepeace swallowed her anger, and decided to change tack. The young aristocrat was no longer waving a sword at her, but it still seemed wise to convince him that she was useful to him, instead of just dangerous.

'Then tell me what you know of ghosts, Master Symond, and let *me* try to save him. In return, I will be a friend to you. I am no kitchen girl here. I am Patience Lott, God's own prophetess. Even Lady Eleanor vouches for me. I will hear your so-called friends plotting against you. I can warn you of dangers. I can even have "visions" of you fighting the good fight.'

An incredulous smile started to pucker the corner of Symond's mouth.

'You may not be haunted by Elders,' he said, 'but you *are* changed. I never thought that *you* would prove to be the ruthless one!'

Makepeace scrutinized Symond. She had never known him well, and even now she felt as if she were slithering across the surface of his icy, unreadable facade. Clearly he was having trouble understanding her too.

'I am not changed,' she said. 'You never knew me. None of you ever knew me.' It occurred to her that perhaps she had not even known herself.

CHAPTER 31

Symond dug out a bottle of rum from behind the bed, along with a wooden cup and an engraved metal one.

'If the men out there knew I had this, they would all be craning their necks and hissing like geese,' he said coolly. 'They're all prayer-mad. God's blood, they have fits of the mother every time I swear! Where is the fun in being a soldier if you don't drink or swear? Of course, the sergeant knows I bring bottles here, but he can't punish me without admitting how often he searches my room.'

He sloshed a little rum into the two cups, and passed the wooden one to Makepeace. She suspected that the wooden cup showed her the terms of the alliance he was willing to offer—with Symond as patron and master, not an equal. Makepeace took it, hesitated, then sipped. It seemed best to humour his pride for the moment.

'My destiny was explained to me when I was ten years old,' Symond said, staring into his cup. 'I was taken to the vast family tree painted on the wall in the chapel, and told about the great ancestors I would truly know some day. I was "a new channel cut to hold a great river from the past".

'That was when my training started. Heirs of the house must practise contracting mind and soul, so as to make space for our future guests. The Infiltrators examine us regularly.' He stared at the tip of his riding boot. 'Sometimes they . . . rearrange our inner architecture. Apparently the results are more satisfactory if done over a long time, like training a hedge for topiary. Far better than having to hack a space of the right size at the last minute.'

'They rearranged your soul?' asked Makepeace, appalled. 'Did that not change you?'

'How should I know?' Symond shrugged. 'I have no idea what kind of man I might have been without it.'

'What else did they teach you?' Makepeace was beginning to wonder if she might have got off rather lightly with her three years' drudgery in the kitchen. A decade of regular brain-pruning was a high price to pay even for lordship and luxury.

'Well, they did not teach me how to fight my ancestors' ghosts! Quite the reverse. I was taught how to yield.' A slightly bitter smirk. 'It was drummed into me that my destiny was not only my duty, but also my greatness and glory. I drank the claptrap down, and was desperate to host my ancestors. After all, what would I be without the "great river" of those ancient souls? Just a muddy ditch.

'But there were things I noticed. I began to work out why the Elders need us.'

'Unhoused ghosts melt into nothing,' Makepeace said promptly.

'They do,' agreed Symond. 'Our bodies protect the Elders, and stop them blowing away in the wind. But there is more to it than that. Normal ghosts burn themselves out faster the more they move, talk or do. Have you noticed that?'

Makepeace nodded. She remembered Bear charging at his erstwhile tormentors, his essence steaming away from him.

'Ghosts inside a living person's body wear themselves out too, but they renew themselves. Strength passes from the living person to the ghost. They're like mistletoe boughs, drinking the strength from a living tree. We are not just their shelter. We are their food.'

The thought made Makepeace shiver, but it also made sense to her. Her own guests were sometimes active, sometimes dormant. They lent her strength and skills she did not have, but now she thought about it, she often felt exhausted afterwards.

'Have you ever watched an Inheritance?' Symond asked suddenly.

Makepeace flinched, then shook her head. She did not want to admit to what she had seen at Twelfth Night.

'I have,' said Symond, and for a little while his face had absolutely no expression at all.

'My father,' he said, after a pause, 'was my hero, my teacher, my pattern for life.'

'I liked Sir Thomas,' Makepeace said, very gently. Symond gave her a puzzled, distracted glance, and she realized that her likes and dislikes had no meaning for him at all.

'You never knew him,' he said dismissively. 'With everyone else he could be bluff and merry, but he was stern and exacting with me, because our conversations *mattered*. I feared him, admired him, and tried to please him. You cannot understand the bond between a lord and his heir. Sharing such a destiny means so much more than sharing blood. Lordship is a sacred trust, a duty of guardianship—the estate and title own us, as much as we own them, and we must pass them on unsullied.' For a moment Symond did not sound quite like himself, and Makepeace could imagine Sir Thomas saying those words.

'He always spurred me to be the best at everything, and eventually he admitted why. Not all Fellmotte souls were preserved, only those judged to be of the greatest worth to the family.

'So I knew that one day, when the Elders came for me, I would be weighed in the balance. My own private Judgement Day. If they approved of me, I would live on forever among the Elders. If not, my body would be stolen from me, and my soul crushed to pulp. I had everything to gain and everything to lose, so I wore myself threadbare trying to please them.

'Then my father's "Judgement Day" arrived. My father. I knew how hard he had worked for the family, how learned he was, how loyal . . .' Symond shook his head, his face still showing a tranquillity that did not match his words. 'All for nothing. He was found wanting. They crushed him. I stood there and watched it happen.'

Makepeace listened, uncertain what to feel. There was so much in Symond's story that made her want to pity him. Yet he had shown little pity himself at the Battle of Hangerdon Hill. Even now, his reactions seemed off-kilter.

'Do you want me to describe it?' he asked suddenly, his tone jarringly offhand. 'I had a ringside seat.'

Makepeace nodded slowly. She had seen some of it, but Symond had been closer. He refilled his cup.

'The Infiltrator poured out of my grandfather first,' he said, 'and I saw her slip in through my father's mouth. The others followed one by one. I think perhaps he fought back at the very end . . . but it did him no good.'

Makepeace said nothing, remembering Sir Thomas's tormented face. She felt sick with pity.

'Do you know something interesting?' Symond continued in the same, cool tone. 'The ghosts were not all the same. The Infiltrator looked smaller, but healthier, more whole. The others were larger but . . . cramped. Ill-formed. Have you ever seen two apples sprouted from the same stem, too close to each other, so that they grew misshapen?'

Now that is interesting, the doctor remarked silently in Makepeace's head.

'Why would she be smaller?' asked Makepeace, now intrigued.

'She has to venture out of the shell more often than the other ghosts,' Symond answered immediately, 'so I daresay some of her essence bleeds away now and then.'

Makepeace had never even thought of this before. Being 'Infiltrated' had been so unpleasant that she had not stopped to wonder about the dangers to the Infiltrator.

'But perhaps that also explains why she looked different,' Symond went on. 'An Infiltrator *needs* to be able to hold herself together outside the body, and the other Elders do not. Perhaps living in the shell allows them to become . . . soft.'

'What do you know about that Infiltrator?' Makepeace wondered whether the ever-stealthy Morgan was listening in.

'Lady Morgan Fellmotte,' Symond said promptly. 'By Elder standards, she's a foot-soldier. She is only the third lady who has ever joined their ranks, and she is not even of our blood—just Fellmotte by marriage. She is one of their youngest, too, dead only thirty years. Why do you ask?'

'I just wondered how the Elders choose their Infiltrators,' Makepeace said meekly. 'Do they draw lots?'

'I warrant the job goes to the lowliest ghost,' Symond said. 'Who would want it? Infiltrators wear out over time.'

'If the Elder ghosts are so soft, how do they crush living spirits?' asked Makepeace. 'Why couldn't Sir Thomas hold his own against them?'

'I cannot be sure. The Elders have the advantage of numbers and experience. But they also have no doubts to weaken them.

The Elders may be monstrous, but they are sure of themselves. They are their own religion.'

Certainty, said the doctor in Makepeace's mind. Ah. Yes, perhaps.

'I knew that the Fellmottes were *likely* to preserve my spirit,' Symond added quietly. 'They approved of me. But their favour was slippery, and selfish. I could not be sure of them, and even if they preserved me, I might have found myself serving as their Infiltrator. So I started to make contacts and plans of my own.'

'Why did the Elders never suspect you?' Makepeace asked. 'They can tell when somebody is lying, or hiding something. They never paid much attention to me because I was beneath their notice—but you were the precious heir! You plotted for years and they never guessed. You put a knife in Sir Anthony's side and he didn't see it coming. Why not?'

'Elders do not read our thoughts, though they are happy to let us think they do,' said Symond. 'They are very old, that is all. There is an alphabet to people's faces and manners, and they have had longer to learn it. Everyone gives away their feelings in tiny ways—a glint in the eye, a wobble in the voice, a tremor in the hands.'

'Then how did you stop them reading your feelings?' asked Makepeace.

'Oh, that is quite simple,' said Symond. 'I can force myself to stop feeling anything, whenever I choose. I have been learning the trick of it for years. It is not as hard as people seem to think.'

Makepeace nodded slowly, trying to maintain her carefully thoughtful expression. Living people didn't usually make her skin crawl, but Symond was apparently an exception. She could not help wondering whether the rearrangement of his 'internal architecture' might have caused some problems after all.

There was one other question that had been bothering her.

'Master Symond,' she said, 'when you stuck a knife in Sir Anthony . . . how did you escape getting possessed?'

A smile crept back on to his face. Makepeace suspected that he did not particularly like her, but apparently she was just clever enough to interest him.

'You're not entirely stupid, are you?' he said. 'You are right, two of the ghosts leaped out of his body and tried to do exactly that. One of them got in before I could do anything about it.' Symond laughed at Makepeace's appalled expression. 'Don't faint. There's only one spirit in this body now, and it's mine.'

'So you *do* know how to fight Fellmotte ghosts!' Makepeace's spirits rose again.

'In a sense.' Symond knocked back the rest of his rum. 'Over time I found ways of protecting myself. Ghosts became my hobby and study. I have been quite the scientist. Do you really want to know how I rid myself of that ghost?'

Makepeace nodded.

'Then perhaps I shall show you tomorrow. There will be a . . . hunting trip of sorts then. Once the hunt is on, stay close to me.'

'My lord,' Makepeace asked carefully, 'would it not be simpler if you explained it to me?'

'No,' said Symond, who now seemed to be enjoying a private joke. 'I would rather not prepare you. I want to see what you notice, and how you handle it when the time comes. Consider it a test of character.'

Makepeace tried to wrestle her unease. Against the odds she

seemed to have an alliance of sorts. She had learned a great deal, and James's case no longer looked completely hopeless.

However, the exhilarating tingle of power she had felt at the start of the conversation had melted away. Whatever was happening now, she was no longer in control.

He is a detestable villain, said the doctor later, but clever.

Makepeace had brought her conversation with Symond to an end for fear of being missed. She suspected it might hurt her reputation as a saintly prophet if she was found drinking with a man in his bedchamber. Instead, she had retreated to a closet for 'private meditation'.

I don't think he noticed any of you, thought Makepeace. *I am not sure why.*

Lady Morgan appears to be an expert in self-concealment, remarked Quick. Your bear was in one of its dormant phases, in case you had not noticed. The Puritan and myself thought it best to keep a low profile, and remained as still and quiet as possible.

So you and Master Tyler are talking to each other now? Makepeace could not suppress a very small smile.

No more than we can help. The doctor's tone was sullen. Tyler believes that he is going to Hell. I think so too. That appears to be the only thing we can agree upon. However, last night while you slept we reached a practical understanding of sorts.

Do you intend to tell Symond Fellmotte about us? In particular, are you planning to tell him that an angry Fellmotte spymistress was listening to your entire conversation with him?

No, Makepeace answered firmly. *He might be useful as an ally, but I don't trust him. I'd sooner thrust my hand in a bucket of vipers.*

Then why are we here? asked the doctor.

Because I don't have a bucket of vipers that can help me save James, answered Makepeace with a sigh.

Speaking of vipers, Lady Morgan still appears to be lying low, commented the doctor. It's only a matter of time before she attempts something, however.

You're right, Makepeace replied silently. *We have one thing in our favour, though. Lady Spymistress Morgan is an idiot.*

The lady may well be listening to us, remarked the doctor cautiously.

I hope she is! Makepeace answered. *Only an idiot would be scrabbling to get back to serving a gaggle of evil old greybeards who don't care whether she gets worn down to the nub! What if they had decided to recruit Symond's ghost to their coterie? Who would they have pushed out to make room for him?*

If Morgan was listening, she did not respond.

In any case, continued the doctor, with an air of suppressed excitement, I believe that your new ally is right about something very important. His theory would explain an oddity I have noticed.

We passenger-ghosts are plunged into darkness whenever you close your eyes. I thought at first that this was because we used your eyes to see the world. But if your Bear does see through your eyes—your human eyes—then why is he able to see in the dark like a beast?

So ghosts are mysterious and unnatural, and break God's laws, Makepeace answered, confused and a little impatient. *You can't make sense of some things. You might as well ask how witches fly.*

Oh, come now! snapped the doctor. Our existence may be the stuff of waking nightmares, but there will be rules to it. I believe Symond Fellmotte has unravelled the truth. The key is expectation. Belief.

I think ghosts can see without using their living host's eyes. However, we are used to the bodies we once had. Your bear believes that he can only see through eyes that are open. However, he also expects to be able to see in the dark.

If I am right, then that explains why there are so few ghosts. Dead souls only become ghosts if they expect to do so.

Bear never expected it! Makepeace frowned in thought. *But . . . he was very angry when he died. In fact, I'm not sure he noticed he* had *died.*

So his spirit lingered, said the doctor, sounding pleased. Then there are those who die in desperation and doubt, thinking their souls lost, like your Puritan friend, and the favoured Fellmottes, who die knowing that their ghosts will have a new home . . .

And you, said Makepeace, feeling her spirits sink guiltily. *You expected to become a ghost because I told you that you could.*

Never mind that, said the doctor briskly but firmly. The Fellmotte ghosts survive from century to century, triumphing over the spirits of their hosts, because they utterly believe in their right and ability to do so. Their certainty and mad arrogance is their strength.

If you want to weaken their spirits, find a way to shatter that certainty. Break their faith. Make them doubt.

CHAPTER 32

The next morning, Symond completely ignored Makepeace, which was only sensible. It was best that nobody suspect a connection between them, lest they also notice that both had the same faint cleft in their chin.

It did, however, mean that she was left no closer to knowing what Symond had meant by a 'hunt'. In fact, Whitehollow seemed to be preparing for a rather different sort of gathering.

The ballroom was cleaned, its windows polished, and tables and chairs set out as if for a party. On pewter plates a small spread was laid out—tongue, veal, partridge pie, bread and cheese. It was nothing compared to the magnificent banquets at Grizehayes, but fine enough to suggest that guests of quality were expected.

'What's going on?' Makepeace asked a private who was putting candles back into candlesticks in the ballroom. Such extravagance suggested an important event.

'It's a wedding, Mistress Lott,' he said politely. 'The general's nephew's marrying the daughter of a member of Parliament. They'll be turning up this afternoon—and some of their friends and family too.'

They might decorate the place a little, remarked the doctor morosely. The rafters were bare, and no flowers adorned the room.

Marriage belongs to God, said Livewell matter-of-factly enough, and He doesn't care about frills and ribbons.

Makepeace was glad to hear Livewell's voice. He had been quiet for a while. She could not guess what it must have been like to find himself surrounded by soldiers of the army he had abandoned. She worried that he might start tearing himself apart again.

The first visitors to arrive were three black-clad, severe-looking men. To Makepeace's surprise they gave the sergeant and other officers only the briefest, coolest nod, before stepping aside with Symond, and holding a quiet, earnest conversation with him.

Afterwards Symond maintained his usual air of cool detachment, but Makepeace detected hints of excitement. At one point he caught at her sleeve.

'Remember—once the hunt starts, stay close to me.'

'When is the hunt?' she asked. 'Is it after the wedding? I can't find a reason to join it if I don't know when it is!'

He laughed under his breath.

'This whole wedding is a hunt of sorts,' he whispered. 'The families were planning to hold it back on the general's estates in a few months . . . but holding it here right now allows them to invite certain guests, who cannot really say no. This –' he gestured through the door at the wide ballroom—'is an opening trap.'

'A trap?'

'One of the guests secretly spies for the King,' Symond explained with visible relish. 'We have proof of it now, but unfortunately the spy is a member of the gentry. If we knock on their door and ask to arrest them, their household will probably try to spirit them away to safety. That's why we've lured the spy here, far from their servants and reinforcements.'

The conversation left a bad taste in Makepeace's mouth. Allying with Symond meant nailing her colours to Parliament's mast for now, but her little time on His Majesty's secret service left her with a reluctant sympathy for the unsuspecting spy.

After lunch, the damp morning mist thickened into fog,

robbing the lawns and outhouses of all detail. The sergeant sent more men down the drive to guide guests to the house, and in the mid-afternoon the wedding party and others arrived.

The general was a grim-jawed man with a well-trimmed beard, and his nephew a slimmer, younger, clean-shaven version of him. The quiet, nervously smiling bride was ushered in by her talkative mother. However, Makepeace barely noticed any of them.

Instead, her attention was drawn by a well-dressed couple who rode in on the same horse, the woman sitting behind the man. The gentleman dismounted and handed down his wife with a courtesy that seemed formal rather than affectionate.

The wife had vivid red hair just visible under her hat, and a long, bold face dotted with black silk patches. It was 'Helen', the Royalist spy, adventuress and bullion smuggler.

Makepeace ducked behind a corner before Helen could catch sight of her. From her hiding place she saw Helen's husband shaking the general's hand warmly. The two men seemed to be good friends.

What was Helen doing here? For a moment, Makepeace wondered whether Helen had been a Parliamentarian all the time, infiltrating the Royalist spy network as a double agent. But that seemed unlikely. No double agent sent by Parliament would smuggle so much gold to the King.

No, it was far more likely that Helen really was a spy for the King, but posed as a Parliamentarian in her everyday life. Symond had told Makepeace that he had proof of the identity of a secret Royalist spy. It was a member of the gentry, someone with their own household . . . somebody like Helen.

Makepeace's heart plummeted. Her camaraderie with Helen

had been a sham built from her own lies, but she *liked* the older woman.

What should Makepeace do now? The safest and most logical option was to stay out of Helen's sight. If Helen did not know that her erstwhile comrade was at Whitehollow, she could not betray her if caught. Yet Makepeace recoiled from this option.

What else could she do? Even if she was mad enough to try to warn Helen, how could she do it? Helen would be watched, so there would be no chance to whisper in her ear unobserved. There were probably ways in which the King's spies warned each other of danger, but Makepeace did not know what they were.

And then it occurred to Makepeace that somebody else probably would. She found a quiet corner where she could concentrate, then closed her eyes and took a deep breath.

Lady Morgan, she thought, *I need your help. I want to tell Helen that she has walked into a trap. Is there some way I can warn her?*

Are you mad? demanded the doctor. If that woman leaves here alive, she will have seen both yourself and Symond! Word will reach the Fellmottes!

I think I am mad, yes! Makepeace answered. *I know Helen would never have risked her mission for me . . . but in a pinch I think she would have risked her neck. Oh, I'm not planning to ready a horse for her, or pull out a pistol to protect her. But . . . I want to give her a fighting chance.*

The silence rolled on.

Morgan, Makepeace tried one more time, *you may be determined to be my enemy. But Helen never hurt you—she's your comrade. You were a spy too, weren't you, when you were alive? Can you remember what it was like to live like her?*

There was a pause, and then from the shadowy depths of her own mind Makepeace heard a familiar, hard-edged voice.

Find a paper that you can pass to her without drawing remark, said Morgan. The bottle you stole from Lady April is artichoke juice—you may use it to write invisibly.

Makepeace hastened to the entrance, acquired some of the religious tracts pinned to the door, then hurried back to her room. She dipped a pen into the artichoke juice as though it were ink, and wrote a short message in the margin of a tract.

Wedding is a trap. Flee if you can.

Sure enough, the juice only damped the paper, and dried leaving no mark.

How will she read it? Makepeace asked.

The writing will appear if held to a candle flame, said the spymistress. Nick the corner with your fingernail, so that she knows there is a hidden message.

Hands shaking with nerves, Makepeace carried the pile of tracts into the ballroom. She got a few odd looks as she started handing them out, but only a few. Strange, religious behaviour was to be expected from prophets.

Most of the guests were sitting in the little window seats, with their backs to the vaporous white beyond the tiny panes. Helen was sitting between the bride and another lady, and seemed to be dominating the conversation easily. To judge by the way her companions smothered their giggling with their fans, her jokes were a little scandalous.

Makepeace paused by the window seat, bobbed an uncomfortable curtsy, and placed a tract in the reluctant hand of each lady. Then Helen's gaze flicked to Makepeace's face.

For the tiniest moment the red-haired woman's eyes flared with shock and recognition. But the expression was so fleeting that only Makepeace caught it. A moment later Helen was throwing back her head to laugh at something the bride had said, as if Makepeace were utterly invisible to her.

Makepeace moved on, handing out more tracts, and gave only stumbled, dazed responses to one red-faced gentleman's jokey attempts to flirt with her. She was aware of Helen light-heartedly excusing herself from her companions, and leaving the room.

A little later Helen returned, her smile looking rather fixed. The red-faced gentleman greeted her as an acquaintance, with a flurry of jovial compliments, and tried to persuade her to step aside and let him read poetry to her. However, she brushed him off and quickly made her way to her husband. Passing by, Makepeace overheard a little of their muted conversation.

'Something has turned my insides,' Helen murmured. 'I feel quite ill. My dear . . . I think I should return home.'

'Can you try not to embarrass me, just for once?' her husband snapped. 'If you are well enough to ride, you are well enough to stay and make pleasantries. And if you take the horse, then how should I come home again?'

The severe-looking black-clad men entered the room. There was something fundamentally unfestive about them, like Grim Reaper figures stalking through a picnic. They made eye contact with Symond and nodded. Helen noticed them too, and turned pale.

Time had run out. The three black-clad men walked silently and politely through the room, towards Helen and her husband . . .

. . . and past them. They came to a halt in front of the ruddy man who had tried to flirt with Makepeace.

'Sir,' said one of them, 'I hope you will step outside with us and spare the company unpleasantness.'

He stared up at them, and opened his mouth as if he were about to bluster some protest, or pretend ignorance. Then he let his mouth close again, and released a long, slow breath. He offered an apologetic half-smile to the other guests around him, all now watching him with fear, curiosity, confusion or suspicion.

The exposed spy rose heavily to his feet, and downed his goblet. Then he threw it into the face of his nearest enemy, and sprinted for the door, taking everyone by surprise. Makepeace flung herself out of the way as he barrelled past.

'Keep the main door barred!' she heard somebody shouting. There was a crash. 'He's out through the window—on the front lawn!'

All the military men in the room surged out of the ballroom, followed by most of the servants and guests. The front door was flung open and everyone poured outside. Through the fog, Makepeace could just see a distant figure running in the direction of tree cover. As she watched, it halted, then zagged in a new direction. Other figures that had been waiting in the shadows of the trees leaped out and chased after him. Evidently those who set the trap had placed men in ambush just in case.

Glancing over her shoulder, Makepeace could see most of the wedding guests clustered in front of the house. Helen looked astonished and aghast.

The leader of the black-clad men advanced with Symond

beside him. The former was dabbing at a cut on his forehead, left by the flung goblet.

'You were right,' he said to Symond. 'He *did* try to run. I expected a bit more dignity.'

'I did not,' said Symond. As the black-clad man walked on, Symond caught Makepeace's eye, and grinned.

'Halloo the chase,' he whispered. 'Stay close to me.'

The confused crowd poured into the fog, and promptly lost track of each other. Shouts echoed through the gloom.

'Over there! I see him! Halt!'

'Don't let him reach the trees!'

Then there were two sharp cracks, like boughs breaking in a storm.

'The traitor's on the ground—fetch the chirurgeon!'

Symond sprinted towards the last call, and Makepeace hurried after him, mouth dry. There were two men standing over a third, who lay sprawled at their feet. A man with a leather bag ran out of the house and across the lawn to kneel next to the fallen man. Makepeace guessed that he must be a chirurgeon.

'Can you mend him?' called one of the officers. 'He has questions to answer!'

'Some genius put a bullet in his head at close range!' retorted the chirurgeon. 'I'd need a ladle even to collect his brains!'

Makepeace could smell gunsmoke. It was not like the sweet, half-living smoke from cooking or woodfires. It had a bitter, metallic tang, and for a moment she wondered if hellfire smelt that way.

'We need a stretcher!' called one of the soldiers. The other had pulled a bible out of his pocket, and was peering closely at the page as he tried to read it aloud, half blinded by the fog.

Symond approached the body, and knelt next to it. He reminded Makepeace of a cat at a mousehole. Then he stiffened, as if that cat had seen the shadowy flick of a mouse's tail. Makepeace had seen something too, a hazy tendril above the body that was neither smoke nor mist.

It was a ghost, sure enough, a very faint and ragged one. It had sensed the haven inside Symond, and was wavering unsteadily towards his face.

Only Makepeace was close enough to see Symond smile. As it drew closer, he suddenly bared his teeth and hissed in a deep breath, as if to draw the whole ghost into his lungs. His eyes gleamed with predatory excitement.

The ghost recoiled. For a second it flailed in confusion, then Makepeace saw it streak away across the lawn, the grass blades flattening slightly as it passed. A little bush shivered almost imperceptibly as if nudged, little beads of moisture falling from its leaves. Only Makepeace and Symond noticed; everybody else nearby was focused upon the body.

Symond leaped nimbly to his feet and pursued. Makepeace followed a few yards behind, trying to keep him in sight. He zigzagged, and she guessed that the spy's ghost must be weaving in an attempt to throw off pursuit, as the man had when alive. Now Symond was sprinting towards the treeline. Perhaps the ghost was still clinging to its last hope while living, that if it reached the woodland it would be safe.

Makepeace followed her kinsman into the woods, bracken thrashing at her knees. Now and then mist-veiled boughs loomed suddenly at face-height, forcing her to duck. Still she could see Symond's pale hair and dark coat ahead of her, weaving between the trunks.

Scrambling over a fallen tree, she stumbled into a little clearing, and found Symond on his knees, both hands gripping the dead leaves, and his eyes shut.

At the sound of her approach, he opened his eyes and gave a grin of perfect complacency.

'I have him,' he said.

For a fraction of a second, his face spasmed. Just for that moment it seemed that somebody else was looking out of his eyes in an agony of terror and despair. Then his predatory grin returned and he was Symond again.

'What have you done?' she asked, too aghast to be respectful.

'I've captured a traitor,' said Symond, and Makepeace suspected that he was enjoying her reaction.

'The spy's ghost is inside you?' Makepeace saw the little spasm occur again. 'Why? Why did you do it?'

'Well, you see, my "new friends" in Parliament's army are very demanding. They keep wanting me to provide them with more information they can use against the Royalist side. I need to keep them happy if I want to inherit my rightful estates. The problem is, I've already told them most of what I know. They want me to find out more by turning spy, but that would mean risking my neck. I've found a better way of getting information. Are you squeamish?'

Makepeace shook her head slowly.

'Good. I wouldn't want you fainting, and distracting me from my interview. Let's see if he's ready to talk.' He lowered his eyes, and when he spoke again his words did not seem to be directed to Makepeace.

'Now then, my good fellow. Why don't you unburden your soul, and give me a list of your accomplices? Then you can tell me where you hide your papers, and help me with a couple of ciphers . . .'

There was a pause, then Symond tutted and laughed.

'Now he's panicking, and demanding to know where he is, and why it's so dark. They usually do. But when I start drinking away their soul a little at a time, they become a lot more helpful. For a while, at least. Until their minds break.'

'What do you mean?' croaked Makepeace.

'I told you I had made a study of ghosts. I also told you that ghosts inside our bodies can draw on our strength. But I have discovered something much more interesting. If we are stronger than a ghost, *it can work the other way too.* Someone with my gift—our gift—can draw the strength out of a lone ghost, and burn it up like fuel.

'It took a lot of practice, starting with the weakest and most tattered ghosts I could find. Bedlam was a good place for those. Ever since, I've been taking on stronger and stronger spirits, so that *I* became stronger. Thank God I did, or that wounded Elderghost from Sir Anthony would have done for me!

'Do you understand? Do you see what God intended us to be? We're not ditches waiting for rivers, or trees meekly feeding mistletoe. We're hunters, Kitchen-Makepeace. We're predators. And if you serve me very well indeed, I will teach you the tricks of it.'

Symond looked away, and to judge by his smile he had turned his attention to his captive once more. His face spasmed again and again. Each time the fleeting expression was more terrified and anguished.

Makepeace had said that she was not squeamish. She had skinned countless animals. Even cutting gangrene out of a man's flesh had not turned her stomach like this.

She did not have well-considered ideas on the subject of evil.

There were sins that sent you to Hell, of course, and she had heard them listed often enough. There were terrible things that she did not want to happen to her or anybody she cared about, but the threat of those was just the way of the world. Goodness was a luxury, and God clearly had no time for her.

But she discovered, to her surprise, that her gut had opinions of its own. It knew that there were unbearable evils in the world, and that right now she was looking at one.

And deeper in her soul, she could hear Bear's answering rumble of a growl. It understood pain. It understood torture.

'Stop it,' Makepeace said aloud. 'Let the ghost go.' She was warm now, and shaking from head to foot. Bear's breath was in her ear.

Symond gave her a look of mild contempt. 'Don't disappoint me now. I was just starting to hope that you might be useful. And don't distract me. My traitor friend is just about to break . . .'

As Symond looked away from her again, Makepeace snatched up a piece of broken branch, and swung it at him. Mid-swing, she felt the movement gain extra strength from Bear's anger. It hit Symond in the back of the neck, pitching him forward. She thought she saw a faint, mutilated strand of shadow wisp away from him as the captive ghost escaped and melted.

Makepeace roared. For a moment her vision blackened, and she wanted to hit Symond again. No. If she did, she would kill him.

She dropped the branch and backed away. He was already rising, and reaching for his sword.

'You miserable jade!'

Makepeace turned and ran.

She darted between the misty trees, the crash and rustle of

Symond's steps close behind her. Every moment she expected to feel his blade slice into her back.

The trees unexpectedly ended, and she was running through bracken and then grass. A huge murky oblong loomed into view ahead, and she realized that she was back on the front lawn of Whitehollow.

Three figures were walking hastily towards her across the lawn. As she neared them, she made out their black clothes, and realized that they were the trio who had tried to arrest the spy.

'Catch her!' Symond bellowed behind her. 'She's one of *them*! She's one of the Fellmotte witches!'

The three men instantly spread out to block her passing. As she tried to dart around them, the tallest drew back his arm. She barely saw his fist fly forward, only felt the jarring shock as it hit her jaw. The world exploded into pain, then darkness.

CHAPTER 33

When Makepeace first edged back into consciousness, for a while she was only aware of the pain in her chin. It seemed as big as a sun, but a sun that pulsed red and orange. Becoming reacquainted with the rest of herself was not an enjoyable experience. Her head hurt, and she felt sick. Opening her eyes, she found that she was lying on a mattress in what looked like someone's writing closet.

She staggered to her feet, and tried the door. It was locked. The window was barred, and she felt a swimming sense of déjà vu and panic. She was a prisoner again.

Is everyone all right? she asked silently, suddenly frightened for her troublesome companions.

I believe so, said the doctor with an air of tortured calm. So . . . after all the trouble it cost us to find Symond Fellmotte, you found it essential to hit him with a log?

The man needed a smacking, said Livewell with feeling. 'Tis just a shame we couldn't hit him with the whole tree.

In spite of her situation and stinging jaw, Makepeace gave a small snort of mirth. With relief, she realized that she could feel the warm vastness of Bear as well.

Morgan? Are you still there? There was no response, but then again that was not surprising. *Where are we?* Makepeace asked instead.

I do not know, answered Livewell. I have seen nothing since that fellow struck us in the jaw.

I thought you could all still move my body and open my eyes while I was asleep? Makepeace gingerly sat up, and felt her bruised chin.

During ordinary sleep, yes, said Dr Quick. During true unconsciousness, however, it seems we cannot manoeuvre the body at all. A fascinating discovery, but rather inconvenient right now.

Makepeace clambered up on to the bed, and peered out through the tiny window as best she could. She could see trees, and the chimneys of Whitehollow beyond them. She guessed that she was being held in the gatehouse.

She started as the door opened, and a servingman entered.

'You're to come with me,' he said.

He led her out of the closet into a bare, little chamber. The man in black who had punched Makepeace sat in a chair at a desk. Symond lounged by the wall, with his usual mask-like sangfroid.

The man in black appeared to be about thirty, and his dark hair was already receding. His eyes were keen, but he blinked too hard, and Makepeace imagined him reading for long hours by candlelight.

'We already know everything important,' he said, looking up from his papers. 'All that is left is for you to admit the truth, fill in the gaps, and tell us who else is steeped in this corruption.' He leaned back in his chair and looked at her. 'There is still time for you to convince us that you were led astray by others. You are young and unlearned, easy prey for the Devil's tricks.'

Makepeace flushed as she remembered the word that Symond had shouted.

Witch.

'What Devil's tricks?' Perhaps Makepeace could still play the frightened little girl. 'Why did you hit me? Who are you? Why am I here?'

'Why did you come to Whitehollow?' asked the interrogator, ignoring her questions.

'I was seeking Lady Eleanor,' she said defiantly.

'I have an account here from Private William Horne.' The interrogator shuffled his papers. 'He says that he came upon you one day by surprise. You were capering almost naked on your hands and knees, snarling like a beast, and ripping a live fish with your teeth.'

'I hitched my skirts to wash my feet in the stream, and was lucky enough to scoop a fish out of the water. I was on my hands and knees on the bank trying to stop it jumping back in!' It was worse than expected. Her enemies had clearly been collecting accounts from the household.

'He also says that you plucked a memory from his very head, and taunted him with it. You knew the feelings of his heart, the fancies in his brain, as you should not have done.'

'I saw it in a vision!'

'Not all visions are sent by the Almighty. Some are the delusions of a weak mind . . . and some are deceptions by the Evil One.'

Makepeace's heart sank. It seemed there was only a narrow line between prophetess and witch.

'I hear you also have an uncommon way with animals,' the interrogator went on. 'At Whitehollow there is a yellow cat called Wilterkin. They say it spits and scratches at everyone else, but within five minutes of meeting you, it was nuzzling your face as if whispering to you.'

'I dropped a scrap for it,' said Makepeace. 'It's a *cat*. You can buy any cat's love for an inch of bacon rind!' She could not believe that her great joy, the company of animals, was now considered evidence against her.

'Did you let it suck on your ear?' he asked, in the same calm, severe tone.

'What?'

'A witch will suckle the devils and familiars that are sent to her. Sometimes their teats are strangely placed. One woman was visited by a pale mouse with a man's face, who drank milk from a nipple in her ear lobe.'

There it was at last: the word 'witch'. Makepeace could feel her skin tingling.

'No,' she said, with all the scorn she could muster. 'No cat has been drinking milk out of my ear. You have let someone feed you a platter of lies.'

'Have we?' he asked coldly. 'We heard you ourselves. We heard the Devil inside you, bellowing in the woods.'

So they had heard Makepeace roaring Bear's roar, down in the foggy woodland. They were already convinced that she was an unnatural being. The interrogator had just been letting out rope so that she could tell lies and hang herself.

His eyes were severe, and a little reddened from lack of sleep, but Makepeace saw a spark of something in them. He was not handsome, tall or bold—not the sort of man to draw notice on an ordinary day. But these were uncommon times, and people had to pay attention to him. He was doing God's work.

Bear was drowsy and drained, but awake, and he could smell the man in black. The man smelt of good soap and other people's pain. He smelt a little like Young Crowe.

'We know that you tried to kill Lord Fellmotte,' the man in

black said. 'He has told us all about you. Now it is your turn to tell us about the Fellmottes.'

Symond was still calmly watching from the sidelines. He had a cat's way of smiling without smiling. But even cats had limits to their cruelty, unlike people. The sight of him filled Makepeace with fury.

'The Fellmottes are devils,' Makepeace said with feeling. 'I ran away from them. I ran to Lord Fellmotte, because I hoped he would keep me safe. But he's worse than any of them! I cried out because I was afraid of him!'

'I know that he tried to exorcise the demon in you,' said the man in black.

'Exorcise?' It was not a word Makepeace knew.

'To banish it back to Hell. The Lord has bestowed on him a great gift—the ability to drive out devils, and send unquiet spirits to their eternal rest—'

'*The Lord has bestowed . . . ?*' This was too much. 'You gulls! He's leading you all by the nose! He doesn't send ghosts to their rest! He *eats* them. I saw him do it, and *that* was why I screamed.'

'You should show him a little gratitude,' the man in black said severely. 'He thinks you can be saved.' He jotted something in a notebook, then sighed and looked at Symond. 'You were right, a most mischievous and vengeful tongue. Well, if a woman is a witch, she is usually a scold and a brawler as well. Are you sure you can win her back to God?'

'Give me some time with her,' said Symond solemnly. 'I'll see if I can drive the devils out.'

'No!' said Makepeace. 'Don't leave me with him! Listen to me! He eats ghosts! He eats *souls*!'

But they would not heed her, and she was carried back to her little room. Symond followed, and asked the guard to wait outside.

'You need to be careful with these Fellmotte witches,' Symond told him. 'If she starts throwing curses around, I can protect myself, but I cannot shield you.'

Once Symond and Makepeace were alone, he smiled. 'You should thank me,' he said. 'If I had not spoken up for you, these fellows would be trying harsh methods to win you back to righteousness.' He laughed. 'Here is the bargain. You will tell me where the charter is hidden, and I will tell our self-styled inquisitors that I have driven the demons out of you.

'Then they will sit you down, and you can confess to everything. They already have some pretty fancies about the happenings at Grizehayes. Tell them that the Fellmottes are all witches, and fly around the countryside in eggshells and mortars. Tell them that the family forced you to frolic on the hillside with the Evil One. Tell them that Mistress Gotely taught you poisons and potions, and that the kitchen dogs walked on two legs and did your bidding.

'I was in a quandary, you see. I had won these fellows' interest and protection by telling them a little of the Fellmottes' customs. But I could not prove anything unless I gave them the charter, which would leave me no threat to use against my family. But *you*, and your confession, will do very well as proof.'

'I will not confess,' said Makepeace. 'And I will not tell you where the charter is. If I tell you, you will have no reason to keep me alive. So I think I shall hold my tongue, *Master Symond*.'

The demotion to 'Master Symond' seemed to sting him even more than the rejection of the bargain.

'There's a ghost inside you, isn't there?' Symond narrowed his eyes. 'A mad one. I heard it roaring. And I suppose you didn't have the skill to consume it or kick it out, did you? I might have helped you with that, if you'd passed my test.

'Those fellows think you're possessed, and they're right. If they start to torment you, sooner or later they'll prove it.'

These men want proof that the Fellmottes are witches, said Livewell, after Symond had left. Why not give it to them? Why not tell them where to find the charter? Why are we still lying to them? You said you wanted to be the Fellmottes' undoing.

Yes, but I would like to live to see it, replied Makepeace, massaging her swollen jaw. *And I need to live so that I can save James! If I give them the charter, they will work out soon enough that I am one of the Fellmotte gifted. And what would they make of me then? I never signed a pact with the Devil in my own blood, and I don't have nipples in my ears . . . but I do consort with spirits, don't I? You said so yourself. Bear does follow me everywhere like a familiar. And I am possessed.*

And if I give up his precious charter, Symond will do his best to see me found guilty. Do you think I'll breathe free air again?

No, said the doctor grimly. We'll be lucky if they don't hang you, then congratulate themselves on saving your soul.

The charter's the only bit of power I have right now, Makepeace said bitterly, *and that's looking feeble enough.*

These are good men, persisted Livewell.

Are they? retorted Makepeace. *Their leader looks like a man who enjoys a little righteous power over people. I've seen that look before. And Bear does not like the smell of him.*

Do you trust your Bear's judgement? Livewell asked, very seriously.

Yes, said Makepeace, after a moment's thought. *I'm learning to listen to him. He's a wild brute—there are many things he lacks the wit to understand. But he knows when something's wrong.*

Then we shall not trust these men, said Livewell, with surprising firmness. What else can we do?

Could Bear fight our way out of here? the doctor asked hopefully.

It's not that simple, answered Makepeace. *I can't set him on someone, like a dog. Sometimes when he and I are both angry . . . then it's hard to stop us. But we couldn't punch our way through the door to this room, and we can't bat a bullet out of the air. There are a lot of soldiers in these woods, and they'll know by now that I've been arrested for witchcraft.*

Then your smuggler friend Helen will probably know as well, commented the doctor. Could she be an ally?

Perhaps, answered Makepeace. She suspected that the red-faced spy had been one of Helen's secret Royalist contacts. If it had not been for Makepeace's warning, Helen might have stepped aside to talk to him, and fallen under suspicion as well. The older woman might well be thankful. *But we have no way of asking for her help.*

Was that really true?

Oh, Makepeace said silently, *I am wrong. There is a way of contacting Helen. A dangerous way.*

I don't much like the sound of this, said the doctor.

Neither do I, murmured Makepeace. But she could see no other way forward. *I need to speak with Morgan.*

How could that possibly help? exclaimed Dr Quick.

Lady Morgan! Makepeace thought as loudly as she could. *I want to talk to you. I know I tried to chase you before, but I won't this time. Please, I won't harm you.*

There was no response.

I do not think the lady trusts us, **said the doctor.** She prefers to appear and disappear at will, so that we cannot keep track of her, and right now I fancy she is hidden away in her lair.

Makepeace recalled the shocking deluge of emotions and mangled memories that had assaulted her mind when she tried to 'follow' Morgan.

You told me that she was hiding in a part of my mind that was shut off from the rest, she answered silently. *I think I know what that is now. All these years, there's been a chapter of my memories I couldn't look at—wouldn't look at.*

If that's her lair . . . then I know where to find her.

CHAPTER 34

Makepeace lay on her little bed with her eyes closed, hearing herself breathe. To comfort herself she imagined herself lying on the stomach of an enormous Bear, bigger than Whitehollow, bigger than Grizehayes, his fur deeper than summer grass, the rise and fall of his breathing like the swaying of a galleon.

But she could not stay there forever. There were mind-places to go, and things to remember. There was an abyss to brave, and an enemy to face.

You can wait here for me, Makepeace told Bear. *I will come back soon. I need to face this alone.*

But Bear did not really understand. He was coming with her, of course he was. And after a moment she realized that she was the one being foolish. There was no longer any such thing as 'alone'.

So when Makepeace took a deep breath and started to remember Poplar, the younger self she pictured in her mind's eye walked with a Bear at her side. She let herself sink into the image. It was memory, it was imagination, it had the power and vividness of a dream.

There was Poplar, after all this time, with its reek and roar. The clatter and thunder of the shipyards, the fluttering poplar trees, the lush green marshlands where brown-and-cream cattle grazed. It was so vivid that the smoke stung tears from her eyes. Like clothes tucked away in a chest from the light of day, the memories had not faded. Their dyes were still bright.

And . . . Poplar itself was small, she realized. Far smaller than

Oxford or London. Just a few houses clustering around a road, like grass seeds about a stalk.

In her imagination she walked the road to London, as she had three years before. Nobody gave twelve-year-old Makepeace a second glance, or seemed to notice Bear at her side. The sunset was vast. The sky was darkening. With every step, the air became murkier and more oppressive. But there was somebody she needed to find.

Bear was still beside her. She could reach out and touch his fur, even as the roar of an angry crowd filled her ears. And when she ran, he ran beside her, on all fours.

Now they were in the crush of the apprentices' riot, a mad, screaming darkness torn by gunshots. Looming adult bodies stampeded and shifted in panic, knocking Makepeace this way and that, crushing her and blocking her view. Makepeace looked all around, desperate to see one specific face.

Where was she? Where was she? Where was she?

There. Right there.

Mother.

Every line of her face clear. The witchiness of her hair escaping from under her cap. The deep-set eyes with stars and riddles in them. Margaret.

And a carelessly swung cudgel was heading towards her undefended brow . . .

But Makepeace and Bear could prevent it! They were here now; they could block it! A bat of the paw deflected the cudgel.

But now a bottle shattered nearby, shards heading for Margaret's face . . .

Makepeace's imagined self raised a hasty arm to shield Mother.

But now a hoe was knocked out of somebody's hands, so that its blade careered towards Margaret. A thrown stone ricocheted off a wall in her direction. A bullet fired blindly took its relentless course for her temple . . .

Mother screamed.

Then she was standing in front of Makepeace, her pale face half covered in dark rivulets of blood. She stared at Makepeace, her face deathly, and then her expression twisted.

'Stay away from me!' she screamed, striking Makepeace's face with a blow that shuddered the world. 'Go away! Go away!' She shoved at her daughter with a giant's strength.

Makepeace tumbled back into a different darkness. She landed among thistles, and stared up at stars. She was in a little overgrown clearing, flanked by reeds that whispered in the wind. She sat up, and saw not far away a lowly oblong of disturbed earth. It was Mother's grave, on the edge of the Poplar marshes.

Bear was a little cub now, his soft muzzle opening to give a small bleat of dismay. He had died in these marshes, and he recognized them. Makepeace scooped him up in her arms, feeling herself shiver from cold and fear.

Beyond the edge of the clearing, among the reeds, stood the smoky silhouette of a woman. She was motionless but for her loose, wild hair, which stirred and wavered in the breeze.

'Ma,' gasped Makepeace.

You were the death of me, whispered the wind, the reeds, and the stealthy click and gurgle of the streams. *You were the death of me.*

'I'm sorry, Ma!' The words came out in a little sob. 'I'm sorry we argued! I'm sorry I ran!'

The woman-shape did not move, but suddenly it seemed to be

a lot closer, still faceless and implacable. *The death of me*, breathed the lonely marshes. *The death of me*.

'I tried to save you!' Makepeace felt her eyes sting with tears. 'I tried! But you pushed me . . . and that man carried me away . . .'

The death of me. The wind rose, and the woman's hair billowed. All of a sudden she was standing on the very edge of the clearing, silent and ominous, her face still lost in shadow.

Soon the shape would swoop at her, and Makepeace would see its terrible smoky face, and hear it slur in her ear as it clawed at her brain. And yet Makepeace was filled with an anguish and longing even greater than her fear.

'Why couldn't I save you?' Makepeace shouted at the figure. She thought again of the scene she had just left, and all her hopeless attempts to shield Mother from a fatal blow. 'Why does it have to happen? Why can't I stop it?'

It turned out that, deep down, she already knew the answer.

'It was just bad luck, wasn't it?' she whispered, and felt tears slide down her face. 'There was nothing I could do about it.'

Bear was warm and heavy in her arms. She bowed her head over him protectively, and felt his rough fur against her cheek.

'Why did you push me away, Ma?' asked Makepeace in anguish. 'I could have helped you! I could have taken you home!' She was afraid that at the end Mother had hated her so much that even her help was unbearable.

And then, at last, Makepeace finally understood.

'Oh, Ma,' she said. 'You were afraid. You were afraid for *me*.

'You didn't hate me. You guessed you were done for, and you were scared that your ghost might turn on me! You were trying to protect me. You were always, always trying to protect me.'

At last, Makepeace felt that she had begun to understand the wild, secretive mother who had brought her up. Margaret had been too inflexible, but how could she be otherwise? Nobody with a will less stubborn could have escaped the Fellmottes.

But she had loved Makepeace. She had defied the Fellmottes for Makepeace, fled house and hearth for Makepeace, worked her fingers to the bone for Makepeace. She had loved her with the cruel purity of the mother bird who forces the fledgling out of the nest to test its half-formed wings. She had done what she thought was best for her daughter. She had been right, she had been wrong, and she would never have apologized anyway.

'You loved me,' said Makepeace, hardly able to voice the words.

The night seemed to breathe out for a long, long time. Afterwards, there were no longer voices in the wind-blown reeds, and now the marshes were simply dark and cold, not seething with menace and pain. There was still a female figure at the clearing's edge, but the outline looked different now. Makepeace's eyes cleared, and she could see who the woman was, and who she was not.

'Hello, Lady Morgan,' she said, and slowly approached. Bear was larger and heavier now, and Makepeace had to put him down.

Morgan was indistinct, a woman-shape of smoke and silver pins, but as Makepeace drew closer, she could make out a clever, narrow face with heavy-lidded eyes, a high brow and a subtle, curling mouth. There was no visible sign of injury, but nonetheless she seemed subtly askew, like a picture on a slightly bent card. Evidently she had not fully recovered from her first fight with Bear.

'This was a good hiding place,' admitted Makepeace. 'You knew I couldn't face Mother's death. Even though I am haunted by you, Bear and the others, I think perhaps I have been haunted by Mother most of all. And she was never even a ghost, was she?'

Morgan sighed.

'Probably not,' she said sounding incredibly bored. 'I certainly do not think her ghost found its way back from Lambeth or the marshes to your house, in order to attack you. That really *was* a nightmare, you stupid girl.'

The Infiltrator shook her head wearily.

'I will not miss this stronghold,' she continued. 'The problem with spending time in someone else's memories, is that they start to feel like one's own, and then one is a stone's throw from starting to care about them.'

The clouds split to show a splinter of moon, and light winked on Morgan's silver eyes, her pearl-studded ruff, the rings on her fingers.

'Enough gossip,' she said abruptly. 'You may have found your way into one of my lairs, but this battle is far from over. There are several others I can use. Humans are always strangers to their own brains, and you have the usual supply of blind spots.'

'Then why were you waiting here for me?' asked Makepeace. 'Why not run to the next hiding place? I think you're bluffing. You're wounded, you're alone, and I have friends looking out for you.'

'I wanted to speak with you in private,' said Morgan, 'to demand your unconditional surrender. Let me talk to our captors, and I guarantee that I can negotiate a ransom for us. Once I am talking to the right people, there will be a price, and the Fellmotte family will pay it to have us back safely.'

'No,' said Makepeace.

'Then why are you here? Ah . . . I see.' Morgan glanced at Bear, who was now a lot more bear-sized. 'You brought your beast here to finish me.'

'No. I've come to ask you to join my side.'

'What? You really *are* desperate. Delusional, too. Why would I side with you against my own family?'

'Because you sweated out your whole life to serve them, and they treated you like dirt. And even now, they're *still* treating you like dirt. The Infiltrator is the one that has to take all the risks that Elders hate taking, isn't it? You have to slide out of the body to scout things out, or prune the minds of heirs, even though that means your spirit starts to leak away. That must be torture. And they make you do it over and over again. After everything you did for them, you're still the expendable one. And that won't ever change.

'Do you even like the other Elders? Did you ever like them? Because if not, being stuck in the same head as those arrogant, selfish, cold-blooded toads doesn't sound like immortality to me. It sounds like Hell.'

'What makes you think I am so different from them?' asked Morgan.

'I don't know for certain that you are,' said Makepeace. 'But you helped me warn Helen. Maybe you just did that so that Helen would survive and report seeing me and Symond. But maybe you saw a fellow spy in danger, and wanted to protect her.

'And . . . you knew about all of *this*.' Makepeace waved a hand at the grave, the marshes, and Poplar somewhere in the darkness. 'You knew my darkest secrets and griefs. You could have used them to torture me, weaken me and break my heart. Yet you never did.

'You're a ruthless harpy, Morgan, but you're clever and brave.

And you know what it means to have to earn something—that makes you better than the other Elders. I don't want to destroy you. I want to learn about you, and learn from you. I won't surrender to you, but there's a place here for you if you'll work with me.'

'You're only saying all this because you want something from me.'

'I do want your help, yes. But I mean what I say, too. Morgan, you're two lifetimes old. You can tell when people are lying. And you're sitting inside my brain. You *know* I'm telling the truth. Trusting you is a risk. It would be really easy for you to betray me. But if you do, I suppose it won't make my situation any worse than it is already.'

'The Fellmottes always win,' said Morgan. Little spasms of lightning flickered indecisively through her smoky form. 'I can serve them, or I can lose everything. That is the world we live in.'

'And what if the world is ending?' asked Makepeace. 'Something *is* happening, isn't it? Everything's turning upside down, and everybody feels it. If the world ended in fire tomorrow, would you be glad that you'd been the Fellmottes' faithful servant to the end? Or would you wish that you'd rebelled, and risked everything, and used all your cunning against them, just once?'

Morgan had a clever face, but not a happy one.

'I make no promises,' she said. 'But you can tell me your plan.'

CHAPTER 35

Symond was right. The witch-finders were no longer in a mood to be kind. The little window was covered over with a piece of sacking, which allowed only a thin, seeping light. The bed was removed.

Makepeace was left to herself. Just as she was wondering whether she had been forgotten, three deafening knocks sounded at the door. She jumped out of her skin, wondering why anybody would knock. To her greater confusion, nobody opened the door, and the footsteps outside passed on.

Some time later the same thing happened again. And then again, about an hour later. That strange knock became her only clock. Without light it was easy to lose track of time.

No food or drink arrived. Bear was growing ravenous and restless, and Makepeace could not stop him pacing.

When night swallowed the little prison, and faint owl quavers ruffled the cool air, Makepeace settled in a corner of the room, and tried to sleep. However, she was jolted into wakefulness by the knocks, over and over again. Each time she woke to darkness and confusion, until Bear's night-eyes told her where she was.

And then the door swung open with a crash, and there were lanterns in the room, making her blink. She was pulled to her feet and dragged out into the little study where the quiet man in black was waiting.

He had questions for her. Did the Fellmottes ever put curses on their enemies? Could they pass through stone walls? Did they rub ointment on themselves and fly? Had *she* ever flown?

He had pictures to show her. Woodcuts of witches' familiars. Had she seen anything like these at Grizehayes? A black hare leaping. A crudely drawn fish with a grimacing woman's face. A cow with a snake-like spiralling tail. A bristle-covered frog the size of a baby being fed blood with a spoon.

'No,' she said. 'No.' All the while, a vast Bear made of shadow and rage stirred in her mind, wanting to rear up and strike off heads. 'No,' she said, and the men in black thought that she was talking to them.

Not yet, Bear.

She was put back in her cell, and left in darkness. The knocks came ever and anon. The men meant to rob her of sleep and soften her will, she could see that. The thirst was even worse than the hunger. Her head ached and her mouth was like glue.

After this broken, sleepless night, when the birdsong told Makepeace that it must be morning, Symond came to visit.

He was clearly gratified to see her huddled in a corner of the room, the very picture of misery. He made a show of holding a handkerchief to his face to shield it from the stuffiness of the closet.

'I thought you might be ready to talk, but you're clearly enjoying your repose. Perhaps I should go, and come back in a couple of days . . .'

'No!' cried out Makepeace, in tones as plaintive and piercing as she could make them. 'Don't go! I'll tell you! I'll tell you where I hid the—'

'Hush!' Symond swiftly closed the door and locked it. 'Keep your voice down!' And then, as Makepeace had hoped, he crossed the room so that she could murmur to him.

At the last moment, he saw her body tense, but before he

could react she was leaping to her feet. Bear had Symond's scent. Symond smelt of thrown stones, dragged chains, blood and cruelty.

Makepeace let the roar erupt from her, knowing that it would echo through the woods. She lashed out at Symond's face, knocking him backwards. He struck his head against the wall, and slid groggily down it.

Makepeace grabbed Symond by his collar. For a moment she felt that she might break his neck. Then she remembered herself, and her plan.

Now, Morgan!

There was a brief, shuddersome sensation as though a piece of clammy gauze had been pulled out of her ear. A smoky, sinuous shape was weaving its way down her arm towards Symond's face.

Outside the room she could hear muffled shouts and loud attempts to kick the door in. Morgan's wraith reached Symond's mouth and was drawn in by his breath, half a second before the door yielded with a splintering crash.

The new arrivals managed to wrestle Symond away from Makepeace, and drag him from the room. They were too wise to try to subdue her straight away, though. Only when there were four of them did they venture back into the cell, throw a blanket over her head and bind her with ropes.

Later, when they thought she seemed calmer, they brought her back to see their leader. They kept her bound, for they had a hearty, superstitious respect for the strength of the Evil One.

'You are leaving me few options,' the man in black said.

'You could let me go,' said Makepeace, with sudden boldness. 'All I ever wanted was to be left alone. Let me go and I swear I will never harm anybody.'

'You know that I cannot do that,' he answered. 'Such powers as yours can come only from an evil source, and can only lead to evil. We must save you, and save others from you.

'There are burns on your hands,' he continued, leaning forward and lacing his fingers, 'from cooking pots and kettles. Such pain when an inch of our flesh burns, even for a second! But imagine that your hand was held against that red-hot kettle for ten seconds, not one. Now imagine the agony of a full minute, unable to pull away, or do anything but watch your skin blacken.

'Now . . . imagine a searing anguish through every inch of you, that went on for a week, a year, a lifetime, a million lifetimes. Imagine the despair of knowing that this, and a thousand other torments, would never, ever end. Imagine the grief of knowing that you might have known true happiness, but that you traded it for an eternity of horrors.

'That . . . is Hell.'

Makepeace felt goosebumps prickle over her arms. There was something about this man that reminded her of the minister in Poplar. His faith was fierce like a blade, but one more likely to cut others than himself.

'It would perhaps be a kindness,' he went on, 'if I held your hand in the candle-flame, to give you taste of the suffering that might be yours if you do not forswear evil. Better to lose a hand than your soul.'

'The Bible says we should know a tree by the fruit it bears,' Makepeace replied, a little sharply. 'If you burn my hand off, what should I think of you?'

'Suffering is sometimes the greatest blessing,' the witch-finder answered calmly. 'The child learns from the cane as well as the book. The sorrows of our lives teach and cleanse us.'

'God send you many blessings,' muttered Makepeace, but too quietly for him to hear.

'You can perhaps be saved, you see,' he went on. 'Would you not wish to be clean and free again? Would your soul not sing?'

Makepeace stayed quiet for a long time, pretending to consider his words, then broke down into choking sobs that she hoped were convincing.

'It would,' she whimpered. 'Oh, if such a thing were possible! There *is* a demon in me—'tis all true—but I never asked for it! I think the Fellmottes sent it to plague me!'

'And why should they do that?'

'Because I . . .' Makepeace dropped her gaze again and let herself stammer. 'I . . . stole from them when I ran away. There was a piece of parchment they treated as more precious than gold, so I took it with me to see if I could sell it. But when I looked at it, I was frightened—it was a fancy-lettered thing, talking of the family's dealings with spirits. And there was the King's signature on it too, and a wax seal as big as a conker.'

'Are you sure?' All the blood drained out of the interrogator's face. His eyes had the exultant but panicky expression of one who has just hooked a whale while fishing for trout, and now needs to haul it to shore. 'The King's signature? Where is it now?'

'I sent it to a friend and asked her to hold it for safekeeping,' Makepeace lied blithely.

'Where?'

'Oxfordshire—not far from Brill.'

His face fell. As Makepeace knew all too well, Brill was in the perilous zone between the two armies. But she could see him calculating the risk, and judging the worth of the gamble. A document linking the King to witches!

'Where is her house?' he asked. 'How should we find it?'

'Oh, she will not give it to anybody but me,' Makepeace said promptly. 'I told her anyone else who came after it was probably a Fellmotte spy, no matter what they looked like.'

'Then you must come with us,' he said grimly. 'This can be the start of your penance, and proof of your repentance. No time must be lost, for the Fellmottes will be seeking this paper too, and who knows how their imps may help them trace it! We shall set off today—as soon as Lord Fellmotte is well enough to ride.'

A few hours later, in warmer clothes, Makepeace was led out into daylight that seemed uncommonly bright. *What strange beasts people are*, she thought. *We adjust to everything so quickly. Perhaps we would even get used to Hell.*

To her dismay, she found that she was to share a horse with Symond. He did not look happy about this either. There was a storm-coloured bruise on his jaw, but it looked as though it were fading, not darkening. Perhaps adding ghosts to his diet allowed him to heal more quickly.

Makepeace was helped up to sit sideways in front of him, and her wrists and ankles retied. Evidently they were taking no chances. Makepeace's interrogator and his two colleagues each had their own horses.

How far can we rely upon Morgan? asked the doctor.

I asked her to tell the Fellmottes that I was being taken to Brill, Makepeace answered him silently. *I fancy she'll do that whether she decides to betray us or not.* With luck, by now the cunning spymistress had used Symond to write a coded letter while he slept, and placed it somewhere Helen would find it.

Makepeace had been dealt a poor hand, and her only hope was

to dash the cards from the other players' grasps. Chaos sounded better than hopelessness.

'Whatever you're planning, it won't work.' Symond's muttered words cut uncomfortably into Makepeace's thoughts. 'Sooner or later you'll need me as a friend. If you get that charter to me somehow, I'll pardon you. But if it ends up in anyone else's hands, I swear I'll see you hanged for a witch on a hawthorn tree. And then I'll come for your ghost. I'll flay your mind away, one sliver at a time, over a whole week, until there's only a whimper of you left. Then I'll keep that forever to frighten other ghosts, like a hunting trophy on my wall.'

Makepeace said nothing, sitting as straight as she could on the horse's broad back. Being slowly digested by Symond sounded more like Hell than a cauldron of fire.

PART SEVEN: WORLD'S END

CHAPTER 36

On the long ride, Makepeace felt exposed, the ropes around her wrists and ankles drawing every eye. Thin, nervous rain trickled down her neck and nestled in her eyelashes, and she could not wipe them away. Before her, Symond's gloved hands gripped the reins, and the horse's neck bobbed.

After time, however, the motion started to lull her. Bear wanted to sleep, so Makepeace let him have his way. There was nothing she could do now, and she would need to be awake later. She let her eyelids droop, leaving her enemy with the task of keeping her on the horse.

Makepeace woke again at a little riverside village stuffed to the gills with troops, horses and tents amid the sloping woods. Her interrogator was talking to some of the soldiers.

'We can spare a few men, but no horses,' said one of the officers. 'We've trouble enough. That truce is fraying like a slut's hem. The King talks a good peace, but wise heads say he's keeping us dangling till his queen can raise more troops and smash us to splinters. His promises aren't worth a fart.'

Four soldiers joined their group. Two carried muskets and wore bandoliers strung with little wooden gunpowder bottles. Makepeace was helped down from the horse, and her ankles untied. From here, she was told, the journey would be on foot.

The little group stayed close to the hedgerows, one man moving ahead of the rest. Makepeace guessed that they were trying to avoid being seen.

At last she glimpsed ahead the cottage where the Axeworths

had lived. She was relieved to see that the chickens were gone, which probably meant that the little family had left. The barrow was missing too, along with the sorry relic that had lain beneath it.

'That is my friend's house,' Makepeace said.

'It seems very quiet.' The interrogator peered at the cottage, and seemed to be weighing his options. 'Come—let us go to the door. You can talk to your friend.'

'Like this?' Makepeace held up her bound wrists. 'She'll see I'm a captive!'

With evident reluctance, he untied her hands. The two of them walked to the door, and the interrogator knocked. As Makepeace expected, there was no reply.

After a few more knocks, he opened the door, and entered with two soldiers at his back. A couple of minutes later, he emerged again.

'This house is empty,' he said.

'Then she must be out,' Makepeace said quickly. 'If we wait, she'll come back.'

He took hold of her arm, and pulled her in through the front door.

'Will she?' he asked. 'This place looks abandoned to me.'

The little cottage had been stripped bare. All the portable furniture was gone, along with the pewter, the rush-light stand, and all the firewood and kindling by the hearth. Even the chair in which Makepeace's patient had sat was missing.

'I don't know what's happened!' She looked at the interrogator with a prepared expression of bewildered innocence. 'My friend said she would wait for me here!'

'Did she hide the charter in the house, or take it with her?' he demanded.

'How should I know?' Makepeace retorted.

'Search the house,' the interrogator ordered the soldiers. 'I'll have a man at the window, and another in that tree out there, to look out for trouble.' The soldiers began taking up floorboards, knocking holes in walls and poking sticks up inside the chimney flue. 'Don't forget to check the rafters and the thatch!'

Makepeace stayed near the door, gazing out across the fields, looking for some sign of movement. Behind her she could hear smashes, and even the occasional swear word. The interrogator's snapped insistence that the soldiers 'mind their Billingsgate tongues' sounded just as ill-tempered. There was anger everywhere, she realized, just under the surface. Somehow she had grown used to tasting it in the air.

'Soon they'll realize that you've been selling them a tarradiddle,' Symond said in Makepeace's ear. 'How do you think they'll all react when they know you've been wasting their time? Give me one good reason to stop them from shooting you in the yard.'

He was right. Time was running out.

Out across the fields, a hovering kestrel caught her eye. It tilted and fluttered in the air above a hedgerow, and she could almost imagine some small, oblivious creature below it. Then, instead of a straight swoop, it sped off in a long, low slant, as if its little quarry had suddenly raced away. At the same moment, she saw two small birds flit from the same patch of hedge in the opposite direction.

'There's something out there,' she said under her breath.

'What?' Symond sounded sceptical. 'What are you talking about?'

There was an angry thunder of steps and Makepeace was swung round to face the interrogator.

'Mistress, we have bared this cottage's very bones—'

'There's something out there,' Makepeace said again, louder this time. 'Behind that far hedge, near the meadowsweet.'

'Ignore the crafty little baggage,' Symond said with contempt. 'She's lying again.'

'What did you see?' The interrogator frowned.

'Nothing,' said Makepeace. 'But the birds did. Something scared them.' She saw his caution wrestling with his doubt and annoyance.

'Make sure your muskets are ready,' he muttered to his comrades, 'and let's get those matches lit!'

One of the men busied himself with flint and steel. When the match cords were smouldering, they were handed out to the musketeers in readiness.

'I see something!' called the man in the tree outside. 'There, by the elm—'

There was a thud, and a thump as he fell from the tree, a gash in the back of his head. A heavy rock tumbled down beside him.

'That came from behind the house!' shouted someone, and then somebody else yelled, 'There!'

There was a loud crack as one of the musketeers fired, and the room filled with smoke. Just before the gunshot, however, Bear had smelt something else. A familiar scent, from above . . .

'Roof!' was all Makepeace had time to shout. Half her companions heard her and looked up. Half did not. The latter had no chance when the Elder in James's body crashed through the ragged thatch and landed in the middle of the room, sword drawn.

He was snake-fast, kestrel-fast. He lunged to impale the musketeer that had not fired, slashed across the throat of another soldier, and carved into the face of one of the men in black. Three men fell. They leaked thin, shimmering ghosts that rippled and faded.

But Makepeace's warning had marred James's perfect attack. The interrogator tumbled backwards, and the cut that would have blinded him knocked his hat off instead. His other colleague managed a desperate parry. The surviving musketeer dropped his ramming rod mid-reload and leaped backwards, reversing his weapon to use it as a club. Meanwhile, Symond swiftly stepped behind Makepeace. Reaching an arm over her shoulder, he fired his pistol at James's head from close range.

James was darting to one side even as the trigger pulled. The bullet missed him, cracking the brickwork behind him, but he gave a snarl, clutching at a red powder-burn on the skin around his right eye. The smoke from the pistol blinded him for a fatal instant. Makepeace flung herself forward and lunged for his sword hand, jolting the hilt from his grasp. The musketeer struck him in the face with the butt of his gun, knocking him to the floor.

'Kill him!' shouted Symond, taking a step back.

'No!' cried Makepeace. Now for a gamble of all gambles. She looked appealingly at the interrogator. 'We need him alive, so his men will surrender! And . . . I *know* this man! He's not a witch, just demon-cursed, like me! He needs Lord Fellmotte to exorcise him!'

'Don't listen to her!' bellowed Symond.

'Lord Fellmotte!' erupted the interrogator, losing patience. 'Exorcise the prisoner!'

Symond gave Makepeace a fleeting glance of pure hatred. He put away his sword, and drew his dirk instead. He ventured closer, making sure that at all times the blade was pointed firmly at the prisoner. Slowly and carefully, he dropped to a crouch, and laid a hand on the prisoner's shoulder.

And then, to everyone's surprise including his, his right hand gave an odd little spasm, and tossed his dirk away across the room.

Elder James promptly grabbed Symond by the shoulders to stop him pulling away, and let his jaw drop wide. He breathed out with a sound like a broken bellows, and only Makepeace saw the smoky forms of ghosts surge from his throat towards Symond's face.

Symond gave a short gargle of shock as spirits seethed in through his eyes, ears, nostrils and mouth. Then his face, usually so mask-like, jittered helplessly between different paroxysms of terror.

Makepeace quietly backed against a wall, her skin crawling. Given the choice between a half-blinded, captured bastard, and a well-trained heir with a blade in his hand, the ghosts had seized a golden chance to trade up. She had hoped for this, but the sight of it still made her feel sick.

James released Symond and fell backwards, looking shocked and stunned. Symond stood shakily, then staggered across the room, his arms jerking and twitching.

'My lord?' The interrogator's free hand was fumbling at his pocket, and Makepeace wondered if he was looking for his bible. 'My lord . . . are you well?'

Symond stooped to pick up his dirk, then straightened. He wobbled on his feet for a moment, so that the interrogator reached out to steady him. Then Symond drove his dirk into the interrogator's stomach with shocking force.

He drew his sword with unnatural speed, and hacked swiftly into the side of the remaining musketeer's neck. The last soldier had just time to scream as he was run through.

There was a ragged sound of steps outside, and the front door was flung open. White Crowe burst in, with a young soldier in Fellmotte colours by his side. Both immediately pointed their weapons at Symond.

'Oh, put those away!' snapped the Elder in Symond's body. 'Can you not see who I—'

There was a crack, and he stiffened as if listening intently. A round, dark hole was suddenly visible in his forehead. Makepeace could smell smoke, that same metallic hellfire gunsmoke.

'Oh, I know who you are,' said the young Royalist soldier, 'you toad-licking traitor.' A wreath of smoke surrounded his pistol. Symond collapsed to the ground, still wearing an expression of intense concentration.

'You fool!' shouted White Crowe. 'We were supposed to capture Master Symond alive!'

'I'll hang before I regret it,' said the young soldier with feeling. 'My brother died at that battle, thanks to him.' Other soldiers piled in behind him, took in the scene at a glance, and pointed their weapons at Makepeace.

'Are you badly hurt, my lord?' White Crowe stooped beside James.

James gave Makepeace a dazed, haggard glance. And yes, it *was* James at last, the real James. When she saw his hand start to move towards hers, she gave him a tiny, urgent shake of the head, willing him to understand. To her relief, she saw realization dawn across his face.

Groggily James glanced at White Crowe instead, and shook his head.

'A powder burn, nothing more,' he rasped. 'A minor inconvenience.' It was not a perfect impression of the voice he

379

had used as an Elder, but close enough. 'One of them was lucky . . . briefly.'

'My lord, let me help you to the carriage,' said White Crowe, wrapping one of James's arms over his shoulder. He helped James to his feet and guided him out through the door. 'Bring the girl,' he said over his shoulder.

Nobody but Makepeace paid any attention to Symond's body. White Crowe's men were not gifted. They heard no faint, spectral screams, like fingernails against the mind. And they saw nothing when ghosts swirled out of Symond like dirty water.

But Makepeace saw them as she was manhandled towards the door. They rose and mingled, writhing, thrashing and smokily bleeding into the air. These were the 'wolves' for which Mother had prepared her. Soon they would sense her, and the haven at her core. Then they would come for her.

But she could not leave without Morgan.

The two closest ghosts were locked in battle, tearing vaporous strands from each other. The larger was already badly tattered, perhaps savaged by Symond's predatory mind. The smaller one looked different from the other ghosts, and moved more quickly and sinuously.

Morgan.

Makepeace feigned a stumble, and fell from her captors' arms to the floor. Steeling her will, she threw out one arm, with her fingers almost touching the Infiltrator's ghost. It broke from its fight, and spiralled swiftly up her arm. She breathed deeply to draw in air and one spymistress-ghost, repressing a shudder as she did so.

As the soldiers picked Makepeace up and dragged her out of the cottage, the other ghost streaked towards her head. She had a brief glimpse of a hazy, misshapen face. Then for a fearful moment everything was twilit, as the phantom tried to pour in through her eyes.

But this ghost was panicky and already fraying. It was not ready for her defences, battle-hardened by her graveyard vigils. It was not ready for her angels of the mind. And most of all, it was not ready for Bear. When Makepeace's vision cleared again, the shreds of her attacker were floating on the air like dark gossamer.

Are you hurt? Makepeace asked quickly, trying to get a sense of Morgan's presence in her head, while her captors hurried her down the path after White Crowe and James.

A minor inconvenience, came the wry response in Morgan's familiar hard-edged voice. And that is not a question I have been asked in a very long time.

Makepeace cast an anxious glance back towards the cottage, looking for more spectral pursuers.

They will seek us, but they are wounded, murmured Morgan. And they have just lost their Infiltrator.

'If we hurry,' White Crowe was saying, 'we can reach Grizehayes before the enemy's reinforcements, and slip past the siege in darkness. With luck Lord Fellmotte is still alive—we still have a chance of getting the girl to him in time!'

James and Makepeace exchanged a fleeting, panicky glance, but what could they do?

'Lead on,' James said huskily.

After all Makepeace's plans, struggles and escapes, it seemed that she was going back to Grizehayes after all. For a moment she felt as though it had been biding her time and watching her efforts, before putting out one long, lazy cat paw, and pinning her like a wounded bird.

CHAPTER 37

Only when she was tucked inside the Fellmotte carriage alongside James did Makepeace dare to speak.

'Is anyone listening to us?' she murmured.

'I don't think so,' James whispered back. 'The driver won't hear us, and everybody else is on horses.'

'That's not what I mean,' said Makepeace, meeting his eye and raising an eyebrow.

It took a moment for her meaning to sink in. James looked rueful and shook his head.

'Just me in here now,' he said.

'Let's look at your eye, then,' Makepeace whispered. James showed his face, and she noticed the singed spatter pattern on the skin of his cheek, and the painful redness of his eyeball.

'I can't see properly out of it,' murmured James, with commendable composure. 'Everything is blurry . . .'

Makepeace spent a few moments in silent consultation with the doctor.

'Your eye should mend,' she said, 'in a day or two. A friend of mine says he's seen the like before. And he says that if we wash out that burn and dress it you'll lose that leper-look in a few weeks.'

'Friend?' James's brows rose in consternation. 'Makepeace— what have you done?'

'Me? What did *you* do?' Makepeace could not resist giving him a small, fierce punch in the arm. 'You used me to hide that charter! Then you ran away without me! I waited at those stocks for ages! I thought you'd been caught and hanged!'

'I always meant to come back! But everything happened so fast. Symond had a plan—he said he'd use the charter to threaten the family, and get some of his estates ahead of time. Then he'd set up his own manor, with no Inheritance or ghosts, and he'd bring us there to join his household. And nobody would trouble us while we had that charter.'

'You should have told me!'

'He made me promise silence,' James said simply. 'A man who breaks his word is better dead.'

'Well, you broke your word to me when you threw yourself face-first on a pile of Fellmotte ghosts!' Makepeace gave him a sharp little pinch, as if they were much younger children. There was an angry joy in voicing her frustration.

'I'm sorry!' hissed James, and seemed to mean it. 'If I could take it back I would! If you had been there that day, you would understand. When I found Sir Anthony bleeding on the ground, and he beckoned me over . . . it felt like Providence. As if some star of my birth had shaped me for that moment! That one chance to become something . . . great.

'And it *was* greatness, Makepeace! You don't know the things I could do when I'd Inherited. The languages that sprang into my head, the sword moves I suddenly knew, and all the dealings of the court laid out for me like a web on a loom! And to give orders and see things done, to watch doors open, to have everything possible—'

'To chase your own kin across two and a half counties,' Makepeace interjected sharply.

James put an arm around her shoulders and squeezed her tightly for a few seconds, then kissed the top of her head.

'I know,' he muttered into her cap. 'I was the Lord of Fools. I thought I would still be myself, and change everything. But I was just a puppet. The bean in the cake—that's what you said, wasn't it? Giving up my freedom for a game of lordship.'

He sighed.

'I felt . . . sorry for him too,' he admitted, sounding embarrassed. 'Sir Anthony. He was still one of those devils, but when he was lying there in his own blood he looked frightened, like any dying man. It was hard to say no. I know, 'tis a stupid reason.'

'Yes.' Makepeace remembered her own helpless desire to save Livewell's disintegrating ghost. 'A stupid reason. But not the worst kind of stupid reason.'

She hugged him back, and sighed.

'You'll have another game of lordship to play when we reach Grizehayes,' she said under her breath. 'You must play Lord of Misrule in good earnest, and play it well, or we're both for the pot.'

'What about you?' James studied her face with a concerned frown. 'What *have* you done to yourself, Makepeace?'

'Don't worry.' Makepeace squeezed his hand, and searched for the right words. 'I'm not haunted against my will. I just made some new friends.'

'So there are ghosts inside you?' James seemed to be struggling with the idea.

'James.' It was Makepeace's turn to admit to a betrayal. 'I have *always* been haunted, for as long as you have known me. I brought a ghost with me to Grizehayes, and nobody guessed. I should have told you. I wanted to tell you. But you were right, I *am* a coward sometimes. Trust frightens me more than pain.

'He is my friend, and my battle-brother. We are woven into

each other. I want you to understand him, so you can understand me. Let me tell you about him.'

During the long and wearying ride, the carriage stopped now and then for a change of horses, but not to break the journey. Occasionally there would be sounds of challenges outside and muffled voices. Sometimes passwords were exchanged, sometimes coins or papers, sometimes gunshots.

With a sense of inevitability, Makepeace saw the countryside change and revert. Lush fields yielded to moorland. Damp lambs followed the black-faced sheep down the paths between the gorse mounds. Everything was so familiar it hurt. The sights and colours locked around Makepeace's mind like a familiar shackle.

The convoy halted in a little copse, just after sunset. The driver and one soldier stayed to look after the carriage and horses. White Crowe, Makepeace and James continued on foot, accompanied by five other soldiers wearing Fellmotte colours. Makepeace recognized a few of them from the neighbouring villages, and was sure she had once bought ladles from one of them. But war had recast them all. They had new costumes, and new roles to play.

White Crowe had found an eye-patch of black cloth for James. Thankfully nobody expected James to lead the troop while he was injured and half blind. If he had, the others might soon have guessed that he no longer wielded the skills and knowledge of an Elder.

Grizehayes they saw from a distance, its distinctive towers silhouetted against the last violet glimmer of the fading day. However, it was no longer alone.

On the darkling expanse around it, where once there had been flat, unbroken ground, a straggling, ramshackle town seemed to have risen up from the very earth. Clusters of dun-coloured canvas tents had sprouted, and among them campfires glowed like scattered embers. The camp was a crescent shape, curling its tapering arms to embrace Grizehayes. However, it did not encircle the great house completely, and there was still a wide, wary distance between the nearest tents and the ancient grey walls.

It was true, then. Grizehayes was under siege.

One soldier vanished into the darkness to scout ahead, and soon returned.

'Our guards on Widow's Tower have seen our lantern signal and returned it,' he said. 'They know we're here, so they'll be ready to let us in through the sally gate.'

'If the enemy saw the signal in the tower, they'll know the household is signalling to someone in the dark,' said White Crowe. 'They'll be watching for us. Quiet as death, everyone. They'll have scouts of their own outside the camp, far away from the fires so that their eyes can adjust to the dark.'

Gingerly they crept through the darkness skirting the edge of the camp, following White Crowe's lead. They nearly blundered into a clutch of enemy musketeers, but noticed them in time, thanks to the quiet rattle of their bandoliers, and the pinpoint glow of their slow matches.

Makepeace briefly wondered about grabbing James's hand, running towards these strangers and surrendering. It would save her from Grizehayes, but seemed like an excellent recipe for getting shot.

At last the group cleared the tip of the camp's crescent, and now there was only a dark expanse of uneven ground between them and the distant walls. Makepeace could make out the dark, arched outline of the small sally door at the top of its flight of steps.

'Run,' said White Crowe, 'and stop for nothing.'

As they sprinted for the door, there were a few cries from the direction of the camp. A single optimistic shot rang out, but the bullet flew wild into the darkness. Only when Makepeace reached the portcullis with the others did she dare to glance back. A few dark figures were running from the direction of the tents, but faltered as rocks were hurled at them from the tower above.

The portcullis was hastily hauled up, and when it was half raised, Makepeace and the others quickly ducked beneath it, into the short, unlit tunnel beyond. The portcullis dropped behind them with a clang, and shortly after, the door at the far end of the tunnel opened, to reveal Young Crowe with a lantern.

'Welcome back, my lord,' he said. 'Your arrival with Lady Maud is not a moment too soon.'

'His lordship is sinking like a stone,' said Young Crowe, as he hustled the new arrivals towards the chapel. 'He will not last the night—I doubt he will see out the hour.'

Once again Makepeace was being hurried to Lord Fellmotte's side, so that ghosts could be crammed into her shell.

I do not know what will happen, Makepeace silently told her invisible companions. *I do not know if James has a plan. The Crowes may tie us down and flood us with Fellmotte ghosts. We might have to fight.*

Well, at least our practice fighting each other will not have gone to waste, said Dr Quick.

If we leave our enemies sicker than we found them, Livewell said laconically, then today is a good day.

Bear made no sound, but Makepeace could feel him in her head, and it strengthened her.

Morgan was also silent. It occurred to Makepeace that such a battle would give the spymistress the chance to switch sides again, and rejoin her old coterie. *If it happens, it happens*, she told herself. *Until then, I trust her.*

En route, Young Crowe also gave a rapid report on the progress of the siege.

The army had been outside for about a week. The siege force had only three big guns—two mortars that flung larger stones and flaming grenadoes, and a demi-culverin with better range. The Old Tower had taken a few knocks, and some of the turrets now had a broken-toothed look. So far, however, Grizehayes's thick walls had shrugged off the worst of the damage.

'They have asked for our surrender repeatedly, of course,' said Young Crowe. 'The traditional offer—all the women, children and civilians allowed to leave, and then terms of surrender to be negotiated. Of course, Lady April has said no each time.'

Lady April was at Grizehayes. This was bad news. Makepeace had been hoping that no other Elders were in the great house.

'How is Lady April now?' James asked carefully. The same thought had clearly occurred to him.

'Oh, still recovering from her injuries.' Young Crowe gave Makepeace a brief, cold look. 'She remains in her sickbed except when she is needed.'

'And the rest of the family?' asked James.

'Sir Marmaduke is hoping to bring troops here to break the siege—though it's God's own guess whether they arrive before the enemy's reinforcements,' said Young Crowe. 'The Bishop is in the north, winning hearts and minds to the cause. Sir Alan is still in London, fighting in the courts against the sequestration.' Makepeace had heard of these powerful members of the Fellmotte family before. Thankfully, it sounded like they were busy elsewhere.

Makepeace listened to Young Crowe's account with slight relief. If Lady April was still keeping to her quarters and the other Elders were away, perhaps James might yet avoid coming face to face with someone who could see that he was not possessed.

'Our cellars are well stocked with gunpowder and two months' supply of food, and we have all the water we need from our well.' Young Crowe was thinner than usual and a bit less dapper. 'The towers are manned with the local trained band, and some of the best shots amongst our fowlers and game keepers. Whenever the rebels get too close to the walls, we drop rocks and hot oil on them.

'The rebels have set sappers to dig a trench running from their camp towards the west wall. They are probably hoping to set mines at the base, but they won't reach it before Sir Marmaduke's forces arrive to relieve us. Grizehayes has been besieged before. These walls never fall. You might as well hurl cherries at a mountain.'

Makepeace could feel the weight of the ancient house crushing in on her again, pressing her thoughts and will like flowers. Had she really imagined that this place might lose its power over her?

The door of the chapel swung open. In the great chair, as if he had not moved since her departure, Lord Fellmotte was waiting for Maud.

Makepeace could not help noticing that the chair next to that of Lord Fellmotte now had metal shackles attached to confine the sitter's wrists and ankles. Clearly the household were no longer willing to put their trust in mere rope and wood.

'Lady April asked to be notified as soon as we returned,'

declared White Crowe, then gave a hasty bow and strode away. James and Makepeace exchanged a panicky look, but there was no good excuse to stop him.

Old Crowe was in the chapel, fussing over Lord Fellmotte, who looked greyer and thinner than ever. Lord Fellmotte's feet were bare, and rested on a pair of dead pigeons that lay in a pool of their own fresh blood. It was an old and desperate remedy, used when death was thought imminent, as a last-ditch attempt to draw out sickness.

The steward glanced up as they entered, and looked almost tearfully relieved to see both Makepeace and James.

'My lord! Oh, my lord, you have her! I shall fetch the drug straight away!'

'No!' snapped James, in a harsh, Elder-like voice. The chapel echoed the word, adding its own gilded echoes. 'The drug will not be needed. Fasten the girl into the chair.'

'But . . .' The steward faltered, and exchanged a glance with his son. 'The girl has a monster inside her! Last time she—'

'Did you hear me?' James asked, his tone coldly menacing.

There was a flurry of obedience. Makepeace was dragged over to the chair, and shoved down into it. The cold of the shackles as they fastened around her ankles and wrists gave her a chill of panic, but she fought it down.

'Now leave!' commanded James, snatching the key from Young Crowe's hand. 'All of you!'

The two Crowes stared at him with astonishment and dismay. Makepeace thought she saw a glimmer of suspicion in Young Crowe's eyes.

'Now!' bellowed James.

Still looking shocked and doubtful, the Crowes left the room, taking the soldiers with them. James quickly barred the chapel door, then ran over and unlocked Makepeace's shackles, his hands shaking with haste.

'The Crowes know something is wrong,' he said under his breath. 'They couldn't say no to an Elder, but when Lady April gets here they'll flock to her instead. That door will hold them out for a while, though.'

'James,' whispered Makepeace as the shackles loosened. 'We can't stay in here! Lord Fellmotte might die at any moment!'

She saw realization dawn across her brother's face. If the lord died, seven ancient, desperate ghosts would be released . . . and would sense the two tempting vessels trapped in a room with them. Makepeace had ghostly friends to defend her, and could at least try to repel boarders. Her brother, however, did not.

James muttered a word unfit for chapel.

'What in scarlet Hell do we do?'

CHAPTER 38

The siblings stared at the sick man's slack face and seething, antagonistic gaze.

'We need to get out of here,' Makepeace said.

The stained-glass windows were too small. As she looked around frantically, inspiration struck.

'James, there *is* another way out!' Makepeace pointed to the raised gallery at the back of the chapel. 'There's a door at the back of it, and a corridor leading to the family's chambers! Can you climb there, then lower something so you can help me up?' She remembered him nimbly scaling the tower to visit her on their first meeting.

'I can't leave you down here with him!' James pointed to the dying lord.

'If you get possessed again,' Makepeace said sharply, 'you will turn on me. You need to keep away from him for *my* safety.'

'You're going to win every argument from now on by talking about "that time you were possessed", aren't you?' James muttered, as he clambered on to a sarcophagus, then placed his foot cautiously on a marble head protruding from the wall. It promptly broke away under his weight, and fell to the floor with a loud smash.

There were sounds of confused voices outside the main chapel door. Evidently Inheritance did not usually involve property damage. Makepeace heard Old Crowe shout a question. This was followed by loud, insistent knocking.

James swore, still hanging off the wall.

Makepeace's gaze crept back to the slumped shape in the great chair. It still hurt her to see the kindly features of Sir Thomas looking so pale and ill.

'I'm sorry, Sir Thomas,' she whispered, even though she knew he was just a shell. 'I liked you. I'm sorry you never had a proper deathbed. I'm sorry to leave you like this. And I know you died for the sake of the family . . . but I have to stop them. Forever.'

Something had changed in his face, she realized. A light had gone out of it. She had already started backing away when the first ghost seeped out of the corner of his mouth like smoke.

'James!' she shouted. 'They're coming!'

Her brother was just scrambling over the rail into the gallery. He tugged down a hanging that decorated the back wall, knotted one end to the rail, and tossed the loose end down to dangle from the gallery.

'Climb this!'

Makepeace ran over and grasped the cloth, and started to climb, using the few treacherous footholds in the wall. Behind her, the air was thickening with whispers.

She was precariously perched on a slender ledge when something shadowy swooped towards her head. She felt it tickle, moth-like, in her ear as it tried to tunnel its way in. Her left foot slipped off, and only her grip on the cloth rope stopped her falling.

Let me do the climbing! hissed Livewell urgently.

He was right. Makepeace could not fight and climb at once. She gave him her hands and feet, and braced for the fight.

She did not know who he was, the Elder-ghost clawing his way into her mind. As their minds bruised each other, she glimpsed memories—a thousand arrows darkening the sky like a thundercloud, ships on fire, bishops kneeling, a library the size of a cathedral. His certainty hit her like a battering ram, and for a moment it shook her will.

What was she doing, refusing to accept her destiny? How could she want so many centuries of memories to be lost? It was like sawing down a millennia-old tree.

But it was a tree with roots that strangled. She was killing the past in self-defence.

I am sorry, Makepeace told the Elder-ghost. *Wherever your soul goes next, I hope you find mercy. But I cannot show you any.*

Makepeace lashed out with her mind at the attacking ghost, and she could feel the doctor add his will to hers. Bear's wrath was a furnace. But this ghost was no desperate wisp. It was powerful and cunning, and she could feel it sliding its claws into the weak parts of her defences.

Then Morgan chose her side. She suddenly surged from hiding, and appeared at the other Elder's side, mingling her strength with his. Makepeace sensed the Elder's recognition and exultatation—shortly followed by horror as the spymistress tore him in two.

That, remarked Morgan, as his screaming fragments melted away, is a trick that will only work once.

Makepeace reached the rail, and James pulled her on to the gallery. They hastily opened the door, and sprinted down the corridor. Behind them, the air quivered with a thin, musical sibilance as more spirits rose out of Lord Fellmotte and set off in pursuit. The siblings fled down corridor after darkened corridor, then dived into the Map Room to catch their breath.

'We need to think!' James pressed his knuckles against his temples and let out a breath. 'We can't get out of Grizehayes.

Everything's guarded and locked. But if we keep running long enough, the loose ghosts will melt away. Then, even if we do get captured, at least we can't be possessed!'

'We can still be killed!' Makepeace pointed out. 'We let Lord Fellmotte's ghosts bleed into mist! Do you think the family will ever forgive that?'

'We're valuable spares, and you're the only person who knows where their charter is hidden, remember?' countered James. 'At least we have a *chance* of bargaining! They need allies right now, and so do we. That army out there is a bigger threat to all of us. Like it or not . . . we're all on the same side.'

'No, James!' hissed Makepeace with feeling. 'We're not!'

'Then what's *your* plan?'

Makepeace steeled herself.

'We do what the enemy sappers wanted to do,' she said. 'We blow a hole in the outer wall. We force Grizehayes to surrender.'

For several seconds, James stared at her in disbelief and horror.

'No!' he hissed at last. 'That's treason! That's not just betraying the Fellmottes, that's betraying the King!'

'I don't care!' Makepeace spat back. 'I only care about the people who live in this county!'

She drew a ragged breath, and tried to force her thoughts into words.

'Maybe Sir Marmaduke will turn up and break the siege,' she said. 'But Parliament *needs* this county. They'll have to send another, bigger army.'

'So what if they do?' exclaimed James. 'You've seen how strong our walls are!' There was an unmistakable note of pride, and Makepeace noticed the 'our'.

'Then there's another siege,' she answered. 'A long one. Food runs short in Grizehayes. People start eating dogs, rats and horses. The army outside takes food from all the villages around because otherwise they'll starve. Winter comes and *everybody* goes hungry. The trees are cut down and there are fights over firewood. Then people start dying of camp fever.

'Right now the enemy's willing to let Grizehayes surrender, which means everybody here would get out alive. What happens to all the women and children and old people if we *don't* surrender, and the walls fall later anyway?'

'Then . . . it could get very ugly,' James admitted, scowling. He did not go into details.

'The Fellmottes won't surrender,' said Makepeace. 'And they don't even care about the King! They'd sacrifice everybody here to keep Grizehayes. Because Grizehayes is their heart, James! I want to strike at their heart.'

The siblings were relieved to find the nearest stairway unguarded, and descended as quickly and stealthily as they could. All was quiet in the darkened passageways around the kitchens. In the fuel store, next to the stacks of logs, they found a number of promising barrels.

'Are you sure you can make this explode?' James whispered, as he started carefully rolling a barrel out of the room.

I watched the sappers preparing them, Livewell told Makepeace. There's no great trick to it. The hard part was always getting close enough to the wall without being shot by the enemy.

Makepeace nodded to herself.

'That won't be a problem,' she told James.

'Those little pauses,' said James, 'when you listen to voices I can't hear, are not getting any less disturbing.'

They manoeuvred the barrel down into the wine cellar, laying it against the foundations of the western wall.

Following Livewell's advice, Makepeace pulled the cork out of the side of the barrel, and inserted a short length of match cord.

'We need to pile things on top of it,' she said, relaying his words. 'Earth, rocks or anything heavy.' They clustered other full barrels around it, then crept to the kitchen to find other pileables.

It was strange to be back in the kitchen again, and to see everything that had filled her days and worn her hands rough. The dogs flocked to Makepeace as if she had never been absent. Bear was wary, feeling that the kitchen had started to smell different in his absence, and wanted to rub his shoulder against the table until it was his again.

Not now, Bear.

James and Makepeace carried down heavy pans, sacks of grain and pailfuls of salt from the meat safe. All of these were piled on top of the little barrel, until it was almost buried, but for the jutting match cord.

Her hand shaking, Makepeace lit the end of the fuse, so that it glowed red.

Grizehayes must fall. It was Makepeace's only way of striking at the Fellmottes' terrible certainty. Grizehayes was their arrogance made stone. It was proof of their centuries. It told them they were eternal.

'Now let's get out of here!' whispered James. The pair of them hurried up the cellar stairs, then came to a halt as they noticed half a dozen figures standing at the top.

White Crowe and Young Crowe had their swords drawn. Around them stood three of the Grizehayes manservants, now armed. At the back, Lady April's metallic white face gleamed like a poisonous moon.

How did they find us? wondered Makepeace. Too late she remembered Bear's unease. The kitchen, and particularly the table, had smelt different—and slightly frightened.

Of course. With Makepeace gone, Grizehayes had recruited a new kitchen boy or girl to keep an eye on the fire at night. So some child had lain terrified as intruders lumbered around the kitchen talking of gunpowder, and had taken the first chance to slip away and report . . .

Sorry, Bear. I forgot to listen to you.

James did not even hesitate. He immediately straightened, raising his chin imperiously high.

'What is this foolery?' he demanded, in an impressively irritable impression of his voice as an Elder.

'If you please . . . If you might be willing to come with us . . .' said Young Crowe, in a tone that managed to sound grovelling and aggressive at the same time.

'What mean these swords?' James glared. 'How dare you wave bare blades at Lord Fellmotte!' He gestured towards Makepeace.

'That is not Lord Fellmotte,' said Lady April coldly.

Do you trust me to speak? asked Morgan.

Yes, answered Makepeace quickly.

It was not the first time she had felt Morgan take control of her throat and use her voice, but this time at least it was done with permission, and did not feel as if it might choke her.

'Galamial Crowe,' said Morgan's hard-edged voice through Makepeace's mouth. 'If you lack the wit to know your own lord, then we wasted the money we gave your father for your schooling. Was the advice we gave you on your twentieth birthday also wasted?'

Makepeace could feel her own body language changing too. Her posture became more stooped, in Obadiah's old fashion. There was an inexpressible strangeness in feeling her own expression change, her brow puckering, and her mouth moving in ways that it seldom did.

'That *is* his lordship!' exclaimed Young Crowe, lowering his sword.

'And you, Myles Crowe.' Morgan spoke again through Makepeace. 'Have you forgotten the day we vouched for your character at Gladdon Beacon?'

White Crowe started to put up his sword, then paused, his eyes fixed on the little turnspit dog, which had trotted down the steps towards Makepeace's feet. Without thinking about it, she had moved one foot to stroke under the dog's chin with her toe. It was a gesture of habit, but not the habit of a lord. He stared at her, his gaze cloudy with indecision and doubt.

'Seize them!' commanded Lady April.

'No!' Young Crowe moved to stand in front of James and Makepeace. 'Forgive me, Lady April,' he said shakily, 'I never did think to disobey you in anything. But my first loyalty is to Lord Fellmotte.'

'Defend the head of the steps!' shouted James, and two of the other men obediently moved to stand alongside Young Crowe. White Crowe still did not move. A man on Lady April's side tried to bat Young Crowe's sword aside, and immediately a cramped skirmish broke out, blades clashing and striking sparks off the walls.

Taking advantage of the confusion, James grabbed Makepeace's hand and ran with her, back down the cellar stairs. It was their only line of retreat. They hid among the maze of barrels.

'How long do we have?' whispered James, and she knew he was thinking of the smouldering fuse.

'I don't know,' answered Makepeace. 'Minutes, perhaps.' They had intended to be far from the cellar when the powder exploded. There might still be time to put out the match, of course. But what could await them after that, but defeat and capture?

I do not know how big the explosion will be, admitted Livewell. It might well blow us apart. But I say we do it anyway.

I have seen enough of this hellhole to agree, the doctor said, sounding surprised at himself.

Morgan laughed, very quietly and sombrely.

Let it burn, she said.

'Let's bring Grizehayes down,' said Makepeace.

'Ah, well.' James snickered. 'We might as well die spitting in their Evil Eye!'

The shouts and clashes of weapons at the top of the stairs had hushed, and Lady April's voice could be heard giving commands. Evidently she had triumphed over Young Crowe and his allies, through force of will or arms.

'They'll be coming for us,' whispered James.

'Let them,' hissed Makepeace. 'The more the merrier when the powder blows.' She put out her lantern and plunged them into darkness.

She could tell from James's wide eyes that he could not see a thing.

'Trust us,' she whispered.

'Can you hear us?' Lady April called down the stairs. 'Come up and surrender, or we shall send down the dogs!'

Both siblings tensed. Once again, the Grizehayes dogs would

be loosed on them. But now they had no moors to flee across. They were cornered prey.

Nonetheless, neither of them spoke a word, or moved to surrender.

Seconds crawled by, and then Makepeace heard a faint clatter of claws from the direction of the steps. Panting rough as sawdust. The flap of soft jowls.

Makepeace knew all of them by their smell. The hulking mastiffs with their great jaws and terrible bite. The wolfhound, its long sinews aching for large prey to chase. The greyhounds, swift and deadly like hawks of the land. The bloodhounds, scenting her fear like wine.

She smelt their fast blood, their hunt-hunger. The claw-skitter neared their hiding place. One deep bark reverberated in the darkness, and a moment later a cacophony of barking echoed throughout the cellar.

'Shh!' Makepeace rose from her hiding place, even as her heart raced, and her skin tingled in readiness for a bite. 'Nero—Star—Catcher—Caliban! *You know me.*'

She could see their pale forms tensed in the darkness. Then one large shape drew closer. A wet nose nudged her hand, and a tongue licked her palm.

They knew her smell. She was the gravy-giver. She was pack, perhaps. And she was a beast whose temper should not be tested too far.

'You will need to come up eventually,' called down Lady April.

'Why?' shouted James, his teeth chattering. 'We have friends down here, and enough wine to make merry. We might sing a few songs.'

'Or perhaps we'll hold out until your enemies take Grizehayes tomorrow,' suggested Makepeace.

'Don't be absurd,' snapped Lady April. 'We can hold out against a siege until the end of the war, if necessary! We have enough provisions and shot for two whole months.'

Makepeace laughed out loud. 'Do you think the war will be over in *two months*?'

'The Queen is back in the country with money, arms and troops for the King's cause,' declared Lady April. 'London will soon lose heart. The rebels are already crumbling.' Her certainty was cold and monumental, like marble.

'No, they're not!' exclaimed Makepeace. 'And London's *fierce*, my lady. It's a quarrelsome, stinking madhouse, but it has a will like the Juggernaut. I don't care how ancient and clever you are. If you say the war's ending, you're blind.'

'How dare you!' Lady April sounded angry, but Makepeace thought she detected the tiniest hint of something else.

'I watched two Elders die today,' Makepeace declared loudly. A shocked silence pooled like blood. 'Sir Anthony's ghosts possessed Symond, and one of your soldiers killed him. And those ghosts—those wise, all-knowing ghosts—didn't see it coming. They had never really noticed that soldier, you see. They didn't care that he'd lost a brother at Hangerdon Hill. And then he shot them in the head.

'You've been missing things, important things, because there are people you never notice. And now it's too late for you all. This isn't like the other wars you've fought. Your wits and centuries won't help you this time. This is new. This is the world ending, Lady April.'

'Enough!' rapped Lady April. 'You have exhausted our patience.'

Men were venturing carefully down the steps, two of them carrying candles that underlit their faces. At their rear descended Lady April, armed with a pair of wicked-looking knives.

Carefully James lifted one of the smaller barrels, hefted it to his shoulder, then flung it at one of the candle-carriers. The barrel struck his hand, and the candle flew against the wall and went out. The other turned too quickly to see what had happened, and the motion killed the candle flame. There was consternation and confusion.

'Something leaped at me!'

'I saw something before the candle went out! The red of the light reflected in a dozen eyes! I . . . do not think they were all dogs.'

'There's something in the dark! I can hear it growling!'

'If you can hear it,' Lady April rasped, 'then you know where it is!'

But the growler was on the move. Makepeace relaxed into Bear. She dropped to all fours, and it felt easy and necessary. His nose was hers, her eyes were his. She let her throat vibrate with deep and ominous rumbles.

Bear's not a child I have to humour. He's not a Fury to keep on a chain. I don't need to be ashamed or afraid of him. He's me. Whatever we were, now we're us.

The first man was knocked unconscious by one long side-swipe. A second aimed a slash of his sword in the direction of Makepeace's growls, and was knocked over backwards by a mastiff and a greyhound. A third tried to run to the stairs for more light, and was flung bodily into a little stack of barrels.

'I have the boy!' shouted White Crowe suddenly. There were sounds of a scuffle.

Makepeace lurched towards the noise, but suddenly thin, strong fingers clasped the sides of her head and gripped fistfuls of her hair.

'Mongrel!' The hard voice of Lady April rasped in Makepeace's ear. 'Ingrate!' And Makepeace screamed as a spirit lunged out, and bit into her mind's defences like an axe. It caught her off guard and she had no time to brace for it.

Makepeace had been attacked by ghosts before, but they had always been trying to make a home in her. This was different. This was a bombardment, and Lady April did not care what she destroyed. Makepeace fought back and felt her secret allies do the same.

All of us. We learned to fight together in the end. Even as she felt painful cracks appear in her mind's shell, there was a sad jubilation in that thought. At the same time, she could sense the Elder's frustration. Makepeace was losing, but much more slowly than expected.

Then Makepeace smelt fear that was not her own, and sensed the hairline cracks of doubt now running through Lady April's marble souls.

'My lady,' called White Crowe, his voice anxious. 'There is something here. A glowing red star. It looks a bit like a lit match . . .'

The assault on Makepeace's brain abruptly halted as she was physically thrown aside.

'Fools!' shouted Lady April. 'That is gunpowder!' Makepeace saw the old woman speed like a greyhound through the darkness, towards the glowing, crimson star of the lit match . . .

And that bright red dot was the epicentre when the world broke.

The explosion was deafening, and the force of it knocked Makepeace back, the way a careless hand might fell a house of cards. There was a brief rush of heat, and then a lot of things seemed to be raining around her. The air was full of smoke and flour. She sat up coughing, just in time to see a large, jagged chunk of the wall and ceiling buckle and crash down on to the slabs.

Ashen and astonished-looking sky gawped down through the gap. James stumbled over rubble to her side, and helped her up. A small distance away, White Crowe sat dazed and dust-covered. If there was anything left of Lady April it was under the great fallen pile of masonry.

James was mouthing something. Makepeace's ears were ringing, and his voice was as faint as a ghost, but she thought she understood. She hurried up the cellar stairs with him, stepped carefully past Young Crowe's unconscious body, and gaped at the beautiful crack that had appeared in the wall.

It was just wide enough for two young people to slip through, and let themselves fall on to the grass outside. It was even easier for the dogs as they followed.

CHAPTER 39

Many hours later, in the early afternoon, Makepeace and James stopped to rest near a spinney at the top of a hill. It had been an old hill fort in ancient times, but now there was just a strangely shaped mound with views across the surrounding countryside.

Both were feeling battered and exhausted inside and out, and it had caught up with them at last. James was still recovering from playing host to five arrogant Fellmotte ghosts, and being crushed into a corner of himself. Makepeace's own battles with the Elder ghosts had left her battered and a little melancholy. They had left a dusting of their memories, like the ashes of singed moths, and for the moment it flavoured everything she saw.

Both siblings had a fine collection of bruises, which were showing through their skin in all colours of the rainbow. Furthermore, Makepeace's arms ached from carrying the turnspit dog, whose short legs tired more quickly than those of the other dogs.

'What's that?' said James.

In the far distance, the two of them could see a tall whisker of brownish-grey smoke. It was too large to come from a chimney or campfire, and the wrong colour for woodsmoke. It was the wrong time of year for stubble fires.

Makepeace got out the diptych dial, and looked at the compass. She tried to remember the maps that she had so carefully pieced together, but she already knew in her heart where the smoke was coming from.

'Grizehayes,' said James in a whisper. He looked numb and

shocked, and Makepeace knew that her face wore the same expression.

Grizehayes the invulnerable. Grizehayes the eternal, with centuries encrusted upon it like barnacles. Grizehayes the unchanging rock in the world's river. Their prison, their enemy, their shelter, their home.

Grizehayes was burning.

'Is the world ending?' James asked huskily.

Makepeace moved over, wrapped her bruised arms around him and hugged him tightly.

'Yes,' she said.

'What do we do?'

'We walk,' she said. 'We find food, and a place to sleep. Tomorrow we do it again. We survive.'

Worlds ended sometimes. Makepeace had known that for a while. She had known it since the night of the riots and Mother's death, when her own world had neatly and completely fallen to dust.

One of the dogs snarled at something in the spinney. Makepeace leaped to her feet, but then saw the small outline lumbering through the undergrowth, and the livid white streaks on its pointed face. It was a badger, going about its business as if there were no wars to be fought.

Makepeace watched it with fascination. She remembered all that she had learned about badgers in the bestiary book at Grizehayes. The badger, or brock, whose legs were longer on one side, to help it on sloping ground . . .

. . . but they weren't. As it ambled through a patch of daylight, she could see it quite clearly, and all its short legs were the same humble, sturdy length.

Perhaps none of the old truths were true any more. This could be a new world entirely, with its own rules. A world where badgers were not lopsided, and pelicans did not feed their young with their own blood, and toads had no precious stones in their heads, and cubs were already bear-shaped at birth. A world where castles could burn, and kings could die, and no rule was unbreakable.

'We survive,' she said again, more firmly. 'And we try to lick this new world into shape while it's still soft. If we don't, there's others that will.'

It was only much later that a news-sheet told them the full story of the fall of Grizehayes.

The explosion in the dead of night was commonly blamed on powder stored too close to the walls. When dawn came, white cloths had hung from the battlements of Grizehayes, signalling a willingness to talk. A man called Crowe had emerged to negotiate the surrender.

The siege commander had let all the civilians leave, and even take some provisions and possessions with them. In peacetime he had not been an unkind man, and the siege had been relatively short. His fighting zeal had not had time to curdle into hatred.

The Parliamentarian force that had taken Grizehayes had barely had time to raid its stores before they received word that a large Royalist force, headed by Sir Marmaduke, was less than a day away.

The siege commander faced a hard decision, and made it quickly. Better to torch the house, so that it could never be used again, than risk the King's forces using it as a stronghold, albeit a broken one.

The account said that when Sir Marmaduke saw his ancestral

home in flames, it 'killed his heart'. He refused to wear his protective buff coat, led the cavalry charge and fought like a madman. Afterwards both sides spoke highly of his bravery. But then again, the dead are often easier to praise than the living.

Not all battles were reported in the news-sheets, and not all of them involved full armies or neat battle lines under the gaze of eagle-eyed commanders. Months were passing, and there was still no peace. Sometimes there was a great battle that everyone said would decide things, one way or the other. But somehow it never did.

Humans are strange, adaptable animals, and eventually get used to anything, even the impossible or unbearable. In time, the unthinkable becomes normal.

The inhabitants of one forest hamlet were very glad to be visited by someone who could dress wounds. They had been attacked by an armed band wearing sashes. There had been shots fired and blows struck. In the end the villagers had hidden in the church, and dropped rocks on the strangers until they tired of trying to set fire to the building and left. Nobody was quite sure whether they had been paid troops, brigands or a group of marauding deserters.

The villagers could only pay Makepeace and James by offering shelter, meals, and bones for the dogs, but these were very welcome. James did most of the talking. He cut a good figure, even as a wanderer.

When I think of the fees my services might once have commanded, muttered Dr Quick, as Makepeace's latest patient left through the door with a clean strip of linen around his head. Nonetheless, the doctor complained less about such things these days. Perhaps rich patrons were less grateful than struggling householders. *You are sentimental, as ever.*

It's sense, not sentiment, Makepeace told him, as she cleaned her hands. *We needed somewhere to stay for a few nights.*

You had good solid reasons to help these people, said the doctor. *You always do.*

Did I ever tell you about another chirurgeon I knew before the war? He was a rising star, with better patrons than many physicians. But one day a child died under his knife— the little daughter of his closest friend. After that, he was hopeless. Suddenly he could deny nobody. He ran himself ragged, taking up every case, even where there was no hope of payment. And he could always give excellent, sensible reasons why it was in his interests to do so. He never admitted that he was trying to save everyone, to soothe the ache of failing to save that girl.

Did he ever find peace? asked Makepeace. She knew perfectly well what the doctor was suggesting.

Who can say? He still lives, as far as I know. Perhaps he will, some day. And in the meanwhile, the stupid man is saving a lot of lives.

Do you want to write some more today? asked Makepeace.

If we can spare the time and paper.

Whenever she had the chance, Makepeace bartered for paper. It was seldom cheap, and often used on one side, but it allowed the doctor to write up his discoveries and theories concerning battlefield surgery.

Makepeace had also written two letters, not long after the fall of Grizehayes. The first was sent to Charity Tyler in Norwich, sending back her brother's prayer book, and breaking the news of his death. It told her that he had wished to be reconciled to his cousin, and for an end to bad blood between them, and that he had loved his sister with all his heart. The letter also told her that Livewell had helped breach the walls of a Royalist stronghold and end a siege that might have cost many lives. It did not mention that this had happened after his death.

Livewell would vanish soon, she was sure of it. There was something calmer about him now. Some day she would wake and find a hole in her mind like a missing tooth.

I have polished my soul as much as I can, he had said recently. *If I stay much longer I will only scuff it again.*

The second letter had been written with the help of Morgan. It was addressed to Helen, and was a very dull missive about children getting measles. On the back, however, a second encoded message was written invisibly in artichoke juice:

> Helen,
>
> By now you will have heard strange things of me. The truth is stranger still. I was not in the service of the Fellmottes when you met me, but nor was I working for your enemies. I am your friend and mean to prove myself so.
>
> The charter that you seek is at Whitehollow. Symond Fellmotte hid it in the lining of the secret door in the master bedroom. I moved it from that place, but not far. It is still under that same lining but up in the top corner, held there by a pin. I told him I had hidden it somewhere new, and thought it likely he would put his hand in the base to feel if it was still where he had placed it, and would find it indeed gone. I fancied that

he would not search the rest of the door, but rather make himself mad searching everywhere else in the house. Folk look for things far and wide, but seldom close.

If God wills it, we shall meet again, and if so I hope we shall still be friends.

Judith-as-was

Makepeace remembered the gleam in the witch-hunter's eyes when he had heard about the royal charter. It would be better if the King's spies found it and quietly destroyed it. She could not rid the world of witch-hunters, but there was no need to feed them. From the little she had seen, they were a hungry breed.

Besides, it pleased her to imagine Helen exchanging cool, bland pleasantries with her unsuspecting Parliamentarian husband with Makepeace's note hidden in her glove, and then sneaking out at night to adventures and espionage in the service of the King.

I would like to write up my studies of ghosts as well, remarked the doctor, if I thought we could do so without being burned as heretics.

I wonder sometimes whether your family had fallen into a colossal error. The more ghosts I see, the less sure I am that we are the same souls that once were living. For all we know, perhaps the real souls pass on happily to the Maker, leaving us behind. I think sometimes that we ghosts are . . . memories. Echoes. Impressions. Oh, we can think and feel. We can regret the past, and fear the future. But are we really the people we think we are?

How does that change anything? It was too late for Makepeace to think of her spectral allies as anything other than friends.

I do not know, **said Dr Quick**. It is a blow to my vanity to consider the possibility that I am nothing but a bundle of thoughts, feelings and memories, given life by somebody else's mind. But then again, so is a book. Where is my pen?

Makepeace let him use her hand to write. Not for the first time, she wondered whether the doctor would leave some day too, after he felt he had lived his afterlife to some account.

Not Bear, though. Bear would never be parted from her.

She could find no join, no place where she ended and Bear started. In that first clumsy embrace of the spirit, they had tangled themselves hopelessly, she supposed. Whatever happened, wherever she went, there would always be Bear. Whoever knew her, or liked her, or loved her, would have to accept Bear.

She could even love herself a little now, knowing that she was Bear.

For a good few days after her death, Hannah was very confused.

She had been brought to the front line by love and desperation, in equal measure. It was all very well Tom saying that he must march with the Earl's army, but if he left her all alone with a baby coming, then how would she pay for food, and where would she go? So she had packed her things and come along to war, even as she started to get thick about the waist.

Hannah was not the only one. The baggage train of the army was full of other women—wives, lovers and the other sort—all pitching in with the cooking, nursing and fetching. She liked them, or a lot of them, anyway. It was muddy trudging, but she was young, and sometimes the whole adventure had a mad, exciting holiday feel. Her singing voice, so often praised in church, sounded even better by the campfire.

But then a cart loaded with gunpowder had exploded, killing Tom. The shock of it caused her to fall down in a fit and lose the baby. Afterwards she had no stomach for returning to her own town without Tom. She had no home now. But where could she go? And without Tom's wages as a soldier, how would she eat?

Another woman whispered to her that if she dressed as a man and was willing to take the worst watches, she might 'enlist' and get a soldier's wages. There were a couple of others in the camp who did so, and an officer who turned a blind eye.

So Hannah became Harold. She was too slight to hold the line with the pikemen, so she was taught the tricks of the matchlock, and joined the lines of musketeers.

During the great battle, after the musketeer line had broken in disorder, she had heard yells that the enemy were attacking the baggage train. She had run to the rear of the camp, through a fog of gunsmoke and chaos, to see men on horseback chasing the camp womenfolk and hacking them down with swords. She put a bullet in one of them, and wounded another with her sword, before a slice from behind ended her efforts and her life.

No! she thought as she died. *No! No! It is too soon. It is not fair. I was discovering a new life and I was* good *at this!*

But that thought was all that kept her company for the next few days. She was in darkness. It was a warm, strange darkness, and she did not think she was alone.

Now and then, somebody tried to talk to her. It was a young man's voice, and at first she thought it might be Tom trying to guide her to Heaven, but it didn't sound like him and the accent was wrong.

At last her vision returned. She was so relieved to see blue sky above her that she wanted to sob. However, she found that she

414

could not. She appeared to be walking, but had no control over her own body. When she looked down, she found it was not her own body at all. It was still in male clothing, but now it seemed to be male indeed.

'Can you see?' asked the same insistent voice, sounding a little wary. 'Can you hear me? My name is James.'

What happened? she demanded. Where am I?

'You're safe,' he answered. 'Well . . . actually you're dead, but also safe . . . in a sense. Makepeace—can *you* talk to her? I'm not used to this.'

The person whose eyes Hannah was using turned to look at his companion, a girl a couple of years younger than Hannah. She could have been any market-girl, in her faded wool clothes and linen cap, but there was a knowing, serious look in her eye as if she had already watched the whole of Hannah's life unfold.

On her cheek, Hannah saw two faint smallpox scars, so small they might have been flecks of rain. They reminded her of the two large freckles that had sat on Tom's cheek in almost exactly the same place, and Hannah took this as a good omen. Desperate as she was, she would make do with any omen she could find.

'You don't have to stay if you don't want to,' said the girl called Makepeace. 'But you're welcome to travel with us as long as you like. We believe in second chances, for the people who don't usually get them.

'You're among friends, Hannah. You're home.'

ACKNOWLEDGEMENTS

I would like to thank my editor, Rachel Petty, for showing superhuman patience and calm while I was half-witted with stress over my own delays, and for helping to lure Bear out of the shadows; Bea, Kat, Catherine and everyone else at Macmillan for being supportive, fun and perpetually on my side; Nancy for wisdom and common sense; Martin for putting up with my most frantic months of writing and editing, and for only mocking me gently when I worked until 4 or 5 a.m.; Plot on the Landscape; Rhiannon; Sandra for taking me to the exhibition on Sir Thomas Browne at the Royal College of Physicians; Amy Greenfield for introducing me to Chastleton and its wonderful secret room; Ham House; Boswell Castle; Old Wardour Castle; *The English Civil War: A People's History* by Diane Purkiss; *The King's Smuggler: Jane Whorwood Secret Agent to Charles I* by John Fox; *The Weaker Vessel: Woman's Lot in Seventeenth-Century England* by Antonia Fraser; *Family Life in the Seventeenth Century: The Verneys of Claydon House* by Miriam Slater; *Women in early modern England, 1500–1700* by Jacqueline Eales; *Her Own Life: Autobiographical writings by seventeenth-century Englishwomen* edited by Elspeth Graham, Hilary Hinds, Elaine Hobby & Helen Wilcox; *55 Days* by Howard Brenton; *The History of England Volume III: Civil War* by Peter Ackroyd; and Lady Eleanor Davies, the abrasive, self-styled prophetess who managed to annoy virtually everybody, not least with her tendency to be right.

I would also like to apologize to King Charles I, for forcing a fictional version of him to sign a highly nefarious document. I hope he will forgive me, and refrain from sending spectral spaniels after me in revenge.

ABOUT THE AUTHOR

Frances Hardinge spent a large part of her childhood in a huge old house that inspired her to write strange stories from an early age. She read English at Oxford University, and then got a job at a software company. Her first children's novel, *Fly By Night*, was published to huge critical acclaim and won the Branford Boase First Novel Award. She has been nominated for, and won, several other awards, including the *Los Angeles Times* Book Prize, the *Boston Globe-Horn Book* Award, and the coveted Costa Book of the Year Award for *The Lie Tree*, only the second young adult novel to earn this designation.